The Adventures of Serendipity Brown
Book Two

The Fairhaven Home for Wayward Time Travelers

Jeanette M. Bennett

Flight of Fancy Publishing

THE FAIRHAVEN HOME FOR WAYWARD TIME TRAVELERS
Published by Flight of Fancy Publishing

PUBLISHER'S NOTE
This is a work of fiction. Names, characters, places and incidents are products of the author's imagination or are used fictitiously. Any similarity to actual persons, living or dead, business establishments, organizations, locales and/or events is purely coincidental.

The publisher does not have any control over and does not assume any responsibility for third-party websites or their content.

If you want authors to keep writing, you have to feed us.

ISBN 978-1-939524-06-5

Library of Congress Control Number: 2015921148

Visit http://scablander.com for ordering information
As well as reviews, interviews and some fun surprises.

In Loving Memory of
Josephine and Donald Farley

*Thank you for all your love and support
and for making me part of your family.*

You are missed.

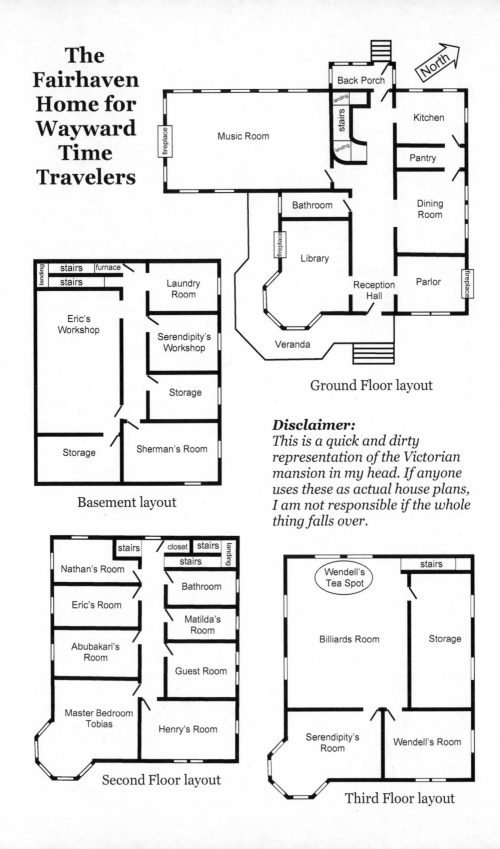

The Fairhaven Home for Wayward Time Travelers

North

Back Porch

landing

stairs

landing

fireplace

Music Room

Kitchen

Pantry

Dining Room

Bathroom

fireplace

Library

Reception Hall

Parlor

fireplace

Veranda

Ground Floor layout

landing

stairs | furnace

stairs

Eric's Workshop

Laundry Room

Serendipity's Workshop

Storage

Storage

Sherman's Room

Basement layout

Disclaimer:

This is a quick and dirty representation of the Victorian mansion in my head. If anyone uses these as actual house plans, I am not responsible if the whole thing falls over.

stairs | closet | stairs | landing

stairs

Nathan's Room

Bathroom

Eric's Room

Matilda's Room

Abubakari's Room

Guest Room

Master Bedroom Tobias

Henry's Room

Second Floor layout

stairs

Wendell's Tea Spot

Billiards Room

Storage

Serendipity's Room

Wendell's Room

Third Floor layout

Chapter One

Dressed in saffron robes, his head shaved, his face serene, Shiro looked like the archetype of the Japanese Buddhist monk. Kneeling on the floor, he carefully placed the yellow chrysanthemum in the earthen vase sitting on the low shelf of the tokonoma recessed into the wall. The flower drooped a bit over the pinewood picture frame that held a photograph of a gentleman in a Victorian suit. One could tell the man in the picture was English just by looking at his face. From the low light of the cast-iron lantern, Shiro noted the sepia tones of the photo went well with the gold petals of the mum.

The moon outside shone brightly enough to throw shadows from ornamental maples onto the translucent mulberry paper covering the bamboo lattice of the sliding door. The teahouse in this ancient roji garden served as Shiro's home when he resided in the "now." A Buddhist monk was supposed to live in the "now," but Shiro spent more time in the "then." The man in the photo had also spent most of his time in the past, which made him Shiro's "brother."

Dr. Shiro Suzuki bowed to the photo. "Please, my apologies, Dr. Wendell Howe, for missing your funeral ceremony. I was in the Field. You understand. I wish I had known you better, but our paths were too far apart to work together in the Field. I enjoyed what little time we spent together. You were a considerate, patient man, well on your way to enlightenment. I wish to honor your memory. I think for you, a tea ceremony is best. Others saw tea only as a drink. You saw tea as history brewed in a cup."

Shiro crawled across the tatami mats to the nearby round iron brazier. He dunked the bamboo dipper into the iron pot fitted on top of the brazier, then poured the heated water into a ceramic tea bowl. Stirring the water with a bamboo whisk a moment to heat the bowl, he then discarded the water into a kensui pot. He wiped the bowl by holding the white cloth still and turning the vessel. He did all this in a slow methodic manner.

"I remember the first time I performed this ceremony for you." Shiro spoke to the spirit of his fallen comrade. "Even though I am no Tea Master, you seemed delighted to find someone who still knew how to perform the ancient ceremony. I was honored you wanted to record me for your book on the history of tea. You had a child's curiosity, the mark of a true scholar. I recall our last conversation when I explained reincarnation to you. The unenlightened think reincarnation is a punishment. It is a learning process. Evil men come back as victims not to torture them, but to teach them compassion. Those who suffer are reborn in a better life that they might learn joy. This life you came back as a scholar, a seeker of knowledge, as did I. You gave your life for that quest. I pray you find what you seek in your next life, Dr. Howe."

Shiro used a tiny scoop to take green powdered tea from a clay caddy and tipped it into the bowl. He again added hot water with the dipper. This time he used the whisk to whip the tea into a frothy brew.

Someone knocked on the doorjamb of the host's entrance, and not the low guest door one had to crawl through, as would be proper. Shiro wondered who would be calling at this late hour. The University of Tokyo's tea garden was closed this time of night, although anyone could just walk in. The only deterrent was a polite sign and a shut bamboo gate. Teahouses were never meant to be lived in, but Shiro was allowed to stay here because it was the most anachronistic part of the campus and where he felt most at home. Universities indulged their temporal anthropologists when possible.

Shiro sat the tea bowl down on the mat and got up. The intruder was probably an overeager student who wanted to be a temporal anthropologist too, and hoped Shiro could tell him "the secret." He would patiently tell the brash youth to come back tomorrow.

Shiro slid the door open. There stood a man in a twenty-seventh-century one-piece jumpsuit of dark grey with a black fringed sash draped over his right shoulder, across his chest and fastened at his left hip. On his head clung a dark-grey skullcap. Shiro found it hard to believe this fashion was now popular in 2662.

Then he saw the emblem on the sash. It had two hands grasping the stand of an ancient hourglass. It took all of Shiro's will to retain his composure.

"Are you Dr. Shiro Suzuki?" the Caucasian spoke in English with an American accent.

"Hai!" Shiro bowed. "I mean, yes. I am Dr. Suzuki Shiro." If he had to speak English in his own home to an intruder, he at least would put the name in the traditional Japanese form with the family name first.

"You will let me in." This sounded like an order, not a request.

Shiro had no choice, having been programmed to fear and obey these men. He stepped aside and let the intruder in. Shiro peered past him into the darkness. "Are you alone, sir?"

"I'm alone."

"I always see you in groups of three."

"One is enough."

Shiro slid the door shut. "May I ask what brings you out at this hour?"

This visit did not bode well to Shiro. He had never heard of the Institute of Time Travel's Enforcers coming to a temporal anthropologist's home. They normally just ordered them to Headquarters.

Shiro turned around to face his guest. The Enforcer had a pistol leveled on him. Shiro suddenly felt cold as a corpse as he studied the slim silver weapon. "So, the rumors are true? You have come back to erase me. What will I do in the future to warrant my death?"

"You have no future, Dr. Suzuki. You are condemned to die for the crimes you have already committed."

"My crimes?"

"Are you not a time traveler?"

"*Licensed* Time Traveler, but you know that"

"Have you not played God with time, treating history as though it were a plaything?

"No, I have been studying the monasteries of ancient Japan."

"You couldn't just read historic records like everyone else? You had to go back and see for yourself, just to satisfy your own curiosity. Your selfish indulgences have played havoc with our history, polluted our time stream."

"Never. I have sworn to *leave no footprint in the sands of time.*" Shiro quoted the motto of the Institute of Time Travel. "I have always been careful to have no impact on the past. Who are you? Are you even with the Institute?"

The man ignored the question. "Just by going into the past, you have changed it, Dr. Suzuki. In doing so you have given us a different, a defective, present. That is why you must die. That is why all time travelers must die."

"No, we are trained to change nothing. We only observe as historians and scientists."

"You are monsters." The leader put his weapon to Shiro's forehead. "All of you."

Begging would do no good, Shiro could tell that by the hatred in the man's eyes. Perhaps Shiro had lived as a monk, but he would die as a samurai. He held his head up and stiffened his jaw.

The energy discharge burned through Shiro's skull, leaving a charred hole on the wall behind him. His body collapsed on the ground.

The assassin looked down at the crumpled remains of the peaceful scholar. A puddle of blood formed behind Shiro's head, soaking into the tatami mat. The killer then adjusted the pistol to a fine beam. He sliced off the corpse's sandaled feet.

He stuck the weapon in his sash, and pulled out a card that read: *Leave no footprint in the sands of time—The Time Keepers.* "*That* should get the message across." He tossed the card on the body. "Another time meddler gone. We will kill them all." The assassin told Shiro. "And then we will go after the greatest criminal of them all. We will go back to where it all started and eliminate the villainess who invented time travel itself. We will kill Dr. Serendipity Brown."

Shiro, of course, made no response, his unblinking eyes staring into space.

Chapter Two

The sound of a jangling 1940s-style alarm clock shredded the silence, jarring Sherman Conrad to semi-consciousness. He reached over to the table next to his bed and slapped at the nuisance, trying to turn it off.

"Hey, mac!" yelped a female voice. "Watch it, will ya?"

Sherman sat up, bouncing on the waves his sudden movement made on his water bed. "Huh?" He tried to peer through the black hair hanging in his face. There was no clock on the stand, just a small silver box the size of a pack of cigarettes and as thick as a Hershey bar. "Uh, sorry Lauren. I thought you were my alarm clock back home."

"That's the fifth time you've done that this month!" The sultry voice from the box scolded. "You wanna knock me off onto the floor again? I know I'm made to survive anything short of a bomb, but...well, it makes me feel unwanted, if you know what I mean!"

Sherman picked up his Personal Assistant Liaison computer or PAL. He was sure some dork in some company's marketing department came up with that name, but he did feel like Lauren really was his pal. "Like, I wasn't trying to be lame. It's just reflex."

"Ah, applesauce! It has been months since you had another alarm clock. Say, when are you going to realize that you aren't in Kansas anymore, sport?" Sherman's boss had programmed the computer with the voice and personality of Lauren Bacall, or more accurately the personality of "Slim" from the movie *To Have or Have Not*. However, the computer seemed to be taking on a personality of its own.

"I never was in Kansas, just Washington and Oregon." Sherman pushed his hair out of his eyes. "Well, until I met Serendipity, anyway."

"Yeah and that was months ago, or more to the point, three hundred and sixty-eight years ago."

Sherman struggled out of the rolling bed. "So, I haven't gotten over the jetlag yet."

He set Lauren on the top of his dresser and dug around for something besides the briefs he slept in. Life could be weird. One minute he was in 1985, the next in 2353. It still seemed like a dream. His accidental kidnapper, Dr. Serendipity Brown, had wanted to take him back, but he talked her into letting him stay on as her assistant.

Sherman pulled on a black Def Leppard T-shirt and whistled—the prompt for his computer.

"Yes, Steve?" Lauren always called Sherman "Steve," the name Slim had given Bogart's character.

"What's the weather report today?"

"Let me check. Hmm, partially cloudy with forty-per-cent chance of rain."

"Like yesterday and the day before." Sherman peered into his mirror and combed his shaggy hair with his fingers.

"Well, we are in Beaverton, Oregon. What'd you expect? We're in the middle of a stinking rainforest."

"Yeah." Sherman grinned. Lauren was pretty cheeky for a computer, but he liked her.

Sherman put on his tennis shoes and stuck on his black horn-rimmed glasses. Twenty-fourth century medicine had mended his eyes making the glasses unnecessary, but Serendipity paid him to wear them, because they were "so twentieth century." She also allowed—well, more like encouraged—him to wear his native costume from the 1980s. Sherman felt certain Serendipity had initially just kept him as a souvenir of her first time trip.

Sherman looked in the mirror at his baby-face and felt his chin. "Better shave." It disgusted him that at nineteen he could still go days without shaving.

He grabbed Lauren, stuffed her in his jeans pocket and staggered out of the room and down the hall to the nearest bathroom. His bedroom didn't have a bathroom of its own, being simply one of the huge mansion's many spare rooms. He felt at home here because Serendipity had done the whole place in twentieth-century antiques and reproductions. She was very proud of her priceless treasures, but Sherman thought most of it looked like she had gone dumpster diving. As for Serendipity, she was easy enough to live with, even if she was quirky.

In the bathroom stood the third person residing in the house, leaning over the sink as he shaved with a straight razor. Dr. Wendell Howe wore a Victorian shirt without the attachable collar and cuffs, and brown wool slacks held up by buttoned suspenders. This was "half-naked" for Wendell. The Englishman had a flawless but unremarkable face that few remembered.

Wendell looked over at the door. "Hello, old boy. Are you ready to greet the morning?"

"Eh, I'd rather just flip it off," Sherman mumbled.

"I daresay someone is in dire need of some caffeine." Wendell's sedate voice reflected the long line of Cambridge University professors from which he had descended. Even when he made a quip he showed little expression, save for a slight smile. "Would you like me to step out and allow you to...erm...use the facilities?"

"Just came in to shave. I can come back." Sherman started to twist around to leave.

"No, you are fine. I can share the mirror if you don't mind my rudely hogging the sink."

Wendell turned back to the mirror and pulled the straight razor down his cheek he was holding taunt, careful to miss his sideburns, and flung the soap suds into the basin.

"Dude, isn't that dangerous?" Sherman watched with morbid fascination.

"Not if you know what you are doing. Frankly, I prefer shaving this way." Wendell set the blade down and lathered up some more suds in the shaving mug for his second pass. He reapplied the soap on his face with the badger-hair brush.

Wendell wasn't from the twenty-fourth century or the twentieth, but another time altogether, although there was much debate as to which time he really was from. Dr. Wendell Abercrombie Howe had been a temporal anthropologist from the twenty-seventh century but had spent most of his life in the nineteenth. He was more at home in the Victorian Age than his own.

Temporal anthropologists were registered time travelers who were trained to fit into the time period they chose to study, so as to make no impact or attract attention. Wendell was the most inconspicuous wallflower Sherman had ever met. Still, he liked Wendell. He had become like a big brother to Sherman—or was that father figure—or maybe grandfather figure? Twenty-seventh century science had slowed aging down. While Wendell looked like he might be pushing forty, he was in fact, eighty-five.

Sherman pulled his electric razor out of his drawer and plugged it in. He started shaving using the side of the long counter mirror not over the sink.

"I don't believe it," a voice came from the doorway.

Sherman looked up to see Dr. Serendipity Brown still in her pink robe, leaning on the door frame, her dark-brown curls exploding from her head. She was a middle-aged woman who refused to disclose her true age. Sherman found her face pleasant enough. No great beauty, unless you asked Wendell who seemed to think she was the most magnificent creature that ever walked the Earth.

"What don't you believe, my dear?" Wendell asked.

"Why anyone in their right mind would want to shave with one of those inefficient contraptions when you can use twenty-fourth-century technology!"

"I have just gotten used to shaving this way." Wendell rinsed off the straight razor.

"No, I mean that stupid twentieth-century electric shaver Sherman is using. It doesn't remove stubble, just shortens it."

Sherman looked at his razor, knowing she was right.

Wendell pulled his upper lip down and started to shave under his nose, then stopped. "I say, Serendipity, how would you feel about my growing back my mustache? I only shaved it off to hide from the Enforcers. Jolly lot of good that did."

"Hmm." She studied him, rubbing her chin. "Never kissed a man with a mustache before. Not sure if—"

A ringing noise came from Serendipity's robe pocket.

"Hold that thought." She told Wendell and pulled out her own PAL computer, now acting as a phone. "Hello?" Her eyebrows sloped down into an angry frown. "He what! No! Where? That jerk! Thanks, Charlene."

Serendipity stuffed the computer back in her pocket. "That stinking mole rat!" She snarled and took off down the hall.

Wendell quickly rinsed off his face, and followed after her. Sherman likewise set his own razor down to see what was going on. Wasn't Charlene the name of Serendipity's lawyer? He ran down the hall, nearly tripping on a meandering two-foot-high robot vacuum cleaner that looked more vacuum cleaner than robot. Its top was domed, reminding him of R2D2 from Star Wars, only smaller and plainer.

Sherman found Wendell and Serendipity in her office. "Tom!" she cued her own computer. "Office screen. Rebecca Russell Show broadcast. This morning's show. Bruce Dawson interview."

"You got it, pussycat." Her computer crooned in Tom Jones' voice. Sherman was sure Tom Jones didn't really talk like that.

A slender woman came up on the screen, her blonde hair moussed into something reminiscent of an ice cream cone. "I am sure you have all heard of the wealthy inventor Dr. Serendipity Brown. She made the news last month when she unveiled her newest invention, an improved compact Neutrino Dark Energy Generator. What everyone really wants to know is what Dr. Brown is *really* like? Are the rumors true that she is eccentric, peculiar, even crazy—a genuine mad scientist? We have here this morning someone who knew her *intimately*. Please welcome her ex-husband, screen heartthrob Bruce Dawson."

The camera flashed over to a handsome middle-aged man with a smug smirk above his cleft chin.

Serendipity looked like she wanted to punch the screen. "I wouldn't give that vulture an interview, so she went to my ex?"

Wendell came over and put his arm around Serendipity's waist. "Why would anyone appear on the telly to talk about his ex-wife? That seems a bit caddish."

"Bruce will do anything for money."

"So," said the Rebecca on the screen, "what was it like to live with a woman who is such a genius?"

"A nightmare!" Bruce shook his head. "Dippy is a total squirrel snack."

"Dippy!" Serendipity hated that nickname. Her mouth curled into a snarl, but her eyes looked betrayed.

"Tom, pause!" Wendell said firmly. Bruce's face froze in a surly sneer. "Serendipity, darling, you don't need to watch this slander."

"I need to find out what Bruce said." Serendipity looked up at Wendell. "I need to watch this."

"Very well, but you must promise me one thing." His face was its usual bland expression.

Serendipity frowned. "What?"

"You must promise to remember that you are wonderful and that I love you."

"Ah!" Serendipity melted and gave Wendell a hug. "Tom, continue."

Sherman watched the screen, and he watched the other two in the room. Wendell held onto Serendipity as she endured the abuse from her ex-husband.

"Don't listen to the dweeb, Ser," Sherman said. "Maybe they should interview me and Wendell. We'll tell them what you are really like."

"Thanks, kid. But what happens when they try to find out anything about you two? A man from the past and one from the future?"

"So sue the scumbag."

"I'm a celebrity, I guess, so that makes me fair game. People can say what they want. Besides suing Bruce would just draw more attention to him and the interview. Then everybody will be sure to see it."

Sherman nodded. "Yeah, you're probably right. Bummer." He went back to watching the screen.

"Would you believe it?" Bruce leaned toward the show hostess. "Dippy actually talked about making a time machine? How off is that?"

"A time machine?" Rebecca's voice held derision. "Isn't that impossible?"

Bruce snorted a laugh. "Yes, but not half as impossible as keeping that woman satisfied."

Serendipity grinned up at Wendell. "So, your achievement was twice as hard as mine."

Wendell fought to keep a straight face. "Not in front of Sherman."

Serendipity looked over at Sherman. "Yeah, because Sherman has no idea you're sleeping with me."

Sherman held up his hands. "I know nothing. Nothing."

They watched the rest of the fifteen minute interview. Serendipity groaned when it was over. "Why did he have to tell that story about the torn pants? Is he going to tell everything? Why does he want to make me a laughing stock? I used to think maybe I hated that man. Now, I know I do."

Wendell held her tighter. "History will remember Serendipity Brown. No one will remember Bruce Dawson. He is nothing more than a flea."

"Yeah, but he's an annoying flea." Serendipity looked over at Sherman and then up at Wendell. "I am so glad I have you two now. You're both such good friends. Okay, so you are a bit more, Wendell, but I feel you're my friend too."

"No matter what the future may bring, my dear. Even if you decide you no longer want a dull Victorian and kick me out of the house, I will still be your friend."

"You aren't dull so much as understated." Serendipity winked at Wendell, then sighed. "Those dashing Don Juans like Bruce can never love a woman as much as they love themselves. From now on, I'm staying with my own kind. I'm sticking with awkward geeks."

"I shall assume that was meant to be a compliment." Wendell wrinkled his nose as if he had something sour in his mouth.

"Yes." Serendipity patted his arm. "I'm saying I'm glad I have you."

"Don't let Bruce bum you out," Sherman said. "More people were probably laughing at *him* than you. Anyone can see he's a loser. No one will remember what he said next week. Bet he would have a cow if he knew you really did build a time machine."

"Yeah, I hate to admit it, but Bruce was what most inspired me. When I suggested someone might be able to break the time barrier, the jerk made fun of me. I had to show him."

"You aren't announcing your invention to the world yet, are you?" Wendell raised his eyebrow.

"Not ready. This is big. Real big. Someone might be tempted to steal my Timemobile and try to change history. I'm not sure how to handle this, so I'm taking it slow."

Wendell studied her concerned. "You look like you need cheered up. Might I suggest that we get you out of the house? Go for a holiday?"

"My luck I'd run into Bruce."

"I know." Sherman got a sly smile. "How about we go somewhere he can't? Ya know, like go shopping for antiques while they are still new?"

"Ooh! Twentieth-century shopping trip." Serendipity grinned. "This will give us a chance to try out those new modifications on the Timemobile. Now, where should we go? Maybe the 1980s and that way you could pick up stuff for your room too."

"You mean my personal stuff?"

Serendipity stared at Sherman. "That's right! You only brought the clothes on your back, literally, didn't you? Maybe we could go back and get your belongings."

Sherman sighed. "Nice thought but it has been months. I'm sure the guys cleared out my junk and got a new roommate."

"Surely they wouldn't..."

"They really got no choice. It takes four of us to make the rent."

Serendipity rolled her eyes up at the ceiling, then looked back at Sherman. "Not if we go back to the day after you left."

Wendell frowned. "Wouldn't that change history?"

Serendipity patted his cheek. "Yeah, someone not getting Sherman's hand-me-downs will change the world. Besides, maybe this is the way it happened. Sherman can tell everyone he got a better job and is moving instead of disappearing into thin air and becoming an urban myth."

Sherman shrugged. "I don't think Kelso qualifies as urban."

"Still we can keep the cops from dragging the river for you. Problem is I don't know if there's much room in the Timemobile for a lot of furniture."

"All I got is a bed, and it's a piece of junk not worth moving. I do have a few things I would like to save."

Serendipity tugged at her hair. "Let's see, we met on April 10th, my very first trip."

"May 18th, 1985 from my side."

"All right then, we'll have breakfast, Wendell and I will change our clothes to something twentieth-century, I'll make some period money, and we'll be off to 1985. Sound like a plan?"

Wendell rolled his eyes up, like he was thinking. As their official Time Travel Consultant, he was no doubt going over all the possible disasters in his head. "I can't think of any foreseeable problems with your proposal."

"Awesome." Sherman grinned at Serendipity. "Now I can get my gaming supplies."

Sherman leaned on the wall, waiting in the hall outside the workshop. Serendipity arrived dressed in the full skirt and peasant blouse she had worn to the First International Monterey Pop Festival in 1967. Wendell followed behind her in the black suit with a thin tie he had worn when they snuck into the Ed Sullivan Show to see the Beatles in 1963.

Sherman hadn't gone inside the workshop, because Serendipity had been working on a secret project. She did that occasionally and wouldn't let either him or Wendell watch. Now she wanted to unveil her latest improvement with as much fanfare as could be mustered with an audience of two. Sherman figured humoring her didn't hurt anything.

Serendipity threw open the door. "There! Now it really *is* a Timemobile."

The large scarlet metal box with a silver swoosh across it now sat on the back of a truck.

"It looks like a lorry." Wendell went up to the time machine.

"Looks like a delivery truck to me." Sherman studied it.

Wendell frowned at him. "That's what a lorry is."

Serendipity pulled open the driver's door of the cab. "It's a hovertruck, with my time machine in place of the cargo box. Now our time machine can just levitate or roll to another location so we won't have to fire it up just to move it a short distance. I also hooked up the hovertruck motor to one of my Dark Energy Drives so we don't have to worry about fuel. I've expanded the Holographic Skin so we can disguise the whole thing as a wagon, a stage coach, or any period delivery truck."

Sherman nodded. "Yeah, a wooden shed rolling down the road would attract some attention."

"I kept the profile boxy, so we can still disguise it as a shed or whatever if we want. I put a computer in the cab part, too, so in an emergency it can drive itself. I want to key it to your voices so either of you can move it in a crises situation. Get in and sit down, Sherman."

Sherman climbed into the driver's seat and sat down.

"The cue is T.M.," Serendipity told Sherman.

"T.M.?"

"Short for Timemobile."

Sherman cleared his throat. "T.M. turn on!"

"Yes?" the computer spoke with an English accent.

"T.M.," Serendipity said. "This is Sherman Conrad. Record his voice and face. He is to be given full access, you will obey his commands."

"Affirmative, Dr. Brown."

"Now, kid, say something to the nice computer."

Sherman looked at the dashboard. "What do you want me to say?"

"Voice and face recorded," the computer said.

Serendipity pulled on Sherman's arm. "Okay, get out, kid."

Sherman crawled out.

Serendipity grabbed Wendell's arm. "Now you get in, Wendell. T.M., record voice and face for full access."

Wendell climbed in and sat down. "Hello, T.M. This is Dr. Wendell Howe a.k.a. Professor Howellingsworth. Please record my voice and image."

"Recorded, as requested."

Sherman frowned. "Why does that voice sound familiar, Ser? Who is it?"

"Exactly." She grinned at him.

"What?"

"Who. Doctor Who. Fourth Doctor. Tom Baker."

"What!" Sherman yelped. "You can't give it Tom Baker's voice."

"Why not? He's not using it now."

Sherman realized this was the twenty-fourth century, so Tom Baker would have been long dead. Sherman thought the joke in very bad taste. "Why would you want to give it Tom Baker's voice?"

"The Doctor was a time traveler. So is the Timemobile. Would you prefer Peter Davison or Sylvester McCoy?"

"Who's Sylvester McCoy?"

"Seventh Doctor. I think he came after 1985."

"Ser, you can't give the Timemobile Tom Baker's voice!"

"What?" Serendipity frowned. "You would rather have David Tennant, or Clive Ashton or Walter Humphrey?"

"Huh? Who are these guys?"

"David Tennant was the Tenth Doctor, Clive Ashton was the Thirty-Second Doctor, and Walter Humphrey was the Forty-Fifth Doctor. But I'm sticking with a Doctor from the first series from the twentieth century."

"What? *First* series?"

"Yeah, they would cancel the show and then bring it back, then cancel it, then bring it back. Heard rumors BBC is going to start it up again with the Fifty-Fourth Doctor."

"Wait a minute!" Sherman protested. "I thought the Doctor could only regenerate twelve times?"

Serendipity rolled her eyes. "Oh sure, like the writers couldn't figure out a way around that one. I don't know how many times they destroyed the Master, the Daleks and Gallifrey, just to bring them back later."

"Gallifrey?"

"Yeah, you wouldn't believe how often they blew up that planet. After about the tenth time, I don't think anyone took it seriously."

Wendell shook his head at them. "I'm surprised anyone ever took any of that silly show seriously."

With that blasphemy, Serendipity and Sherman both turned and gave Wendell withering glares.

"Erm, sorry," Wendell stepped back. "I did not mean to offend anyone."

Serendipity snorted. "And you call yourself a Brit! Shame on you. That's like an American scoffing at Superman!"

"Yeah, no one bad-mouths the Man of Steel." Sherman poked out his chest.

"I'll flagellate myself later, when I have the time," Wendell said. "Now can we get back to reality? What does it matter what voice the computer has?"

"It just seems sacrilegious to give it the Doctor's voice." Sherman pushed his hair out of his eyes.

Serendipity shook her head. "It's meant to be a tribute! Like when they named the prototype for the Space Shuttle after Star Trek's *Enterprise*."

"Oh," Sherman said. "Well, if you put it that way. Okay, that will work."

"Ridiculous twentieth-century science fiction." Wendell rolled his eyes. "Now Jules Verne, H.G. Wells, Grant Allen—*that* was science fiction."

Serendipity snorted at him. "Do you like anything that's not Victorian?"

"You." Wendell tried to pacify her with a disarming smile.

"Yeah, and I bet you fantasize about me in a bustle, don't you."

Wendell got a funny smirk. "Actually, bit more like an Alphonse Mucha poster with the flowing gown and a wreath of lilies on your head."

"Okay, much better than the rubber corset and dog collar my second husband tried to get me to dress in. We'll talk about this later, stud." Serendipity stopped and peered at him. "Good lord, are you blushing, Wendell?"

Wendell cleared his throat and tried to compose himself.

"Bashful!" Serendipity grinned at him. "I swear you must have a lusty twin brother who sneaks into my room and makes mad passionate love to me while you're hiding under the bed."

"Serendipity, please, don't."

"Don't what, fuddy-duddy?"

"Don't ridicule me." His voice still had that composed tone it usually had, and his face was stoic, but his eyes appeared wounded. "I can deal with others making fun of me, but not you."

Serendipity's grin dropped. "Yeah, I went too far, didn't I? I'm clueless sometimes." She put her hand on his cheek. "Maybe six failed marriages wasn't completely their fault. Don't let me blow this, Wendell. I really don't want to lose you. You can't help that you're too Victorian. And I guess I can't help being a jackass sometimes."

"You could never be a jackass, my darling."

"Ah."

"You would be a jennet."

"Jennet?"

"A female jackass." Wendell said with a straight face.

Serendipity blinked at him surprised, then started laughing. "Okay, I had that one coming. Maybe you can teach me not to be such a jennet."

"Maybe you can teach me to not to be such a dry old stick." Wendell smiled at her.

Serendipity looked over at Sherman. "We better get this Timemobile on the road before I rip this man's clothes off."

"Serendipity!" Wendell raised an eyebrow at her.

"Yeah, went too far again, right?" Serendipity flashed him a nervous grin.

"Yes, behave yourself," Wendell scolded, fighting back a smile. "Here, allow me to unlock the door for you." Wendell pulled out his pocket computer hidden in a Victorian pocket Bible and clicked his tongue twice to turn it on. "Computer, open Timemobile door." He pulled open the door to the interior of the Timemobile behind the cab, and gave a slight bow. "After you, my dear."

Serendipity started in, then stopped on the step, turned back and winked at Sherman. "He's only doing this because he knows if he stepped in with his back to me, I'd grab that cute tush." She giggled and went in.

"Woman is as mad as a March Hare, and I think for the same reason." Wendell shook his head, then smirked and followed her in.

Sherman pulled out his computer, and gave a soft whistle.

"Yes, Steve?"

"What does the term 'mad as a March Hare' mean?"

"To act crazy. English slang. It's in reference to the fact that March is the mating season for hares and they bounce around acting loony."

"O-kay," Sherman said slowly. He stuck Lauren back in his pocket and hurried into the Timemobile.

Chapter Three

The world quit convulsing as the Timemobile came to a stop. Serendipity, as always, was the first out of her seat. Her two companions followed her out of the time machine onto the asphalt. Sherman looked over his shoulder to see the Timemobile now disguised as a Rainier Beer delivery van.

Wendell gazed about. "You appear to have hit the car park, Dr. Brown. Spot on."

"Yeah." Sherman scanned the area. "I figured the high school parking lot would be pretty empty on a Sunday morning. Want me to drive to my apartment?"

Serendipity shrugged. "Hadn't thought of that. Suppose you have more experience driving a land vehicle, and you know the town. Sure, you're the chauffeur, kid."

They closed the door of the time machine. Sherman crawled into the driver's seat of the cab. Wendell insisted on opening the passenger door for Serendipity and helping her in. She gave him an amused smile, like he was being silly, but she tolerated his eccentric behavior. Wendell got in and closed the door. It wasn't overly snug, but Sherman was glad there was no gear shift.

Wendell gazed out the window. "I've never been in an antique late-twentieth-century lorry before. This is very exciting." His bland voice held a touch of enthusiasm.

"Well, technically it's not," Serendipity said. "But I suppose it has the same feel since we will have to stay on the ground."

Sherman looked over the dashboard. "Where's the ignition?"

"T.M., turn on motor," Serendipity ordered.

"Yes, Dr. Brown," Tom Baker's voice said as the motor started up with a faint purr.

"Okay, kid." Serendipity looked over at Sherman. "You steer. There's a gas and brake pedal just like my hovercar you've driven."

Sherman thought it was funny that hovercars had kept the names for things from the gas powered cars, even when the original item was obsolete. Hovercars still had "gas pedals," even though they didn't use gas. But then again cars in his time still had "dashboards," "trunks," and "tires," terms they had inherited from horse-drawn carriages.

Sherman took it out of park, then pulled out of the school parking lot and onto the road. They had driven a block when something odd hit him. "Uh, Ser." Sherman cocked his head, listening. "There's no motor sound."

"Of course not, it's an electric hovervan powered by a Dark Energy Drive."

"But shouldn't it sound like a diesel truck for the disguise to be convincing?"

"Oh, yeah, you're right kid." Serendipity leaned forward. "T.M., give us some diesel engine sounds."

"Vroom, Vroom," T.M. said.

Sherman shook his head. "That doesn't work, Ser."

"Yeah, going have to work on that." Serendipity put her hand on the dashboard. "Going to have to work on the shocks too. This rides awfully bumpy."

"That's the roads, Ser. That's what happens when the road crew puts asphalt patches on top of patches. You're just use to cars that hover in the air."

They drove under the I-5 overpass to the old section of town, through the neighborhood of houses from the 1920s, 1940s and 1960s, all looking equally worn and tired. Sherman pulled up and parked in front of a two-story unpainted cinderblock building that managed to cram a four-apartment building onto a small one-house lot. The only landscaping was weeds in the cracks in the driveway that took up what would have been a front yard. The cars parked there were definitely used.

"This is where you lived?" Serendipity stared in horror.

"Yeah, there in Apartment B at the top right." Sherman pointed to the large "B" that had lost a nail and was now hanging upside down. "Place is a dump."

Wendell opened his door. "Let's get those containers out of the back and pack up your belongings, shall we?"

Sherman crawled out of the cab and went around to the other side to join Wendell, who had already opened the door to the time machine. Wendell climbed in, then handed out large plastic storage containers to the other two. Sherman appreciated the fact that the prim Englishman didn't comment on the place.

The three carried the containers up rusty metal steps, to the landing in front of the apartment. Serendipity wrinkled her nose when Sherman opened the door.

"Sorry." Sherman stepped in. "I was on a sit-down strike. I got tired of cleaning up after these pigs. I only cleaned up my own messes. I think the hosers are waiting for their moms to magically appear and scrub the place."

The three of them went into the tiny living room. In front of a ripped dirty green couch sat a scratched-up coffee table covered with empty pizza boxes. Behind it the thick layer of paint failed to disguise the cinderblock wall.

A closed door opened, and a young man stepped out of a cluttered bedroom, wearing only jeans. "Hey, dude," he mumbled, half asleep. "McDonald's called about six. Said if you didn't show up for work in a half hour, you were fired." He looked at his wristwatch. "I guess you're fired. What's up?"

"I'm moving out, Norm. Got a better job, but I have to blow this town."

"No way," his voice showed little emotion.

"Yes way." Sherman assured him

"Who's this with you?"

"New boss."

"Is this your boss's old lady?"

Serendipity walked over and glared at Norm. "I beg your pardon, pipsqueak!"

"*She* is my new boss," Sherman said. "Meet Dr. Serendipity Brown, genius inventor and this is Professor Wendell Howellingsworth, Dr. Brown's consultant." Sherman used the alias Serendipity had given Wendell to cover his tracks in the twenty-fourth century.

Wendell set the container down on its side and walked over to Norm, his hand held out. "Glad to make your acquaintance, Norm."

Norm let Wendell shake his hand. "Cool."

"We've come to get my stuff," Sherman told his roommate. "You can have anything I leave."

"Awesome, dude. What about your car?"

"The junker is yours. I'll leave the title. You can fix it or have it hauled away as scrap."

"Thanks, dude."

"Nice knowing ya, Norm." Sherman didn't say it sarcastically, but it did lack sincerity.

"Yeah, you too." Norm turned and stumbled back into the room and closed the door.

"Nice guy." Serendipity frowned.

"Norm just got off nightshift at the gas station, so he's a little spaced."

"I mean he doesn't seem upset at never seeing you again."

Sherman fought back a smile. "Dude is probably sick of me. It's not easy to share a cramped dump with three other guys. Just being able to put up with one another is sometimes the best you can do. The apartment only has two bedrooms so there's really no privacy. Mine's over here."

They stepped through the door of a small room lit by a window on the other end. A sun-faded piece of gingham material hung over the curtain rod. On the left side of the room lay a mattress on the floor with a few blankets wadded on it. Between the foot of the "bed" and the closet sprawled a pile of clothes. Tacked on the wall beside this mess hung a few magazine photos of sports figures.

On the other side of the room, where the door opened out, sat a beat-up bunk-bed frame, a coat of black paint trying to fill in the dinks in the wood. On top lay a foam pad with frayed blankets smoothed out in an attempt at neatness.

"This is my side," Sherman walked into the room. "I bought the bunk bed real cheap at a yard sale. Thought it would save space. We can just toss my clothes in a container."

Underneath the top bed a wooden dowel hung down. On it suspended coat hangers holding shirts, pants and a denim jacket. Down by the window, on the slats of the bottom bunk, sat a couple of milk crates that served as bookcases holding paperbacks, magazines and comics. Behind them sat a large cardboard box full of dirty laundry.

Sherman bent down a pulled a cardboard box from under the bed. "I found these boxes behind a print shop. I think they held reams of paper. They had lids so I thought they would be good for storage. I just cut them down so they would fit under the bed. This one has my gaming supplies and tapes for my Walkman, these two have clothes and this last one has odds and ends."

"Looks like you are already packed, kid."

"Yeah, pretty much."

"I congratulate you on your clever use of space." Wendell studied the layout with interest.

"It's all junk."

"But it's an ingenious use of junk."

"Thanks. When you don't have much space you learn to be kind of neat and organized. I grew up in a single-wide trailer. I shared a room smaller than this with two brothers." Sherman picked up the Walkman sitting on one of the milk crates and put it into one of the storage boxes.

"You had two brothers?" Wendell sounded excited.

"And three sisters. They had their own room."

"Oh my, five siblings! I was an only child. Most folks are in my time. With people living so long they had to cut back on the birthrate. I always wondered what it would be like to have siblings—someone to play with and talk to. That must have been marvelous for you."

"It was hell." Sherman walked around to the foot of the bed.

"Hell?"

"Everybody fought for space, food and attention. I was the youngest boy, so my two brothers bullied me."

"Oh, then you were the baby in the family?"

"Hardly. I had two younger sisters. They expected everyone else to take care of them."

"Perhaps I had it better than I knew." Wendell sounded disappointed.

Sherman climbed up the ladder attached to the back of the bunk-bed. He crawled up the bed to his alarm clock balanced on a board he had nailed on the headboard as a shelf. "You want my alarm clock, Ser?"

"Please!" Serendipity reached up eagerly as he handed it down to her. She studied it and grinned. "A real battery powered Westclox with a snooze button! Touchdown!"

"I don't suppose the blankets are worth keeping. I do want my posters though." Sherman flopped on his back and pulled the tacks out of the map of Middle Earth he had on the ceiling. He then detached from the wall the pictures of bikini-clad girls he had salvaged from an old Sports Illustrated calendar.

Sherman lowered himself off the bed and put the pinups into the gaming supplies box.

Serendipity was already taking shirts off hangers and packing them into the plastic container they had brought up.

Wendell picked up half of Sherman's library by the handles, with the cardboard box full of clothes on top of it. "I shall go ahead and take these down to the lorry." Wendell turned and left.

Sherman picked a couple of his storage boxes stacked on one another. "I'm with you."

"Wendell is right, you know." Serendipity folded a pair of jeans. "This does show organizational skills. This is the only part of the apartment that is tidy."

Sherman shrugged. "Jerry says I'm just neat because I'm a fag. Dork! I think *he's* gay." Sherman glared at the unmade mattress on the floor underneath the photos of athletes—*male* athletes.

"Yeah, I guess they are homophobic in this time period. Don't listen to people. Just be who you are."

Sherman almost asked if that meant Serendipity was telling him not to let people talk him into thinking he was gay, or if she meant he shouldn't be ashamed if he was gay. He decided to let it drop. Sherman liked girls *way* too much to even wonder about his own sexual orientation. Pity girls didn't seem to feel the same way about him.

Sherman did a quick tour of the apartment to see if there was anything he had forgotten. He looked in the kitchen cupboards. "I got a few dishes I guess I'll let the guys have."

Serendipity looked over his shoulder. "Is this your cupboard?"

"Yeah."

"Can I have your stuff?" she asked.

"It's just some give-away glasses, some Melmac plates and a couple of aluminum pots."

"Yeah, I'll pay you five thousand for them."

Sherman managed not to roll his eyes. "Ser, just take them."

Serendipity carefully wrapped the Camp Snoopy glasses Sherman had gotten from work in brown paper bags and stuck them in the box with the dirty laundry.

"Well, that's it, Ser." Sherman headed for the door. "Ser?"

Sherman looked behind him to see Serendipity running her hand lovingly over the decrepit kitchen table that needed wiped off. "A circa 1960 Formica and chrome table. What would your roommates sell it for?"

"Ser, that table is a piece of garbage. The top is all scratched; the legs have dents. You have a nicer one at home."

"But it's a replica. This one is *real*."

"You can go back and buy a brand new one, you know. Come on." Sherman walked back into the living room. "I'll grab the last of my stuff and we'll get out of here."

"Do you want to go by work and tell them you won't be coming in?" Serendipity followed him out, clutching her treasures.

"They already fired me even though for all they know I'm lying in the hospital, croaking. And I worked there three years." Sherman sighed and shrugged. "I guess they are used to people quitting by just not showing up for work."

Sherman carried the last container down the steps.

"What about your family?" Serendipity negotiated the rickety stairs.

"What about them?"

"Sherman! You have to at least tell your mother goodbye."

"Yeah, you're probably right."

They got down to the truck with the Rainier Beer logo with its large calligraphic red "R." Wendell stood waiting, looking about at the neighborhood. His expression didn't show disgust, but sadness. No doubt the Englishman could feel the vibes of this depressed neighborhood. Wendell forced a smile as Sherman came over, then took his container and packed it away.

Serendipity took the box with her new-found treasures into the Timemobile and tied it down with bungee cords and netting. She looked over at Sherman at the door. "So where does your Mom live? Do we get to meet her?"

"I'd rather you didn't. You would probably have to fight her for Wendell."

"What?" Wendell whirled around. "I wouldn't—"

"Mom would. You aren't butt-ugly, you got class and you look like you have a decent job. You're a huge step up from anything she's ever had. She'd be all over you. Hell, you could cause a riot in the trailer court. All the women would be fighting over you."

"You are joking, right?" The usually ignored Wendell raised a skeptical eyebrow.

"Look around, Wendell." Sherman motioned with his hand. "This place is full of desperate people. This is a lumber town, so there's been high unemployment since the timber industry went south. Longview Fiber was about the largest producer of paper bags and milk cartons. They're laying-off now that everyone is switching to plastic. Mount Saint Helens blowing just made things worse. Why do you think I jumped at the chance to work for Serendipity and get out of here?"

"I had no idea, old chap. If you like, you can leave us at a restaurant and we will wait for you."

Serendipity looked unconvinced. "If I had a kid I would want to meet the people he's going to work for."

Wendell put his hand on her arm. Serendipity looked up at him, and he shook his head at her. "Leave Sherman his dignity."

"Yeah, maybe I should listen to you, Wendell." Serendipity nodded. "You're the sensitive one."

"I wouldn't say that."

"But you seem to know what others around you are feeling better than I do."

"That's because you get preoccupied with your inventions. You are focused on solving problems. As for me, I'm an anthropologist. I've spent my life studying people. I think I have an unfair advantage."

Serendipity smiled at Wendell and turned to Sherman. "Okay, kid, you can drop us off and we'll wait for you to return." Then she looked hopeful again. "Would it be too much if you dropped us off at the McDonald's you used to work at? You don't have to go in, but I would like Wendell to see where the very first time trip in history took place."

The historian perked up. "Oh my word, that would indeed be exciting!"

Sherman fought back a laugh. "Yeah, sure."

Serendipity and Wendell might be right, Sherman decided. He should tell his mother goodbye. He didn't want any regrets twenty years later. He left his boss and her consultant at the McDonald's near I-5 and drove under the freeway again, then turned off Allen Street to follow South Pacific Avenue to the tiny trailer court in south Kelso. He found a vacant spot at the side of the narrow lane separating the two rows of trailers and parked the van.

"T.M. lock the doors. Don't let anyone in until I return."

"Understood, Mr. Conrad."

"Just call me Sherman."

"As you wish, Sherman."

Sherman got out of the cab, and walked past the rusting trailers to the one he had once called home. He went through the gate of the chicken-wire fence that enclosed a narrow yard hardly big enough to bother mowing. He carefully walked up the rotting wooden steps that bowed under his weight to knock on the aluminum door. It rattled like it would fall off if he rapped too hard.

The door opened, revealing a fourteen-year-old girl with over-moussed black hair. "Hello, ugly!"

Sherman ignored the insult. It wasn't personal. His sister talked that way to all her siblings, trying to start a fight. He had no idea why she did this. Maybe it was for the excitement—maybe for the attention. Sherman was the only one smart enough not to take the bait.

"Hello Terry. Is Mom home?"

"Yeah. Why?" Terry turned and flitted off, without waiting for an answer.

Sherman stepped on in. The single-wide trailer smelled of mold and stale tobacco smoke. Sherman found his Mom sitting on the couch watching a soap opera, with a cigarette in one hand and a coffee mug in the other. An ignored pile of unfolded laundry took up the rest of the couch.

"Hello, Mom."

She looked up, dark roots showing under her blonde hair. His mom disproved the theory that one could never be too skinny. Even so her jeans were still too tight and the short stretchy top failed to cover her belly button. The outfit was too young for her and made her look ridiculous. "Shhh! It's getting to the good part. They're going to tell who the father of Monica's baby is. I hope it's not Cliff; he's a jerk."

"Mom, this is important."

"How come you never visit, Sherman? You kids only come by when you need money. I don't have any money."

"I didn't come to borrow money, Mom. Have I ever borrowed money?"

She kept her eyes on the television. "No, I guess not. You're the only one that doesn't. Your brother Clyde borrowed a fifty from me yesterday. Now I'm short. Can I borrow some money from you for cigarettes?"

"Sure, Mom." Sherman took out his wallet, pulled out the replica hundred dollar bills Serendipity had given him for shopping. He handed it all to his mother. She counted it, actually forgetting the TV. "Hell, this is seven hundred dollars! Where did you get this?"

"That's what I came to tell you. It's an advance. I got a real good job. Problem is it's a long way from here and I'll be traveling."

"It isn't drugs, is it?"

"No, Mom."

"Good." She stuffed the bills in her purse at her feet. "I found a marijuana joint in your brother Bobby's jacket pocket again. I told him to shape up or ship out." His mom put her cigarette in her mouth and sucked hard, the tip turning red, then black.

"Yes, Mom."

"I don't want him becoming like Harvey next door. He got arrested. Be doing six months in the County Jail. It doesn't surprise me. His mother is such a tramp. She stole my last boyfriend. Don't know what he saw in her. She's so fat."

"Mom, it will be a long time before I see you again, if I ever do. The job is in—uh, the Amazon. There's no phones, no mail."

"Why do you want to go to the Amazon, Sherman? You could get a job at Longview Fiber."

"Mom, they aren't hiring, they're laying-off. There aren't any jobs in this area. Why do you think I was working at a fast-food joint? If I'm going to make anything of myself I'm going to have to leave."

"What about me, Sherman? Did you ever think about that?" She took a sip of coffee.

"Mom, you're not that old. You're healthy. You're grownup. You can take care of yourself."

She snorted. "Yeah, none of you kids ever appreciated anything I ever did for you."

Sherman sighed and reached into his jacket pocket and pulled out a couple of gold coins Serendipity had given him in 1886 at Laramie. "Here Mom."

"Crap, Sherman! Did you steal these?" She stared at them.

"No, Mom."

"These real?"

"They're real gold. It's all I have. I can't stay. I have an appointment."

"Thank you, Sherman. This will help." She managed to wedge them into the pocket of her tight jeans.

Sherman knew it would probably all be spent within the week with nothing to show for it.

She held out her arms. "Now, come over here and give your mother a hug." She didn't bother to get up or put down her cigarette.

Sherman went over and gave her a hug. "I love you, Mom."

"Yeah, love you too."

Sherman walked to the door. He looked back and saw his mother was already hypnotized by the television. He looked over at his youngest sibling. "Goodbye, Terry."

"Goodbye, stupid." His sister stuck out her tongue.

Sherman walked back to the Timemobile. As lousy as his apartment had been, it seemed a step up from this. Still he felt a little guilty. Should he stay and take care of his Mom? How can you take care of someone that hopeless? He would never be able to bring her up. She would only wind up dragging him down into her bog of despair.

Yet Sherman sometimes wondered if all of this was completely his mother's fault. Or was it this town? This place seemed to suck the very life out of you. Sherman looked at the trees around him covered with moss. Even the trees here seemed to start rotting before their time.

Sometimes Sherman had felt like Serendipity had saved his life. Now, he was certain of it.

Sherman drove the Timemobile back to the McDonald's. He had no choice but to go in to retrieve his companions. He found Serendipity and Wendell sitting on plastic benches in a booth, eating Egg McMuffins. She drank a cup of coffee, while Wendell held a Styrofoam cup with a teabag in it. Sherman smiled at the ludicrous scene, for this was the tea gourmet who carefully timed his brew and served it in porcelain cups. He then noticed Wendell wore his Victorian spectacles, which hid a twenty-seventh-century camera. Wendell kept looking around, occasionally touching the hinge at the eyepiece, which meant he was taking pictures or video. Sherman came over and sat down next to Serendipity, who moved over for him.

Serendipity pointed out the window. "Hey kid, you know the lot over there where the Timemobile landed my first trip?"

"Yeah?" Sherman looked past the small playground outside to the tiny vacant lot covered with weeds and Shasta daisies.

"Wendell says they built a fifty-foot obelisk there in the twenty-sixth century, marking it as the sight of the first time trip!"

"You're kidding."

"I haven't actually visited it." Wendell studied the empty ground. "But I've seen 3-D holograms. This establishment will be long gone but they will build an exact replica here for the museum."

"Some temporal anthropologist came back and recorded it?"

"Are you kidding? Dr. Eugene Carson from the University of Washington was sitting in that booth over there recording your meeting with Serendipity Brown more than two hundred years ago on the one-hundredth anniversary of the first time trip. That was before the Institute of Time

Travel started regulating time travel. Well, two centuries ago from my time. It will be several centuries in the future from your time. Well, actually five months ago in your current Base Time. Yesterday from this point." Wendell shook his head as if trying to clear it. "Problem with time travel is one should never try to create a timeline. It winds up looking like a bowl of spaghetti."

Sherman stared over at the now empty booth, trying to remember if he had noticed anyone there yesterday five months ago.

"Would you like something, kid?" Serendipity asked, breaking his reverie. "I wanted Wendell to taste a Big Mac, but they said they're still making breakfast. They did offer us these McMuffin things. They're really good!"

Sherman shook his head. "I'm fine."

"How did it go?"

"Okay." Sherman shrugged. "I gave her all the money I had on me. Told her it would be awhile before I ever saw her again, if ever."

"Was she upset?"

"Not really. She was kind of engrossed in her soaps."

"Soaps?"

"Soap operas. Daytime dramas on TV."

Serendipity looked horrified and started to say something, but Wendell shook his head at her. "I do believe, Serendipity dear, you wished to go shopping?"

"Yeah, right," Serendipity said. "So, where is a good place to go shopping, kid?"

"Portland, maybe Vancouver."

"No, I meant locally."

"Ser, would you mind awfully if we left? I just want to get out of this town."

Serendipity studied him a moment, and then nodded. "Sure, kid. Maybe we ought to just take your stuff home, plan a shopping trip later."

"Yeah." Sherman nodded. "I'd like to go home."

Serendipity smiled at him. "It's your home as long as you want to stay, kid."

"Thanks, Ser."

Serendipity drank the last gulp of coffee and got up, heading for the door. She tossed the empty cup in the trash on the way out. Wendell followed, with the tray. Sherman hurried after the two, when a hand grabbed his arm.

"Sherman!"

Sherman whirled around to see the assistant manager, Gilbert, glaring at him. Gilbert wasn't much older or bigger than Sherman. He always rode Sherman's butt, but then he rode everyone's butt. Gilbert used bullying to make up for his lack of managerial skills. "You were supposed to be in here at six o'clock this morning!"

"Sorry, wasn't able to come in. I couldn't get to a phone."

"You're fired, you little twerp!"

"You already fired me once. You can't fire me twice." Sherman kept his voice calm. "Besides, I think only the owner can do that, not you. You can tell them I quit."

Serendipity came over and managed to look down at the slightly taller man. "Excuse me, but Sherman couldn't call you because he was busy working for me."

"Who the hell are you?" Gilbert glared.

"Someone who can buy and sell you, sweetheart. I'm rich beyond your wildest imagination. I'm paying Sherman more every week than you probably make in a year, because Sherman is smarter and more talented than you." She reached out and patted Gilbert on the cheek. "He's too good to work for you." She looked over at Sherman. "Come along, Mr. Conrad. We have pressing business."

"Of course, Dr. Brown." Sherman walked out of his old workplace with as much dignity as he could muster. He beat Serendipity and Wendell back to the Timemobile, however, and climbed into the driver's seat.

Serendipity slid over next to him. "Pull her around behind a building where there's no one to see us. Don't want anyone having a heart attack watching the van disappear."

Sherman drove behind the old vacated *Hilander Bowl* building. They crawled out of the cab and got into the Timemobile proper. Sherman strapped in as Serendipity set the dials.

She plopped down in her own seat. "Everyone ready?"

"More than ready," Sherman assured her. "And thank you."

"For what, kid?"

"For rescuing me from this place...from that job...from this life."

"Accidentally kidnapping you was the smartest thing I ever did, kid." Serendipity smiled at him as the machine began thrashing like an animal escaping from a leg noose.

Chapter Four

The Timemobile settled down and everyone undid their seatbelts. Serendipity picked up the box full of dishes and dirty clothes and headed for the door. She swung it open and yelped, dropping the crate, her precious McDonald's Camp Snoopy glasses crashing to the floor of the workshop.

Serendipity slammed the door shut, locked it, then put her back against it. "I am going to have to put a monitor on this thing so I can see what's outside before I open the door."

Wendell and Sherman were out of their seats, coming to her aid.

"What is it, Ser?" Sherman asked.

"THEM!"

"Them?"

"No, *THEM.*" Serendipity turned to Wendell. "Your worst nightmare."

"Enforcers?" Wendell's left eye started jerking with that nervous tic that only the Institute of Time Travel Enforcement Agency seemed to stimulate.

Serendipity nodded.

"But they promised to leave us alone," Sherman protested.

One of the invaders outside banged on the Timemobile door. "Dr. Brown! We need to talk to you."

"You can't have Wendell!" Serendipity yelled back. "He's mine. You *promised* him to me!"

"Dr. Brown, we are not here to arrest Dr. Howe. We just need to talk to *you*. We came to warn you that your life is in danger."

Before Serendipity could stop him, Wendell scooped her away and swung open the door. "What? Dr. Brown is in danger?"

"Yes, Dr. Howe, we just need to talk."

Sherman peered around Wendell to see three men in identical dark grey twenty-fourth-century suits and identical emotionless expressions. Dark glasses hid their eyes and any feeling that might be in them. Sherman recognized them as Agents Five, Eighteen and Twenty-Two of the twenty-seventh century's Institute of Time Travel Enforcement Agency. It was their job to make sure no one traveled in time from their own time period without the Institute's overseeing the entire trip.

At first glance they looked identical, but Sherman had learned from their previous contact to see them as individuals. Agent Five, the leader, a pit bull of a man, looked like he might have some distant African ancestry. Agent Twenty-Two, the interrogator, had a leaner build with reddish-tinged hair beyond a high forehead. Maybe, Irish? French? Jewish? Agent Eighteen, the muscle of the group, looked Mediterranean or Middle Eastern or Polynesian or Hispanic or something. Sherman couldn't tell.

Sherman followed Serendipity and Wendell out of the Timemobile and glared at Agent Five. "I thought Serendipity was outside your jurisdiction."

"She is, and we would not be here if it wasn't critical." Agent Five stood stiffly. "We are taking a chance just coming here, but felt any of our interactions that might inadvertently change history was not as risky as Serendipity being murdered."

"Murdered!" Wendell drew Serendipity to himself in a protective manner.

"Murdered?" Serendipity gently untangled herself from Wendell and stepped forward. "Aren't you meddling with history by warning me?"

"You aren't supposed to die at this time. The assassins are from the twenty-seventh century. They are from a new terrorist faction of the Time Purists who call themselves the Time Keepers. These insurgents have decided the Time Purists are not effective enough and the only way to keep time pure and free of possible time manipulations from time travelers is to go into the past and assassinate Serendipity Brown, the inventor of time travel."

"How do you know this?" Serendipity moved closer to Agent Five.

"One of our agents infiltrated the Time Keepers and discovered their plan."

"So, go arrest them," Sherman said.

"The Time Keepers are set up in cells, so our agent only knows a few of those involved. There is no way we could arrest enough of them to make an impact. It would only serve to warn their leaders that we know their plans."

Wendell came up to Serendipity and once more put his arm around her defensively. "So, how do you know they won't go into the past and assassinate Dr. Brown when she was a child?"

Agent Five shook his head. "We know that they want to eliminate her before she announces her invention to the world, but after the rumors had started."

"Bruce!" Serendipity said. "That jerk. I'll bet that interview started the rumors."

"But why after the rumors?" Wendell asked Agent Five.

"They want Serendipity to die of mysterious circumstances after stories surfaced that she had created a time machine. They want it to be a warning to others not to try and invent time travel."

"But that makes no sense."

Agent Five raised an eyebrow. "Agent Twenty-Two is our trained psychologist. Ask him."

Agent Twenty-Two stepped forward. "The terrorists are what we refer to inside the profession as *total nut jobs*." He said this with his usual straight face.

Agent Five nodded. "We want you to evacuate, Dr. Brown, so we can set a trap for them."

"You want us to leave town?"

"We want you to leave this time period and go into the past. We want you to go where they'll never find you."

"Where's that?"

"We do not know and we do not want to know, in case they capture and torture us. We suggest you make your plans, pack and get out as quickly as possible." Agent Five scowled at Wendell. "And make certain she stays out of the future. We have enough problems."

"Wait a minute," Sherman said, "if these wackos are so all fired worried about changing history, won't they being changing history if they kill Serendipity?"

"The Time Keepers feel this one alteration will correct all the changes that time travelers have created."

Wendell nervously brushed his upper lip, a habit he had developed after having had a mustache for fifty years. "But being able to go back in time and study the past has allowed us to stop more than one disaster in our own time. Won't billions die if they stop time travel?"

"Yes, Dr. Howe." Agent Five's face looked even grimmer. "You don't think we are just here to protect our jobs, do you? I suggest you pack what you will need to survive and get out of here as soon as you can. I would recommend you discuss any plans where neither we nor any surveillance cameras can overhear where you are going. Just pick the last place on earth and time in history they would expect you to go."

"How will we know when to come back?" Serendipity sounded far calmer than the situation warranted.

"Come back in exactly three months Base Time to check if it's safe. Send Dr. Howe or Mr. Conrad out in case there is an ambush, so you can get away in your time machine."

"I do not use my friends as alligator bait." Serendipity raised her eyebrow. "Why don't I just jump ahead three months in my machine with you and shove *you* out?"

Agent Five shook his head. "Bad idea. That's what Base Time is all about. When you are hopping about in time, you need to keep your Base Timeline, your own present, in actual time. Otherwise you could be growing old before your time or meeting yourself coming back."

"Agent Five is correct," Agent Twenty-Two said. "It is far better for your sanity."

"Yeah, yeah." Serendipity rolled her eyes. "I've had this lecture before from Wendell."

This was still too much for Sherman. "How do you know these Time Keeper bozos can even do this? Maybe it's just a lot of talk."

"Our terrorists have already struck." Agent Five pushed on the bridge of his dark glasses. "They have assassinated three temporal anthropologists back home. Executed is more accurate. They cut off the dead men's feet and left a card with the Institute's motto: 'Leave no footprints in the sands of time.'"

"Cut off their feet!" Sherman yelped. "That's gross."

"No kidding." Serendipity wrinkled her nose in disgust. "But why go after a bunch of harmless history geeks? I mean if they kill me there never will have been any time travel, right?"

Agent Five shook his head. "Perhaps they want to eliminate them before they can do any more time traveling, though it looks more like they are punishing them for imagined crimes."

Wendell appeared nauseous. "Who were they? Who were the temporal anthropologists?"

"Dr. Walther Hoffmann, Dr. Shiro Suzuki and Dr. Kahn Shamar."

"Shamar...Suzuki...Hoffman?" Wendell whispered. "Dead?"

Serendipity put her hand on his arm. "Isn't Shamar that guy you told us about that you once worked with in 1800s India?"

Wendell nodded. "Yes and Dr. Suzuki is the chap who did the tea ceremony I recorded in my book on tea. I never had a chance to work in the Field with him or Hoffman because Shiro was studying Japanese monasteries and Walther was studying the Goths. They were always nice to me. There aren't many of us temporal anthropologists. We are a rather close knit group of introverts." Wendell turned to Agent Five. "What about the surviving T.A.s? Are they safe?"

"We have guards on all the remaining Registered Time Travelers in the twenty-seventh century."

"What about the T.A.s in the Field? Have they been warned or retrieved?"

"There are only seven remaining. We just have to assume the Time Keepers won't be after them, and are going after Dr. Brown. The terrorists only have one time machine."

"The terrorists have a time machine!" Wendell's normally calm voice bordered on hysteria.

"We are assuming they do. One of our time machines is unaccounted for."

"But how could they run it? Only trained technicians can set them."

"They got the knowledge...somehow." Agent Five's brows dipped even lower behind his dark glasses.

Sherman read the worried expression. "You suspect one of your own, don't you?"

Agent Five shook his head. "It would make sense, but everyone at the Institute down to the tour guides has been interrogated using Compliance Disks. No one can lie with one of those on the back of his neck."

Sherman winced at the memory of his own interrogation just a few weeks before.

"So the T.A.s in the Field are not safe," Wendell said. "If the terrorists have access to time travel technology, you don't know what records they might have. They might know exactly where the T.A.s in the Field are. Why don't you send agents after them?"

"All time travel into or out of the twenty-seventh century present has been stopped by a dampening field. We were the last ones out. The Institute spared us so we could protect Dr. Brown. All other agents are needed in the twenty-seventh century to help protect the remaining registered time travelers and track the terrorists we have identified. We can't afford to go on a wild goose chase to save a handful of people who *might* be in danger."

"If you have stopped all time travel in and out of the twenty-seventh century, how will the people in the Field return?"

"They can't. If they try they will simply ricochet back to where they started." Then Agent Five added, "We hope."

"You hope?" Wendell eyes widened even more.

"It is possible the time machine will bounce into another unknown time period where we probably will never find them, or they will—well, crash into the closed gate as it were."

"You mean they will die?" Sherman yelped.

"It is unfortunate, but we can't risk the lives of billions to save seven."

"What if we were to retrieve them?" Wendell offered.

"Fine with me," Serendipity agreed.

"Too dangerous." Agent Five shook his head. "Your first duty, Dr. Howe, is to protect Dr. Brown at all costs. Make certain she gets somewhere safe to hide."

Serendipity frowned. "We have to pack, figure out where to go, replicate the proper money and find a place to live in the next couple of days?"

"No, Dr. Brown. You are leaving in the next couple of hours."

Serendipity stared at Agent Five a moment, then she gave a soft moan. Her eyes rolled up into her head as she fell backwards in a swoon. Wendell caught her. Sherman rushed over confused. This was so out of character for the unshakable Serendipity Brown.

"Serendipity!" Wendell patted her cheeks. "Are you all right, darling?"

"I need to lie down," she whispered. "Just take me to my room. Please?"

Agent Eighteen, silent as ever, scooped up Serendipity.

"I can show you where her bedroom is." Wendell hovered.

Agent Twenty-Two studied Serendipity concerned. "The shock was too much for her. I have something I can give her."

"No!" Serendipity yelped. "Please, just let me lie down for a little bit. Just a panic attack. I'll be fine if I can collect myself. Just give me a half hour."

"I really don't want to drug her if it can be helped." Agent Twenty-Two told Agent Five. "She's the only one who can operate her time machine."

The entire group followed Wendell as he led Agent Eighteen to Serendipity's bedroom. The tall burly man laid her on the tie-dyed spread on her bed with its padded heart-shaped headboard.

"Don't leave me, Wendell," she whimpered, her eyes closed. "You too, Sherman." She reached out a trembling hand.

Wendell sat on the bed beside her and took her hand. "I'll never leave you, dearest."

Sherman took her other hand. "I'm here for you Ser."

Agent Twenty-Two nodded at Agents Five and Eighteen. "We will leave them alone for a half hour, then check on Dr. Brown. I guess this was a lot to take in."

The Enforcers left, Agent Twenty-Two gently closing the door.

"Serendipity, darling." Wendell leaned down. "Sherman and I will take care of you. Everything will be all right. You have nothing to fear."

Serendipity opened one eye. "Are the Time Nazis gone?" she whispered.

"Yes?" Wendell blinked confused.

"Good!" She pulled her PAL computer out of her skirt pocket, rolled over on her stomach and began typing furiously with her thumbs.

"That was a quick recovery," Sherman whispered. "Did you just fake that attack?"

"What do you think?" Her voice sounded indignant. "Had to get away from those goons."

"Why?" Wendell kept his voice down, too.

"So, I could hack into their computers."

"What!" Wendell managed not to yell. "You cannot. I'm sure they have security blocks."

Serendipity made a face. "Please, don't insult me. I can hack into just about anything. One of my Ph.D.s is in computers."

"Why do you want into their computers?"

"To see if they have any record of who those seven missing time travelers are and where they might be. We're going after them. Nobody tells Serendipity Brown she can't do something."

Wendell fought back a grin. "Serendipity Brown, I love you."

"And I expect you to show me just how much by making mad passionate love to me after we save them." Serendipity didn't look up from her computer. "But for now, watch the door and let me work."

Sherman went over to the door, and kept his ear to it. Serendipity worked while Wendell watched anxiously.

Serendipity suddenly grinned. "Oh, I am so good! Got them downloaded." She sat up. "So, you love me, Wendell?"

Wendell grinned at her. "If I hadn't before, I certainly do now. You are magnificent!"

"Eh, piece of baklava." Serendipity studied the screen. "Oh dear, Henry Darrel is on here. He's a friend of yours, isn't he?"

"Yes!" The normally polite Wendell snatched Serendipity's computer from her, reading the screen with a look of panic. "Henry is in Florida with a Cerwyn Owen and Priscilla Cohen, both temporal zoologists. Abubakari Djata is in Mali, Erik Olafson is in Norway and Matilda Warwick..." Wendell's voice faded. "No, not Matilda."

"You know Matilda?"

"Yes, nice lady studying medieval convents. She doesn't deserve to die. None of them do."

"Who says they have to die? I told you we would rescue them."

"Just knowing the date and place isn't enough. Without the exact coordinates and the signatures from their tracking implants it could take weeks or months to find them all."

"Tom, coordinates and signature for Matilda Warwick."

Wendell's eyes got big. "My word! You got those, too?" He looked torn between laughing and crying.

"Yeah, and after we get out of here and away from the Time Gestapo, we'll save your nun friend."

Wendell bit at his lip. "I would like to retrieve her first, but Henry has two temporal zoologists with him. We would be rescuing three people in one visit. We will have to give them a lift first."

"We'll do her second."

Wendell nodded. Then unable to contain himself he grabbed Serendipity and hugged her. "Thank you, Serendipity. Thank you."

"I noticed one of the names on the list was Tobias Leach."

"I would be hugging you even for his sake."

"Why? He doesn't like you."

"We still must rescue him. All right, we can rescue him last. Henry, Matilda then...Hmm, Dr. Djata is a Mali scholar and Dr. Olafson is a Viking. Both nice chaps." Wendell waved his head back and forth like he was weighing. "Okay, Djata third, Olafson fourth—he's a big Viking who carries an ax and hammer. He can defend himself better against attackers. Then Tobias. He'll probably be in some brothel with bouncers anyway."

"So if the terrorists kill him, he'll die happy?"

Wendell frowned at her. "That is not funny. I do not wish to see any of them die."

Sherman pushed his horn-rimmed glasses back up his nose. "So once we save them what do we do? We can't bring them back here."

Serendipity shrugged. "I guess we are going to have a few guests at our hideout in the past."

Wendell took Serendipity's hand. "Is there any way you could just send me?"

"You need me to run the machine. Besides I have you and Sherman to protect me."

"Neither of us are combatants," Wendell pointed out.

"No, but I am." Serendipity gave him a tiger-like grin. "I'll pack a stunner. So, it looks like we need to establish a safe house somewhere in the past. First, to what year do we go? I'd say twentieth century is the first place they'll look if they know anything about me. I don't want to go too far back. Don't want to rough it too much. Would like access to the internet. How did people survive before then without the 'net'?"

"Internet didn't get really big before the early twenty-first century, if I recall," Wendell said.

"Hmm, how about 2010? Still close enough to the twentieth century for Sherman and me. Now where do we go? Portland area is out."

"The British Isles are also too obvious." Wendell looked disappointed. "There is a chance they might know about me."

"So is the Longview/Kelso area." Sherman didn't look disappointed. "They probably do know about me."

"Be nice if we could keep it in the Pacific Northwest." Serendipity gazed up at the ceiling, looking thoughtful. "Wherever we go, we are going to need a place big enough to accommodate ten people. Don't have time to build. We will have to buy or rent. We can let that help us decide where to go, see what is available. If we rent they will want to do a background check, so that's out. Buying would be best, but it will have to be cash, or again they will want to do a background check if we get a loan. We are going to need a whole lot of money. I don't know if I can replicate that much in such a short time."

"Why don't you go with the obvious?" Sherman suggested.

"Obvious?"

"Yeah, go back to the twentieth century and buy stocks, then go to 2010 and sell them."

Wendell thought a moment. "Normally I would say that's unethical, but this is a matter of life and death—and not just ours. Billions could die if time travel is eliminated."

Serendipity nodded. "Okay, that's the plan. You two pack what you need, what you can't get in 2010 and can't live without. Wendell, you'll have to do some quick research on the history of stocks."

The historian looked uncertain. "I'll try my best. Business was never my strong suit."

"Hey, let me!" Sherman bounced off the bed. "I've always been fascinated with money, maybe because I never had any. My first online college course was on the history of the stock exchange."

Wendell raised his eyebrow at him. "That is an odd subject to choose for your first course."

"All right," Sherman confessed. "At the time I wasn't sure if Ser was going to keep me. I just wanted to know where to invest some money when she sent me back to 1985."

Serendipity shrugged. "Knew you were smart. Looks like that course will come in handy after all. Okay Wendell, try and pack as many of our costumes from the wardrobe room as you can. Looks like we will be doing some time hopping. I'll pack some tools and Robbie, and make some twentieth-century money to buy the stocks. And remember, tell the Time Gestapo out there nothing, except that I appear to be fine now. We got ourselves some temporal anthropologists to save."

Chapter Five

Sherman came into the huge workshop carrying his luggage: a nineteenth-century carpet bag, a twenty-fourth-century suitcase and a twentieth-century backpack. He found Serendipity standing with Robbie and arguing with Agent Five. "I'm not going anywhere without Robbie! It's my cook and housekeeper."

"I'm sorry, but you can't take a twenty-fourth-century android into the past. If anyone discovers it is a robot, it could cause havoc with history."

"I'll starve without Robbie!"

Agent Five snorted. "You're a genius, Dr. Brown. Learn to cook."

"You sound just like my fourth husband. Bet you're divorced, too. Can I at least have Robbie help me pack?"

"That would be acceptable, just don't pack the robot."

"Fine. Robbie." Serendipity pointed to a tool chest on wheels. "Bring that over and put it in the machine."

"I'm sorry, Dr. Brown." Agent Five studied the large chest. "But you can't take that either."

"And what happens if the Timemobile breaks down?"

"Take the bare essentials and the least technically advanced tools you can get by with."

"Fine." Serendipity looked up to see Sherman. "Sherman! I need you to help me fabricate some money for the trip."

"We have already handled that, Dr. Brown." Agent Five turned to his largest companion. "Agent Eighteen, the money please."

Agent Eighteen stepped over to one of the work counters and picked up a leather drawstring bag Sherman had never noticed before. He came over and held out the huge pouch without a word.

Agent Five spoke for him. "We have five hundred dollars in ten-dollar Eagle gold pieces dated 1795. You can use them as legal tender until 1933. Before or after that you can always melt them down and sell the gold—well, any period before the twenty-second century when they started replicating gold. This is about eighteen and a half pounds."

"Five hundred dollars?" Serendipity protested. "Are you nuts? We can't survive three months on just five hundred dollars. I don't know if I could survive one day."

"I'm sorry, Dr. Brown, but you won't be able to pursue your extravagant lifestyle. You'll just have to rough it."

"Don't worry, Ser." Sherman put his hand on her shoulder. "I know how to stretch a dollar."

Serendipity looked over at Sherman. He gave her a wink the Enforcers couldn't see.

Wendell recruited Sherman to help him bring down four plastic storage boxes full of historical costumes since they had no idea what was available in 2010 and where Serendipity might want to go for a quick trip. Agent Five insisted on inspecting the containers and seemed satisfied that it was only clothes and no robots. He in fact congratulated Wendell on his cleverness for covering up their destination from them.

Sherman opened the Timemobile door to pack it. "Oh, man! We've still got to unload my stuff out of here."

Agent Five looked over at Agent Eighteen and Twenty-Two. "You two help unpack the time machine and set the items over there. I'll help you take them up to the attic after they leave. Right now I have to babysit Dr. Brown, and guard against her packing some tool she should not take into the past."

Sherman set his milk crate down next to the other boxes and looked up at Agent Eighteen standing beside him. The man was bigger than the other enforcers and almost never spoke. The man's features were nondescript but his complexion hinted at something other than Anglo-Saxon. Curiosity got the better of Sherman. "Uh, can I ask you a personal question?"

"Yes?" Agent Eighteen grunted.

"What nationality are you? I mean, are you Italian or Greek or Spanish or Arab or Indian or Hawaiian or Mexican or Filipino?"

"Yes." Agent Eighteen turned and headed back for another box.

Sherman watched him confused.

Wendell must have overheard, for he leaned down and whispered. "Remember he's from the twenty-seventh century. Being from one ethnic group is now the minority rather than the majority. Bullies used to tease me and call me *inbred*. Children can be so cruel sometimes."

"Tell me about it."

Wendell gave him a sympathetic smile. "Come on, old boy. Let's make certain the Enforcers pack everything we need in our time machine."

Sherman and Wendell went into the Timemobile to make sure everything had been secured down with netting and bungee cords properly. When they came out, Serendipity wore a defiant but defeated glare directed at Agent Five.

"All right, Dr. Brown, Dr. Howe, Mr. Conrad," Agent Five barked. He didn't raise his voice, but something about it made them snap to attention, including Serendipity. He looked them over, lined up like Marine recruits. "Okay, all three of you pull out your computers. Set Base Time for 12:15 p.m., October first, 2353. You will report here in exactly three months, January first, 2354 at noon precisely. Is that understood? I would suggest you keep the date, if not the year, the same wherever you decide to go, so you won't forget that date. Is that understood?"

"Yes, sir," Sherman yelped.

Serendipity however gave Agent Five a faked seductive smile. "So are you going to throw a party for me?"

"Party?" Agent Five frowned.

"Yeah, New Year's Day party. You can bring the noise makers."

"Just hope you don't have Time Keepers here to meet you, Dr. Brown, with their *noise makers* pointed at you."

Serendipity's smile dropped.

"Now, get in your time machine and vacate the premises. Go somewhere safe. And good luck!"

"Thank you." Serendipity forced a smile.

"I was talking to Dr. Howe and Mr. Conrad. They are going to have their hands full with you, Dr. Brown."

"Yup, definitely reminds me of my fourth husband." Serendipity winked at Agent Five and climbed up the steps into the Timemobile.

Sherman and Wendell followed her in and closed the door.

"Be sure to lock that, Wendell." She went over to the dials. "Now, where are we supposed to go and live on a piddling five hundred?"

Sherman pulled out his computer. "Let me have twenty of those ten-dollar gold pieces and take me back to September thirtieth, 1919. We are about to live every stock broker's fantasy."

Chapter Six

Sherman felt disappointed at how much 2010 looked like 1985. The Timemobile was now disguised as a U-Haul truck in a bank parking lot in Seattle. The three time travelers dove into the cab in a failed attempt to get out of the rain and keep dry. Sherman watched the drops beating against the windshield, trying to get at him. "Bummer, the weather was a lot nicer in 1919."

Wendell shook his head. "I still can't believe you only bought five shares of Coca-Cola for forty dollars apiece and they are now worth over forty million!"

"It's just that high because I had the brokers reinvest the dividends. I only cashed in part of the stocks because they are still going up and still splitting. You should see what they would be worth in 2353!"

"Somehow it doesn't seem...well, cricket. I feel guilty that I had any part in this, letting Dr. Brown use my Bizzy Card computer application to create fake identification documents for you."

"The stock certificates were real." Sherman consoled him. "Could be worse. My textbook said money was pretty much all virtual by the year 2000. We could have had Ser hack into some bank computer and make us billionaires."

"Naw." Serendipity grinned at him. "Might be fun, but could get messy. Don't want any record of me being here. It's why we put the bank account in your name. Besides that would be embezzlement and that's illegal. Traveling back in time to buy stocks isn't against the law."

"Not yet anyway," Wendell corrected her.

Serendipity looked again in her wallet at the bills Sherman had handed her. "Are you sure five thousand dollars is going to be enough cash for the weekend?"

"It better be, Ser. Do you know how many months I could live on that much money? I hope inflation hasn't been that bad in the last twenty-five years. Besides I have this debit card and a brochure on how to use it. I think we are more than set."

"If you say so, kid." Serendipity stuffed the wallet in her purse. "All right then, troops, what's our next move? Do we look for a house?"

"No," Wendell yelped. "We need to save the T.A.s."

"Yeah, that would take precedence. But we are going to need someplace to put our stuff and our rescued temporal anthropologists. The Timemobile isn't going to hold ten people and our luggage."

"That is true." Wendell bit at his lower lip, visibly trying to calm himself.

"Hey guys," Sherman said. "Why not get a motel room?"

"Not a bad idea, but where do we find one?" Serendipity scanned the buildings around them.

"We just go up to I-5 and head north. There should be motels all along the freeway."

"Go for it, kid." Serendipity nodded her approval.

Sherman headed east, away from the waterfront. He fought traffic while Serendipity and Wendell watched for road signs giving directions to I-5. Once on the Interstate, they had to drive some distance to get out of the downtown area. Finally they saw a sign listing several motels at the next right.

Sherman pulled into the driveway of the Steelhead Inn, an older two-story two-star motel. "How about this one?" He turned to Serendipity. "If we get a ground floor room we can park just feet away from the Timemobile so we can unload. It's across the road from a mall, so we can take everyone clothes shopping so we won't look like we're from another time. And there are several restaurants around us. There's even a branch of our bank within sight."

"Perfect!" Serendipity agreed. "It may not be the Ritz, but certainly more convenient. Come on, Wendell, move that cute keister of yours so I can get out."

Serendipity entered the lobby, wearing the 1964 dress she had worn to see the Beatles. It had short sleeves, the blue fabric with pink polka dots ending an inch below her knees. The young female clerk at the desk glanced up. "Hello, may I help you? Ooh, I love that dress. So Retro. So Audrey Hepburn. Where did you get it?"

"'Net." Of course, Serendipity was referring to the Virtual Mall in the twenty-fourth century.

"Yeah, it's amazing what you can get on the internet nowadays. So would you three like rooms? We have rooms with one and two beds, all queens."

"We have seven more people besides us that are going to meet us here. We want the rooms together, and at least one on the ground floor?"

"Non-smoking," Sherman added.

"Oh yeah." Serendipity frowned. "We don't want any rooms that were on fire."

The clerk laughed at what she must have thought was a joke. Serendipity looked confused. She apparently didn't know what a non-smoking room was. Sherman remembered she had once mentioned tobacco was an illegal substance in the twenty-fourth century.

The clerk studied the computer screen. "I'm afraid we are a bit booked up."

"On a Thursday?" Sherman frowned, then remembered October first probably wasn't the same day of the week in 2010 as 2353.

"It's Friday," the Clerk corrected him. "And there's some kind of convention at the local church. We do have four rooms together, all with two queen beds."

"So we'll have to get chummy." Serendipity shrugged.

"All right." The clerk smiled at them. "That's ninety dollars per room, so that will be $360.00. Would you like to use a credit card?"

"Cash." Serendipity plopped four one-hundred-dollar bills on the counter.

The clerk handed Serendipity her change along with several plastic cards. "Here are your key cards for the doors. Will two each be enough?"

"That's fine."

"Now, if you'll pull your truck around to the right side of the building, your rooms are about in the middle. You have rooms 124, 125, 224 and 225."

"Thank you," Serendipity nodded at her. "Come on guys," she turned to Sherman and Wendell. "Let's unpack our stuff."

They drove around the side of the building and pulled into a parking spot just in front of the rooms. The paint was not peeling, so Sherman took that as a good sign. The open walkway above had stairs on either end, as well as here between their lower rooms. That would be convenient for communicating with their guests upstairs.

Serendipity took charge as usual. "Let's unload all our junk into room 124. I don't know yet how we are going to divide up the rooms, so we'll just put it all into one room for now."

After several tries of pulling the plastic card through the lock and much cursing, the genius inventor finally figured out the uncooperative device. They unloaded all the boxes out of the Timemobile and into the room. Serendipity made sure the drapes were pulled and Wendell stuck the "Do Not Disturb" sign on the doorknob. They at last sat down dog-tired.

"Whoa, what a day!" Serendipity slumped into her chair. "I say we go to bed early."

Wendell stood up from the bed, looking anxious. "It's not dark yet. Can't we rescue a few people? Maybe Henry and Matilda at least?"

"You do realize I have a time machine and we can just go back to yesterday."

"No, that will complicate things. We need to keep our Base Time straight."

Serendipity rolled her eyes. "Okay, Wendell, but I'm starving. Can we at least grab a burger?"

"There's a fast-food place across the street," Sherman said. "I can run over and grab us all something. We can scarf it down, then hit the road or time stream or wormhole, or whatever it is we hit."

"Sounds good, kid."

"Thank you." Wendell sat back down. "I know I am being unreasonable but—"

Serendipity got up and came over to him. "Wanting to save your friends is not unreasonable. These are people, not teapots." She sat down next to him on the bed. "Just give me some coffee and I'll be fine."

"I noticed a drip-coffee maker in the corner in the back." Sherman pointed it out. "I'll go get three burgers. Would you like fries with that?" Sherman asked automatically.

Wendell was already going through the boxes of clothes before he had his burger finished. He tossed three brown robes on the bed. "We'll need those later."

Serendipity shoved the rest of her hamburger in her mouth and came over. "What's that?" she asked with her mouth full.

"When I was packing the wardrobe I realized we have nothing to wear for our trip to save Dr. Warwick, Dr. Olafson and Dr. Djata. Since all three are in the Middle Ages, I thought monks robes might work nicely. I didn't have time to do any research. I ordered them on the V-Mall and had it delivered over the wire to your fabber. I put it on your credit card. I hope you don't mind."

"It's why I gave you access to my card. I'm glad you thought of it." Serendipity opened up another box. "What are you looking for specifically?"

Wendell pulled out a Victorian pocket Bible that housed his computer and clicked his tongue to turn it on. "We are going first to Florida, north of Okeechobee Lake, year 1870." He read the files Serendipity had stolen from Agent Five's computer and copied to Wendell's.

"I don't have to wear a bustle, do I?"

"Go with your hippie outfit. My computer shows we will be out in the middle of nowhere. At most we might run into Seminole Indians or homesteaders. I doubt very much if they will be slaves to the current fashions."

"Can I wear my jeans?" Sherman asked.

"They would be period, although the T-shirt is out." Wendell slipped his Bible back in his pocket and went back to digging through the boxes. "Wear your Victorian shirt without the collar. I'll go with my frock coat even if it will look odd in the swamp. Mad dogs and Englishmen, eh? Hopefully we shall not need to stay too long. If we take the coordinates you downloaded to my computer, Dr. Brown, we should materialize right next to their time machine. Let's hope they aren't too far away from it."

Sherman noted that Wendell called Serendipity "Dr. Brown." Wendell did that when he was in business mode. The normally neat Wendell was pulling clothes out and tossing them aside helter-skelter.

Serendipity found her peasant blouse and long skirt and headed for the bathroom to get dressed. Wendell seemed to forget he was overly modest and yanked his 1960s trousers off, to put his Victorian ones on. Sherman managed not to laugh at Wendell's tight-fitting Victorian underdrawers that came just past his knees. Serendipity only took a few minutes to get dressed, but Wendell stood ready when she came out. "Are you ready to proceed?" he asked, his voice held a touch of agitation, which meant he was frantic.

"Wendell." Serendipity came over and grabbed his arm. "Calm down. We'll save your friends."

"Yes, forgive me, Serendipity." Wendell took a deep breath and let it out.

"Okay, let's go to Okefenokee Swamp." Serendipity headed for the door.

"That's Okeechobee Lake!" Wendell yelped. "Please don't put in the wrong coordinates, Dr. Brown."

Chapter Seven

The Timemobile came to a stop after shaking like an alligator tearing apart prey. Serendipity unfastened her strap and stood up.

"Wait, Dr. Brown." Wendell hurriedly unbuckled and jumped up. "Please, may I step out first? Henry knows me. The only time machine that would show up like this would be one full of Enforcers. When he sees we aren't Enforcers he might assume we are dangerous criminal renegades."

"Yes, of course. You make first contact."

Wendell opened the door and stepped out, Serendipity and Sherman following. They appeared to have materialized at a campsite with a couple of canvas tents next to a wooden shack. Sherman guessed that was their disguised time machine. Beyond the small clearing grew tall cypress and short swamp laurels with Spanish moss hanging from the trees. To the left on lower ground was shallow water in which swamp grass grew.

"Kind of marshy." Sherman swatted at a mosquito.

"This is the headwaters of the Everglades," Wendell said. "Some day this spot will be drained for farmland."

A middle-aged but lean man stepped out of one of the tents eyeing them suspiciously. He wore a couple days growth of beard, as well as a white shirt with no cuffs or collar. Black button suspenders held up grey pants with a red strip on the inseam. Was that from a Confederate soldier uniform? Sherman recognized the man as Dr. Henry Darrel, a temporal anthropologist who studied the American working man of the nineteenth century. They had met in 1886. Sherman didn't expect Henry to remember him since he knew the Enforcers had erased that incident from the man's memory.

Henry turned to the other tent. "Heads up, we got company!"

Out of the other tent rushed a tall man and a petite woman, both with dark hair and dressed in what looked like backwoods attire consisting of tan pants and shirts. Unlike the other time travelers Sherman had seen, these two didn't look like store manikins, for he had a memorable nose and hers was even more memorable.

All three stared at Wendell like stunned deer caught in a truck's headlights at night.

"It's all right, everyone," Wendell assured them. "We come in peace."

Henry's wide eyes somehow got wider. He slowly came forward. "Wendell? Wendell Howe? Is that you? What in blazes are you—? Quick, what is your Base Time?"

"First of October." Wendell frowned. "No wait, what day is it back home? It was 2660 last account I had, but my life has gotten so discombobulated. I have no idea what year it should be."

"Then you aren't from the past, but from the present?" Henry cocked his head.

"Yes, Henry."

Henry broke out in a big grin. "Wendell! You no-good, lowdown, egg-sucking dog!" He scooped up the Englishman in a big bear hug, pounding his back. "You're dead! They told us you were dead."

"The reports of my death have been greatly exaggerated."

Henry laughed, stepping back. "Mark Twain, right? It's okay, folks." Henry looked over at his two associates. "This is Dr. Wendell Howe, another temporal anthropologist." He grabbed Wendell's arms like he was afraid he would evaporate. "Let me look at you, you ugly horned toad. I can't believe it! How did you get a time machine? How did you elude the Enforcers? Who the heck have you got with you?"

"Please, old chap," Wendell said, his voice bland as ever. "One question at a time. Right now I don't have time to go into all the particulars. It's a very long story. Let's just say I have a new job and the Enforcers are doing their best to ignore me. I am pleased to be able to introduce you to my traveling companions. Dr. Henry Darrel, I would like you to meet Dr. Serendipity Brown and her assistant, Mr. Sherman Conrad."

Henry let go of Wendell and held out his hand. "Glad to make your acquaintance, Dr. Brown." He stopped and blinked at her. "Serendipity Brown? Your parents named you after the woman that invented time travel and here you are time traveling? How ironic is that?"

"Erm, Henry," Wendell said slowly. "This is *the* Serendipity Brown from the twenty-fourth century. *She* invented time travel."

Henry's grizzled jaw dropped. "How?"

"Yes?" Dr. Howe asked.

"No, how did you—?"

"I helped jump her time machine and then hitched a ride. I'm working for Dr. Brown now. That I fear is a *very* long story. I can explain it all later."

The man and woman came over staring at Serendipity, blinking in shock. Serendipity stuck out her hand. "Dr. Cerwyn Owen and Dr. Priscilla Cohen, I presume?"

They both numbly stuck out their hands and stared at Serendipity as she shook them.

"You are really Dr. Serendipity Brown, the Mother of Time Travel, are you?" Cerwyn spoke in a Welsh accent that purred the "Rs."

Serendipity made a face. "That makes me sound old."

"Wh-what are you doing here?"

"We came to save you." Serendipity rocked up on her toes.

"That is the Enforcers job, isn't it?"

"They are busy, and don't seem to care if you live or die. You're in danger and we are here to take you somewhere safe."

"Why?"

"We time travelers have to stick together." Serendipity patted him on the arm. "Besides if I'm the Mother of Time Travel, then I guess that makes you all my kids, huh."

"You are asking us to leave? Are you meshugge?" Priscilla argued in a Brooklyn accent. "We don't have a viable parrot population for breeding."

"Dr. Cohen is right." Cerwyn crossed his arms. "We couldn't possibly leave yet. We only have three males and four females, don't we?"

"Male and female what?" Sherman asked.

"Conuropsis carolinensis," Priscilla said the name with reverence. She stepped over to three apple-crate-sized cages on the ground. Inside fluttered pigeon-sized green parrots, three with yellow heads and red faces, the rest with just green heads.

"Conu-what?" Sherman scratched his head.

"Carolina parakeets," Henry translated.

"Parakeets? They look like parrots."

"Yes." Cerwyn tried to sound patient. "That's what you Americans call the Melopsittacus undulatus known by the more common name Budgerigar. Parakeet comes from *paroquet* which means 'small parrot.' It's a name given to several small unrelated species of the order Psittaciformes, isn't it?" Cerwyn noticed Sherman's confused look and translated. "Parrot family."

Sherman studied the birds. "I think I've seen these at the pet store."

Priscilla whirled around and glared at Sherman like he had uttered blasphemy. "These are Conuropsis carolinensis! The only parrot native to the eastern United States. They became extinct in the early twentieth century."

Cerwyn came over and put his arm around Priscilla's shoulders. "Can you believe people shot these magnificent creatures because they thought they were pests? Philistines! Dr. Cohen and I are here to save the Carolina parakeet; to bring it back so future generations can enjoy these magnificent creatures, aren't we? We hope someday we can breed enough of them that we can move them out of the safety of zoos and back to their natural habitat where they can once more claim their rightful place among God's creation." He gazed down at Priscilla who looked up and smiled adoringly. Then they both looked back down at the birds even more adoringly.

"But," Cerwyn continued, "to do that we will need more birds. So, we can't leave yet."

Serendipity rolled her eyes. "Aren't you people listening? You are in mortal danger. All time travel to the twenty-seventh century has been stopped. If you try to go back there's a good chance you'll smash into a barrier and die. If you stay here there's a good chance terrorists, who have their own time machine, will come here and kill you. They've already killed three temporal anthropologists. You could be next."

"That's not important, is it?" Cerwyn held his head high. "We are expendable."

"Yes, the birds come first." Priscilla stiffened her jaw bravely.

Serendipity slapped her forehead. "Do you people have birds on your brains, or are you just bird brains?"

Wendell put his hand on Serendipity's shoulder. "Erm, please, let me have a go. I've dealt with temporal biologists before." Wendell stepped toward the two zoologists. "I assume you two are concerned about the welfare of your charges?"

"Of course!" Priscilla sounded insulted. "We must keep them alive at all costs."

"Insane homicidal killers are coming to murder you. Once they have assassinated you, what do you think they will do with the birds?"

"Turn them loose?" Cerwyn asked hopefully.

"Homicidal maniacs normally start out as animal abusers. Not only will they in all likelihood kill these helpless creatures, they will probably torture them to death, mutilating them and chortling the whole time."

"What a horrible thing to even think!" Priscilla's eyes widened.

"It is a horrible thing to think, but it is true. To be a temporal anthropologist I have had to take a few psychology and sociology classes, enough to know that when homo sapiens lose all respect for life, there is no more brutal monster on the planet, with no regard for how rare, beautiful or special another living creature might be."

Cerwyn and Priscilla stared at Wendell in alarm. Then they looked at each other.

"He's right, Cerwyn," Priscilla whispered. "The paskudnyaks probably would."

Cerwyn nodded. "Aye, Dr. Howe, we'll come with you...for the sake of the birds, isn't it?"

"Excellent." Wendell stepped over to the cages. "Shall we release these trapped creatures?"

"No!" Cerwyn and Priscilla screamed at once.

Wendell turned and stared at the two. "Do you really want to be dragging these poor animals around through time? We're all refugees right now. It will be at least three months before you can even contemplate returning to the twenty-seventh century. I don't know how well wild parrots would fare. It could be very hard on these delicate birds. You can come back later when things are normal and catch more."

Cerwyn shook his head, tousling his wavy hair. "These are Conuropsis carolinensis! They are too precious to throw away. The twenty-seventh century needs them, don't they? Dr. Cohen and I are trained veterinarians and zoologists. We can take care of them. The parrots will be our full responsibility."

"We will do whatever it takes." Priscilla sounded like she would cut off an arm to feed them if need be.

"Fine then." Serendipity threw up her hands. "We'll take the stupid birds. Just get in the machine."

Priscilla glared at Serendipity. "They are not stupid." She acted like Serendipity had just insulted a beloved child.

Wendell gave them his most disarming smile. "Please forgive Dr. Brown. She does not mean any insult, but we are all a wee bit impatient. We have to save you from assassins who could show up any minute. And we still have four other people in different time periods we have to save as quickly as possible."

Henry looked concerned. "Other temporal anthropologists?"

Wendell turned and looked Henry in the eye. "Yes, the next person on our list is Matilda Warwick."

Henry's sun-tanned face turned pale. "Matilda? Tarnation Wendell, why in hell didn't you save her first? She's a woman all alone, after all."

"You were first because you have two others with you. We are saving three on this trip."

Henry nodded, and then he turned. "All right, Dr. Cohen and Dr. Owen, you have exactly three minutes to pack up and get the hell out of here! Is that understood? Gather up your personal belongings *now*."

"What about the tents?" Dr. Owen asked.

"Damn the tents! We leave them. Take your stuff and what you need. Clear the camp of all twenty-seventh-century items, but any period stuff can be left. The local Indians can scrounge it if they want. I don't think a couple of tents and cots will make any difference in their fates. We don't have time to take down tents. Well, don't just stand there! Now get cracking!" Henry stepped into his own tent.

Cerwyn and Priscilla looked at each other, then turned and went into the other tent.

Wendell turned to Serendipity and Sherman. "Please be very careful what you say to Dr. Owen and Dr. Cohen about the birds. And for heaven sakes, don't go near the animals. I've worked with temporal biologists before. If you think temporal anthropologists are obsessive, then you haven't met a temporal biologist. They can't be trained to immerse in a culture, because they are too immersed in their plants and animals. They go all over time gathering specimens and some poor temporal anthropologist gets assigned to them to run interference with the natives."

"Sounds like fun." Serendipity's tone was sarcastic.

"You have no idea. I remember the time I had to go to 1865 with a temporal botanist into the Alps looking for wild flowers. Dr. Karl Guggenheim was hoping to find some that had gone extinct. I thought it might be a pleasant mission, since I would have someone to talk to. He only spoke to me if he had to. He spent hours talking to those dash-it-all plants, though. You haven't met obsessive, until you've met a temporal zoologist or botanist. These people are absolutely dotty. Humor them as best you can."

Henry came out of his tent carrying a carpet bag and a Hudson Bay five-point wool jacket, and wearing his black Stetson hat. He handed the luggage and jacket to Wendell. "I'm going to pack what I can throw in crates. You people can help."

Sherman followed after Henry. "Tell me what to do."

Henry smiled at him. "Good man. Go through the camp and grab what isn't nailed down. Don't touch the cages though or you'll set off the zoologists."

They all quickly packed up all the equipment, leaving the tents and cots. They stowed everything in the Timemobile. Cerwyn and Priscilla insisted on securing the cages themselves. It was only when they were ready to go that anyone noticed there were only four seats.

"I don't need a seat. I can sit on the floor." Henry shrugged. "I've ridden shotgun on stagecoaches without a safety belt."

"It's a pretty bumpy ride," Wendell warned him.

Henry just grinned. "So is a stagecoach."

Serendipity shook her head. "The seats have shocks."

Dr. Owen looked at the parrots. "Then we will sit on the floor and put the cages in the seats, won't we?"

Serendipity rolled her eyes. "You have the cages on your bedrolls. That should cushion them. No I was thinking Dr. Cohen can sit on your lap and I'll sit on Wendell's."

Dr. Owen started to open his mouth but Wendell stopped him. "Don't argue with her. You won't win. Please, time is of the essence."

Dr. Darrel and Dr. Owen, with his smaller colleague on his lap, took the back seats. Sherman and Wendell strapped into the front two. Serendipity set the controls on the front wall, then jumped into Wendell's lap.

"Okay guys, here we go," Serendipity warned them

The Timemobile began shaking as it moved through the wormhole. The parrots began squawking and beating their wings in terror. After several minutes the machine came to a stop.

"Yee-ha!" Henry whooped bouncing out of his chair, waving his hat. "Yup, just like a stagecoach ride."

Serendipity stood up, so Wendell could get up. "The rest of you keep your seats. Sherman is going to drive us around to our rooms."

"Drive?" Henry stared at Wendell.

Wendell inclined his head to Serendipity. "Dr. Brown, would you mind if Sherman and I show Henry your latest innovation?"

"Yeah, I'll stay here with the birds and their parents."

The three crawled out of the Timemobile where it now sat parked in the alley behind the motel. Henry looked back at the U-Haul truck and scratched his head. "Just 'cause you have the contraption disguised as a truck don't mean it's gonna roll."

"The wheels are real," Wendell assured him. "Dr. Brown set her time machine on the back of a hoverlorry so it can be moved to a better location when needed."

"That's right. She always did call the dang thing a Timemobile in her records. Pity the Institute doesn't do this."

"Well, get in you guys." Sherman walked around to the driver's side. "Or you'll have to walk the hundred feet."

Henry was already crawling in when Sherman sat down in his seat. Wendell followed and shut the door. Sherman drove the Timemobile around the building and parked in front of their room.

"Stick the zoo in Room 125," Wendell said. "Serendipity has the key cards. Unload all the equipment in there too. Henry, you can take either Room 224 or 225 above. We have to get this unpacked as quickly as possible. We'll help you with some of the unpacking, but Serendipity, Sherman and I have to change into medieval costumes. We have to save Matilda."

"Let me go with you," Henry asked anxiously.

"Sorry, Henry, but you will need to take care of the zoologists."

"I got to hold down the fort, huh?"

"Don't worry, Henry, I'll get her back to you in one piece."

Henry looked taken aback. "How did you know?"

"The way you look whenever I mention her name. The way she looked when I mentioned you. She tried not to show it, of course. She didn't want me to feel ill at ease."

"Yeah, she cried something awful at your funeral."

"I'm glad you are here, Henry. I have someone now. You will need to take care of Matilda. I don't want her to be alone in these unsettled times."

Henry nodded. "Of course."

Wendell smiled at him and opened the door. They piled out to find Serendipity already leading the zoologists to Room 125.

"You put the cages in the bathroom," Serendipity ordered. "Then go over to the mall and get some tarps to lay down for the cages. Don't worry; I'll give you some money. Get lots of drop cloths too. I'll be fried crispy if I'm going to pay for damages to a motel room from wunken parrot poop!"

"Whoa!" Henry grinned. "A woman after my own heart."

"Hands off, old boy," Wendell told Henry. "I'm *not* sharing her."

Henry whirled around and stared at Wendell. "*Her*? Dr. Serendipity Brown? She's your gal?"

Wendell just smiled.

"Why if that don't beat all! Serendipity Brown herself! You do flabbergast me sometimes, Wendell."

"Let's just hope she doesn't figure out she can do a lot better than me."

Henry slapped him on the back. "Well, she won't hear it from me, partner."

Chapter Eight

Twenty minutes later in the year 1438, Wendell, dressed in a brown monk's robe, burst out of the Timemobile into a grove of deciduous trees. By the time the similarly attired Sherman and Serendipity joined him, he was opening up his Bible to the screen page in the middle. He pointed to a large thicket of blackberry brambles that stood eight feet high. "There, that is Dr. Warwick's time machine."

Sherman noticed the white flowers among the thorns. He decided this was a clever disguise since no one would think of bothering the impenetrable mass of clawing vines until they bore fruit. Sherman had grown up with enough wild blackberry bushes to have a healthy respect for those barbs.

Then Sherman noticed most of the trees had long leaves with tiny green fuzzy immature fruit. "Are these peach trees?"

"Almonds." Wendell glanced at one, then went back to studying his computer. "Dr. Warwick says they use them in everything in this time period. Almond milk was used in cooking far more than cow's milk, which had a very short shelf life. It was still popular in the Victorian Age for the same reason." He pointed. "There. Matilda should be in this direction."

"Lead on," Serendipity ordered. "We better get Matilda back to Henry before he busts a spleen. I get the feeling he has a crush on her."

Wendell made no comment, his expression deadpan as usual. Sherman did notice his mouth tighten just a little.

They meandered a few dozen feet distance through the trees and brush until they came upon an open field of tall green grass that looked to be some sort of grain. About a thousand feet away to the right stood more trees beyond which a few church spires were visible. The country looked flat, the highest point being a knoll about a half mile away upon which sat a castle that looked in disrepair. Sherman took that as a good sign that this place had known peace for a while. The closest building dead ahead was a three-story grey stone structure with narrow windows.

"Is that a castle or prison?" Serendipity shaded her eyes. "Is your friend in there?"

Wendell glanced down at his computer. "So it would appear. That is Saint Radegund's Priory, home to a group of Benedictine nuns." Wendell glanced about bemused. "I must say, the place looks so different from my own time, or even the Victorian Age."

"You've been here before?"

"I should say so. I was born and reared here. This is Cambridge, England." He waved his arm out. "Well, it will be one day anyway. We are just beyond the city limits of this time period. In a few centuries this will be the middle of town. I'm happy to say the common grazing land between here and the river will survive into my own time as a park."

"I'm guessing the nunnery didn't survive."

"It did in a way. About sixty years from now, Bishop John Alcock will accuse the nuns of impropriety and seize the priory and turn it into *The College of the Blessed Virgin Mary, Saint John the Evangelist and the Glorious Virgin Saint Radegund, near Cambridge* or as it is more commonly known, *Jesus College*."

"Wait a minute." Serendipity peered at Wendell with one eye. "I didn't hear the name *Jesus* anywhere in that long-winded name."

"Don't blame me, I didn't name it." Wendell pointed toward the priory. "Someday this will be part of the University of Cambridge, and that chapel will be the oldest building on campus."

"So did you guys steal the rest of the university from helpless women?"

"That part of our history isn't taught at the local schools." Wendell followed the narrow dirt path that skirted the field.

Serendipity hurried to come up beside Wendell. "So what did the nuns do that was so naughty? Turn the convent into a brothel?"

"I'm sure the rumors suggested that. Another more probable tale was that the ladies allowed scholars from the local university into the convent to discuss philosophy and news. Saint Radegund had stressed that her nuns be educated. However they later joined the Order of Benedictine which felt nuns should be completely cut off from the world. That the nuns had any contact with men, no matter how innocent, was looked upon with horror."

"Is that why the place looks like a prison?" Sherman noted what looked like bars on the windows.

"Most likely." Wendell agreed. "They sought to keep the nuns in and the world out."

"You certainly know a lot about medieval convents."

"Matilda and I used to talk shop. Henry the Eighth had abolished all the convents when he made himself head of his own church. They weren't legal again until the 1829 Catholic Relief Act. Matilda was always eager to hear any information I brought back from the Field on these new establishments."

As they got closer to the convent, Sherman studied the structure. On the left side corner, a chapel with stained glass windows jutted out of the structure, breaking the blocky look. In the middle of the front stood two large doors of wood and iron that even a bull dozer might have difficulty breaking down.

As they reached the gate of the enclosure Wendell turned to them. "My era is Victorian not Medieval, so we will have to play this by ear. When you don't know the proper etiquette of a culture, politeness and humility can often carry you through. Please, keep your heads down, especially you Serendipity. I don't want them to see you are a woman. Let them think you are my novices, or apprentices or servants or whatever. Please don't say anything. Let me do all the talking."

"You're the temporal anthropologist." Serendipity bowed her head letting the huge hood fall down to hide her face and stuck her hands in the arms of her robe. Sherman followed her example. He hoped their Victorian boots looked medieval enough. They had to be better than his tennis shoes back at the hotel room.

Wendell stepped up to the gate and rang the doorbell, literally a bell on a rope. After a minute a small window in the wood door slid open and two eyes peered through the iron lattice work. "God be with ye, brother," a shy feminine voice said.

Wendell bobbed his head. "Good afternoon and God be with you too, sister.

"Ney be I a sister, but only a lowly servant."

"May we speak to someone in charge, please? We are here on the most urgent business. We need an audience with Lady Matilda of Warwick."

The flap closed, but the door did not open. After a minute, Serendipity started to grab the bell rope. Wendell placed his hand on hers. "Please, Dr. Brown, we must be patient. These are slower times." Wendell smiled at Serendipity. He turned back to the entrance, crossed his arms and stood there a few moments, then frowned at the wooden door. "I do hope she went to fetch someone and isn't just ignoring us."

"At this rate," Serendipity muttered, "if the terrorists don't kill Dr. Warwick, she'll die of old age before we can talk to her."

After several minutes the window slid open again to show two keen eyes with crow's feet around them. "Yea?" asked a stern female voice. "What do ye want? This is a nunnery."

Wendell bowed his head as far as his chin would let him. "I do apologize for the intrusion, but this is an emergency. Lady Matilda of Warwick is in the gravest of danger. If we cannot come in, may she come out? We must speak with her. Tell her a member of the Brotherhood of Travelers Throughout Time is here to see her."

The door flap slid shut again, but this time the door slowly swung open revealing a short stone tunnel. Inside stood three nuns wearing black tunics. Underneath the black veils were white wimples and round white collars. Sherman had expected something medieval, but they were dressed very much like nuns he had seen in the twentieth century.

The older woman in front was short and gaunt with an assertive manner. "I am Mother Agnes Seyntelowe, the prioress. Ye may enter."

"Thank you," Wendell gave her an elegant bow. "My name is Wendell de la Howe. Please excuse any impropriety on my part. I come from far away and am new to your customs and rules. If I do anything inappropriate please feel free to correct me. I mean no harm or insult to you or the other nuns."

The Mother Agnes looked Wendell over carefully, then grunted her approval. "Ye hast the guise of noble blood but meek continence. I ken ye art to be trusted. Follow hence." She turned and led the group through the stone hallway that opened onto a courtyard ringed by covered cloisters in front of the convent's buildings. Sherman expected the nun to lead them into one of the structures, but she just stood there. She finally spoke, "A servant fetcheth Lady Matilda nonce."

Wendell again bowed. "My most heartfelt thanks, my dear lady."

The Prioress raised an eyebrow like that was an inappropriate response, then shrugged like it wasn't worth correcting. Sherman could tell the woman ruled the roost here. He got the feeling that if Wendell pulled out a sword, the woman would have slapped it out of his hand or just glared him down.

At last a woman dressed in a green tunic came out of a building followed by a petite woman, about five-foot-two, wearing a plain dark-blue tunic. Auburn hair peeked out from under the long wool veil covering her head. The only decoration she had was a crude pewter crucifix on a leather thong. The woman appeared anxious. She hurried over to them. "Why hast ye come yon for me? Tis there a problem?"

"Yes, there is Matilda." Wendell threw back his hood.

Matilda's blue eyes widened. "Wendell?" She stepped back blinking, then her knees started to buckle. Wendell rushed forward to catch her.

"Wendell?" She reached out and put her hand on his cheek. "Mother of Mercy! Tis thee! Oh, Wendell. I wast told thou art dead!"

"I got better," Wendell said with a straight face.

Matilda laughed and threw her arms around him. "Oh, Wendell, thou art alive!"

Sherman noticed the silent Serendipity dare to lift her head a bit, cocking it to one side.

Wendell pulled back abruptly. "Erm, sorry. I have a permanent relationship now."

Matilda let go of him and stepped back. "Pray thee, do forgiveth me. But how come thee hither? This be not thy territory. How didst thee come to be here?"

"Very long story. I don't have time to explain. You are in great peril, my dear. You have to trust me."

"Why should I not? I trust thee with my life. But if I be in danger, why were thee sent? Should not the Enforcers come to my rescue? Be these Enforcers?" She gave Sherman and Serendipity a skeptical glance.

"No. The Enforcers are too busy defending those back home. A war has broken out, a terrible war against our kind. Terrorists have already killed three of our brotherhood."

"Killed? Who?"

"Hoffmann, Suzuki and Shamar."

Matilda's hand flew to her mouth. "Shiro? Dead? No, not Shiro."

Wendell stiffened. "Dear lord, did you two have an *understanding*?"

Matilda nodded, tears trickling out of her closed eyes.

"Oh, Matilda!" Wendell put his arms around her and held her close. "I am so sorry. Had I known, I would have broken this news to you more gently. I liked Shiro, too. He was a good man." Wendell rocked her for a few moments, then grabbed her shoulders and pushed her back. "I don't wish to be callous, but we haven't much time. There are others we must save. We shall take you to a safe place to hide."

Matilda straightened her face, and lifted her shoulders, nodding. Sherman could see there was a lion under that mousey exterior.

"You won't be alone, my dear. Henry is there waiting for you."

"Henry!" Her voice rose like a little girl who had been told she was getting a puppy.

Wendell smiled at her, looking sad and delighted at the same time. "Yes, you are going to have to spend the next three months with Henry. But we need to get you out of here. We need to collect your luggage."

Matilda turned to the Prioress. "I pray, Reverend Mother, may these good brethren enter into my chamber and retrieve my chest?"

"I shall attend ye," Mother Agnes said. "Your visitors may go hence to your cell and nowhere else and may stay only long enough to gather your belongings."

The older nun led them across the courtyard to a small building. They entered into the structure and walked up the wooden stairs. "Your manner of speech be most strange, Brother Wendell." The prioress glanced back at him. "Where are ye from?"

"Erm, France."

"Yea, De la Howe dost sounds Norman. Ye hast journeyed far to retrieve your kinswoman."

Sherman ducked his head more, fighting back the urge to say: "You have no idea, lady." Instead he shared an amused knowing glance with Serendipity.

They came to a tiny room with stone walls, bare except for a ten inch wooden cross above a narrow wooden bed. The bed had high sides to hold a mattress through which poked straw. In the corner squatted a three-legged wooden stool and next to it a small oak chest, hardly more than twice the size of Wendell's tea chest. It had a rustic look, held together with black iron bands.

Matilda pointed to it. "This is all I own."

Wendell picked it up, with a grunt. "Do you have bricks in this?"

Matilda chuckled. "No, but tis sturdily built. Wouldst thou desire me to carry it?"

Wendell raised an eyebrow at her.

"Wait." Sherman came over. "Let me help."

"I can manage it," Wendell grumbled.

"Yeah, but you're going to have to carry it a ways. We can make better time if I help."

Wendell nodded. "Grab the other end."

Sherman grabbed the wooden handle on one end of the chest. He and Wendell carried the container out the way they had come, following the women down the stairs.

When they got back to the gate to the outside world, Matilda turned to the prioress. "I thank ye for your hospitality, Reverend Mother. Ye have all been most kind. I do apologize for this disruption, but I must leave anon, least I endanger ye all."

"Thank you, Lady Warwick." The prioress bowed her head. "Ye art a perfect guest. Ye art welcome to return. We wol pray for your safety and the safety of your people. May God protect ye."

"God be with ye." Matilda returned the gesture.

The gate closed behind them and they made their way back through the meadow to the trees. Matilda came up next to Wendell and fell in step. "All right, we mayst speak more freely now. What is going on, Wendell? Who art these two with thee? However did thee get here?"

"I hitched a ride." Wendell looked down at her. "Dr. Matilda Warwick, I would like to introduce you to Dr. Serendipity Brown and her assistant Mr. Sherman Conrad. We came here with her time machine."

Matilda fought back a smile. "Wendell, do be serious!"

"I am serious." Wendell's expression never changed. "Dr. Brown, tell her I'm serious."

Serendipity pushed back the hood of her cowl. "Yeah, he's serious. Little too serious sometimes. I'm trying to get him to lighten up."

Matilda frowned at Serendipity. "But this be not possible."

"Yeah, getting Wendell to lighten up probably is impossible."

"Nay, I mean ye could not possibly be *the* Serendipity Brown." Matilda shook her head.

"I got to be somebody, might as well be her," Serendipity said.

"Go ahead." Wendell smiled at Matilda. "Do a DNA scan on her."

Matilda lifted the dark-grey cross she wore around her neck. She pointed it at Serendipity and gasped. "Saints preserve us, ye art indeed Dr. Serendipity Brown!" She turned to Wendell. "What hast thou done? Thou knowst well none of us are to have contact with Serendipity Brown." She turned to Serendipity. "Ne'er are we allowed to get anywhere near ye or speak with ye for fear it could jeopardize the very invention of time travel." She frowned. "Mercy on my soul! *I* am speaking to ye! Woe is me! This could be the end of my career."

"It's all right, Matilda." Wendell adjusted the chest to his other hand. That looked like a good idea, so Sherman did too.

"All right? Fool! The Enforcers wol have thy head on a platter."

"They decided I should keep my head right where it is. Apparently I am supposed to be where I am. Very long story, I'm afraid."

"So all this time thou hast been dead, where were thee?"

"Here and there, mostly the twenty-fourth century."

"And thou hast a lady friend there? In the past? That be forbidden! Thou cannot do that!"

"Oh yes he can and quite well, I might add." Serendipity winked at Matilda.

Matilda stopped and stared at her with her mouth open.

"The Enforcers know." Wendell sounded apologetic. "Again long story."

Matilda started walking again, staring at Serendipity and then at Wendell. Then she broke out in a laugh. "Wendell Howe! Never dost thou cease to amaze me. Of all the women in all of time, thou hast won the heart of Dr. Serendipity Brown herself." Matilda turned to Serendipity. "I do hope ye know the manner of man ye have. There be none more kind or chivalrous.

You hang onto him with both hands." Then her eyes narrowed. "And ye best treat him right or ye wol answer to me."

Serendipity just grinned at the threat. "You have some very devoted friends, Wendell. Remind me not to kick you out some night because I got bored with you."

"I shall endeavor not to bore you too much then, Dr. Brown."

Serendipity turned to Matilda as they walked along. "So you're a nun? Sounds like a bucket of giggles."

"Nay, I am not a nun. For that a woman hast to take vows of obedience and would need permission to travel. I be only a visitor. Convents were never as wealthy as monasteries and so most were forced to take in paying guests."

"Guests?"

"Nay there be hotels in this age, just inns that be little more than taverns. Convents were one of the few places safe for the female traveler. Convents would prefer to have no guests, for most art wealthy women with fine clothes, servants and lap dogs. Most disrupting. The tale I tell is I am a rich widow on a pilgrimage to visit all the convents and live as the nuns live. I suppose I am a lay nun of sorts."

"Why would you want to live such a dull life?"

"Dull? It be not dull! Convents attracted the female artists and intellectuals of the day. Sadly, history recorded very little of the nuns and their accomplishments. That is why I hast come hither, to save our lost history."

Wendell smiled at her. "Isn't she something? Far braver than me, I must say. I picked a rather civilized and cushy period to study."

"Civilized and cushy?" Serendipity snorted a suppressed laugh. "When I met you, you were living with candles and a chamber pot."

"There were electric lights and flush toilets further into the Victorian Age. And the men were far more chivalrous than Medieval men ever were. All right, Victorian women were still second-class citizens, but they were fighting for their rights and slowly winning. Many men sympathized with their plight. It was a much safer period for women...well, for everybody actually."

"Boring!" Matilda snorted. "Never would thee get me into a bustle and ask how many lumps thee want with thy tea. Middle Ages be far more exciting."

Wendell started to open his mouth, then shut it and grinned at Serendipity. "Every temporal anthropologist believes he is studying the best of all possible worlds. You should hear the arguments we get into at the Association of Temporal Anthropologists Annual Meeting. I don't believe anyone has thrown a punch, but we have been known to actually raise our voices a bit."

"Yeah, I bet you are a wild bunch." Serendipity fought back a smile.

Sherman remembered Wendell calling T.A.s professional wallflowers and that soft-spoken Dr. Henry Darrell was considered a bit rough around the edges by his associates. Heck, Matilda might be one of the spunkier ones. The next three months with this lot should be pretty quiet.

Matilda stared at Wendell, frowning. "Didst thou shave thy mustache?"

Sherman pulled the Timemobile up in front of the motel room. The parking lot lighting was beginning to glow. He noticed the curtain in the upper right room draw back, and Henry's face appeared in the window for a moment. The curtain fell and then the door flew open, Henry ran out and down the platform to the stairs. He had showered, shaved and changed his clothes.

Sherman jumped out of the cab, but Henry had beaten him to the door going into the Timemobile. Wendell was trying to help Matilda down the steps, but when she saw Henry her eyes lit up and she let go of Wendell's hand to get to the cowboy, throwing her arms around him. Henry lifted her off her feet in a big bear hug. They started to kiss, then pulled back and looked back over at Wendell. Henry set Matilda back down.

"I'm glad to see you are safe, Dr. Warwick." Henry shook her hand.

"Yea, Dr. Darrel." Matilda's voice sounded very businesslike. "I hope ye art doing well."

Wendell came over and put his arms around both their shoulders. "No need for that, you two. Let's get Matilda's chest. Do you mind sharing a room with Henry, Matilda?"

"I, uh...," Matilda's voice faded like she couldn't find the words.

Wendell leaned down to give her a quick kiss on the forehead. "It's all right, Matilda. It really is. Don't worry about me." Wendell turned to Henry. "Come on, Henry. You may help me with Matilda's luggage."

Henry nodded, and followed Wendell into the Timemobile. Henry came back out with the chest by himself.

"I say, Henry." Wendell poked his head out the door. "Let me help you with that."

"Ain't nothing," Henry assured him. "You forget I'm a working man. This is lighter than a newborn calf. I'll take care of this."

Wendell looked over at Serendipity. "Can we make another trip tonight and retrieve Dr. Djata?"

Serendipity looked up at the darkening sky. What little light the rain clouds had grudging allowed the sun to sneak in was now almost gone. "Getting kind of late, don't you think?"

"I know, Dr. Brown. I would go by myself if I could operate your time machine. Perhaps you could transport me there and wait in the Timemobile, while I go find Abubakari Djata."

Serendipity patted Wendell on the cheek. "Okay, sweetie, I can't refuse you anything. So, this Abubakari is a good friend of yours?"

"I hardly know the man," Wendell said. "But he always seemed like a decent chap. Besides he's a temporal anthropologist. That makes him family."

"Let me go and help ya, buddy," Henry said.

Wendell shook his head. "I need you here to take care of the temporal zoologists and Matilda."

"I wol be fine," Matilda assured him.

"No, you won't." Wendell turned to Henry. "One of the T.A.'s that was assassinated was Shiro Suzuki. He and Matilda had an *understanding*."

Matilda hung her head, looking at the ground. Henry put his arms around her. "Oh darling, I'm so sorry."

"You need to mourn Shiro," Wendell told her. "Don't keep it in. And you don't need to be alone."

Sherman stepped over to Henry and Matilda. "I'll be with Wendell. I'll help him."

Even though Henry looked down at him, Sherman didn't feel like he was being looked down upon. "All right, Sherman," Henry smiled at him. "You watch this gullible limey's back."

Wendell looked over at Serendipity. "Well then, Dr. Brown? Shall we be off?"

"Okay, but first Sherman takes me through a drive-through espresso. I'll need a triple shot mocha. I have to admit, I've always wanted to go to Timbuktu."

"Timbuktu?" Sherman frowned. "We're really going to Timbuktu?'

Wendell smiled at him. "Now you'll be able to say you've been every-where."

Chapter Nine

Serendipity opened the door of the Timemobile, the dry sub-Saharan heat hitting them like a blast furnace. She stepped out and turned to frown at the Timemobile. Sherman and Wendell joined her. To one side of them was a tall limestone wall and on the other a leather tent. Several yards away were more of these tents in various shapes, many looking like mounds, some rectangular. No one seemed about except a few tethered camels. The sun was directly overhead so Sherman assumed everyone had fled to shady spots. The few withered trees baking in the bronze sand didn't offer much shade and so were ignored. Most of the vegetation off in the distance was sparse scrub brush holding down small sand dunes.

The Timemobile, now appearing as a wooden shed, looked totally out of place. Serendipity pulled out her computer, took pictures of a few of the tents and stepped back into her Timemobile. A minute later the machine took on the appearance of another small tent, just different enough that it wasn't the impossible exact copy of any of them.

Wendell had pulled out his Bible and opened it. "It appears this tent beside us is hiding Djata's time machine. Hmm, the computer identifies this style of tent as Tuareg, a nomadic people in this region. These must appear and disappear all the time, so no one would pay much attention."

Sherman looked around. "So, do we just wait for Dr. Djata to show up?"

Wendell shook his head. "He may not come here every day, if at all. We need to find him as soon as possible." He clicked his tongue twice, cuing his computer. "Search for Abubakari Djata's signature." Wendell looked up from his Bible. "He appears to be in this direction on the other side of this wall. Let's walk around it and see if we can find an entrance."

Following the barrier, they at last came to a gate that was open and unguarded. As they entered Sherman looked about. This was no village, but a good sized town. All about in neat rows stood one and two-story adobe mud buildings with high turrets. Wood beams stuck out the sides of the walls, looking more like decoration than support. The structures all looked very alien, unlike anything Sherman had seen before. If he hadn't known better, he would have sworn they were on another planet. He began to understand why the name *Timbuktu* evoked the exotic.

In the wide dirt streets walked people dressed in robes or loose fitting clothes. The men wore turbans or brimless caps, while the women draped loose scarves over their heads. Some of the men wore heavy dark blue robes and turbans, their lower faces covered, while unveiled women followed them. All the faces were various shades of brown; the three time travelers appeared to be the only pale-skinned people in town.

"Dude, I think we're attracting attention." Sherman glanced about nervously.

Wendell studied the crowd. "We would have done better with Arabic robes than monks' attire. I must say though, the looks we are getting seem only mildly curious rather than hostile. By the variety of costumes, I would have to conclude this town is a trading center. The natives are used to strangers, so they shouldn't be xenophobic. In 1350 I doubt they get many, if any Europeans, so we don't have to worry about a bad reputation preceding us. Just act polite and humble and we should do fine."

They trotted after Wendell as he led them through the dusty streets. Occasionally, a vendor accosted them, then politely left them alone when they showed no interest. Sherman kind of wished they had the right sort of money to try some of the foods offered—it all smelled good. A camel bawled as he knelt to be unloaded of his burden. In the shade of a building a couple of old men sat on the ground playing a game that was a board with holes dished in it. They moved stones from one hole to the next, while others watched intently. Oddest of all, Sherman noticed quite a few people sitting on stools or on the ground reading books. Weren't books supposed to be outrageously expensive in the days before the printing press?

As they walked along, Serendipity studied Wendell pensively. She finally trotted up next to him. "Can I ask you a personal question, sweetie? Just out of curiosity."

"Yes?" Wendell kept his eye on the arrow on the screen of his computer that pointed toward Abubakari's signature. He glanced up ahead often to keep from running into anything.

"Were you and Matilda ever lovers?"

Wendell stopped, whirled around and stared at Serendipity.

"Come on Wendell, you are eighty-five. I didn't expect you to be a virgin."

"I assure you *that* is over."

"Keep going, keep going." Serendipity shooed him.

Wendell started up again looking very uneasy. "Besides, she is with Henry now."

"Yeah, I noticed that. So you two were once a couple?"

"No, not a couple. We had an *understanding*."

"She said she had an understanding with Shiro, too. Just what is an understanding?"

Wendell gave a weary sigh. "It is difficult to explain to an outsider. Being a temporal anthropologist is a lonely life. We aren't allowed to get involved with people in the Field. We are seldom in the present—our present—so it's hard to have a relationship with anyone there since we are seldom around. And when you do find a woman attracted to temporal anthropologists it's usually just a T.A. groupie who wants to see how many time periods she can score."

Serendipity giggled.

"No, really. They carry scorecards. I've seen them. Apparently I'm worth a lot of points. Odd women. Few T.A.s have anything to do with them. Then there are the Romantics."

"Romantics?"

"Yes, they actually want a relationship. However they have read too many historical romances and they want you to be the hero from one. The look of disappointment on their faces when they realize I'm not Heathcliff, but just boring old Wendell. They will break your heart into more pieces than the groupies. Sometimes you can find a woman who loves you enough to wait for those few days you show up every two months. But that grows old quickly and they find someone more permanent. It seems the only one who understands what it is like to be a temporal anthropologist is another temporal anthropologist. Few of us are lucky enough to find someone to partner with us in our selected time period, so we have an *understanding*."

"Understanding?"

"Yes, neither partner can demand the other be exclusive since we are like ships passing in the night and only see each other a few times a year—if we are lucky."

"So Matilda had an understanding with you, then Shiro, then Henry?"

"No, all three of us at once. There may have been a couple of others, too. Probably not too many. Matilda *is* a lady."

"What! Matilda had a half-a-dozen lovers at once? Not bad for a nun, huh?"

Wendell stopped and gave her a stern look. "Dr. Brown! You will not make fun of Matilda. She's a good woman in a bad situation." He snorted. "Civilians. You make us sound like it's a wild orgy. It is just two lonely people trying to comfort each other, especially after one of those dreadful debriefings. The ordeal is like having your soul ripped out."

"Yeah, I remember."

"No you do not." Wendell sounded slightly cross. "You didn't get the full treatment. Enforcers want us to be terrified of them so we will never try to get away with anything in the past. Debriefings leave you vulnerable. You need someone to curl up with. Only another temporal anthropologist really understands."

"So you two haven't broken up yet?"

"Of course we have. You were standing right there."

"When you told Matilda you had a permanent relationship? That was a break up?"

Wendell stopped and gazed at her with those soulful grey eyes. "Yes, at least I hope you are permanent." He cleared his throat and started walking again. "One part of the *understanding* is that when one of your partners settles down and finds a permanent partner, you let them go with your blessing. I ceased to be Matilda's partner when you and I—erm, conjoined."

"Yeah, she didn't seem that upset especially when you mentioned Henry's name."

"Well, he was always her favorite. She tried not to show it, always polite about it, but I got the feeling I was a watered-down version of Henry to her."

"Did Henry know about you and Matilda?"

"I believe so. In fact I get the feeling it was his idea."

"What!"

"Henry knew I would treat Matilda like a lady and I would take care of her."

"So how long were you and Matilda together?"

"Erm, I think around twenty years."

"Twenty years!"

"Yes, and if the two of us are still together by the end of the year, we will have clocked more hours together than Matilda and I ever had. Sometimes it was only twice a year for a few hours together. You have no idea how wonderful it feels to have a woman all to yourself everyday. You are a dream come true, Serendipity—my lucky find."

"So let me get this straight. You only got sex every few months?"

"More or less."

"And you stayed sane?"

Wendell sighed. "More or less."

"So, you had all this passion stored up, and I hit the jackpot?"

Wendell stopped, and turned to give Serendipity a languid smile. "More or less."

Serendipity returned the smile and moved in. They were nose to nose and about to kiss.

"Ah-hem," Sherman cleared his throat loudly. "Shouldn't we be looking for this Abu-whatever dude?"

Wendell's face turned pink. "Yes, of course. We need to save Dr. Djata. Can this wait for a more appropriate time, my dear?"

Serendipity gave Wendell a seductive look. "More or less."

He smirked at her, then turned and took off down the street following his computer's lead. Serendipity trotted after him.

Sherman shook his head. "A sex-crazed woman and a sex-starved man," he muttered. "It's a match made in heaven." He sighed and ran to catch up with them.

Sherman studied the high adobe wall beyond which he could glimpse more than one roof. Beside the enclosure stood a tall tower shaped like a skinny pyramid with four sides atop a square base. Wood beams stuck out all over it.

Wendell looked over at his companions. "Abubakari is either in here, or this is merely in the path. I suggest we circumnavigate this barrier and ascertain that my arrow continues pointing inside."

They circled the wall as the arrow on Wendell's computer screen slowly moved, always pointing to the inside of the enclosure. They came to an open gate and entered into a courtyard of packed earth. A lone shade tree grew in the middle under which sat a wrinkled gentleman dressed in loose white robes. Wendell put away his Bible and went over to him. He gave a slight bow. "Excuse me, sir, can you tell me where I may find Abubakari Djata?"

The man frowned at Wendell and said something unintelligible.

"Yes, of course." Wendell rolled his eyes. "That was daft of me. How would you know English?"

Serendipity stepped forward. "Where...is...Abubakari...Djata," she said very slowly. "We...must...find...Abubakari...Djata."

Wendell gave her an incredulous glance. "Dr. Brown, contrary to popular American belief, not everybody can understand English if you speak it slowly enough."

The dark skinned man seemed amused by Serendipity's idiotic delivery, then cocked his head. "Abubakari Djata?"

"Yes!" Serendipity nodded excitedly. "Abubakari Djata."

The man nodded, stood up and motioned for them to follow.

Wendell shook his head. "I guess I was wrong. Apparently anyone *can* understand English if you speak it slowly enough."

Their guide led them into an adobe building and then to a large room lined with wooden bookshelves. All the books were stored piled on top of one another, rather than stood on end as Sherman had seen in libraries back home. There must have been thousands of volumes. Dozens of men sat on reed mats on the floor studying the manuscripts. One man carefully turned a page that was loose. Sherman glanced around and noticed all the books had loose pages. One scholar opened a very small book. The cover wrapped completely around the pages, keeping the unbound book together. Sherman now understood why the books were stored flat.

"Abubakari Djata?" their guide called.

One white robed man holding a fly whisk that had a carved wooden handle topped with brown horse hair, looked up. "Owo, wa?"

Their guide went over and spoke to him. The scholar looked over at the three of them in brown monk's robes and cowls, and frowned. He got up and came over in a slow regal manner. The man had a round, pleasant but unremarkable face beneath his white turban. He appeared to be in his late fifties, with grey at his temples and scattered in his short neatly-trimmed beard. He bowed his head and said something to them, his baritone voice as rich as a cello.

Wendell shook his head. "Sorry, old chap, I'm afraid I don't speak whatever it is you are speaking. Are you Dr. Abubakari Djata?"

"Anglakan?" the man spoke with a melodic African accent. "You are from England, wa? It will be centuries before any Englishman makes it down here."

"I am English." Wendell pointed to Serendipity and Sherman. "They are from America."

"Ayi, that is not possible! There is no Ameriki, not yet anyway. Who are you?"

"I'm Dr. Wendell Howe, Temporal Anthropologist with the University of Cambridge."

Abubakari peered at his face. "Yes, you do look like Dr. Howe. But how can you be he, wa? You are supposed to be dead."

"Well, my mum always complained I never did what I was supposed to," Wendell said with a straight face.

Abubakari gave a chuckle. "Owo, at the reception after the funeral

everyone said you had quite a sense of humor. Made me sorry I did not get
to know you better. What are you doing in 1350 Mali, wa? Are you not
supposed to be in 1800s England?"

"I have a new employer."

"You left Cambridge University?"

"I left the twenty-seventh century. Dr. Djata, I would like you to meet
Dr. Serendipity Brown and her assistant Sherman Conrad."

"Most unusual name." Dr. Djata shook her proffered hand. "So your
parents named you after the inventor of time travel, wa?"

"No, I *am* the inventor of time travel."

Abubakari smiled at Serendipity. "I see you have a sense of humor too."

Wendell shook his head "No, she really is *the* Serendipity Brown. Go
ahead, do a DNA scan."

"Yeah." Serendipity made a face. "I'd hate to think anyone else got that
ridiculous name."

Abubakari pointed his fly whisk at Serendipity. He stared at it, his eyes
getting big and then stared at Serendipity. "Why is Dr. Howe with *the*
Serendipity Brown, and why are you both here, wa?"

Serendipity put her hand on his arm. "We came to save you, Dr. Djata.
Your life is in danger. There are some crazy, evil people from your century
that mean to eliminate time travel by killing time travelers. They have
already killed three temporal anthropologists."

"Is it not the job of the Enforcers to stop them, wa?"

"Yes, they are doing what they can, but they are overextended. They
decided the few people still out in the Field are expendable. I don't. That is
why we are here to take you someplace safe."

"I was going to return to the twenty-seventh century tomorrow,"
Abubakari pointed out. "So I should be safe."

"*No!*" Serendipity, Wendell and Sherman all yelled at once. Several
people looked up from their books.

"You can't!" Wendell lowered his voice. "The Enforcers have prevented
all time travel in and out of the twenty-seventh century. If you try, your time
machine will either come back, bounce into another time period where they
will never find you, or you will hit a wall and disintegrate. They are not
certain what will happen."

Serendipity nodded. "There is a time machine missing, despite the lock
down. We are afraid they may come after you."

"Why me?" Abubakari frowned. "Begging your pardon, but if they want
to eliminate time travel would it not make more sense to come after you,
wa?"

Wendell put his arm protectively around Serendipity. "Yes, it would.
That's why the Enforcers are setting a trap in her home for the assassins
and why they told her to go into hiding in another time period."

"We want to take you with us, so you will be safe too," Serendipity said.

"If you are in danger, why did you come back to save *me*, wa?" Abubakari
looked confused.

"Because." Serendipity smiled at him, leaning her head forward. "Because you are in danger too, and we can save you. Besides, it would be fun hanging around with someone from Timbuktu. When people ask you where you are from, and you say 'Timbuktu,' I can watch the looks of disbelief on their faces."

Abubakari gave her a perplexed look and then laughed. "You are a little mad, I think, but I like you."

"Good, because you'll have to live with me for the next three months in the year 2010."

"Owo, I will go with you, Dr. Brown, if only to help protect you from your enemies." Abubakari bowed his head to Serendipity.

The four time travelers walked through the dusty streets of Timbuktu back to the Timemobile. Abubakari looked over at Sherman and nodded. "Please forgive me, young man. I believe I was introduced to you and completely ignored you. My name is Dr. Abubakari Djata." He held out his hand to Sherman.

"My name is Sherman Conrad." Sherman shook his hand. "So, what are you doing in Timbuktu in 1350, Dr. Ja-ta?" Sherman tried to pronounce the name.

Abubakari only smiled at the bad attempt. "I am collecting books—digitally, of course. I have a camera hidden in my fly whisk, along with my computer. All the books are hand written so any would be sorely missed if I took even one. You found me at Sankore Madrasah—the University of Sankore. It is the University I am associated with in the twenty-seventh century, although it will be much larger then."

"Awesome! Your university is that old?"

"Owo, it dates back to 988, making it even older than Oxford or Cambridge." He glanced over at Wendell. "No offense."

"None taken." Wendell smiled. "Oxford loves pointing out they are older than us. I'm glad to see someone beat them."

"They certainly have a lot of books," Sherman noted.

"This city is full of books." Abubakari waved his arms expansively. "Timbuktu's major import is books, and its major export is gold. This is one of the wealthiest cities in the world right now."

Sherman glanced around. "The place doesn't look poverty stricken, but it doesn't look like anyone is filthy rich. So everyone is buying books instead of luxuries?"

"Every book is printed by hand, so they *are* an expensive luxury. There are so many manuscripts here, and in the city of Jenne just down river, that 700,000 survived into the early twenty-first century from the Mali and Songhai Empires. About the year 2000 they began recording them digitally. I am trying to find those that did not survive and make copies. I am rescuing the lost books."

"Wow! I didn't know Timbuktu was a real place, let alone a city of books."

Abubakari chuckled and shook his head. "Yes, you Ameriki are odd. Ameriki of African descent want their ancestors to be Zulu warriors when they were in fact probably scholars."

"What?" Serendipity perked up. "African-Americans are from here?"

"Most of the slaves sent to the new world came from West Africa. Many were from the Mande peoples like myself."

"Really?" Serendipity grinned excitedly at Abubakari. "Sometime I'm going to have you tell me all about the history of this area."

They continued on until they came to the outside of the city where they had left the Timemobile.

Abubakari frowned at the tent hiding his own transport. "What do I do with my time machine, wa?"

"You said you were returning tomorrow?" Wendell asked.

"Yes, it was set to return."

"Then empty it out, old chap, because it will return tomorrow and probably smash into a wall. By the way, where are your digs? We should probably gather up all your belongings."

"It is all in here." Abubakari pulled back the tent flap to reveal a sleeping mat, baskets and a fire pit with an iron pot. Against the far wall was a large Persian carpet.

Sherman started walking across the tent, then hit something invisible when he got to the rug. "Ow!"

Abubakari whirled around from securing the tent flap. "I do apologize. The natives normally respect the privacy of others but, just in case, the techs set the machine to be *invisible* by showing what should appear to anyone peeking inside. The illusion of the rug marks where the machine is so I do not break my nose." He pointed his fly whisk toward the carpet and reached into thin air. He felt along, then opened a door, hanging above the ground, revealing the inside like a doorway to another dimension.

"Awesome, dude!"

Abubakari stepped up the invisible steps. "I do have a few emergency items from the twenty-seventh century that could come in handy. All these items in front of the carpet are mine and can go with us, too."

While Abubakari was in the machine, Sherman rolled up the sleeping mat and blanket, while Serendipity and Wendell stuck stray items into the baskets. They loaded up everything into the Timemobile. Serendipity set the dials and everyone buckled in. She smiled over at Abubakari. "Next stop Seattle, 2010. Hope you like coffee and salmon."

Abubakari chuckled. "Seattle. What an exotic name!"

Since Wendell insisted they keep Base Time, it was very late when they got back to the Steelhead Inn. Abubakari climbed down the steps of the Timemobile, looking about at the parking lot lit by street lights.

The African ran his hand over the nearest car. "Oh my, are these ancient gasoline-powered automobiles?"

"Yeah." Sherman saw nothing exciting about a Toyota.

"And this building, is this where we are staying, wa?"

"Just for a few days."

"It is very...quaint. Have they invented flush toilets yet? I'm afraid I am not acquainted with this period of time."

"Yeah. Flush toilets, showers, televisions and hair dryers." Sherman realized Abubakari was gawking at everything not because it was more advanced than fourteenth-century Mali, but because it was so primitive compared to *twenty-seventh-century* Mali.

"It might be fun to study a new time period in the distant past." Abubakari began pointing his fly whisk about, obviously taking pictures. Then he stopped and looked at Sherman worried. "I have not been ingrained into this society. I will stand out."

"Just tell them you are a refugee from Africa, dude, which is the truth. You're new to the country so no one will expect you to fit in. As long as you don't run into another African immigrant from Timbuktu, you'll be fine."

"Howdy, Dr. Djata," a voice called out.

Sherman turned around to see Henry and Matilda coming over to them.

Henry stuck out his hand. "Glad you could make it, Dr. Djata. Don't know if you remember us. I'm Dr. Henry Darrel and this is Dr. Matilda Warwick."

"Yes, I remember you." Abubakari shook their hands. "The Old West cowboy and the Medieval nun."

Henry glanced over at Sherman, then over at Wendell and Serendipity. He shook his head. "You three look plum tuckered out! Go get some shuteye. Matilda and I will show Dr. Djata up to his room and get him settled in."

Wendell looked back at the Timemobile. "What about Dr. Olafson and Dr. Leach? We need to save them."

Henry put his arm around Wendell's shoulders and steered him to the door with a large "124" on it. "Come on, buddy, it's after midnight. You've been rode hard and put away wet. You all need to get some rest. We'll get them tomorrow."

Wendell didn't say anything, but looked at Henry like he knew he was right. Serendipity opened the door and flipped on the light. The beds were piled with the clothes Wendell had thrown on them. Henry scooped them up and dumped them on the containers. Wendell sat down on the bed and flopped sideways. He just lay there with his eyes shut and jaw slacked.

Serendipity studied Wendell. "I think he's asleep. That or he's dead."

Henry and Serendipity pulled off Wendell's ankle-length black boots. They looked like they had built in white spats on top with black buttons—Victorian, of course. It was a good thing the monks robe had covered them up.

Henry pulled Wendell's feet up on the bed and rolled him on his back. "I'd undress him, but we might wake him up. Let's leave well enough alone."

"Thanks, Henry." Serendipity blinked bleary-eyed at him. "We had quite a day today. Moved Sherman out of his apartment in 1985. Got home and the Enforcers told us to pack up and get out immediately. They didn't give us much cash, so we went back to 1919 so Sherman could buy stocks and turn two hundred dollars into forty million. Found a place to stay. Then we made three trips into the past to rescue you guys."

Henry's eyes got big. 'Hoo-wee, little lady. I got tuckered out just hearing about it! You get yourselves into bed and get some sleep."

"Most excellent idea." Sherman sat down on the other bed. He kicked off his tennis shoes. He swung his legs up and fell back over on the bed. He didn't remember his head hitting the pillow.

Chapter Ten

A growling noise woke up Sherman. He slowly opened his eyes, realizing it was his stomach.

"Good morning, sunshine," said a cheery voice.

Sherman looked over to see Serendipity sitting at the table with a cup of coffee, looking far too perky. She wore a twenty-fourth century suit with one inch lapels. "Want a cup of coffee?"

"Okay." Sherman got up and stumbled over to the small courtesy coffee maker in the back of the room by the sink. He noticed Wendell's spirit lamp already set up on the counter beside it, heating a kettle of water. Sherman poured himself a cup of coffee, and came over and sat at the table across from Serendipity. He leaned on his elbow, his hand propping his head up, and tried to keep his eyes open.

A shrill whistle squealed. Sherman almost fell over.

"Ah, kettle's ready." Serendipity jumped up and went to the back counter.

"What? Who? Where?" Wendell popped up in the bed, blinking. He, like Sherman, still wore his monk's robes.

"Making you some tea, sweetie." Serendipity poured a little water in his teapot and swished it around.

"You don't know how to make tea." Wendell forced himself to stand up.

"Don't worry, I think I watched your video on 'how to make a proper cup of tea' as you called it, enough times. I even warmed the pot for you."

"Oh." Wendell staggered over to her. "Rather kind of you, old girl."

"Never call a woman 'old' when she is holding a kettle of hot water."

"Sorry, I meant no offense, love." Wendell kissed her on the cheek. "What time is it?"

"8:30. I let you two get eight hours of sleep."

"8:30! Dear heavens, we still have Dr. Olafson and Dr. Leach to rescue and—" Wendell stopped and stared across the room toward the windows. "My word, what the deuce is that?"

Sherman looked over at where Wendell stared. There in the corner, near the boxes in front of the closed curtains, a young woman stood stiffly, dressed in a short navy-blue skirt and white puffy-sleeved blouse. Sherman jumped back startled. "Dude! Why didn't I see her?"

"You haven't seen *me* yet." Serendipity smirked at Sherman. She looked at Wendell. "Been shopping while you two were asleep. I've been awake for hours."

"Is that a robot?" Wendell studied the girl.

"Yup," Serendipity said proudly. "Translation device to be exact."

"Translation device?"

"Figured we would need one if we were going to visit Vikings. We had problems communicating in Timbuktu. If the natives had been hostile we could have gotten into real trouble. Vikings aren't known for being a cuddly bunch. Yeah, I know we have translation programs in our computers but a talking box is going to freak out anyone in the past. So I figured an android doing the talking would be less scary."

Wendell walked across the room, studying the android. "I must say, it is very lifelike."

"Of course." Serendipity leaned back on the counter. "If we are going to have a translator device that won't raise suspicion, then the android is going to have to look as lifelike as possible. It will only work if the natives think it's human."

"Very lifelike, indeed." Wendell reached out and felt the skin. "Warm, feels real. Hang on a tick, is this thing a—" Wendell placed his hand on one of its breasts, and then jerked his hand away like it had been burnt. "It has *nipples*! It's anatomically correct! Oh, this is disgusting. Is this thing a—a—?"

"Pleasure-bot?" Serendipity helped Wendell out.

"Oh, Serendipity! How could you even think of procuring one of these—these *things*?"

"Hey, you're the one grabbing its breast."

"I-I—just—w-wanted to—make sure—I—"

"Calm down, Wendell before your head explodes. I'm just being practical. If for some reason the robot had its clothes torn off, or someone got too close to it, we want to fool them into thinking that it's a real human. They would probably have to cut this thing open to find out it's not human. Unfortunately, of all the robots, pleasure-bots look the most lifelike. Don't worry I erased the *recreational* programs and put in what I wanted. It's downloaded with every known language and translation program, as well as a domestic program. Got to have someone to scramble my eggs. I picked out the least sexy model. This one doesn't have huge breasts."

Wendell came closer and studied the robot again, then looked even more nauseated. "You do realize why it has small breasts, don't you?"

"Some guys like petite women?"

"No, they want it to look like an underage teenager! Dear heavens! Look, it is wearing a school uniform! This is not just a—a—one of those things. It's one for pedophiles!"

"Oh, really Wendell. It's just some guys like small breasted, baby-faced women. I've known plenty of women in their twenties, even thirties that looked like that."

Wendell shuddered.

"Look at it this way, Wendell. We saved her from white slavery and a life of shame."

Wendell raised an eyebrow at her. "It's a robot, Serendipity. It does not feel or think." He looked back over at the robot. "I suppose you are right. We will need the most realistic looking robot we can get if it's going to be traveling with us to other time periods. I know I'm a prude; I have probably become too Victorian. It is just—well, I never understood the whole concept of one of these things. They make my skin crawl."

"Yeah." Serendipity smiled at Wendell. "You are a hopeless romantic underneath that stoic exterior. You don't see a woman as just a sex object. Well, some losers do. This way they can have their sex object without messing up some real person's life. These robots serve a very noble purpose, I suppose."

"I never looked at it that way," Wendell said.

"Okay." Sherman pushed his hair out of his eyes. "I'm confused. Why aren't all robots made this realistic?"

Serendipity and Wendell both stared at Sherman in horror. "It's a robot, kid." Serendipity sounded like a mother explaining a taboo to a small child. "You can make them look realistic, or you can make them sound realistic, but you never put the two together."

"One must be very careful with artificial intelligence." Wendell's voice sounded even more patient than usual. "You must be very careful not to develop one that is *too* human."

"Why?" Sherman studied their anxiety.

"Because it's just wrong!" Serendipity began to sound Victorian herself. "Back in the twenty-third century a robotic genius named Dr. Fred Hiram lost his child in an accident. He built a robot identical to his son, made the body realistic, programmed in his mannerisms, gave it his voice. It was creepy. He actually began to believe it was his son. Then the robot had a glitch and kept repeating the same phrase over and over. Hiram went mad, completely over the edge. They had to destroy the robot. The whole time it was crying and acting like it didn't know it was a robot. Those poor guys that disposed of it suffered nervous breakdowns themselves."

"That's not the worse event." Wendell crossed his arms. "Remember the Bolivian Incident?"

Serendipity shuddered. "That was scary."

"What happened?" Sherman asked.

Wendell looked grim. "It was back in 2232 at the Bolivian Robot Works. Robots took over the factory and killed everyone. The authorities had to bomb the place."

"Robots are fine as robots." Serendipity shook her finger at Sherman. "But you never want to make them too human, and you never want them to become self-aware. This robot is a translation device and labor-saving machine, but nothing more. It's just a thing, remember that."

"Okay." Sherman took a sip of coffee. He had thought Serendipity and Wendell were pretty open-minded, but apparently they only tolerated robots if they knew their place. "So, they have robots now in 2010?"

"Very primitive ones, nothing close to this." Serendipity poured tea into one of the ceramic cups from Wendell's tea chest and held it out to him on a saucer. "Tea's ready, sweetie."

Wendell came over and accepted the proffered brew. "Thank you, my dear. Erm, where exactly *did* you get this robot?" He took a sip.

"Twenty-fourth century."

Wendell choked on his tea and set the cup down. "Twenty-fourth century! Did you go back last night? Are you stark raving mad? There could have been Time Keepers there."

"Don't worry. I went back to 2352."

"And how did you pay for the robot?"

"With my credit card."

"Dr. Brown!" Wendell slapped his forehead. "Serendipity, you can't go playing fast and loose with time like that! You dare not change the past."

"Didn't change anything. Just made it happen."

"What?"

"Yeah, I woke up last night and remembered something odd that happened last year. I got a credit card bill with a few purchases I had never made. I mean I've never been desperate enough to get a pleasure-bot and why would I want a female one? And why would I buy a monk's robe in its size? I called the company on it, but they insisted whoever bought it not only signed my name, but had my face and DNA. I wasn't sure if the company was ripping me off, or we had a very clever identity thief, but it wasn't worth the hassle of fighting it. I just paid the bill and canceled the card. I looked in my wallet last night and realized I had forgotten to cut up the card and still had it on me. Now the whole thing made sense, I really was the one who had made those purchases."

"So, you bought a robot and reprogrammed it in a couple of hours?"

"Heck, no, I've been gone a couple of days."

"A couple of days!" Wendell yelped.

"Well, not quite two. Had to get some sleep. I remembered there was also a hotel room and some restaurants on that bill too."

"Serendipity, you can't do things like that!"

"Wendell, I had to get a hotel room. It was on the bill. You didn't want me to change the past, did you? I don't know why I chose Boise, Idaho though. I guess because it was on the bill."

"Dr. Brown, you have to keep to your Base Time. You can't go popping back and forth through time like that. You have to keep your personal timeline straight. You can't go putting kinks in it. You are now two days older than you should be."

"So?"

"So, it can add up," Wendell's voice had an uncustomary sternness to it. "In the early twenty-fifth century some printing company came up with what they thought was a brilliant use for time travel. People could get any printing job, no matter how big or time consuming in only a minute. The workers would simply go back a month or two in the past and do the job. They could have given it to the customer yesterday, like they asked, but then the customer would never remember ordering it. The service wasn't cheap, but there were people willing to pay. It made the owner rich, but the workers died of old age within a few years. The families sued, and the owner went bankrupt. They passed laws making this use of time travel illegal."

Wendell made a fist and slapped it on his other palm. "That is why you have to stick to your Base Time. That's why when a time traveler goes into the past and is gone two months he can't just come back a few minutes after he had left. He has to come back exactly two months later. You can't mess with time, especially your own."

"Okay, but this was an emergency," Serendipity said. "If I showed up two days later the people we were going to save might be dead."

Wendell sighed and looked at her defeated. "Just be careful, Serendipity. I'm going to outlive you as it is."

Serendipity blinked at him. "Yeah, you told us science has made people in the twenty-seventh century age slower. I never really thought about what that meant. What are you going to do when I'm old and gray?"

"Love you." Wendell took her hands in his.

Then Serendipity's stomach spoke, growling indignantly.

Wendell looked at her midriff. "If you are going to live to a ripe old age, maybe we should feed you. I believe there is supposed to be a complimentary breakfast with this room. Hmm, I hope that doesn't mean just nutrition tablets, or are they doing that yet? Shall we go check that out so we can be on our way?"

"Yeah, shall we get the others? You get dressed and I'll go wake them up."

"Wait Ser, I'll help." Sherman pulled off his cowl and robe. He had his jeans and T-shirt on underneath.

"Well, you got dressed fast." Serendipity grinned. "Okay, you take the upper deck. I'll try and reason with the parrot people."

"Be diplomatic," Wendell warned her. "Think of them as doting parents with an ailing baby."

Serendipity sighed and rolled her eyes. "Yeah, I'll be as understanding as I can."

Sherman first knocked on the door with the "225" on it and waited a moment. The door opened, revealing Henry wearing a red flannel union suit and a sleepy expression. Sherman tried not to laugh, but couldn't help it.

"What's your problem, kid?" Henry frowned, rubbing his bristly chin.

"I'm sorry. I expected to see you in a nightshirt like Wendell wears. I've only seen underwear like that in old cartoons."

"It's comfortable, okay? So, did you need something, or did ya just come up here to laugh at my sleepwear?"

Sherman straightened up his face. "Uh, I came to tell you that we were going to go to the lobby to get breakfast. Just go inside the main door facing the road."

"Okay, kid, we'll get dressed and meet you."

"Uh, that doesn't really have a flap in the back, does it?"

"Of course. How else am I gonna sit on a honey pot without getting undressed."

Sherman put his hand to his mouth, squelching his laugh to a snort and quickly turned away.

"All right, kid, tomorrow I get to laugh at *your* underwear." Henry closed the door.

Sherman fought to slap on a more serious expression as he walked over to Abubakari's door.

The breakfast room was off the lobby and full of half a dozen round tables with about four chairs apiece. The walls sported lemon paint with bright gold trim and framed photos of sunflowers. No doubt this was supposed to wake up the hotel guests. Sherman found the urn of coffee more efficient.

Sherman sat at the table in the breakfast room eating a bowl of corn flakes. Across the table from him was Serendipity in a twenty-fourth century suit and Wendell in his frock coat. At the next table was Abubakari dressed in his long white robes, Matilda in her dark blue tunic and veil, and Henry in brown button fly pants held up with suspenders over a collarless white shirt.

On the other side of the room sat a half dozen strangers eating breakfast and staring at the weird attire of the time travelers. One middle-aged man got the nerve to walk up. "Excuse me? Are you in a play?"

"Yeah." Serendipity looked up. "Cat on a Hot Tin Roof."

"Hmm, I don't remember any of these characters. I'll have to watch that movie again." The man walked away, looking confused.

Wendell smiled at Serendipity. "The natives don't seem hostile."

"Of course not, this is the Pacific Northwest. They like eccentrics. It's why they put up with me."

Wendell looked around the room. "Where are the temporal zoologists?"

"I told them to come eat." Serendipity cut up her waffle. "I'm not going to drag them here."

At that moment Priscilla came into the room wearing the tan shirt and pants she had worn in the swamp. She grabbed a paper plate, loaded it with food and then left. She neither spoke nor looked at anyone.

"Is she mad?" Sherman watched her.

"Angry, no." Wendell said. "Crazy—well, that is up for debate. She's preoccupied with the parrots. I'm surprised she left them this long. Cerwyn will no doubt come foraging when she gets back. Don't ever expect them to both leave those parrots at the same time."

Henry turned in his chair and tapped Wendell on the shoulder. "You gonna pick up Dr. Olafson today?"

"Yes, as soon as we finish eating."

"How about I go with you, old buddy."

"Sorry, Henry, you don't have the right clothes."

"Yeah, dang." Henry sighed, disappointed.

"You know, Henry." Serendipity leaned toward him. "If you want to help, why don't I leave you some money and you three go get some period clothes. They'll have clothing stores at the mall. You'll need to fit in."

"Yeah, you're probably right. Won't we attract attention though?"

"Tell them Abubakari is an immigrant, Matilda decided to leave the convent and you want something more fashionable. This is the Seattle area. Stranger people than you are walking around."

Henry nodded. "We better have at least one of us here to take care of Dr. Olafson when you return. Will he be rooming with Abubakari?"

Abubakari's eyes got big. "Dr. Olafson? Is he not the Viking, wa?"

"Yeah." Henry gave him a sympathetic look.

"He seems like a nice enough fellow, but I am not certain he bathes. He eats with his hands. He belches and laughs about it. It is just the man is so vulgar."

"You don't have to room with Dr. Olafson," Serendipity assured Abubakari. "You can share a room with Dr. Leach."

Abubakari looked thoughtful a moment. "Forget it, I will take the Viking."

Serendipity laughed, then grinned. "I'm yanking your chain. We can get you all rooms of your own."

"Thank you, Dr. Brown." Abubakari looked relieved.

Chapter Eleven

The Timemobile stopped shaking and the world became still. Sherman noticed that once again Wendell beat Serendipity out of the machine, nearly tripping on his monk's robe.

Serendipity and Sherman came out into the small forest clearing to find Wendell waving his computer about. "Ah! That big rock outcropping there is Dr. Olafson's time machine." He nodded his head toward a huge boulder. "I don't see any buildings so we will have to assume he is some distance away."

Serendipity stepped back into the machine. "Now we know what to disguise our machine as." After a minute the wooden shed became a large rock also. She stepped back out, then looked behind her. "Translation robot, follow us."

The female android, dressed in a brown monk's robe and cowl like the rest of them, stepped out. Its face held no emotion.

Serendipity frowned. "We got to give it a name if I'm going to order it about in front of the natives. What do you think, Sherman? You're good with names."

Sherman thought a moment and then grinned. "How about Rosetta Stone?"

Serendipity laughed and slapped Sherman on the back. "I like it! I can call her 'Rosie' for short, ya know like the robot maid on *The Jetsons*."

"I am assuming that is another inane twentieth-century television show?" Wendell rolled his eyes.

Serendipity turned to the robot. "Your new cue is Rosetta or Rosie. You will answer to those names, do you understand?"

"I understand," the human, if unenthusiastic voice said.

Wendell swept his Bible/computer about, then stopped. "I say, I have picked up Dr. Olafson's signature. He appears to be in this direction about a mile away." Wendell took off down the path.

Serendipity looked amused. "Wendell didn't even say, 'after you, Dr. Brown.' The man must be worried. Follow me, Rosie." She trotted after Wendell.

Sherman followed in the rear as they wound their way down the hill through the tall pine and spruce. Far below, Sherman thought he occasionally glimpsed open water through the trees.

Up the trail Wendell gave a yelp. Sherman hurried around a boulder to find a half a dozen men blocking their path. They wore skull caps made of metal and leather, short tunics and breeches, as well as beards and long hair. All of them were either carrying a long spear or a bow with an arrow already notched in the string. They also wore long nasty-looking swords and daggers at their sides. Vikings?

The strangers did not look friendly. One of them yelled something at them.

"Everyone freeze and put up your hands!" Wendell ordered, putting his own hands over his head. His companions obeyed.

One of the men came closer to Wendell and barked something at him.

"Rosetta!" Wendell kept his eyes on the leader. "Translate."

"On your knees." Rosetta's tone lacked any emotion.

Wendell knelt, putting his hands on top of his head. "Do as he says."

Rosetta and Sherman both obeyed, but Serendipity balked. "Ser," Sherman whispered at her. "Don't do anything stupid."

"I'm not afraid of them."

"No, but you'll get Wendell killed, because you know he'll try to protect you."

Serendipity meekly knelt down.

"Rosetta." Wendell didn't look away from the leader. "Tell them we come in peace. We are looking for an Erik Olafson. It is a matter of life and death."

Rosetta spoke to them with that soft but flat voice. The leader looked at her, then down at Wendell. He grinned and said something.

Rosetta didn't need to be asked. "We go hunting deer and catch men of the cross. So, you are foreigners. You have to have your slave speak to us. You look like those Christian missionaries the upstart Olaf Tryggvason has brought from England. We will take you to our chieftain, Jarn. He will decide if we should sell you as slaves or sacrifice you to Odin. Tie them up."

The other Vikings were already obeying, rushing at their captives. A man grabbed Sherman, while another tied his wrists together in front of him with leather strips in such a manner that his arms were crossed. He found laying them against his chest was the most comfortable position. Sherman looked around to see his companions also being bound.

"No!" Wendell yelled. "You can't have that!"

The leader held Wendell's Bible over his head. Rosetta translated, "So this is valuable, is it not? Is this a book? They bring a lot of gold in the right ports. I think I will keep this." He shoved it into a pouch on his belt.

Wendell looked frantic but held his tongue, no doubt afraid to reveal just how valuable the book really was.

The leader barked another order and Sherman was jerked up to his feet.

"You will now follow us to the village," Rosetta spoke for the Vikings.

Sherman tried to stay close to Serendipity, although he had no idea how he would protect her. He tried to keep his eyes on the ground so as not to trip on any roots or fallen branches in the path. He didn't know how he would break his fall with his hands tied.

The path descended to a bay Sherman could now see below. In it floated a thirty-foot-long ship with a prow carved like some alien animal's head. It seemed rather small to Sherman. Somehow he thought Viking raiding ships would be bigger.

On the shore rested a village of little over a dozen structures. The rectangular houses were made of hewn logs with turf roofs. Many of the roofs came all the way to the ground, making the buildings look like grassy mounds. In the center of the settlement stood the largest structure, a twenty-foot wide, fifty-foot-long building built of rough-hewn planks, with a steep roof of wooden shingles. The wood had been weathered grey reminding Sherman of an old deer's skeleton he once found in the woods.

The captors and captives finally reached the bottom of the hill and entered the village. The inhabitants of various ages were going about day to day tasks. Their clothes were finely woven and dyed in various colors. The men dressed like their captors, in short wool tunics and breeches. The women wore ankle length tunics. Over these were shorter jumper-like garments, oval brooches pinning down the straps in front. Between the two ornate metal brooches were strung beads, hanging down like necklaces.

One by one the villagers stopped what they were doing and watched the passing parade with curiosity. Several followed behind them, no doubt wanting to see what would happen. Sherman remembered hearing something once about a gruesome Viking sacrifice called "a blood eagle" where they ripped your lungs out through your back while you were still alive. He had always wondered if that was even possible. Now he really didn't want to find out. "We're toast," he muttered.

Their abductors marched the time travelers into the longhouse. The pillars holding up the roof created a hallway the length of the building. On either side were two-and-a-half-foot high by six-feet wide wooden decks running nearly the length of the room. On them were bearskins. Under them were chests and gear. Sherman suspected these were used as communal beds, or at least benches. The building was lit by a long narrow hearth in the middle of the room and from sunlight coming through the smoke holes in the roof above the rough-hewn rafters. The place was smoky, reminding him of his mom's cigarettes in the crowded trailer where he grew up. At the far end of the room, a group of men sat on stools and wooden chairs, talking to a man in an ornate chair on a platform just wide enough for his chair and just high enough to make the occupant a foot above his audience. The high back of the throne had intertwining creatures carved into the dark wood.

As the prisoners were dragged forward, the sitting men all turned to look, then rose to their feet, save for the man on the throne. Sherman felt a rough hand shoving him down, forcing him to his knees onto the hard packed earth. He felt nauseous and prayed he didn't throw-up.

The leader of their kidnappers stepped forward, addressing the man on the throne. Sherman decided this had to be Jarn the chieftain his captors had spoke of. Jarn's eyes narrowed as he studied their "guests." He bellowed something at the prisoners.

Serendipity turned to the robot. "Rosetta, what did he say?"

"Who are you? Did Olaf Trygvesson send you? What are you doing here?"

"Rosetta," Wendell whispered, "tell him, we come in peace. We have no idea who this Olaf chap is. We come searching for a man named Erik Olafson. It is most urgent we find him."

Rosetta spoke. One of the men, with a blonde beard, his hair in braids, stepped forward. He was tall with broad shoulders. Despite his build he did not stand out among the other tall broad-shouldered men. The grizzly-bear of a man thumped his chest and addressed them.

"I am Erik Olafson," Rosetta translated.

Wendell struggled to get up, and was pushed back down. "Dr. Olafson?" Wendell yelled. "I'm Dr. Wendell Howe. We need to speak."

"Howe!" Dr. Olafson rushed over. "Wendell?" He pushed back Wendell's hood and grinned. "By Thor, it is you! Ha! My heart laughs in my breast." The Viking scooped up the startled Englishman and hugged him. "I thought you were in Temporal Anthropologist Valhalla! Cambridge had your funerary rites. I was most sorry I missed your funeral." Erik's voice sounded gruff but amiable.

"Well, I missed it too, old boy. Maybe we can both make the next one."

Erik gave a thunderous laugh and set Wendell on his feet. He turned to Jarn and addressed the chieftain in his booming voice. Jarn looked surprised and bowed his head to Erik. Then Jarn barked an order to their captors.

Sherman felt himself yanked up on his feet. One of the abductors pulled out a dagger and advanced on Sherman. Before Sherman could back away, the Viking grabbed his wrists and cut off the leather straps binding him. Sherman looked over and noticed Wendell and Serendipity rubbing their freed wrists too.

Erik turned back to them. "I told Jarn that we are brothers. I offered to buy your freedom but Jarn said there was no need, for I am his friend. He apologizes for any misunderstanding. Why did you not tell these folks your quest was for me?"

"I did," Wendell said. "Either they didn't hear or didn't care."

"Evil times are these." Erik expression turned grim. "People are most suspicious. Olaf Tryggvason is back and is trying to take the throne. He forces Christianity on everyone, and kills any who refuse to convert in the most horrible manners. He has not ventured here yet, since this is a small out-of-the-way village of little importance. Jarn prays to Odin they will be ignored."

"What in the world are you doing in the middle of nowhere?"

"RASIRTing."

Wendell turned to Serendipity and Sherman to translate. "*Recording Archeology Site in Real Time.* That way the archaeologists at the dig will know where everything is, what the original site looked like and who lived here." He turned back to Erik. "Please ask him to return my Bible." Wendell pointed to the culprit who had it. "I hate to be fussy, but it has my computer concealed in it."

"Of course! We cannot have that floating around in the Dark Ages." Erik turned to Jarn and spoke to him again. Jarn glared at the leader of the captors and obviously told him to return it, because the thief handed it back to Wendell, shamefaced. Wendell graciously bowed his head to him, and stuck the computer back in his own leather pouch.

"What are you doing in Norway in 995?" Erik asked. "Are you not

Victorian? How did you even get here?"

"I had a friend bring me." Wendell pulled Serendipity over. "Dr. Olafson, I would like to introduce you to Dr. Serendipity Brown."

"The great woman who invented time travel?" Erik pushed back Serendipity's hood. "Is this another of your jests?"

"Do a DNA scan on her," Wendell said.

"Ho, I believe you." Erik studied Serendipity. "No reason have you to lie to me. Be well come, Dr. Brown. It is a great honor to be in your presence!" Erik gave her a hug.

Serendipity grinned at him. "The shy type, huh? So you're with the University of Norway?"

"University of Minnesota!" Erik thumped his chest. "Lots of us Scandinavians in Minnesota. And who are these that follow you?"

"Sherman Conrad, my assistant."

Sherman was afraid he was going to get hugged too, but Erik just shook his hand. Erik turned to Rosetta. "And what name has the girl?"

"Robot translator," Serendipity said.

Erik jerked back his hand. "Truly lifelike. Ho, is that a pleasure-bot?"

"I needed the most realistic-looking robot to fool the natives."

Erik shrugged. "Makes sense. Very clever. Now how did you all come here? What in the name of Freyja are you doing with Dr. Howe, and why did you journey thus?"

"We all came in my Timemobile to save you." Serendipity gave Erik her most infectious smile.

"Save me?"

"We don't have time to fully explain. Time Purist terrorists called Time Keepers are killing temporal anthropologists and trying to stop time travel."

"Killing T.A.s?" Erik looked concerned. "Who?"

"Sharma, Suzuki and Hoffman so far," Wendell said.

"Hoffman! Walther Hoffman?" Erik's voice sounded anguished.

"You were close?"

"Hoffman was my mentor!"

Wendell bowed his head. "I'm so sorry, Dr. Olafson."

"What's a mentor?" Sherman asked.

Wendell turned to him. "A mentor is an older more experienced temporal anthropologist who accompanies you on your first few trips into the past. They show you the ropes. The Institute picks one that is as close as possible to your own period and persona."

Erik nodded. "There were no Viking temporal anthropologists. Visigoth was the closest. A great mentor was Hoffman and a good friend. I could always go to him for wise counsel. Why would anyone wish to kill such a noble person?"

Serendipity put her hand on Erik's arm. "There's a good chance the Time Keepers could come here to kill you too. You can't just go back home because all time travel has been stopped to the twenty-seventh century and the Institute thinks that your machine will explode, or something, if you try to return. The Enforcers can't come to save you, they are busy trying to save the world, and so, wrote you off. We didn't. We are here to take you to safety."

Erik hung his head. "You have valiantly risked your lives for nothing. I am already a dead man."

Wendell stepped closer and put his hand on Erik's shoulder. "What are you talking about, Dr. Olafson?

"I joined a village hunt last week. A raiding party waylaid us. Out of instinct, I stopped the man trying to kill Jarn by knocking the attacker away. He fell back and hit his head on a rock and died. When the Enforcers find out not only will I be tossed out of the program but they will imprison me for life or more likely *erase* me."

"You mean go back in time and assassinate you?" Serendipity's eyes grew wide in horror. "Why? You were defending yourself and your host. It was an accident the attacker died. No court would convict you."

Wendell looked over at Serendipity. "I fear the Court of the Enforcers would. Dr. Olafson broke two rules. He caused the death of someone in the past *and* saved a life. He changed history twice. If the Enforcers make him have an *accident* before this last trip, it will have never happened."

"That's not fair!" Serendipity took Erik's hand. "Jarn considers you a hero, and so do I. I'll see to it that the Enforcers never find you."

"Dr. Brown," Erik protested, "I cannot let you do that. The Enforcers would come after *you.*"

"They can't touch me. I'm Serendipity Brown and outside their jurisdiction. They can't stop me, not without changing time themselves. Besides, I like you—even if you are a Viking."

"Technically, I am not a Viking, per se. A Viking is a raider, a pirate. I am a blacksmith. That is one craft that may freely travel in this society and is always made welcome."

"Well, I'll make you welcome. I got a soft spot for temporal anthropologists. You gather up your stuff and we'll take you to safety with our other rescues. Please hurry though; we still have one more T.A. we have to save."

"Who is that?"

"Tobias Leach."

"Tobias will be with us?" Erik frowned, then smiled. "Good!"

Wendell looked surprised. "Good? You're the first one to say that. You like Dr. Leach?"

"I am not fond of the little pervert. But with him around none will complain of me." Erik gave a huge grin, showing yellowed teeth with a tooth missing.

Wendell chuckled at that. "Yes, Tobias makes me look good too."

Chapter Twelve

When the time travelers stepped out of the Timemobile in the parking lot of the Steelhead Inn, Henry and Matilda already stood waiting. Sherman noticed they were still in their period costumes. Erik came out last, wearing his black fur cloak and carrying his luggage. Slung over his left shoulder hung a leather satchel holding his clothes and personal items. Over the other shoulder he carried a long wooden chest holding his blacksmithing tools. Sherman hated to think what the thing must weigh.

Erik grinned at them, flashing his horrible teeth. "Ho, what land is this?" He looked about.

Henry stepped forward. "Welcome to Seattle 2010, Dr. Olafson. Would you like some help?"

"Neinn, my burden is small. Just show me where I may lay down my worldly possessions. You will wish me to take a bath. Blacksmithing is sweaty work."

"That wol be most considerate of you, Dr. Olafson." Matilda's smile appeared forced.

Erik frowned at her. "By Frigg, tell me you are not one of those folks who think Vikings never bathe. Where do people get that idea? It was the *Saxons* who never bathed." Erik looked over at Wendell. "No offense."

"None taken," Wendell said. "I'm Victorian English, not Dark Age English. Victorians bathe at least once a week."

Serendipity patted Erik's shoulder. "Put your stuff in our room, it's closer." This time Serendipity opened the door with the key card with no problem. Sherman followed everyone in. The room which had been a rat's nest was now cleaned up.

"Just set the box down anywhere, Dr. Olafson." Serendipity looked around. "Who picked up in here?"

"We did," Henry said. "Matilda and I, while Dr. Djata was out buying some clothes. We just folded all the stuff in the storage containers and added the ones in the piles. I hope we didn't mess up some sort of system you had."

Serendipity jerked her thumb over at Wendell. "Would you believe, Mr. Neat here, made that mess? He was in such a hurry to save everyone. Thanks, Henry, Matilda. Does anyone here mind if I call you by your first names? Old Northwest tradition. I'm Serendipity."

"Fine with me," said Henry. "I'm from Wyoming and Matilda is an Aussie, so it won't bother us."

"Aussie?" Serendipity stared at the woman dressed in a tunic. "Australia? You don't sound Australian."

"Nay. No Aussies about in the Middle Ages. I had to change my accent. My patrons art the University of Melbourne. Where dost you think I got the name Matilda? Old Dad was feeling patriotic on the day of my birth. And if you start singing, *Waltzing Matilda*, I wol have to bop ye."

"Fair enough. I had a father with a weird sense of humor too." She turned to Erik. "The bathroom is right in there." She pointed to the door at the back of the room. "I think there's some complimentary soap and shampoo. None of us have had a chance to use them. Uh, what are you doing Wendell?"

Wendell was digging through the newly packed costumes, trying to be a little more neat this time after Henry and Matilda's efforts. "I need to find Victorian clothes for you so we can go after Dr. Leach."

"Wendell, can we at least eat lunch first? We have everyone important."

Wendell frowned over at Serendipity. "I know no one likes the man—I can't stand him myself—but Tobias is a fellow temporal anthropologist. We can't abandon him."

"All right, how about I send Sherman out for burgers or something else quick, while you look for clothes? And then we will go fetch our last lost soul, okay?" Serendipity turned to Sherman. "I saw a memo pad and pen on the dresser. How about you go get orders from everyone and I'll give you some money. Drive the Timemobile if you like."

"Okay, Ser."

"And you thought your experience in fast food would never come in handy."

Sherman walked up to the door of Room 124, carrying a couple of sacks of burgers. Henry came up behind him, carrying two larger ones, having volunteered to help fetch lunch. Sherman knocked at the door, as best he could.

The door opened, showing Abubakari, now dressed in a pair of white slacks and a long sleeve shirt. The design looked African. All were light cotton and loose fitting, as though he was still dressing for the tropics. "Come in, gentlemen."

Sherman came into the room crowded with boxes, luggage and temporal anthropologists.

"Okay, buckaroos," Henry called out. "Lunch is here, chow down." He plopped the bags on the table.

Matilda came over. "I be verily famished. Good old American cuisine." She picked up a burger.

"Oh great." Sherman wrinkled his nose. "After seven centuries, American food doesn't get any better than this?"

"I'll take care of our zoologists, so they don't starve to death." Henry picked up one of the sacks and stepped out the door.

Wendell stood dressed in his waistcoat and trousers, shaving over the sink at the back of the room. His stiff detachable collar was unbuttoned in front so flared out like wings, only held on to his shirt by a collar stud in back. Erik stood behind him, wearing just his breeches, drying his long loose blonde hair with the small hair dryer attached to the wall. There was just something incongruous about a Victorian and a Viking sharing a mirror.

Serendipity stepped out of the bathroom in her Victorian dress. It was made of lavender satin with a cinched waist and had a small bustle. The waist was created with the corset Serendipity had complained about. She smiled when she noticed Sherman with lunch. "Hey, Wendell, Erik, food is here."

The two men both looked over their shoulders at her. Wendell went back to shaving, but Erik hung up the dryer and trotted over. "By Thor, it feels like ages since I had a real hamburger. We have a place near the campus in Minneapolis that made the most glorious hamburgers. Did you get me three?"

"Yeah." Sherman handed him the first one. "You lived in Minneapolis?"

"Ya, back in the twenty-seventh century."

"I figured you all lived in Cambridge, England, like Wendell. Isn't that where the Institute of Time Travel is?"

"Great Baldur, neinn," Erik talked with his mouth full, pausing occasionally to take another bite. "The Institute of Time Travel is on Long Island in Bohemia, New York. We are all connected with different noble Universities."

"You are?"

Matilda nodded. "Yea, for a University to be able to brag of having a temporal anthropologist on staff is high honor indeed. Not all Universities can afford one. We have the privilege to decide with whom we wish to be connected, and if our old alma mater has not the funds, we find a university that dost."

Erik wiped his mouth with the back of his hand. "Ya, but other universities come to us begging us to investigate this or that, and if we accept their quest, they make a contribution to our university to defray costs. Time travel is expensive."

Matilda snorted. "I dost think most of the expense be payment for the Institute's stupid paperwork."

Abubakari wiped his mouth off with a napkin. "Do not forget one of our duties is to give guest lectures at our home university. Other universities pay for our expenses and time to come and give a presentation with them, when we have time. Usually we are out in the Field."

"So, you guys are rich back home?" Sherman took a bite of burger.

The three temporal anthropologists laughed at that.

Erik slapped Sherman on the back. "Hardly, although we are not reduced to digging through garbage cans. The university usually gives us a dwelling, like someone's attic, and an office on campus. We are hardly ever there, so we have no need of a place of great size. The university gives us a salary most modest and we can make some extra money giving lectures and publishing. Only a fool would go into this to get rich."

"Unless you be Tobias Leach," Matilda grumbled.

Clean-shaved Wendell came over to join the group, nostrils flaring hungrily.

"Hey, Wendell," Sherman said. "Did you live in an attic?"

"Yes." Wendell picked up a burger. "But it was the attic of an old Victorian home, so it wasn't just a crawl space. The couple that owned the house had renovated it into a very lovely studio apartment, located just off campus. It was so nice having someone below me who could keep an eye on my digs, since I was seldom there. Still it's good to have a place to store mementos and call home."

"Did you have an office on campus, too?"

"Of course I did, in the Faculty of History Building. It wasn't Victorian. It was built in the 1960s, I do believe, constructed all in glass. It won a few awards when it was built, I understand. I wanted my office there because so many of my ancestors had had offices in that building. Problem was all the office space had been taken. They did have one room available."

"Wasn't that originally a janitor's closet?" Henry asked.

"Yes, before robots replaced brooms and the custodians needed a larger storage room. I managed to fit a small Victorian writing desk and bookcase in there. I had the only office in a glass building without a window. The University did make it up to me for being such a good sport. I may have had the smallest office on campus, but my door had the largest name plaque."

The outside door opened and Henry walked back into the room. "The parrot folks have their lunch. Cerwyn must have made a trip to the pet store at the mall, 'cause they have a big cage now for the birds. They're still wearing nineteenth-century clothes, though."

Sherman shrugged. "When Priscilla came into the breakfast room, the outfit she had on didn't look that weird. From what I've seen, it would pass."

Serendipity nodded. "Yeah, I think khakis are timeless."

Henry grabbed a burger and came over to Wendell. "Okay buddy, Dr. *Letch* is next?"

Wendell fought back a smile. "Dr. *Leach*, yes. He could be difficult to persuade to come with us. You and Matilda were easy, because we are good friends. Dr. Olafson and Dr. Djata are both intelligent enough to listen to reason. Leach however is arrogant and doesn't seem to like me. Maybe it's because we are both in the same territory."

"Shoot!" Henry said. "I'm tramping around the nineteenth century too. Never felt like you were stepping on my toes."

"Yes, but Tobias and I both have the persona of English gentlemen."

"Tobias be no gentleman." Matilda rolled her eyes. "And thou art hardly working on the same subject matter. Is he not studying brothels?"

"Yes, he is." Wendell wrinkled his nose like he smelled something bad. "I suppose that is a forgotten piece of history, but he's not really studying the lives of these women, or the social impact of the double standard. He's just recording his personal exploits."

"Owo, it is just porn." Abubakari snorted. "His books are written for the masses. It has no redeeming quality whatsoever."

"The man is staying within the boundaries set by the Institute, I must give him that." Wendell sat down on the bed. "Well, if I cannot convince him, maybe the presence of Dr. Brown will impress him. I haven't the foggiest what I'm going to do if he refuses to accompany us."

"Leave him," Serendipity said.

"I can't." Wendell shook his head.

"I could come with you on your mighty quest." Erik rubbed his hands together. "I could throw the little weasel over my shoulder and haul him back like a slain stag." The big man looked like he would have no trouble doing that.

"No, I do think a Viking carrying someone off in the 1890s would attract attention."

"Maybe I could go with you all and help out." Henry shoved the rest of his burger in his mouth.

Wendell shook his head. "The two off us dragging Leach away, kicking and screaming, would most likely get us arrested."

"Pity you don't have one of those compliance disks like the Enforcers have." Sherman wiped his mouth on the back of his hand. "You could just slap that on the back of his neck and order him to leave."

"Maybe the zoologists have a tranquilizer rifle we could borrow," Wendell said deadpan.

Henry got a thoughtful frown on his face. "Uh, I'll be right back, folks." He hurried out the door.

"What is Henry up to?" Wendell cocked his head "I do hope he realizes I was joking about the tranquilizer rifle."

A couple of minutes later Henry walked back in holding an orange-colored square disk.

Wendell got off the bed and came over. "I say, what in the name of heavens is that?"

"I got it from the zoologists. They let me take it, because they can't use it on the parrots. I had noticed this in their tool chest. They called it a Taming Devise. They said they use it to control larger animals, after they come around from the tranquilizer dart. It makes them more docile so they can just lead them anywhere. They apparently just need to slap it on the back of the critter's neck below the skull. I know it doesn't look like a compliance disk, but from the description, I wonder if it isn't and that the Institute just made it look different so no one would recognize it."

"We'll need to test it." Wendell studied the object. "Slap it on the back of my neck."

"Neinn!" Erik stopped them. "Use me as your guinea pig. If it makes Dr. Howe sick or injures him, he will be in no shape to rescue Dr. Leach."

"I don't know." Wendell shook his head. "I couldn't possibly ask you—"

Before Wendell could finish the sentence, Erik snatched the device out of Henry's hand and slapped it on the back of his own neck. His eyes got big and he stiffened like a marine at attention.

"Erik?" Wendell asked. "Are you all right?"

"Ya," Erik said a bit mechanically.

"Tarnation!" Henry studied Erik's face. "I think it's working. How do we test it?"

"We would have to ask Dr. Olafson to do something he would normally not do." Abubakari scrutinized Erik's blank face.

Wendell stroked his upper lip. "Like what? I don't wish to ask him to do something dangerous or humiliating."

"Oh, I know!" Serendipity stepped forward. "Hey Erik, repeat after me."

"Ya."

"Ducks are winners."

"Ducks are winners," Erik repeated.

"Golden Gophers are dinner."

"Golden Gophers are dinner." Erik's eyes looked glazed.

"Okay." Serendipity sat down on the bed.

Wendell frowned at her. "What was that supposed to prove?"

"Just remove the device."

Henry stepped over and pressed a button in the center of the square. The device fell off into his hand.

Erik slumped, then straightened up. He stomped over and glared down at Serendipity. "How dare you say Golden Gophers are dinner!" he yelled. "And who gives a drit about your stupid Ducks!"

Serendipity grinned up at Erik, nearly breaking her neck to look up at the tall man towering over her. "I had to make you say something you never would have, unless you were forced against your will, like the University of Oregon football team is better than the University of Minnesota."

Erik's angry scowl evaporated and he grinned. "Ha, you *are* a genius most great, Dr. Brown."

"Call me Serendipity."

"By Jove!" Wendell broke out in a smile. "The gadget works."

Sherman looked over at the robot standing in the corner. "Maybe we could use Rosetta for bait?"

"What?" Serendipity stared at him.

"Well, you keep saying this guy is a perv so—"

"No!" Wendell looked nauseated. "It is a robot. Leach will be able to tell. I do not think even he would sink *that* low. We'll just reason with the man and if that doesn't work, we'll slap this Compliance Disk on him."

"Maybe I ought to go with ya, buddy." Henry offered. "I'm nineteenth century too. I could pose as one of them American nouveau riche tourists. Done that before. I've been to Victorian England more than once."

"We're not going to England. Leach is in Paris 1897 in the Pigalle District."

"Pig Alley?" Sherman wondered if he heard right.

Wendell smirked at him. "That is what the American servicemen called it in World War II. It is *Pigalle*, the Red Light District."

Matilda rolled her eyes. "Why dost it surprise me not that Tobias would be there."

"Well, if it's in Paris, we'll need to take Rosetta anyway." Sherman looked over at the robot. "None of us speak French."

"Au contraire, Monsieur Conrad." Wendell fought back a smile.

"You speak French?"

"Like a native. Well, a native with an English accent. Most Victorian gentlemen knew French, so I learned to speak it fluently." Wendell looked over at Henry and studied him a moment. "I am not certain if I can refuse your offer, Henry. We need Serendipity to impress Tobias, and I'm not keen on the idea of dragging her into that evil place unprotected."

Serendipity rolled her eyes. "Oh, save my virgin eyes from seeing ladies doing the can-can and showing their bloomers."

Wendell frowned at her. "Dr. Brown, the place is packed with ladies of the evening. Everyone will assume you are one too, if you are unescorted. I don't want some drunk mauling you, and treating you disrespectfully."

"I'll be there." Sherman reminded Wendell.

"And it may well take three of us to protect her."

"Oh, really, Wendell." Serendipity crossed her arms. "I'm sure it's not that bad. Have you ever been there?"

"Good heavens, no! But I have heard stories. Pigalle is in Montmarte, a village outside the city-limits of Paris *and* her legal authority, and so attracts those who wish to be outside the law. It was named 'Mount of the Martyr' because St. Denis was decapitated there in 205 A.D. Men have been losing their heads there ever since." Wendell turned to Henry. "We are about the same size. I think I have a late Victorian suit that will fit you. Sherman can wear his sack suit. Dr. Brown is already dressed appropriately."

"I'll be sure to put on my iron chastity belt, too," Serendipity mumbled.

Chapter Thirteen

It was odd, thought Sherman, but even in a double-breasted suit Henry still looked like a cowboy. Wendell was the only one in the group that looked right in a Victorian suit. Of course, Wendell was wearing his brown top hat, and Henry was wearing his black Stetson.

Wendell hopped out of the Timemobile, pulled his computer out of the inner pocket of his faithful brown frock coat and flipped opened the Bible. Sherman followed wearing his derby and dark blue sack suit. They were on a dirt road beside a narrow river. On the other side of the water sat a cottage with a large vegetable garden being hoed by an elderly man. He hadn't looked up, quite intent on his task.

"I think you missed Paris, Dr. Brown." Wendell looked about.

"Ya think maybe?" Sherman mumbled.

Wendell looked up from his computer. "I am picking up a time machine but it is some distance away. For some reason I'm not picking up Dr. Leach's signature at all."

"Well, I suppose we could go find that time machine and work from there." Serendipity stepped up to him in her long lavender dress nearly sweeping the ground. She looked over at the Timemobile disguised as a shed sitting conspicuously by the side of the road. "I suppose we could drive our Timemobile over. Not sure if I can make a horse and buggy look believable. We need something the same shape." She pulled out her own pocket computer out of her drawstring handbag and cued it. "Tom! 1897. Mode of transportation. Any ideas?"

"Automobiles are starting to become more common," the voice of Tom Jones said. "I'd go with a 1897 Delahaye 6hp Limousine, pussycat."

Serendipity looked at the picture on her screen and shrugged. "Looks good to me." She stepped back into the Timemobile. After a minute the shed disappeared and became a bright yellow and black horseless carriage. Unlike many automobiles of the day this had a roof and a back seat, giving it a boxy look. The engine would have been underneath, so the front was short with three lanterns serving as headlights.

Serendipity stepped out. "So what do you think? I cheated a little. It's a bit wider and longer than the original. I put doors on the sides and curtains in the back windows. I left the front windows alone of course, so people can see us inside. That will make it look more natural."

"Looks convincing enough." Wendell studied it.

"Bang up job." Henry grinned. "Fooled me."

"Are you sure there are cars around?" Sherman looked doubtful. He pulled out his own pocket computer and whistled.

"Yes, Steve?" Lauren Bacall's voice said.

"It's 1897. Are there many cars in France now?"

"They've been racing automobiles in France for ten years now," Lauren said. "The Automobile Club of France got together two years ago. It's still a rich man's toy, but this won't be the first automobile anyone around here has seen."

Serendipity frowned at Sherman. "You won't believe me, but you'll believe your computer, huh?"

"I'm sorry, but it's just hard to believe they had cars this early."

"This is the 1890s, kid." Henry slapped Sherman on the back. "We even got telephones and elevators."

Sherman noticed Henry, like Wendell, spoke about the 1800s like he belonged there instead of the twenty-seventh century.

Henry looked around. "Shall we vamoose and track down old Tobias? You can drive, kid."

Sherman went around, opened up the cab and climbed into the driver's seat. Serendipity, Wendell, then Henry all climbed in the other side and scrunched together. "We are all just gonna have to get chummy." Henry turned sideways. "We need to give Sherman a little elbow room. So Wendell, you'll just have to pretend you like Serendipity."

Wendell put his arm around her and pulled her close.

"Well, this *is* nice." Serendipity snuggled up. "Be even nicer if I was between you *and* Henry."

Wendell raised his eyebrow, but Henry just laughed. "Poor Wendell, you gotta put up with two Westerners now."

Wendell managed to pull out his computer and let Henry hold it since he had his hands full. Henry watched the arrow on the screen and gave directions to Sherman. They drove along the river, passing more tiny farms and crossing several narrow canals. They came to a bridge and crossed the river into the town, the skyline dominated by a tall Gothic cathedral. Wendell looked puzzled at he studied the buildings. "There is something vaguely familiar about this place, but it doesn't seem like Paris."

"The arrow is pointing to the right." Henry jerked his thumb.

They continued a short way until Henry called out. "Whoa! The arrow just did a flip-flop. I'd say we just passed Tobias's time machine. Better park, Sherman."

Sherman pulled the vehicle to the side of the road. They all piled out. A huge gothic cathedral towered in front of them, with its stained glass and flying buttresses. Serendipity scratched her head. "Is that the Cathedral of Norte Dame?"

Wendell studied it a moment, frowning. "Something is definitely not right. May I see my computer, Henry?"

"Sure, buddy." he handed it over. Henry pulled out his pocket watch and stared at it. "Jumping Jehoshaphat!" Henry grinned over at Sherman. "That's the cue to turn on my computer. Okay, show me a picture of the Cathedral Norte Dame from the back." Henry frowned. "Looks kind of like it, but not quite, like something's wrong."

Wendell, however, had already trotted off toward a tiny nearby park. The other three followed after him. They at last caught up to Wendell. He stood frowning at a tall pedestal with an equestrian statue of an effeminate knight on top. "This statue, I've seen it before. The Institute has disguised my time machine like this. It is a statue of Joan of Arc on a horse. I guess they figured that while it might attract attention, no Frenchman would think of touching it. I wonder if the French will notice it keeps getting moved from city to city."

Wendell looked down again at his open Bible. "I still can't pick up Leach. We have his time machine. I wonder if he left for another town. I suppose the Enforcers have better tracking equipment than a pocket computer." He began walking slowly, waving his Bible about. "Maybe if I get this pointed in the right direction I might be able to pick him up." Wendell disappeared behind the granite pedestal.

"Excuse me. I mean, pardonnez-moi, monsieur," Wendell spoke to someone on the other side.

"Oh, I say, English are we?" a familiar voice answered.

Sherman came around the pedestal to see Wendell's mouth hanging open. In front of him stood another man, also with his mouth open and eyes wide. Except for his mustache, he looked identical to Wendell. He was even wearing the same brown top hat and frock coat. The stranger pulled out a small black Bible exactly like Wendell's. They both clicked their tongues at the same time. "DNA scan," they said together. They both looked down at the Bibles, then up at each other. "Oh bloody hell," they both groaned in unison.

Sherman blinked at the two of them. "Uh, Wendell?"

"Yes?" they both turned to Sherman.

"Never mind, I think you just answered my question."

"What the...?" Serendipity came around the corner of the statue. "Why does this guy look like Wendell?"

Wendell sighed. "Because it *is* me."

The mustached Wendell shook his head. "This isn't possible. The Institute makes sure this sort of thing can't happen. They go to great pains to assure we never cross our own paths."

The clean-shaven Wendell nodded. "Yes I know. The Institute also safeguards that we never cross paths with another time traveler, unless we are working with them or at least are on the same Base Time. So why would they send Tobias here to Paris in this timeframe when they knew I would already be here years ago Base Time?"

"Paris?" the other Wendell frowned. "This is Amiens."

Their Wendell slapped his forehead. "Of course, that's why the Cathedral Norte Dame looks odd. It is the wrong Cathedral Norte Dame!"

"What?" Serendipity came over to her Wendell. "What do you mean wrong one?"

"France has countless Gothic Cathedrals named Norte Dame: Paris, Amiens, Reims, Bayeux, Chartres to name a few. This is Cathedrale Norte Dame d'Amiens. It is the tallest complete cathedral in France."

"Yes." The other Wendell looked over at Serendipity. "But the Norte Dame in Paris gets all the attention, just because it is in Paris."

Serendipity gave both of them a look of disbelief. "You're beside yourself, and you're still spouting historical trivia?"

The two Wendells looked at each other again. Their Wendell nodded. "Yes, it is all coming back to me. Five years ago the Universite de Picardie Jules Verne, here in Amiens, asked me to record the city in this time period. A lot of it was destroyed in World War I and II and all they had were a few black and white photos. They wanted me to take color vid of the devastated area. They also asked me to record Jules Verne on video. He died in 1915 before movies with sound. He's a member of the Amiens city council now."

"I got him to autograph my copy of *Around the World in Eighty Days*." The younger Wendell grinned excitedly.

"Yes, and the Enforcers will have a fit when they see the copyright date on that edition."

"Well, Grams Julia gave it to me. It was my first real book. It is very special."

"I know," the current Wendell said patiently.

"So, you are from my future?" The former Wendell suddenly looked distressed. "My word, where's my mustache? Did you shave that? Do you know how long it took me to grow that?"

"Yes, I do."

"And who do you have with you? Oh, hello Henry. I'm so glad we got to work together again. I must say, I will look forward to that."

Henry waved half-heartedly, looking lost for words.

The earlier Wendell stepped forward to Sherman and Serendipity. "I don't believe we have ever met."

The later Wendell made the introductions. "Dr. Howe, I am very pleased to introduce myself to Dr. Serendipity Brown and her assistant Mr. Sherman Conrad."

"I am very pleased to make your acquaintance." The earlier Wendell shook their hands. "You seem quite young, Mr. Conrad. Is the Institute allowing a student program in the future? So how do you like time travel?"

"S'okay. A little weird sometimes...like now."

Wendell nodded at him, then stopped and looked stunned. "I say, did you say Serendipity Brown? She's not *the* Serendipity Brown, is she? Is she in the Program now?"

"Nope." Serendipity got closer. "You are going to become my Time Travel Consultant. Hmm, never did get a chance to kiss you with that mustache." Serendipity grabbed the stunned Englishman and planted her lips on his.

The younger Wendell managed to pull back. "Madam, please! We just met!"

The later Wendell pulled her back. "Serendipity, if you don't mind, you don't know me that well, yet."

"*Yet*?" His earlier version's eyes got big. "Me and Serendipity Brown?"

Serendipity grabbed both their arms. "Whoa, two Wendells! The possibilities are endless."

They both jerked back their arms and cried in unison. "Dr. Brown!"

"If you don't mind." The later Wendell scowled. "I really do not want a menage a trois with myself."

"Wait a minute," his earlier self protested. "I can't have a relationship with someone from a different time period. That is strictly against the rules. The Enforcers would see to it I never time travel again, if they don't erase me outright."

"You are outside their jurisdiction now," the later Wendell explained to himself. "You no longer work with the Institute anymore. You work for someone else, old boy."

"Dear heavens, I've gone AWOL?" The younger Wendell looked horrified. "The Enforcers will hunt me down."

"Yes, they did, but they've left you alone. They have decided that you are fulfilling a greater destiny."

"Greater destiny?"

"You are traveling in time with Serendipity Brown now."

The earlier Wendell's eyes got huge. "That's not possible."

"It is. And it was meant to be."

"It is? But why *me*? I'm just a boring history scholar." The former Wendell looked overwhelmed.

"Don't worry." Serendipity winked at him. "You'll do fine. You save me from being stranded in 1851."

"Enforcers would not like that, me saving someone in the past."

"That's why you ran away with me to begin with. The Enforcers are cool with that now."

"But what are you doing here?"

The later Wendell turned and looked at Serendipity. "Yes, what are we doing here? We are supposed to be in Paris. Why did we land outside Amiens? I'll bet those little farms were the Hortillonnages."

"Horta-what?" Serendipity crossed her arms.

"Hortillonnages," the earlier Wendell explained. "The local swamps were drained into canals and turned into farm plots. It dates back to the Roman Period."

The later Wendell poked a few buttons on the screen of his computer. "My word, it would appear you have the longitude spot on, Dr. Brown, but the latitude is incorrect. I say, this is a major cock up. What is going to happen when my former self is interrogated by the Enforcers? You can't take this version of me with you, or I won't be there for you when you really need me. Not to mention it would be far too confusing. Yet if the Enforcers find out, they will ground me for good before we even meet the first time and I won't be there for you either."

"That is a sticky wicket." The younger Wendell nodded.

The later Wendell turned and clamped his hand on the shoulder of his former self. "I'm afraid, old boy, there is only one solution. I will have to make you forget this meeting ever took place."

"I suppose you are right. But how do you propose we do that? The Theta

Wave Strobe in our pocket watch isn't strong enough to get around an Enforcer interrogation."

"No, but a Compliance Disk would be."

"Compliance Disk?" The former Wendell stepped back, looking frightened. "Where in the world did I get one of those, and more importantly *why* would I even have one?"

"Don't worry, you haven't become a scoundrel. It is for a rescue mission. We got it from a temporal zoologist. They call it something else. We'll just slap this on the back of your neck and make you forget any of this took place."

"Do you even know what you are doing?"

"You'll have to trust me."

The earlier Wendell studied the later Wendell. "Well, I've always tried to be honest with myself. If I can't trust me, who can I trust? Besides if it made me a vegetable then you wouldn't be standing here, now would you?"

"Good man! I didn't know I was so brave."

"Wait a minute." Serendipity came over to the former Wendell. "Before you do that, I want to do something." She grabbed his lapels and pulled him closer. This time she gave the younger Wendell a longer kiss. This time he didn't pull away. In fact he leaned forward a bit as Serendipity stepped back. Serendipity patted his cheek. "Until we meet again."

"I say, I will be looking forward to that! At least I would if I wasn't going to have to forget all this." The former Wendell slumped with a disappointed sigh.

The current Wendell pulled the disk out of his pocket and handed it to Henry. "Here, if you will do the honors."

Henry grimaced as he reluctantly slapped it on the back of the earlier version of his friend. The younger Wendell gave an involuntary yelp through clenched teeth. Serendipity held his hand, looking sympathetic.

The later Wendell cleared his throat. "All right, Dr. Howe, you will close your eyes and count to one hundred very slowly, after I remove the disk. You will then open your eyes and remember nothing of this meeting. However, I will leave you with one subliminal message. When you run into Serendipity Brown in the future you will do all in your power to help her, because you love her very much."

"Yes, I will forget everything, but I will help." The former Wendell closed his eyes and nodded.

Their Wendell nodded at Henry. He pushed the button in the middle and it popped off into his hand.

"One...two...three..." the younger Wendell began counting.

The later Wendell then started walking away and motioned for the others to follow. He then broke into a run, returning to the Timemobile. He leaned against the fake horseless carriage. "All right, Sherman, drive us behind a building so no one will see us disappear. And Dr. Brown, please get the coordinates right this time. If I hated myself, we would be in real trouble now."

Chapter Fourteen

Sherman stepped out of the Timemobile cab into Pigalle. He had expected to find a squalid ghetto, but instead saw a broad boulevard lined with iron street lamps. Across the one-way lane was a park-like median strip planted with trees and beyond it another lane going the opposite direction. The streets were brimming with the traffic of small one-horse hansom cabs, with an occasional wagon loaded with barrels and even one or two horseless carriages sputtered by. Well-maintained buildings as tall as seven stories lined the street. On the sidewalk and on the park strip milled a crowd of people—fine gentlemen, spruced-up working stiffs and women wearing fancy low-cut dresses and come hither looks. No one seemed to notice their limousine pop out of nowhere. Sherman wasn't sure if they were all too occupied or if nothing that happened in Pigalle surprised anyone.

Wendell waved his Bible about, then stared over at a statue across the road on the median strip. It looked like the exact same statue of Joan of Arc they had left in Amiens.

"That must be Leach's time machine. I guess the Institute likes to stay with what works." Wendell looked up at the sky, then over at Serendipity. "It looks close to dusk. You seem to have brought us forward a few hours. I hope it is the same day, at least."

"You want to drive next time?" Serendipity folded her arms. "It's a time machine not a hoverbus. I have to travel in time at least a little bit for it to work."

Wendell tipped his top hat and gave her an appeasing smile. "Yes, of course. Passengers shouldn't tell the pilots their business."

Henry looked around. "So, this is Pigalle, huh. Mighty fancy for the bad part of town."

Wendell studied his computer. "I'm picking up Leach's signature. He appears to be in this direction." He started to take off, then stopped and looked back. "Dr. Brown? Henry, Sherman, each of you, take one of her arms."

Sherman and Henry followed orders, putting Serendipity between them. She rolled her eyes. "Sheesh!"

"Humor him," Sherman whispered to her. "Wendell's being overly protective because he's worried sick. I know he doesn't show it, but his nerves are probably shot and so are yours. Don't attack him when he's down just because he cares about you."

Serendipity forced a smile at Wendell, who returned it with a more sincere one. Then he took off like a foxhound on a scent. The other three, arm in arm, followed.

"Kid's right," Henry whispered to Serendipity.

"Yeah, I know. That's why I keep Sherman around."

Sherman noticed a few gentlemen eyeing Serendipity even though she was middle-aged. They looked like they had had way too much alcohol or whatever. Perhaps Wendell had a right to be overly protective.

Wendell at last came to a stop and stared straight ahead. On the other side of the boulevard crouched a one-story structure sandwiched between two six-story buildings. It would have been unnoticeable if not for the three-story red windmill on its roof.

"Moulin Rouge." Wendell read the sign. "That translates to 'Red Windmill.' I believe it is a cabaret."

"A windmill?" Sherman pushed his bangs out of his eyes. "What's sexy about a windmill?"

"Montmarte was once famous for its windmills when it was a rural district." Wendell stroked his upper lip.

"Looks innocent enough," Serendipity said.

"Make certain your computers are where they cannot be stolen by pickpockets." Wendell closed his and tucked it into his frock coat into one of the many breast pockets he had sewn inside. He headed for the entrance at a slower pace, no doubt not wanting to lose Serendipity and her bodyguards in the crowd.

Inside sprawled a large room with a wooden floor where a dozen couples danced. To the right was a long bar at which men in top hats stood drinking wine and spirits. To the left were tables with customers clustered around them. Wendell stopped to scan the crowd.

Sherman noticed one man at a table with a goblet that had a bulge just above the stem. In the bubble was a green liquid. Lying across the top of the glass was a large slotted spoon. The man set a sugar cube on the spoon then began slowly dribbling a small pitcher of water over it into the goblet. The green liquid spilled out of the bottom section and turned a milky color.

Sherman tugged at Wendell's sleeve. "Uh, Wendell, what's that?"

Wendell glanced over at where Sherman pointed and smiled. "That is absinthe, better known as 'the Green Fairy.' It is a spirit made of wormwood, anise and fennel, primarily. It is reputed to have hallucinogenic properties."

"It does?"

"No more than any other alcohol. Drink enough and I am sure you would eventually see fairies." Wendell went back to studying the bar. "Can any of you spot Tobias?"

"Nope." Henry swiveled his head about.

"I believe there is supposed to be a garden in the back. Shall we try there?"

They headed toward the rear where glass doors between pillars opened onto a large patio. Wendell led them outside where there were several lines of tables and chairs with more customers.

Sherman's attention instantly went to the four-story elephant standing next to a large stage it dwarfed. As wrinkled as a Shar-Pei, the behemoth looked as bewildered as Sherman as to why he was here. "What the—? Why did they put that giant elephant there?"

Wendell shrugged. "Decor, I suppose. I understand they picked it up cheap after the 1889 Paris Universal Exposition. It is just plaster. Rumor has it that for a franc you can go inside and watch belly dancers in the elephant's belly. Only men are allowed. Personally I think ladies aren't permitted so hen-pecked men can go in there and smoke a cigar in peace."

The band in front of the stage struck up a tune and ladies in frilly skirts pranced out onto the stage. They lifted their skirts to reveal their lacey petticoats and pantaloons, flouncing them to the fast music. Even Sherman recognized the can-can. The dancers impressed him with the sheer gymnastic skills they showed, bouncing on one leg, while kicking the other. And they *were* cute girls. He lost all interest in the elephant.

"Hey, Fancy Pants!" Henry yelled over the music. "Is that Tobias? Over there sitting at the far end in the green suit and brown derby."

Wendell followed Henry's finger and nodded. "I do believe you are right."

Sherman was shorter than the two temporal anthropologists so he took their word for it. They worked their way through the maze to the table where Tobias sat with a young woman in a sleeveless low-cut red dress that showed off some cleavage. He wore a double-breasted suit with a gold satin waistcoat, his derby at a rakish tilt. The Englishman was about the same height and build as Wendell, except he looked a bit younger and had black hair. Tobias and his companion both held stemmed glasses full of milky Green Fairy.

"How do you do, Dr. Leach?" Wendell spoke loud enough to be heard above the din of the orchestra and the crowd. "Enjoying the absinthe, I see?"

Tobias looked up, his face registering shock. "Howe? What the hell are you doing here? They told me to stay away from Amiens because you were there now in Field Time—seven years ago in my Base Time. There is no record of you coming down to Paris."

"We need to talk, Tobias."

Tobias looked over at his female companion and said, "Excusez-nous s'il vous plait, mon cher."

The lady pouted, disappointed, but stood up and left. She made sure to take her drink with her.

"What are you doing here, When-Dull?" Tobias glared, setting down his glass. "They told me I could have September 1897, Paris. I was very specific about the time slot. This here and this now are *mine*! You can't have them! Go back to Amiens." Tobias stopped, and looked past Wendell. "Is that Darrel with you? What the hell is he doing here? Shouldn't he be somewhere punching a cow?"

"What are you doing in Paris? I thought you were studying the homosexual scene of 1870s London." Wendell sat down uninvited. The others also pulled up chairs.

"That was two years ago. Wait, how would you know that?" Tobias looked suspicious, nervously twisting the end of his black mustache. "That would have been five years in your future." Tobias pointed at Wendell's lip. "And when did you shave your mustache? What is going on here? There was a rumor going around that you had gone AWOL. Then the Enforcers said you had been killed in the Field. They threw a big funeral for you and everything! That still didn't kill all the rumors. I don't know what you are up to Howe, but you are just going to have to leave."

"So, you finished with your previous project?" Wendell asked.

"As if that is any of your business." Tobias leaned back in his chair. "My publisher told me to shelve the other project, said what I had gathered wasn't that exciting. Their accounting department decided they needed a book on the famous Red Light District of 1890s Paris. I picked this year, because it is special, and I'm not letting you take it from me."

"What's so special about 1897?" Wendell cocked his head.

"This is a critical point for the Pigalle." Tobias studied his fingernails. "At this point the Moulin Rogue has started hiring failed ballet dancers instead of prostitutes for their chorus line, but they haven't cleaned up their act yet for the tourists. If anything, the can-can is getting raunchier. The Folies-Bergeres are showing more and more skin, though they haven't gotten to bare breasts yet. And the Grand Guignol plays are getting more provocative with their subject matter. They are currently featuring plays about prostitutes and gory murders. And of course the Maisons Closes are still here." Tobias looked pointedly at Henry. "That's cathouses to the cowboy here." He turned back to Wendell. "So, I'm not leaving. I have this time and place already reserved. You two and your playmates will have to leave."

Tobias leaned forward. "So which one of you gets the boy and which one gets the old trout? You couldn't do any better than her?"

Wendell snarled and started to get up, but Henry pushed him back into his seat.

"Leach, you jackass," Henry growled. "Mr. Conrad is the assistant of our lady friend here. And if you knew who *she* was, you'd be eating crow without catsup!"

"Oh, is she a music hall entertainer?"

Wendell stood up and glowered down at Tobias. "This, you git, is Dr. Serendipity Brown! *The* Serendipity Brown. Now you will apologize."

Tobias frowned confused, then laughed. "Yes, of course she is and I'm Toulouse Lautrec."

Henry smiled. "Yeah, I found it hard to swallow myself, when he first told me. Go on, Leach, do a DNA scan on her."

Tobias pointed the cut-glass knob of his walking stick at her. His eyes got big. "Bloody hell! What are you doing with *her*? Does the Institute know about this? How did you get here?"

"I brought them here." Serendipity smiled at Tobias. "We came in *my* time machine."

"Why are any of you here?" Tobias glanced about nervously. "What is going on?"

"We're here to save your worthless hide." Henry leaned his elbow on the table.

Tobias picked up his glass again. "You are here to save me from myself?"

Wendell bent forward, lowering his voice. "We are here to save you from assassins called Time Keepers. A renegade offshoot of the Time Purists have become terrorists and they are killing temporal anthropologists. They have already killed three. All time travel in and out of the twenty-seventh century has been stopped, so if you try to go home, you will never make it. There is one time machine missing and we are certain the terrorists have it."

"So why are you here?" Tobias looked suspicious. "Shouldn't the Enforcers be here if I really *am* in danger?"

"The Enforcers are too busy," Wendell said. "They wrote you off, along with the few others left in the Field. So we are here to save you."

"Is this one of your practical jokes?"

Serendipity stared at Wendell stunned. "You're a practical joker?"

"I put pepper in Henry's coffee at a banquet once."

Henry shrugged. "I had it coming after that whoopee cushion. I just like watching Wendell blush. He turns such a bright shade of pink."

"No, this is not a joke," Wendell assured Tobias.

Tobias got a smug sneer, like he had figured it all out. "No, it is not a joke. It's a scam! You are here to trick me into going AWOL, too. You just want to ruin my career."

Wendell groaned, putting his face in his hand.

"Well, there you go." Henry rolled his eyes. "You caught us, Leach. Wendell and I have destroyed our careers, ruined our lives, made ourselves marked men just so we could ruin your day. I'm surprised you can find a hat big enough for that head."

Serendipity stood up and leaned forward. "Dr. Leach, I don't know you. Why would I risk my life to get back at someone I never met, and who never did me any harm."

"Maybe these two kidnapped you."

"Sweetheart, do I look like someone who would placidly go along with kidnappers? I'm a twenty-fourth-century woman, not a nineteenth-century one. We are only here because Wendell is worried about you. The man wants to save your life. Now either come along, or we can slap a Compliance Disk on you, or we can leave you here to die."

"Compliance Disk!" Tobias stared horrified at Wendell. "How could you get your hands on a Compliance Disk? Now, I know you are criminals!" He flipped up the collar of his jacket like that would protect his neck.

"I wish you hadn't mentioned that," Wendell whispered to Serendipity.

"Oops."

Tobias raised his walking stick with both hands. "If you try to use it, I will cause a scene. The cabarets have hired bouncers to protect gentlemen such as myself from riffraff like you."

"Fine we won't use it. We will just leave you here to die." Serendipity started to get up. "Come on guys, we did our best."

"No, Dr. Brown." Wendell grabbed her hand. "We can't just leave him. I know he's insufferable, but he is the great-nephew and nearest descendant of Sir Albert Leach."

"So?"

"Sir Albert was my greatest inspiration and mentor. He was one of the great pioneers in Temporal Anthropology and one of the greatest scholars of Victorian history and culture that ever lived. He founded the Association of Temporal Anthropologists. They knighted him for it."

"And don't think my life hasn't been hell living in *that* shadow," Tobias muttered.

Wendell sighed frustrated. "Tobias, what can I possibly do to convince you we are really here to save you?"

"Give me the Compliance Disk." Tobias held out his hand.

"What?"

"Give me the Compliance Disk. I'm not going anywhere with you if you can slap that thing on me and make me your puppet so you can humiliate me."

"I would never..."

"Then hand it over." Tobias snapped his fingers a couple of times and held his hand out again.

Wendell sighed and handed it over.

"This doesn't look like a Compliance Disk." Tobias studied the orange square.

"No, it doesn't. It is one the temporal zoologists use on large animals."

Tobias turned the disk over, then nodded. "Wrong shape and color, but otherwise—" Tobias stuffed it into his pocket. "Now, if you will excuse me I don't wish to miss Loie Fuller at the Folies Bergere. I understand she is going to do her famous Serpentine Dance. It is not really that risqué, but there are other less clothed acts too." Tobias smiled at them and got up, leaning his walking stick over his right shoulder. He turned his back on them and started walking out.

Serendipity jumped up and ran after Tobias. She grasped his arm. "Hey!"

"Yes?" Tobias turned and raised his eyebrow at her.

"Don't you know who I am? I'm Serendipity Brown, the inventor of time travel. If it wasn't for me, you wouldn't have a job! Doesn't that mean anything to you?"

Tobias appeared bored. "Not unless you can do a fan dance or something even more amusing I can record for my next book. You've wasted enough of my time; I have to get back to work." He removed her hand and continued toward the door.

Serendipity stood there with her mouth open. She turned to her companions who were now standing beside her. "What a jerk!" Serendipity fumed. "I say we leave him to his fate."

Henry watched Tobias making his way through the crowd. "If nothing else, we got to get that Compliance Disk back. I hate to think what that slimy polecat would do with it." He turned and gave Wendell an accusing scowl. "I can't believe you just handed it over."

"I-I didn't know what else to do." Wendell shrugged. "I didn't dream he would walk off with it."

"You always were too gullible, Fancy Pants. Now we gotta roundup the hombre."

"I don't think Tobias would actually use it on someone." Wendell assured him. "But the Enforcers will want to know where he procured it. We cannot have that."

They started after Tobias but lost him in the sudden rush of men coming in. Sherman finally waded through the crowd and got out into the street, but found himself separated from his companions. The sky was growing dark enough that the street lights were now on. He looked around frantically, then felt his arm grabbed. He turned to punch his attacker.

"Whoa, kid! Just me." Henry grinned at him. Next to him Sherman saw Wendell with his arm in Serendipity's.

"Did you find Tobias?" Sherman asked.

Henry snorted. "Scalawag got away."

"Take Dr. Brown, Henry." Wendell let go of his charge and pulled out his Bible and opened it up. "Tobias is in that direction," he pointed. Wendell took off down the sidewalk. Sherman linked with Serendipity's other arm and navigated through the maze of people. They caught up with Wendell, who stood rigid, looking down an alley between two buildings.

"What's up, buddy?" Henry asked

Wendell just pointed. Although the passage was darkened by the twilight, there was enough illumination cast from the street light behind them to see what was going on. There among the garbage cans, three men, dressed in grey suits, roughed up a fourth man in a green suit.

"I think that's Tobias. He's being mugged!" Wendell cried and rushed in. Henry let go of Serendipity and ran after him. Sherman hung back, intending to protect Serendipity. The adventurous inventor however shook free of Sherman and took off right behind Henry.

"You will unhand that man at once!" Wendell demanded.

One of the three hooligans turned and glared at Wendell. "Stay away! This is none of your concern, savage."

"Savage?" Sherman frowned. That was an odd thing to call an obviously civilized gentleman like Wendell.

"Run!" Tobias screamed, cowering on the ground. "It's *them*. It's the Time Keepers!"

The name "savage" now made sense to Sherman. The assassins from the twenty-seventh century must have viewed Victorians as primitives. However, Tobias's valiant warning had become an accidental betrayal. His attackers now knew the rescuers were not from the nineteenth century. They turned and stared at Wendell, Henry, Serendipity and Sherman.

The mugger that had told Wendell to go away stepped forward—no doubt, the leader. He wore a beard that somehow didn't seem quite natural. "How do you know about the Time Keepers? Are you temporal anthropologists, too?" He pulled out his computer from his pocket and pointed it at them. "Yes, these two have signatures. One is Dr. Henry Darrel, who's on our list. The other is Dr. Wendell Howe, but he is recorded as dead."

Wendell's eyes got big. "Where did you get those signatures? We don't even have mine. You must have gotten into the Institute's main records. How could you have done that?"

The leader frowned at Serendipity and Sherman. "They have no signatures. Who are they?"

"Commander?" One of the other men pointed. "Look at that woman's face. Doesn't she look like the last person on our list?"

"Dr. Serendipity Brown?" The leader pointed an odd-looking silver object he had in his other hand at Serendipity. It was shaped like a pistol, but far too skinny. Sherman didn't know what it was, but it seemed to scare both Wendell and Henry. However, they both stepped forward, without a word, putting themselves between the assailant and Serendipity, grim determination on their faces.

There came a commotion behind the other two attackers. They turned to find the forgotten Tobias, no longer curled up in a sniveling ball. Tobias stood there with the Compliance Disk he had pulled out of his pocket. He slapped it on the neck of the attacker closest to him.

"Knock out your partner!" Tobias ordered.

The controlled man turned and socked his startled associate in the jaw, knocking him to the ground.

As the leader turned, Serendipity pushed past her two stunned protectors and pulled a small red cylinder the size of a lipstick case out of her handbag. It sparked and she shoved it into the leader's side. He screamed and also crumpled to the ground.

The man with the Compliance Disk on his neck looked down shocked at the fellow he had just punched out. He collected himself and moved toward Serendipity.

"Freeze!" Tobias screamed at him.

The attacker went stiff. Serendipity shoved her weapon into his gut. He jerked like someone struck by lightning and dropped.

The five of them stared down a moment at the three prone men. Tobias looked over at Wendell, his face pale. "Bloody hell, you were telling the truth! They said they were going to kill me for crimes against history or some such rubbish. They said I was to be their first victim in the Field because I was the most well-known."

Henry scratched his head. "Well, your dirty books did make the bestsellers list."

Sherman came over to Serendipity. "What the hell is that thing you got, Ser?"

"Stunner. Told ya I would pack one."

Wendell however made no comment. He glared down at the leader and grabbed up one of the twenty-seventh-century weapons that had been dropped. Snarling, Wendell pointed it at the head of the leader.

"What are you doing, Wendell?" Serendipity watched in disbelief.

"They wanted to kill you, Serendipity." Wendell did not look up, his voice level but tight. "They won't stop until they do. They must be destroyed."

"Don't do it, Wendell."

Wendell's expression was cold, but his eyes looked tortured. He continued to point the weapon. Then he gave a groan and threw it against the brick wall, smashing it. "I can't do it." He bowed his head. "I'm sorry. Forgive me, Serendipity. I'm too much of a coward."

Serendipity came over and put her arms around him. "You aren't a coward. You just aren't a killer. Don't think I'd like you if you were one."

"We still need to render them helpless." Sherman looked around. "What if we take their weapons so they can't use them?"

Henry smiled at him. "Good idea, kid. Let's take their computers too. Hell, just go through their pockets and take everything. That will slow them down." Henry knelt down and started frisking the closest assailant.

Sherman retrieved the Compliance Disk from Serendipity's second victim and put it in his own pocket, then started searching for anything else.

Tobias knelt down and started patting down the last man.

Serendipity took Wendell's hand. "We'll go where they'll never find us. We'll be fine." Then she got a wicked grin. "Maybe we ought to steal their clothes too. That'll teach them."

Wendell slowly smiled. "This is Pigalle, Dr. Brown. Would anyone notice they were naked?"

Henry stood up. "I got everything off this polecat."

"Let's get back to our time machine." Serendipity got that take charge look.

Tobias nodded submissively. "All right, Dr. Brown."

"Wait, Ser." Sherman grabbed her arm. "Shouldn't we take away their time machine? We could send it into the twenty-seventh century and these guys will be stranded and they'll be no threat."

"We would have to track it down first." Henry said. "These guys could be awake by then. Besides we have their computers, it has the key signal to open their machine, so they can't get in."

"Then we could steal it."

"We can't use the key signal either. We don't know what the verbal password is to turn their computers on. It won't recognize our voices even if we could."

"Wait a minute." Tobias frowned. "If we have them rendered helpless, why do I have to leave? I have a book to research, video to take."

"Leach, you moron." Henry didn't even try to sound patient. "How do you know these yahoos won't come after you with Colt 45s?"

Serendipity pursed her lips in thought. "Maybe this year isn't secure, but now they can't get to the twenty-fourth century. I'm safe to go home."

Wendell peered down at her grimly. "Are we absolutely certain there are only three men? What if there is a fourth? What if he was acting as lookout? What if he is watching now?"

Serendipity's confident expression melted into a nervous frown. "Let's get the hell out of here." She turned and headed in the direction of the Timemobile.

Tobias came up beside her. "I don't suppose we could go to my digs and pack my..." His voice trailed off. "No, we need to get out of here before they become conscious and come looking for us."

They ran back to their own time machine across the lane from the statue of Joan of Arc. Serendipity pointed her computer at the door of the yellow limousine to unlock it, then let herself into the back.

"Dr. Brown!" Wendell hurried in after her. "Don't take us straight to 2010. Take us somewhere else first, just in case someone is watching. I don't know the extent of their equipment, but I have heard rumors that if someone makes an illegal trip in time, the Enforcers can track where they go."

Serendipity nodded and began setting dials.

"Shouldn't we move the Timemobile into an alley so no one will see us disappear?" Sherman asked.

Tobias snorted. "They're Parisians. They'll just think Georges Melies is advertising his magic act at the Theatre Robert-Houdin."

"You sit in the back seat, Tobias." Wendell pointed. "Henry, you can sit beside him. Dr. Brown can sit on my lap."

They all sat down and strapped in while Serendipity set the dials. She bounced over and sat on Wendell's lap. "So, you finally invited me to your place, huh? You romantic devil, you!" She threw her arms around him and fastened her lips on his.

Sherman looked behind him to see Tobias sitting with his mouth hanging open. Sherman turned around grinning and buckled his own belt. He looked over at Serendipity and Wendell to see them still in a lip lock, the Victorian gentleman making no attempt to make the lady behave herself. They kept on kissing even as the Timemobile began vibrating like...well, never mind what it was vibrating like.

The machine finally settled. Serendipity sat up and winked. "So, did the earth move for you, too?"

Wendell just grinned at her.

Tobias turned to Henry. "Don't tell me, Wendell and she are—"

"A couple?" Henry drawled. "Ee-yup.

Serendipity looked around the chair and smirked at Tobias. "Finally got me a man who can keep up with me. Now, who's the old trout?"

She stood up. "Stay seated gentlemen, unless you really want to see Toledo, Ohio in 1959." She went over to the dials again. "Okay guys, Seattle 2010."

Serendipity finished and threw herself again in Wendell's lap. This time she didn't kiss him, just hung on tight, as he hugged her back. Again the Timemobile began quaking like it was sitting on a fault line. It stopped. Serendipity grinned at Wendell. "I always liked this seating arrangement."

"I'll move the Timemobile around to our room." Sherman undid the belt and stood up. "No, don't get up, Wendell. You look like you have your hands full."

Tobias jumped out of his own seat. "Howe can't do that!"

"Can't do what?" Serendipity raised an eyebrow at Tobias. "Kiss me?

Seems to be doing just fine."

"Howe can't have intimate relations with someone from the past! It is strictly forbidden!"

"I'm from the twenty-fourth century, not the nineteenth."

"You are still from the past! You are a historical figure! He cannot go poking—"

"I say!" Wendell got up as fast as he could, without throwing Serendipity onto the floor. "You will not speak of Dr. Serendipity Brown in that manner!"

"Fine then." Tobias stepped closer. "You cannot be sampling her charms."

"Whoa, now." Henry jumped to his feet, glaring at Tobias. "Like you ain't been sampling the charms of half the ladies of the evening in the nineteenth century?"

"That's different! I don't get emotionally involved. I didn't make an impact on the lives of any of them!"

Serendipity sneered at Tobias. "Sweetheart, I don't think I'd be bragging about that."

Tobias sputtered like a lawn mower out of gas.

Before he could compose himself, Sherman stepped forward. "Lay off, Leach! Serendipity's happy. Wendell's happy. I'm happy Ser's not tied up with some jerk. Nobody is getting hurt."

"But it's against the rules!"

"So was saving your sorry butt!" Serendipity came nose to nose with Tobias. "Besides, Wendell has the Enforcers' seal of approval. The man is right where he's supposed to be. I'm Serendipity Brown. I'm outside the rules. So unless you want me to take you back and hand you over to those terrorists, you better just learn to live with Wendell and me being lovers."

"Dr. Brown!" Wendell turned pink.

"All right, Wendell, what would you call us?"

"Erm, serious, perhaps?"

"Fine." Serendipity turned back to Tobias. "You will just have to live with Wendell and me being serious." She turned back to Wendell and winked. "I just love it when you get *serious*, Dr. Howe." She looked over at Sherman. "And now, Mr. Conrad, if you will pull our Timemobile around to our rooms."

"You got it, Ser." Sherman gave her a cocky salute.

Chapter Fifteen

Henry came back into his motel room carrying a couple of six packs of beer. The room was stuffed full of temporal anthropologists in an impromptu celebration. Now, with everyone rescued, Wendell finally appeared relaxed.

Serendipity however looked agitated. She sat at the small desk in the room, holding a telephone receiver, arguing with someone on the other end. "What do you mean you don't have pesto and artichoke pizza? Everyone has pesto and artichoke pizza. Fine then, oysters with clam sauce. What! No clam sauce? No, this isn't a crank call. What sort of broken down place is this?"

Sherman came over. "What's wrong, Ser?"

"I'm trying to order four large pizzas, and these bozos don't have anything. I don't know why the motel let them leave their menu in the room."

"So, order what's on the menu."

"They have fewer than a dozen varieties here. This can't be their full menu."

Sherman motioned for her to hand him the phone. "Sorry, my cousin is from—uh, New Zealand. Got different pizzas down there. We'll take a pepperoni, a cheese, a Hawaiian and a Supreme. Deliver it to Steelhead Inn, Room 225. Thanks." Sherman looked over at Serendipity. "Go with the classics."

"But I really like pesto and artichoke."

"Sorry, Ser, but this isn't the twenty-fourth century. This is the Dark Ages for pizza."

Serendipity sighed and looked disappointed. "Yeah, I'll have to learn to rough it."

Henry came over and handed her a beer. "Got the pizzas ordered?"

"Yeah, but not much variety in this time period."

"Even fewer in the 1800s." Henry held up a six pack. "Okay, who wants a beer?"

Sherman wasn't the only one raising his hand.

"All right, buckaroos." Henry surveyed them. "First you have to answer this question: How many temporal anthropologists does it take to change a light bulb?"

"None!" Matilda piped up. "Temporal anthropologists use nay but candles."

Erik raised his hand. "None, because a temporal anthropologist may only watch to observe who comes to change it."

"Oh, I know!" Wendell broke out in a grin. "None, because temporal anthropologists don't change anything."

"Wendell wins, I think." Henry handed him a beer. "Okay, the other two were good also"

Wendell shook his head. "No, I better not. Dr. Brown says I embarrass her when I get drunk."

"Oh, does Fancy Pants have a wild side we don't know about?"

Serendipity came over and put her arm around Wendell's waist. "No, Wendell starts singing Gilbert and Sullivan."

Erik slapped Wendell on the back. "I am a Viking, nothing scares me."

"One beer wol not harm thee, Wendell," Matilda said. "Besides there be eight of us and only twelve bottles. Can any man get drunk on just two beers?"

"I'm Victorian, not medieval." Wendell raised an eyebrow at her.

"Nay, I guess not all drinketh four pints a day as we did at the convent."

"Four pints?" Sherman yelped. "Nuns? Every day?"

"Nary but a fool would dare drink the water back then." Matilda shrugged.

"Oh, great!" Henry put his arm around Matilda. "Looks like the nun can drink us all under the table."

"Speak for yourself." Tobias muttered, taking a beer.

Sherman started to reach for a bottle, hoping no one would remember he was underage.

"Sherman!" Serendipity called.

Sherman yanked his hand back, then realized her voice hadn't sounded angry. "Yeah?" He turned to face her.

"Would you mind going downstairs and telling the antisocial zoologists that we have pizza coming? They'll have to come up and get it. We aren't waiting on them."

Sherman descended the stairs to the room underneath the party and knocked.

Cerwyn swung open the door. "Get in, don't let in a draft." He grabbed Sherman and yanked him in.

Sherman saw they had moved the furniture around to accommodate a large cage, five feet high, and four foot square. The parrots hopped about on the perches. In the center of the enclosure stood a tree branch held up with a heavy stand. The newspaper lining the bottom of the cage was pristine. Sherman wondered how many times a day they changed it. He also noticed that the floor and everything in the room within a five foot radius from the cage had been covered with clear plastic drop cloths.

"Uh, I just came down to tell you that we ordered pizza. Should be here soon. Come up and help yourself."

Cerwyn nodded. "I can come up for a few minutes and pickup a few pieces for the two of us."

Priscilla stepped over and pulled Sherman to a spot two feet away. "Don't stand too close to the cage, please. You'll upset the birds."

Sherman almost protested, then remembered what Wendell had said about temporal zoologists being overly protective. Best he make himself an ally in their eyes. "Uh, these are really pretty parrots. I think it's awesome that you want to bring them back from extinction. I can't believe anyone could actually shoot anything this beautiful."

Cerwyn and Priscilla both seemed to melt.

"Aren't they lovely though?" Cerwyn beamed.

"Would you like me to save them the pizza crust, or is that good for them?" Sherman asked.

Cerwyn shook his head. "Inappropriate, isn't it? We are trying to feed them a balanced diet. Priscilla walked down to a market and picked up some fresh carrots and apples to supplement their food pellets. I hope we can get better conditions for them."

"Serendipity wants to get a permanent place." Sherman watched the green parrots flit about. "Once we get a house we can take better care of them. I'm sorry you have to make do for now. If there's anything I can get you or do for you, let me know. We want to take care of everyone we saved, and that includes the small feathery ones."

Sherman looked over to see Priscilla smile. "Thank you, uh, what was your name?" she asked.

"Sherman."

"Thank you, Sherman. You're a mensch. That was very thoughtful."

Cerwyn smiled at him too. "Most people don't understand, do they? These birds are our chance to make amends, to bring back a great treasure our ancestors destroyed. They are priceless. Worth more than all the tea in China."

"Don't let Wendell hear you say that," Sherman said.

Cerwyn looked at him baffled. "Why?"

"Dr. Howe wrote a book on tea. I was making a joke. Uh...never mind. I can phone and let you know when the pizza is here. That way you can come up and get what you like."

"Ooh!" Priscilla perked up. "Did you order a pastrami and sauerkraut pizza?"

"Sorry, it's the early twenty-first century now." Sherman tried to sound sympathetic. "Varieties are a little limited. Would you like me to bring you down a beer?"

They both shook their heads. "We need to keep our full faculties." Priscilla held her head up. "We must be vigilant."

"Yes." Cerwyn nodded. "We take turns keeping watch at night."

Sherman looked at the lively parrots again. They all looked perfectly healthy to him. "Right, I'll call you later."

Erik finished up the leftovers as they all sat around Henry and Matilda's hotel room in chairs or on beds. Sherman sat on the floor leaned against the wall. The room seemed to shrink with eight people in it.

Serendipity and Wendell took turns filling the other temporal anthropologists in on the full details of what the Enforcers had told them about the Time Keepers, how Serendipity got the information on how to find them, and how their episode with Tobias had validated their worst suspicions—that the Time Keepers would have hunted them all down and killed them.

They discussed possible plans for the next day, as well as the next three months. The best strategy they could come up with was to play things by ear.

The talk then drifted to questions on how Wendell ever met Serendipity, where Sherman came from, and what had been happening to Wendell since his supposed death. It finally came to letting everyone in on the happenings of the last two days. Henry took over the retelling of Wendell's meeting his own self a few hours before. It seemed a lot funnier the way Henry told it. Everyone laughed, including Wendell.

Sherman noticed however that Serendipity's smile dropped when Henry got to the part where he and Wendell used the Compliance Disk on the younger Wendell. She got up quietly, unnoticed by everyone except Sherman, and stepped out of the room. Sherman stood up and followed Serendipity out to find her halfway down the stairs to the landing, leaning on the railing. She stared at the cars in the parking lot below.

"Hey Ser." Sherman sidled up to her. "Something is bothering you, isn't it?"

She shook her head, but her face looked haunted.

"Come on, Ser. My job is to take care of you. Agent Five said so. I can't do that if I don't know what's going on."

Ser hung her head. "I just suddenly realized something, that's all."

"What's that?"

"Wendell doesn't really love me."

Sherman stared at her mystified. "What are you talking about? The man is gonzo about you. Why would you think he doesn't? Is it Matilda?"

"No, it's not Matilda. Wendell is right; Henry *is* her favorite. She can't take her eyes off him. She's not the problem."

"Then why do you think Wendell doesn't love you?"

"Oh, he loves me, it's just not real."

"Huh?"

Serendipity continued to stare at the parking lot. "Do you remember when they put the Compliance Disk on the earlier Wendell today to make him forget he had ever seen us?"

"Yes?"

"Remember the subliminal message he left himself?"

"That when you met again that he would help you?"

"That wasn't all of what he said. He said 'you will help Serendipity Brown *because you love her very much.*'"

"Yeah, he does."

"Sherman!" Serendipity turned and peered at him. "Don't you see what happened? He told himself that he loved me very much while he was wearing the Compliance Disk. He *brainwashed* himself into loving me! He has no control over how he feels about me. He has no choice. He has to love me whether he wants to or not. I can't say anything to him about it, because he will deny it to me and himself. And if I do the right thing and quit taking advantage of him, it will crush him, because he isn't thinking straight. I don't know what I should do."

"Ser, how do you know that happened? Remember when you kissed the earlier Wendell? The first time he pulled away, the second time he didn't."

"The first time I took him off guard. The second time he was being polite."

"Besides when you first met Wendell, he didn't throw his arms around you and start kissing you, did he?"

"No, but then he's too reserved Victorian to do that. He did seem smitten from the beginning."

"No, he seemed in awe, and so have the other time travelers we've run into."

"Not the same way as Wendell." Serendipity looked on the verge of crying. "It all makes sense now. Matilda is the sort of woman he's attracted to, not women like me. We are complete opposites. He would never be attracted to me if he hadn't tricked himself into it. Wendell is a nice guy. I feel bad that I'm just using him."

"You aren't just using him."

"But he loves me against his will. I finally meet a nice guy and he has to be forced into loving me. I don't know why I thought someone as great as him could ever love me."

"Why wouldn't he love you?"

"Because men always leave me. I'm impatient. I'm annoying. I'm insensitive. I'm not very girly or beautiful. Why would any man love me?"

"You just risked your life to save seven strangers in the last two days. Hell, you saved me from a lame existence and I'm nobody. You took in Wendell because you felt sorry for him. Sure you aren't perfect, you got faults, but so does everyone else. You got a lot going for you, Ser. You aren't that hard to get along with. How many people would even want to live in the same house as their boss?"

"I saw what you were living with before, kid. Anything would be an improvement, even me."

"No, Ser, it's because you're nice. You don't treat me like your gofer. I consider you a friend. I'm not at all surprised that Wendell loves you."

"Friends and lovers are two totally different things, kid. Friends have a little space between them, lovers don't. It's easier putting up with a friend; they aren't in your face. Maybe Wendell would have liked me anyway, but been passionately in love with me? Probably not."

Sherman heard the door open behind them. Footfalls sounded on the stairs and Wendell came up behind Serendipity and put his arms around her "Was it getting too stuffy in there for you, my love? Or were we boring you? You think one temporal anthropologist is dull, wait until you get half a dozen of us together."

Serendipity didn't turn around, but she did put her hand on his arm. "No sweetie, just getting too warm in there."

"I must say, it's a bit nippy out here. Shouldn't you have on a coat?"

"I'm fine."

"I can never thank you enough for saving those people in there. I am again forever in your debt. I believe you told me yesterday how you wanted me to thank you. I may have to give you a rain check or else we can ask Sherman nicely to give us a little privacy for an hour. I could tell our guests we are both exhausted and are going to turn in early. Of course, you probably *are* exhausted. I could just give you a good cuddle or a back rub or whatever you would like tonight. I am yours to command. Consider me your slave."

Serendipity closed her eyes. Wendell couldn't see her face, but Sherman could. She looked miserable, like a recovering drug addict being offered a hit; afraid to say 'yes', and yet unable to say 'no'.

Wendell held her tighter, with an innocent smile, unaware that anything was wrong.

Serendipity faked a convincing smile and turned around. "Okay, sweetie."

Wendell kissed her forehead. "You wait here a tick, my darling. I will just step back in and make our excuses." He turned to Sherman. "You don't mind, do you, old boy? You can see if the desk clerk can get you a room of your own. Either that or give us an hour before you come down. I would just like to spend a little time with the most wonderful woman in the world."

"Sure thing." Sherman nodded at Wendell. "Hang a tie on the doorknob."

"Good man." Wendell returned the nod and went back into the room.

As soon as Wendell closed the door, Serendipity whirled around to Sherman. "What am I going to do? I don't want to lose him, but how do you lose someone you never had?"

"Wendell doesn't act like he's being forced into anything. He doesn't act like a robot; his eyes aren't glazed. I think you're wrong."

"Am I? Weren't you listening to him? I'm the most wonderful woman in the world? Whatever I want to do? I'm yours to command? Consider me your slave? He's always like that. It's not natural! Wendell's too nice to me."

Before Sherman could answer that, Wendell stepped back out and came down. "Come along, dearest." He held out his arm to Serendipity. She again forced a smile and took his arm. Sherman watched them walk down the metal steps to the ground floor. He heard their door close.

Sherman sighed and leaned on the railing. He reached in his pocket and pulled out his computer and gave a soft whistle.

"Yes, Steve," that sexy voice purred.

"Did you hear any of that, Lauren?"

"Of course, Steve. You usually leave me on."

"I think Ser is just freaking out over nothing, don't you?"

"Maybe. But what if she's hit the nail on the head? She is a pretty smart cookie."

"Yeah, what if Wendell has accidentally hypnotized himself into being gaga for Ser? How will any of us know for sure?"

"Say, that's a tough one, isn't it?"

Sherman looked up at the clouds overhead, glowing from the reflected light below. "How does she get herself into these messes? Who else but Ser could find a righteous dude and then find out it could all be a rip-off? Worst part is the con artist is an innocent victim himself. I know that Agent Five said my job was to take care of Ser, but I have no idea how I'm going to get her out of this one."

"Nuts." Sherman's computer gave a sympathetic sigh. "Ya got me floored on this one too."

Chapter Sixteen

Sherman woke to the sound of the shower running. He sat up and rubbed his eyes. He assumed it was Wendell in the bathroom, for Serendipity was sitting at the little table in the motel room, drinking a cup of coffee in a Styrofoam cup and dressed in her white peasant blouse and long hippie skirt. She smiled at him. "Good morning, kid."

"Morning." Sherman stretched. He got out of bed and pulled down his pajama top, then went over and sat at the table. He was glad he had thought to pack a pair of pajamas. He really didn't want Serendipity or Wendell seeing him in his usual sleeping attire of just his briefs, and he really didn't want to borrow a dorky nightshirt from Wendell.

"So you decided not to get a room?" she asked.

"Couldn't. Everything was taken. I think Abubakari took the spare bed in Henry and Matilda's room, and Erik and Tobias shared a room."

"Erik okay with that? I know none of the temporal anthropologists seem to like Tobias."

"I don't think Erik really likes him either, but I think Erik was cool with it, because Tobias seemed horrified that he had to share a room with a Viking. I'll bet Erik hammed it up."

Serendipity chuckled. "Erik may be an uncouth slob, but he's a *classy* uncouth slob. I don't think he's going to be hard to live with."

"Yeah, I like him too." Sherman looked around. "Where's Rosetta?"

"Standing in the closet."

"She okay with that?"

"It's a robot," Serendipity said slowly.

"Yeah, right." Sherman scratched his head. "So, how did things go last night?"

Serendipity's smile dropped. "Well, we got in the room and Wendell gave me a big hug and told me how much he loved me. I don't think he really expected it to go any further than a snuggle, but...hey, what can I say. I'm weak. I had to rip his clothes off."

"Uh, Ser, too much information. That wasn't what I was asking. Did you tell him?"

"Like I said, I'm weak. Couldn't bring myself to do it. He would hate me if he knew I'm using him against his will."

"First off, Ser, *you* didn't brainwash him. Secondly it was an accident, and thirdly Wendell is a guy. Trust me, he won't be upset you are using him like *that*. Every guy dreams of being a sex-object."

"I still feel bad." Serendipity bit at her bottom lip. "What happens when it wears off? Maybe if I'm at least nice to him he won't hate me. I'll give him anything he asks for, do whatever he wants."

"You do that now."

The sound of flowing water in the other room stopped. Serendipity leaned forward, lowering her voice. "Do I? Wendell lets me lead all the time. Guys always want to be in control.

"Wendell's just laid back. Besides he did kind of take over when we went after his friends the last two days."

Serendipity shook her head. "I'm not going to tease him anymore. He can't defend himself."

"He's been telling you to back off when you go too far."

"But he never fights with me."

"Yes, he does."

"Not really."

Wendell stepped out of the bathroom with his pants and shirt on. "Oh, good morning, Sherman. The lavatory is all yours, old chap."

"Yeah, I need a shower." Sherman went over to his suitcase and dug out some clothes.

Wendell looked at the mirror above the sink outside the bathroom. "I had better shave." He stroked his upper lip, and turned back to Serendipity. "I say, darling, you never did give me an answer."

"Answer? To what?"

"I asked if I should grow my mustache back and then you were interrupted by a phone call, and one thing led to another. So, do you think I should grow my mustache back?"

"Why are you asking *me*?" Serendipity said slowly.

"Well, you are the one who kisses me. I do not wish for a mustache to come between us, my dear."

"If you want to grow it back, go ahead." Her voice had a slight touch of panic to it. "It's your face. You don't need my permission."

"Uh guys?" Sherman held up his finger. "When the Enforcers were interrogating me and I told them Wendell was this Howellingsworth dude Ser made up, they compared his photo to one they had of Wendell's alias. He wore a mustache."

"Well then, I have no choice. History dictates." He turned back to the mirror. "Good. It will make shaving easier. The upper lip is always the tricky part." He began lathering up his badger-hair brush.

Serendipity shot Sherman an "I told you so" look.

Sherman sighed and headed for the bathroom.

The television in the upper corner of the breakfast room was turned to the weather channel, reporting on the sunshine Back East. The buzzer went off on the do-it-yourself waffle maker. Sherman flipped it over, then dug out the waffle that didn't seem to want to leave its place of birth. He plopped the wreckage on his paper plate, and slapped on some margarine and imitation maple syrup. Not the Ritz, but better than a stale donut.

He went over and sat down at an empty spot next to Erik. Sherman didn't know why everyone called Erik a barbarian. The man acted more civilized than any of his roommates back home. He had his hair and beard both washed, combed and braided. "Mind if I sit here, Dr. Olafson?"

"I would be honored to have you sit with me, Sherman," Erik spoke with his mouth full. "Call me Erik. Can you tell me what these tiny donuts are?" He looked down at his bowl.

"Fruit Loops. They don't have them anymore in the twenty-seventh century, huh?"

Erik shrugged. "I know not. I never ate cereal much as a kid except oatmeal. Norwegians prefer a more substantial breakfast. It is mostly Norwegians in Sunburg, Minnesota where I grew up. A lot of Norwegian has survived in the local slang. Ya!"

"So you're Norwegian?"

"Ya, and Swedish, Danish and Icelandic as well. I got Viking blood in my veins." Erik took another mouthful of the cereal. "Not brisling but these loopy things are not bad."

Priscilla stumbled into the room like she had the day before. She grabbed a banana and a couple of pastries and plopped them on a paper plate. She glanced around the room, and then stopped and smiled. "Good morning, Sherman."

"Hello, Dr. Cohen. How are the birds?"

"Doing well." She set a muffin on the plate. "Well, must get back to my babies. You have a nice day."

You too."

Priscilla nodded and hurried out.

Sherman noticed Erik staring at him. Then he noticed Serendipity out of the corner of his eye. He turned his head to see she and the other temporal anthropologists were also gawking at him.

"What did you do?" Serendipity leaned toward Sherman. "Give one of those parrots mouth to mouth resuscitation?"

"I just showed an interest in the birds and told them to let me know if they ever needed anything. The zoologists are okay, just a little wrapped up in the birds is all."

"A little wrapped up? More like obsessed."

"They're rare birds," Sherman said. "Only ones of their kind now. Priscilla and Cerwyn just feel a lot of pressure to keep them healthy in less than perfect conditions."

The couple across the room, got up and tossed their dirty paper plates in the trash and left. Serendipity stood up. "Okay troops, now that we are the only ones in here, we're having an impromptu meeting. Abubakari was the only one able to get clothes yesterday. We are all going to have to buy period attire over at the mall. I'll give everyone some money. Don't get a whole wardrobe for now, just enough for a couple of days. Also pickup any toiletries you might need to get by on. I know Tobias just has the clothes on his back."

Tobias's mustache twitched, but he said nothing.

"I have to buy a primitive period computer," Serendipity continued. "I've seen people around the lobby with them getting on the internet. My

PAL can't seem to get on it though. The binary code is just too primitive for it I guess. Don't think they have artificial DNA in computers yet. If I can get on the internet I should be able to find us a permanent place to live. I hope the internet is at least that sophisticated now."

"Excuse me, Dr. Brown." Henry interrupted. "I noticed people talking into boxes that look kind of like pocket computers. I looked it up on my computer's history files and it seems to be something they call 'a cell phone.' They are currently evolving into something similar to a primitive version of the PAL. Apparently we will need a cell phone if we want to communicate with people in this era."

"Good idea." Serendipity nodded. "We'll get everyone one. We also need transportation. I think it might be too stuffy to ride around town in the back of our current transportation and we won't all fit in the cab. Sherman, since you are the only one with a period wardrobe and know how to drive these gas bombs, I'm going to let you shop for a vehicle."

"What!" Sherman felt overwhelmed.

"See if you can find something that will hold ten people."

"I'm hardly a car expert, especially on cars twenty-five years in my own future."

"You are still our resident expert. You have the best chance of getting it right. Meet me back at our room when you're done." Serendipity sat back down. "I should be back there by noon."

When Sherman got back to the motel at 12:00, he found Serendipity sitting at the table in slacks and a blouse. Wendell sat on the other side of the small table wearing a dark blue suit. Next to him Henry sat on one of the clothes containers. He wore a flannel shirt, jeans and cowboy boots. Sherman assumed the clothes were all from 2010 but they didn't look that different from 1985.

Serendipity was engrossed in a computer that was nothing more than an eighteen-inch flat screen connected to a keyboard. Wendell and Henry were studying an identical one. At least the computers had changed a lot since his time.

"How the computers working? Sherman asked.

"Slow." Serendipity grumbled. "Salesman said this was the fastest model. Called it a 'laptop.' Stupid name. It's too hot to leave on your lap for long. Works better on a table." She looked up at Sherman. "Did you find us transportation?"

Sherman jerked his thumb toward the door. "Yeah, it's right outside."

The three excitedly got up and followed Sherman. In the parking spot sat a long maroon van with three back seats. All the passenger doors were on one side. There were also doors at the rear for loading things.

"Is this thing a bus?" Henry walked around it.

"It's called a Ford E-Series Wagon 350-XL. Salesman says it will seat up to twelve people. There's not much room in the back for luggage, but you can remove any of the back seats for more cargo space."

"Have any trouble driving it?" Serendipity opened one of the doors to look inside.

"Drives the same as an eighties car, just has more bells and whistles is all. It has even got a compact disc player. Guess they caught on. I figured they would go the same way of the eight-track tapes. Hope the color is okay."

"You done good, kid." Serendipity stepped into the wagon.

Wendell and Henry followed her in, looking the vehicle over.

"Looks nice and roomy." Henry plopped down in the driver's seat.

Sherman watched them from the door. "So, any luck with finding us a place to live?"

"I found an old motel for sale." Serendipity said from the back. "Wendell and Henry are trying to talk me into a Victorian mansion they found, but it's way up in Bellingham."

"But it would be perfect," Wendell assured her.

"I'm sure we can find you an old Victorian mansion in Seattle."

"They have all been converted to restaurants and surrounded by twentieth century architecture. This mansion is surrounded by Victorian and Edwardian homes. It is downhill from a university and uphill from a lovely bay."

"We could walk down there in the morning to go fishing," Henry chimed in.

"I suppose we don't have to live in Seattle. I only brought us here because it seemed the most likely place to have stock brokers in 1919."

"Please, Serendipity," Wendell asked wistfully. "It is less than eighty miles from here."

She shook her head and rolled her eyes. "All right, we'll go look at it as soon as everyone gets back."

Late that afternoon they headed north on I-5 toward the Canadian border. Sherman looked in the rearview mirror to see the Timemobile still behind them, stuffed with all their luggage. Henry had been elected to drive "TM" since he bragged he had once driven an 1897 Oldsmobile, which made him the second most qualified driver of the group. Serendipity had said the Timemobile cab could drive itself, but was it good enough to drive I-5?

In the cab with Henry were Wendell and Matilda who volunteered to keep him company. Sherman thought that would have been awkward considering their past history, but the three seemed fine with it.

In the very back of the Ford Wagon, they had pulled out the last bench seat to accommodate the smaller birdcages. Cerwyn and Priscilla had decided this was the best option for the birds. To have them stuck for a couple of hours in a stuffy time machine would not be a good idea. The Timemobile had not been designed for long trips on the road, but for short trips through wormholes.

The seat in front of the parrots held the two temporal zoologists. They both kept undoing their seatbelts to get on their knees to look over the back of the bench at their charges. In the seat behind Sherman, Serendipity was excitedly pumping Abubakari about the Mali Empire. Sherman wasn't sure why Serendipity seemed so interested in African history all of a sudden. On the other side of her sat Erik, dressed in sweatpants and a Minnesota Vikings T-shirt, watching the scenery out the window.

In the bucket seat three feet away from Sherman, sat Tobias, wearing a sports coat, turtleneck and a disgruntled expression. He had grabbed the front passenger seat, and no one had tried to stop him. The Englishman stared out the window at the farms and tall evergreens, with the Cascade Mountains looming in the distance. He seemed lonely. Sherman remembered how Tobias had acted heroically when they had been attacked in Paris. Maybe he wasn't as bad as the others imagined.

"So do you like being a temporal anthropologist, Dr. Leach?" Sherman tried to make conversation.

Tobias looked over at him and said nothing for a moment. He finally spoke. "What I like best about being a temporal anthropologist is not having to make small talk with total strangers, especially children and servants who obviously don't know their place." Tobias looked back out the window.

Okay, maybe Leach really was as bad as the others imagined. Sherman decided to spend the next three months avoiding the snob as much as possible.

So, no conversation to entertain him. Sherman reached over and turned on the radio. After poking buttons he finally found a station playing Heavy Metal rock. That cheered him up, until the station jingle came on telling Sherman he was listening to KZOK, home of Classic Rock. *Classic Rock?* That's what you called music from the 1960s, not the 1980s. Then he remembered this was 2010.

Sherman suddenly recalled his driver's license was woefully expired. The one Wendell's fabber had made him to sell his stocks would be revealed as a fake if a state trooper tried to call it in. He turned off the radio and concentrated on driving.

Sherman made it to Bellingham without getting pulled over. Serendipity immediately wanted to go look at the house for sale, but the zoologists started squawking louder than the birds. So they found an older one-story motel that had a sign that said "Pet friendly." Sherman had no problem getting separate rooms for anyone who wanted them. He passed out keys and told Henry where to park. They opened up the Timemobile and unloaded the luggage.

Sherman grabbed his suitcase, backpack and carpetbag and put them into his room. The room only had one double bed along with a small table and a dresser with a TV on it. The bedcover was a little faded, and the room a bit threadbare, but it looked and smelled clean enough. It would do just fine.

Sherman stepped back out to help with the parrots, but Serendipity grabbed him. "Come on, kid. You have to drive me and Wendell to the real estate office."

"Ser, it's 6:55 on a Sunday evening. Nothing will be open. You'll have to wait until tomorrow morning."

"Okay, but I want to get us a house as soon as possible," Serendipity said. "Maybe we can get some semblance of a normal life back."

Wendell smiled at Serendipity. "And when have either of us had a normal life, Dr. Brown?"

Sherman shook his head. "Trust me guys, normal lives are overrated."

ᏟChapter Seventeen

Sherman and Wendell sat in the back seat of a Nissan while the real estate agent, Connie, talked a mile a minute. She peered over her bifocals at Serendipity, who was riding shotgun. "So you are interested in the Albert Brown house, are you?"

Serendipity nodded. "I figured with a name like Brown it couldn't be all bad. Was he the guy that built it?"

"Yes, 1899. He was a prominent businessman with ten kids. The house has nine bedrooms, two baths, four stories if you count the basement. There is plenty of room. I take it you have a large family?"

"There'll be ten of us."

"My, you and your husband have certainly been blessed." Connie looked back at Wendell.

"Oh, Wendell and I aren't married. I'm divorced."

"What? Your husband ran out on you and eight children?"

"Oh, they aren't my children. Just friends."

Wendell leaned forward. "We are trying to set up a sort of boarding house for professors and scholars visiting Western Washington University."

"Oh!" Connie nodded. "That is an excellent idea. Nicer than a noisy dorm full of students. This house isn't very far from the campus."

Connie kept chattering, outlining all the cultural plusses of the area, as well as shopping spots. The car began going up a hill into a neighborhood of old houses.

Wendell sat up, staring wistfully out the window. "My word, these are some very nice Victorian homes."

"Yeah, the South Hill District is full of them. There was a lot of money in this town back in the late 1800s and early 1900s." Connie gave a quick glance back at Wendell. "Bellingham was a major departure point for Alaska during the Yukon-Alaska Gold Rush. We also had a gold rush up at Mount Baker at that time, though I think more people made fortunes selling supplies to fortune hunters than prospectors striking it rich. We have several dozen buildings on the National Register of Historic Places. This house you asked to look at is one of them."

"Dr. Brown had a beautifully preserved Victorian home back in Beaverton," Wendell said.

"Uh, Wendell." Sherman tugged at his sleeve. "That wasn't really from the Victorian Era. Serendipity built it."

"Really? I had no idea you were that interested in Victorian architecture." Wendell smiled at Serendipity.

"Actually," Sherman said, "it was a replica of the Addams Family's house."

"John Adams?"

"No, *The Addams Family* was a sitcom from the 1960s."

"Sitcom? What is that?"

"A television situation comedy."

"A telly broadcast?" Wendell's normally bland face showed horror. "Why am I not surprised?"

Connie glanced over at Serendipity. "You actually built a house based on the Addams Family?"

"Just the outside."

"I'm glad to hear that." Connie turned a corner. "I would hate to think you had a torture rack and bed-of-nails in *your* playroom."

Wendell raised an eyebrow at Sherman. "Torture rack? Bed of nails? In a playroom? And this was a comedy?"

"The reruns I've seen were hilarious." Sherman assured him.

Wendell sighed and shook his head. "Americans."

"I take it you never saw *Monty Python* or *Fawlty Towers,* huh?"

At last, they pulled up in front of a white three-story Victorian gingerbread structure that faced southeast toward the top of the hill. Rose bushes, still valiantly blooming beyond summer, were planted in front of the railing of the covered veranda that extended across the front of the house and around to the left side. On the left front corner of the building was an octagonal tower which created bay windows on all three stories. The tower was capped with a pointed roof. The rest of the sloping roof of the house was broken up by jutting dormer windows.

Wendell jumped out of the car and stared at it, his mouth hanging open. "Oh my word!"

Sherman walked up beside him. "You do realize you have just ruined any chance of our talking them down on the price."

Wendell closed his mouth, and looked over at Sherman. "Looking too eager, eh?" Wendell glanced back up at the house.

"You haven't seen anything yet." Connie walked up the stone front steps. "Wait until you get a peek at the inside."

They all walked onto the sturdy porch. Connie unlocked the heavy wood door that had an elliptical stained-glass window over it. "The door and transom are original. In fact a lot of the fixtures are original."

She swung the door open onto an eight-foot wide reception hall that extended straight through the empty house to the back door. It was lined with local Pacific red cedar pillars and cross beams. The bare floors were polished oak. This time Sherman's jaw dropped. Poor Wendell looked like his knees were going to buckle.

Serendipity surveyed the house. "Wow, looks like something out of *Gone with the Wind.*"

"Yes, I love these old Victorian mansions. This one is ten thousand thirty-five square feet. It is three stories plus a full basement." Connie looked around. "I wish I had the money to buy it myself, but I don't think I'm up to the task of furnishing a place this big."

Serendipity smiled like a pool shark that had just been challenged by a yokel.

"Oh no," Wendell whispered to Sherman. "She's not going to fill this house up with more *priceless* twentieth-century antiques, is she?"

"Look at the bright side. At least now she can pick that junk up at the Salvation Army really cheap."

"Marvelous. Now she can do it even faster."

Connie took them into the first room on the right. It was about seventeen foot square, with the walls painted off-white. A large double window in the front offered a view of the covered porch and the house across the street beyond. On the wall facing the side yard was a brick fireplace. Even devoid of curtains and rugs, the room looked cozy. "This is the parlor—the sitting room."

"Ooh, a fireplace." Serendipity went over to inspect it. She winked at Wendell. "Maybe the two of us could cuddle up in front of it?"

Connie went over her notes. "The fireplace is original and has been inspected. There are two others in the library and music room. The rest were removed when they converted the house to a coal boiler and then to electric."

"The house has a library?" Sherman's asked wistfully.

"Right across the hall." Connie led them out.

Sherman had expected walls of shelves with a rolling ladder to reach the top books. There were just a couple of narrow built-in bookcases on either side of the fireplace. After he got over his initial disappointment, he had to admit the huge bay window created by the tower did make the room look pretty cool. There was enough glass to let in a lot of light despite the covered porch just outside. The room was at least a third again as large as the parlor.

Wendell studied the walls, again painted off-white. "I take it none of the original wallpaper survived. Of course we can fix that."

"Yeah." Serendipity held up her thumb like an artist. "Needs wood paneling."

Wendell looked slightly nauseous at the suggestion. Even Connie's smile became rather forced. "Uh, let me show you the bathroom in the next room."

The bathroom was painted light green, with high frosted windows on the outside wall. Most of the light came from the wall lamps on either side of the mirror over the sink. Blue and green linoleum surrounded a modern toilet and an antique bathtub. It was cast-iron, lined with white porcelain, with high sides and lifted a few inches off the floor by clawed feet. Sherman was sure the only reason the tub had never been replaced was because it was so big you would have to take out a wall to remove it. "Gnarly! It's a swimming pool."

Wendell hovered dotingly over it. "You don't have to tell me this is original. I love these old tubs."

"Oh, you had a tub like this?" Connie asked.

"No, unfortunately I could never fit one in my—erm, vehicle."

Sherman was sure Wendell meant his time machine.

Connie looked confused. "You couldn't hire a delivery truck?"

"None went on my route." Wendell smiled nervously. "Oh look, a pedestal sink. This looks original, too."

Serendipity ran her hand around the tub. "You could easily get two people in here." She gave Wendell a sideways glance.

Wendell didn't answer but he did raise an interested eyebrow.

Connie showed no signs of noticing the exchange, although she did seem eager to continue with the tour. They crossed the reception hall to a room as large as the library. The room was again painted off-white, but it had a large chandelier in the middle of the ceiling. On the outside wall was a line of windows that gave the room an airy feeling.

"This is the dining room."

"Dining room?" Even Serendipity was impressed. "Holy Hanukah! You could get a banquet table to serve a couple of dozen people in here. Heck, you could get two!"

Sherman tried to decide if that was an exaggeration or not. "It's more like a cafeteria room."

Wendell didn't seem surprised. "I imagine whoever constructed this house was building to impress. They would have invited people over for dinner and the more guests they could manage the better. A large dinner party would get a write up on the society page."

"The newspapers wrote about someone just having people over?" Sherman found that hard to believe.

"Yes, if the occasion was large enough. People were very interested in local gossip back then. To be asked to such a party would have been a great honor and something to brag about."

"Did you get invited to such parties?"

Wendell snorted back a laugh. "Of course not. I was no one. No one noticed me." Wendell noticed Connie staring at him. "Erm, Cambridge is a bit old-fashioned. They still have a society page."

Apparently Connie had never been to England for she bought that.

"Where does that door go?" Serendipity pointed to the back left hand corner.

"That goes into the butler's pantry." Connie walked over to the door. She opened it and turned on a light. Florescent ceiling lights came on showing a long narrow room lined with shelves painted white and covered with white and blue floral plastic shelf liner that was in dire need of being replaced.

"Whoa!" Serendipity said. "That is a lot of storage room. You could lay in enough food to last all winter." She turned to Connie. "Do you people get snowed in here?"

"We are in the Banana Belt. The winters are pretty mild. We get rain, but not much snow except up in the mountains. When this house was built, people used to can fruits and vegetables to last all year. The original owner had ten kids so they probably needed a pantry this big."

Wendell shook his head. "Later occupants may have used this as a larder, but a butler's pantry is where all the dishes, silverware, linens and service items were stored."

Sherman frowned at him. "Who has that many dishes?"

"Someone who would throw elaborate dinner parties, I daresay. Not only would they need numerous place settings but several dinnerware sets to match the various occasions. You only had one set if you didn't feel the need to impress anyone or couldn't afford to impress anyone."

Connie crossed the narrow space to another door. "In here is the kitchen. This was a shortcut for the servants to go directly into the dining room with hot food."

The kitchen walls and cabinets were painted an obnoxious mustard yellow to match the yellow and brown geometric pattern in the old linoleum. Against the wall was an outdated green stove and refrigerator. Sherman held his tongue. It was obvious the previous owners had taken their own refrigerator and stove and substituted these yard-sale rejects.

Serendipity noticed them, too. Her eyes got big as she came over to them. "Oh my gawd!"

"Uh, the owner assured me they still work." Connie sounded apologetic.

"They still work!" Serendipity clapped her hands together. "Do you know what these are?"

"Uh, no. I guess not."

"This is a circa 1970 matching Frigidaire refrigerator and stove, in vintage condition. And it's in classic avocado green! Aren't they beautiful?"

Wendell looked around. "I see they have updated the kitchen."

Sherman studied the well-worn cabinets that appeared to have several layers of paint on them. "Updated? These cabinets look original."

"They probably are not, if the house was built in 1899. Cabinets didn't come into fashion until a decade later. A late Victorian kitchen might have a few narrow shelves to display cups—thus the name *cupboard*. There might be a freestanding hutch or two for dishes. Pots and pans would have hung on the wall. There would be a table in the middle of the room to work on. The sink would have only had one basin instead of two, possibly with a pump. Above the stove you can see a metal plate covering where the wood stove pipe went into the chimney. Pity they painted over it. Next to it would have been a large tank—the hot water heater that would have been heated by the wood stove. On the other side of the room, away from the heat, would have been a metal-lined wooden box with a large block of ice for perishables. There might have been a butter churn in the corner, although they probably just had their butter and milk delivered every morning. It was 1899 after all."

Connie was listening to all this enraptured. "Wow, you describe it like you were there."

"Erm, I have a PhD in Victorian history. I've studied the culture for many years. Shall we continue with the tour?" Wendell tried to change the subject.

They followed Connie out of the kitchen door into the hall, where they faced an ornate staircase of polished mahogany. The bottom curved out, giving it a graceful look despite the heavy square posts with beveled corners that held up the thick handrail. It looked sturdy enough to hold the weight of a grown man if he decided to slide down the banister. Sherman resolved he would have to try that when no one was watching.

To their right was the back door on the northwest wall and under the stairs was a doorway to more steps going down. Connie ignored both of these and headed for the door just to the left of the staircase. "You have got to see the music room."

Sherman wondered what a music room was. Maybe a small well-insulated room for practicing a screechy violin?

Sherman's mouth fell open when he stepped in. This was at least twice as big as the dining room. It was so big the house could not contain it, and it jutted far out into the side yard. Tall windows lined the three outside walls, letting in plenty of sunlight, making the polished oak floors gleam. In the middle of the far wall was a large fireplace. "Awesome! It looks like a freaking ballroom."

"Yes, I understand they hired quartets to entertain guests here. They had the very first Victrola in town and showed it off at dances in this room."

Wendell leaned toward Serendipity. "Remind me to teach you the waltz, my dear."

"Let me show you the upstairs." Connie led them up the ornate staircase to the second floor. A large bathroom was the first room on the left at the top of the landing. This one looked more modernized than the first one, having a shower/bathtub combo, as well as a vanity sink and a medicine cabinet. Even so Sherman was sure this was renovated before he was born. The rest of the floor was taken up with a long hallway, off of which were seven bedrooms of various sizes and shades of pastel paint. The one on the far right had the large bay windows of the tower and overlooked the street.

"Now let me show you the third floor." Connie led them back to the landing and continued up the next set of stairs to a large open room. "This is the Billiards Room. Although you can make it whatever you like."

Sherman noticed the right wall of the large open room sloped in at the top third, no doubt pushed inward by the slanting roof outside. In two spots the wall continued past the slope to allow dormer windows, which produced the gable roofs he had seen outside.

Connie opened up a door on the left side of the room. "This is a storage room, although you could make it whatever you like, too." She showed them the room that extended from the stairwell to the rooms in the very front. It was lined with shelves on the inner most side. The other wall had two dormer windows letting in light.

The two rooms in the front were again bedrooms. The one on the right also had the tower bay window. Wendell studied the room. "Attic rooms were usually for the servants, but how many servants get a bedroom this fancy? This is even nicer than my own attic digs back in Cambridge."

"You lived in an attic apartment?" Connie asked.

"Yes, above the home of a couple of music teachers. I rather enjoyed hearing the Wilkins practice sessions coming through my floorboards."

As they walked back to the stairs, Sherman saw two large windows facing the backyard, providing light to the billiards room. Wendell gazed out them curious, then took in a quick breath. "Oh my word! It looks like a picture postcard no matter where you look."

Connie walked over. "Fantastic view, isn't it?"

Sherman followed Serendipity to find out what the fuss was about.

At the bottom of the hill lay a harbor with small fishing boats and pleasure yachts moored at the docks of the marinas. To the right a few miles away stood old brick buildings in what must be downtown. Beyond that lay hills of verdant forest in front of tall jagged mountains.

"Down below is Bellingham Bay." Connie pointed out the sites to Wendell. "In front of you, over the bay, is Lummi Peninsula. That's where the Lummi Indian Reservation is. They have a real nice casino. To the right is downtown. That huge brick building there is the old city hall—oldest one in the state. It's now a museum. Those mountains are the Cascades."

"Is that Mount Baker?" Sherman pointed to the largest peak.

"No. Mount Baker is to the east, and you are pointing north. You can see Mount Baker from Bellingham, just not from here where you are standing now. It's probably over your right shoulder behind the hill we are on." She pointed, even though the wall was in the way. She turned back. "Those mountains you are seeing are the Canadian Cascades. Canada is only twenty-one miles to the north." She frowned. "Or maybe that is the Coast Range, or the North Shore Mountains, or the Garibaldi Range, or the Golden Ears Peaks. They have so many mountains up there running together no one can keep them straight. I just know they aren't the Rockies, although a few idiots in town insist they are."

Wendell gazed enthralled at the mountains. "Whatever they are, they are beautiful."

Connie smiled proudly, then continued her travelogue. "Over to the left is Portage and Lummi Islands. I don't think you can see Fairhaven from here, although this might have been part of it once."

"Fairhaven?"

"It's a little shopping district just southwest of here down by the bay. I'm not sure if it's even a mile away. Over a hundred years ago, the towns of Fairhaven, Sehome and Whatcom all decided to consolidate into the City of Bellingham. Fairhaven hasn't changed much since the 1890s. The merchants are now renovating it back to its Victorian glory as a tourist attraction. It's a cute little neighborhood."

Wendell made a soft almost indiscernible noise that sounded like a dog whining for a pork chop.

Serendipity stepped up next to him. "Feels like you are home, huh?" She turned to Connie. "Wendell is not only a Victorian historian but a Victorian nut."

"Well, this town oozes Victorian history. We have managed to preserve much from that period. This is probably the most Victorian town in

Washington."

Serendipity raised an eyebrow at Wendell. "So, that's why you and Henry wanted to come to Bellingham."

Wendell smiled at her, and looked back out the window. "You know what this window needs?"

"Curtains?"

"No, a couple of comfy overstuffed chairs and a tea table, so we can sip our tea while gazing at this charming view."

"Actually Wendell," she spoke slowly. "I was thinking with the two bedrooms and this large room here, we might give it to the zoologists and their birds. Be nice and quiet up here."

"Yes, you are probably right." Wendell sighed and stared back out at the view. "I am sure I can find another window facing this way. Still this window needs a chair, whoever gets it."

Connie took them back down to the main floor. Beneath the highest point of the curved staircase was another set of stairs leading to a full basement with more rooms, including the laundry room. Underneath the stairs was the furnace. After that she took them back up to the main floor and through the back door into a large enclosed back porch she called "a mudroom" and then outside. The backyard sloped toward the nearby harbor, save for a spot leveled off for an ancient toolshed. Off the alley was a weathered wooden garage as well as a newer and wider steel structure.

Connie turned to them. "As you can see there is plenty of room for visiting scholars. The house is old, but it was built back when homes were built sturdy. The place is sound and the wiring and plumbing are up to code."

Serendipity looked over at her two compatriots. "Well, guys?"

"I love it." Wendell looked pleadingly at her.

She turned to Sherman. "What about you, kid. It's your money."

"It's big enough we won't be tripping over one another. More than two bathrooms would be nice, but yeah, I think it's awesome."

She turned back to Connie. "Okay, we'll take it. When can we move in?"

"So you want the house?"

"Yeah, so can we move in today?"

"The owners are asking $1,365,000."

"Okay." Serendipity didn't bat an eye.

Connie looked a little taken aback. "Well, you will have to wait for your loan to go through."

"What loan? We'll pay cash."

"Cash?" Connie blinked in disbelief.

"Yup! So when can we move in?"

"Well, there are inspections and closing and so many things. It could take up to a month."

"A month! We need a place to live now."

Connie swallowed hard, then collected herself. Sherman wasn't sure what her commission would be, but it had to be hefty on a house that sold for over a million. She wasn't about to lose this sale if she could help it. "Well, I might be able to arrange with the owners to allow you to pay rent and live here while you are waiting. The rent will be applied to the final payment. I will do my best to get you in here tomorrow."

"Sounds good." Serendipity smiled, pleased.

Chapter Eighteen

The next morning the "U-Haul van" and the Ford Wagon pulled up in front of the house. Connie stood there on the porch with the keys waiting for them.

"Hello, Dr. Brown." Connie smiled sweetly. "I have made a list of all the companies you need to contact such as the phone company, the utilities and the cable company. I can help you with the calls if you like. You may use my cell phone if you don't have one. I also brought a phone book and map of the city."

"Why thank you, Connie." Serendipity turned to the others. "Okay everyone, start unloading. Go up on the second floor and pick out rooms for yourselves. Cerwyn and Priscilla can have the third floor. After that I guess we will have to start shopping for furniture and necessities."

Connie was talking with Serendipity in the entrance hall when Cerwyn came storming over to them from the stairs. "I am very sorry, Dr. Brown, but the third floor will *not* do."

"What's wrong with it?" Serendipity frowned.

"Heat rises, doesn't it? Conuropsis carolinensis are very delicate. Too much heat in a stuffy room could make them sick, even kill them. We need something on the ground floor where we can control the temperature better."

"Fine, what room do you want?"

"The large room over there would be the best." Cerwyn pointed to the music room door. "It has lots of windows so we can allow sunlight in. Parrots need full spectrum light to absorb calcium properly, don't they?"

"You want the largest room in the house?" Serendipity's voice showed annoyance. "I suppose you each want the largest bedrooms, too."

"Oh, no." Cerwyn shook his head. "Dr. Cohen and I will be sleeping in the same room as the birds, won't we? We'll just sleep on the floor in our bedrolls. That will work just fine."

Serendipity groaned and looked over at Sherman. Sherman shrugged. "Let them have it, Ser. They just want what's best for the birds."

Connie frowned. "Birds? Why do they need such a large room? How many do you have?"

Before Cerwyn could explain that they were extinct Carolina Parakeets from 1870, Sherman grabbed him by the arm and led him off. "Right then, Dr. Owen, let me help you with setting things up." Sherman figured Serendipity could come up with an answer to Connie's question without saying too much.

Sherman got Cerwyn and Priscilla squared away and came back out to find Serendipity still in the hall, now talking to Wendell. Connie was no longer there.

"You selfish, self-centered polecat!" a voice yelled from the stairway.

Sherman looked over to see Henry and Tobias coming down the stairs together in what looked like a heated argument. They appeared to be headed toward Serendipity—although it looked like they might first make a detour to the backyard for a fistfight.

"Tobias, you jackass, you can't have that room!" Henry glowered at him.

"Oh, I suppose you want it."

"Hell, no, but it's the master bedroom. Dr. Brown should get it."

Sherman came over to them. "Guys! Hold on! What's the matter?"

Henry jerked his thumb at Tobias. "He wants the fancy master bedroom with the bay window on the second floor. I'm sure Dr. Brown wanted that one. It's her house, she ought to get first pick."

Serendipity shook her head. "Wendell fell in love with a window on the third floor. He and I can take the bedrooms up there, since the zoologists don't want them. Besides, the bank account is in Sherman's name. If anyone should get the master bedroom it should be him."

"Uh, Ser," Sherman spoke up. "Can I pick my own room?"

"Kid, you can have any bedroom you want."

"I saw a nice room in the basement. I think it's under the parlor."

"Basement?" Serendipity's voice rose. "Why would you want a room in the basement?"

Wendell stepped closer to Serendipity. "You don't suppose the poor soul would like to get away from us lot, do you? Sherman not only has to wait on us, chauffeur us, but apparently has to make peace among us. I think he needs a refuge."

Serendipity looked at Wendell, then at Sherman. "Okay kid, if that's what you really want. Anytime you want to trade though, let us know."

Tobias puffed out his chest. "So, do I get the room?"

"Sure, fine." Serendipity waved him off, annoyed.

Tobias went back up the stairs looking triumphant.

Henry whirled on Serendipity, perturbed. "Why are you letting him have the best room?"

"Do you want it?" Serendipity asked.

"Hell, I don't care if I sleep in the garage. It's just I'd rather see anyone else *but* Tobias get that room since he's being so greedy. Right now, Matilda, Erik and Abubakari are up on the second floor discussing who should take the *smallest* room. They each insist that they take it. I would be tickled pink if any of them got the master bedroom. Tobias picked out the best room with no thought of anyone else. The man is so dang self-centered."

Wendell held up his hand. "Henry, you must remember, Tobias comes from a privileged background. Also he probably feels a little helpless now that he is a refugee. That room probably makes him feel like he has some control of his life."

"Tarnation Wendell, aren't we all in that same boat? The rest of us are trying to make the best of it and help one another. Don't know why you're defending that selfish polecat."

"Let him have the silly room if it means that much to him, old boy."

Serendipity snorted. "Yeah, if we are lucky maybe he'll stay in there and leave us all alone."

Sherman sighed and shook his head. "We can only hope."

Just getting the essentials like towels, bedding, kitchenware, soap and such took up most of the day. Since Sherman was a native of the late twentieth century, he was their closest expert to this period so it fell to him to try to figure out what they had to have to survive. Trying to think while herding curious time travelers through Kmart, proved to be nerve wracking. He kept losing a temporal anthropologist intrigued by some stupid gadget or whatnot. You would have thought they were rummaging through King Tut's tomb. Erik was so mesmerized by the hand-cranked eggbeater he was playing with, Sherman had to pull it out of the Viking's hand to give it to the cashier to ring up.

Sherman suggested they just buy blow-up mattresses, lawn chairs and a folding table to tide them over until they could buy proper furniture. Of course that would mean more baby-sitting later. Maybe he could get the appliances by himself, although he knew Serendipity, the shopping queen, would insist on coming.

That evening Sherman, Serendipity and the temporal anthropologists all sat around the dining room in lawn chairs eating the Chinese food Sherman had ordered. He had the meal delivered to the house, figuring the driver would have an easier time finding them than he would have trying to find the restaurant.

Serendipity dipped her spring roll in sweet and sour sauce. "So what do you want to do tonight for entertainment?"

"We can get a TV tomorrow. The cable guy will be here Wednesday." Sherman tried to spear the broccoli on his paper plate with a plastic fork. "I'm afraid I'm a little out of my element there. Most everything else looks pretty much how it looked in 1985, but the TVs I saw were out of *The Jetsons.*"

Wendell fished his pocket Bible out of his waistcoat pocket. "I suppose we could entertain one another with recordings we collected from the past." He clicked his tongue twice to turn his computer on. "Computer. Virtual recreation of the Louvre 1885."

Sherman almost dropped his fork, suddenly finding himself in an art gallery with the Mona Lisa on the wall. Would he ever get use to this?

"Nah." Henry shook his head. "We've all seen the Louvre."

"Computer, off." Wendell said. Sherman found himself back in the dining room.

Erik grinned and grabbed his Thor's hammer amulet he wore around his neck on a leather cord. "By Frey, I know something Wendell at least has never seen."

"Oh?" Wendell stuffed his computer back in his pocket.

"Ya! How many people can brag they have watched their own funeral?"

"I beg your pardon?"

"I told you I missed your funeral. So, when I returned home, I down-loaded the vid to my computer so I could watch it."

"Someone put it on the internet?"

"Ya, I found it on the University of Cambridge site. You have the honor of being their first temporal anthropologist, so they made the funeral a great event. The whole town turned out."

"Really?" Wendell blinked at Erik in disbelief.

"I shall show you." Erik took the amulet off his neck and laid it on the table between the open cartons of fried rice and chow mien. "Odin's blood!" he cued his computer. "Five-foot virtual screen. Play funeral of Dr. Wendell Howe."

A screen popped up a foot over the medallion, and hovered there. On it was a scene of a Victorian hearse pulled by six black horses with black ostrich feather plumes on their heads. Behind them a crowd dressed in dark clothes lined the street.

"Oh my!" Wendell leaned forward. "Where did they ever find that carriage? I can't believe they went to that much trouble for me."

"Yup." Henry grinned at him. "University of Cambridge pulled out all the stops for your funeral, partner. Wyoming U will probably just cremate me and toss me into a cow pasture."

Matilda leaned forward. "I heard tell that Cambridge campaigns to get thee knighted posthumously. I understand the Crown wol only do that for gallant acts of valor, but the University dost argue that thee fell in the line of duty."

"Knighthood? Me?"

Henry chuckled. "Don't let it go to your head, Sir Wendell. Cambridge probably just wants you knighted because Oxford has Sir Albert Leach. They can't let the competition get ahead of them."

The camera followed the procession to a tall medieval structure— *Church of Saint Mary the Great* Wendell called it. It was much larger than the church at St Radegund's Sherman had seen a few days before. He wondered how many ancient churches the campus had and why they needed any.

Six solemn pall bearers dressed in historical clothing from various periods pulled the casket out of the hearse and carried it into the church. One of them was Henry, who looked quite distraught. Wendell named off the other temporal anthropologists. The coffin was taken to the altar dais and laid on a long, short-legged table.

"It was closed casket." Henry explained. "Enforcers said they found you in little pieces. They said you were in a train wreck and wound up buried in several cities which is why it took them so long to collect you. I think they just cloned some bits of you to fool our DNA scanners."

"Ew!" Wendell wrinkled his nose.

There was a long program of organ music of Victorian hymns and then speeches—lots of speeches. Everyone from the mayor and the University president down to a local school teacher and the owner of Wendell's favorite fish and chips shop spoke of Wendell's contribution to scholarship and the local community. Several temporal anthropologists came forward and told stories about Wendell.

"My, I never knew what a marvelous chap I was."

"Heck, people always say nice stuff about people after they die and they don't have to put up with them anymore," Henry quipped.

Matilda punched Henry in the arm. Wendell fought back a smile and went back to watching his tribute.

It was during one rather long recollection that the camera panned across the audience. The pews were packed with hundreds of people. More stood along the wall. Wendell looked pleased, then suddenly his smile dropped. "Computer, stop vid!" He stood up and stepped closer. "Computer back up ten seconds."

The computer obliged, freezing on a group in the front row, which looked even sadder than the rest of the mourners. A woman who appeared to be in her sixties sobbed uncontrollably while a man of the same age tried to console her, although he looked as distressed as she. There was something vaguely familiar about the man. It was then Sherman realized he had Wendell's nose and chin.

"Dear lord," Wendell whispered.

"Who are they?" Serendipity asked.

"Mum and Dad. And look there is Grams Julia and Aunt Beatrice and my cousin Clive and..." Wendell trailed off. He whirled around and headed out of the room.

Erik's shoulders dropped. "Sorry. I thought Wendell would find this amusing. I knew not it showed his lamenting family."

Serendipity bounced out of her lawn chair and headed after Wendell.

"Wait, Dr. Brown!" Henry called after her. "Let the man have some time to himself."

Serendipity turned back at the door. "Like hell I will." She then disappeared.

Serendipity found Wendell in his room on the third floor. He had picked the one in the east corner, since it was the smaller of the two bedrooms. The room was empty, save for his carpet bag and tea chest, so Wendell sat in the corner, his knees pulled up, with his arms folded on them. He had his forehead laid on his arms. Serendipity tiptoed in and a floorboard creaked. He looked up, his face unreadable but his eyes looked tortured.

Serendipity came over and sat on the floor next to him. "Talk to me, sweetie."

Wendell said nothing for a minute then gazed at the far wall. "I remember years ago, in the 1860s I believe, I was in a hamlet in Ireland. In the village square they were throwing a huge party. I asked someone what the fuss was about. He said that Sean—or was it Donald?—was going to catch a ship bound for America in the morning. 'Oh,' said I. 'This is a going away party?' 'No,' the gentleman replied, 'this is a wake.' I told him I thought wakes were for the dead. He assured me that it was a wake because their family member was going over the western ocean and they would never ever see him again. It was the same as his being dead."

Wendell looked into Serendipity's face. "My family thinks I'm dead, and for all expressed purposes I am to them. They can never see me again. And I will never see any of them. They might as well be dead to me too." He pursed his lips and swallowed hard.

"You are mourning them?"

He gave a slight nod. "Yes, I am mourning the deaths of people who won't be born for several centuries." He closed his eyes. "I have forgotten the first rule of time travel—always live in the moment. You know Mark Twain died centuries ago, and yet there you are, in the past interviewing him. He's no ghost. He's very much alive and cracking jokes. And you try not to think about his future. You just enjoy the moment."

"It's not the same, Wendell. You don't have any more moments with your family."

"No. No, I don't. Poor Mum. I have been nothing but a heartbreak to her and the rest of the family. I was always in the past, seldom in the present. They would have preferred I had been a history professor and stayed home. And I can't even tell them I'm sorry."

Serendipity put her arm around his shoulders. "This is all my fault."

"No, I made my own decisions. I have no one to blame but myself."

Serendipity felt a twinge of guilt, remembering Wendell's subliminal message to his earlier self to help her no matter what. She held him a little tighter. "I'll never forget your sacrifice, hon. I'm your family now. We're all your family."

He patted her hand. "Yes, in a manner of speaking, even if it is not blood kin. Still...poor Mum. Poor Dad. Poor Grams." He choked back a sob.

"It's okay Wendell. You have a right to mourn lost ones."

Wendell stiffened his jaw. "I'll be fine. Please, I would like to be alone."

Serendipity gazed into those overcast-grey eyes and shook her head. "No, sweetie. You don't need to be alone. Stop being so macho. Everyone needs at least one person they can be vulnerable with. Let me be yours."

He pulled her closer and laid his head on her shoulder and wept.

Chapter Nineteen

Sherman walked up the stairs from the basement, trying to wipe the sleep from his eyes. It was day five at their new home. He came out into the reception hall, where Rosetta, dressed in a white apron and a grey maid's dress that reached past her knees, polished the carved banister of the stairs curving to the second floor.

"Morning, Rosetta." Sherman gave her a wave.

"Good morning, sir." The robot responded mechanically, her face showing no emotion.

"Sherman, you do know that's a machine, don't you?"

Sherman turned to see Wendell fighting back a smile.

"Uh, yeah."

"Good, because I would really hate to see you getting into an argument with the toaster, old boy. Just remember, Rosetta is an *it*. It may look real, but it has no more personality or feeling than the banister it is cleaning. Talking to a cat would be far less barmy. A cat might not comprehend what you are saying, but at least they might enjoy the sound of your voice."

"Yeah, I know." Sherman tried not to look foolish. "I guess I expect her to at least—well, I don't know. I just don't want to be rude."

"Being rude to it would be as daft as being polite. Just treat it as a household appliance." Wendell studied Rosetta a moment and shuddered. "I daresay it is a little disturbing to have a household appliance that looks *this* real. Still Dr. Brown is right. An android that looked like an android would upset the natives in this period."

Sherman recalled Serendipity's butler back in the twenty-fourth century. Even though he looked human, he didn't look real. His skin was too dull, his moves too stiff. He looked more like a mannequin than a person. Rosetta however moved more naturally. Her skin had a "healthy glow." She even blinked about every ten seconds.

Wendell shook his head, and headed for the dining room. Sherman followed after him. A banquet table with ten chairs was one of the first pieces of furniture Serendipity had bought. Even though it was long, it did not crowd this room at all.

Sherman noticed everyone was sitting in their usual spot. Serendipity was at the far end of the table furthest from the door. On her left sat Abubakari and next to him was Erik. Next to Erik were the two empty seats left for the temporal zoologists, which they never used. Wendell sat down in the chair on Serendipity's right. Sherman sat down next to him. The two empty seats next to Sherman were Matilda's and Henry's. The empty captain's chair at the far end was Tobias's spot. This was the head of the table, which is probably why Tobias had grabbed it, but because Serendipity was at the other end and everyone was focused on her, it had become the bottom.

Sherman looked across the table at Abubakari and Erik studying a laptop. Serendipity had bought laptops for everyone as well as cell phones, until she could figure out a way to access the internet with their twenty-seventh century computers.

"Really, Erik," Serendipity said. "We can just buy everyone a bed."

"But I'm a builder, by Thor." Erik sounded disappointed. "My major research was Viking technology. I have gotten good at blacksmithing and carpentry. I plan to decorate my room with Viking furniture. I promised Matilda I would make her a medieval-style bed. She wants to make her room look like a convent cell. It is why she desired the humblest bedroom."

Sherman got the idea that the only reason Erik and Abubakari really accepted Matilda having the smallest room was because they knew she would probably spend most nights sleeping in Henry's. Everyone was too polite to point this out, but that also was why they insisted Henry take the second largest bedroom on the second floor.

"Why would she want to decorate her bedroom like that boring room we found her in?" Serendipity frowned.

Erik grinned at her. "Ho, same reason you were hunting through the thrift stores to get twentieth-century furniture for your room."

A faint smile twitched Wendell's mouth. "Yes, I think Dr. Brown would have made a good temporal anthropologist, except she sometimes gets a little too involved with the natives. She would have been something like Sunshine."

Erik got a wistful smile at that name. Sherman wondered if they had an "understanding."

"Why would I be like sunlight?" Serendipity stared askingly at Wendell.

"Sunshine is a person," Wendell explained. "Her real name is Dr. Veronica Drew, University of California-Berkley. She goes by the nickname 'Sunshine' in the Field. Her latest project is hitchhiking across late 1960s, early 70s America studying the Hippie culture."

"And she's allowed to get involved with people in the past?"

Wendell shrugged. "From what I understand, it was the era of Free Love and everyone was taking hallucinogenic drugs. I daresay, no one would remember her the next day."

"Well, I have to admit *that* sounds interesting." Serendipity looked around the table. "No offense, guys."

"None taken," Erik assured her. "Can I build you anything? I can do other periods besides Viking. I'm endeavoring to talk Abubakari into a bed."

Abubakari shook his head. "I am quite comfortable sleeping on my mat on the floor."

"I could not interest you in this?" Erik turned the laptop screen to Abubakari.

Abubakari's eyes lit up. "Owo, that I would not mind."

Erik grinned at the others and turned around the laptop. On the screen was a low wooden bed frame that had a woven rope instead of wooden slats.

"I searched the internet for medieval African beds. This is what I found. By Thor, it is almost impossible to navigate the internet in this time period. The search engines are most primitive and inefficient. And everything is so slow. I must type everything in."

"I think I saw a program on mine for vocal commands," Abubakari said.

Erik snorted. "Tried it. Useless. Ho, part of the adventure, ya?"

The side door from the kitchen through the pantry swung open. Henry walked into the room carrying a platter of hotcakes. Matilda followed with a plate of bacon. "Belly up, folks," Henry called out. "Grub is on."

"You really don't have to cook, Henry." Serendipity leaned on the table. "That's what Rosie's for."

"Machine made food?" Henry wrinkled his nose. "Anywho, I wanna keep busy and I like to cook. I worked on a lot of chuck wagons, railroad diner cars, and I spent a year working at a Harvey's as a hash slinger."

"Harvey's?"

"A chain of restaurant's on the Kansas, Topeka and Sante Fe Railroad line." Henry sat the platter on the table. "People riding the trains knew they could get a decent meal there. It might have been the first restaurant chain, at least in America anyway."

"Oh, yeah!" Serendipity grinned excited. "Wasn't that the restaurant in that Judy Garland musical?"

Wendell fought back a smile. "Yes, I can see Henry singing as he slings hash."

"Is there anything you haven't done, Henry?" Sherman asked.

"Jack of all trades, master of none." Henry pulled out a chair for Matilda. He sat her down in her spot on the other side of Sherman.

Tobias entered from the hall, dressed in his sports coat and turtleneck. He sat down at the end without a word, and made eye contact with no one. Everyone else ignored him.

"Hey, kid," Serendipity turned to Sherman. "Would you mind telling our other guests breakfast is ready? They seem to listen to you. Tell them at least one of them is going to have to come out because I have an important announcement."

Sherman nodded and got up. He walked across the wide hall to the music room, then knocked and waited. After a few moments the door was opened by Priscilla. "Hello, Sherman, please come in."

He stepped in, scanning the room. The two zoologists had made use of the large room by building a huge cage made of lumber and wire mesh in the middle of the room. They had rolled out linoleum to protect the wooden floor. Everyone, except Tobias, had helped them with the construction, although Erik and Henry did most of the work. Inside the cage were small potted trees, a basin water fountain as well as hanging feeders. They had installed blinds on the windows to control the amount of sunlight allowed to enter. Tranquil music came from Cerwyn's PAL computer sitting on a cardboard box, the tiny built-in speakers sounding like top of the line acoustic equipment. The parrots flew about, chattering and playing with one another. This had to be parrot paradise. On the other side of the room were two blow-up mattresses on the floor alongside carpetbags.

Sherman studied the poor accommodations. "You know, now that we've taken care of the parrots, we could get you guys some furniture or something."

"Oh, we're fine, aren't we? Cerwyn said.

Priscilla looked at the cage and smiled. "What else could we need?"

"Dr. Brown sent me to tell you breakfast is ready. She wants at least one of you to come out because she has something important to say to us."

"Oh?" Cerwyn looked uncertain.

"I can watch the birds, Dr. Owen," Priscilla assured him.

"All right," Cerwyn sounded reluctant. "I'll just be a tick. I'll bring back our breakfast. You be sure to call me if there's a problem, won't you?"

"Why wouldn't I?" Priscilla watched the birds intently.

Sherman followed as Cerwyn hurried to the dining room. Cerwyn came over and stood between the two empty seats next to Erik and began filling the plates without sitting down. Sherman went back to his seat.

"Thank you, Dr. Owen," Serendipity said. "I thought I would make an announcement while I had you all in one place."

"Who died and made you queen?" Tobias grumbled.

"I believe I did." Wendell said. "They did have my funeral after all."

Matilda and Abubakari chuckled.

Tobias snorted. "Yes, you would defend the woman you are shagging!"

Wendell jumped up. "You will not use that sort of language in front of the ladies." Wendell's quiet voice took on a dark edge. "And you most certainly will not use *that* word in reference to Dr. Brown!"

Tobias stood up and glowered at Wendell. "I just want to know who put her in charge."

"We all did!" Henry glowered at Tobias. "The woman saved all of our lives, you ingrate."

At that moment Cerwyn set down his plate and leaned toward Tobias. "Dr. Leach, Dr. Brown has something to say. I want her to say it so I can get back to my birds. So you will sit down and shut up, or I will make you, won't I? I have wrestled with white rhinos and won, so don't push your luck, boyo."

Tobias started to say something, then closed his mouth, Cerwyn's dark glare forcing him to sit.

"Thank you, Dr. Leach." Cerwyn turned to Serendipity. "Please continue, Dr. Brown."

Wendell sat back down, giving Cerwyn a grateful nod.

Serendipity cleared her throat. "Thank you, Dr. Owen. I was able to hack into the Department of Licensing Computer and give Sherman a new driver's license record. He can go down to the Driver's License Office and tell them he lost his license and get a real one. However, he will need to take in a birth certificate, so I hacked into the Vital Records computer. Neither of these were easy, because they are using archaic binary. I realized I was going to have to get all of you birth certificates, so for expediency, you will all be Washington State natives."

"What!" Wendell couldn't help yelping.

"It's not that horrible." Sherman frowned at him.

"What about our accents, wa?" Abubakari asked. "I do not know if I can do a Western accent."

"You were born here. No one said you had to spend your life here. Your parents moved to another country, or you spent 'X' number of years overseas, or you just spent too much time watching shows from the BBC." Serendipity looked pointedly at Wendell. "I don't care. You can come up with your own story. You each need to pick a town in Washington State you want to be born in, just be sure it has a hospital. Also figure out what year you were born, you can keep your real birthday."

"So I was born 1885, wa?" Abubakari did the math.

Serendipity's eyes widened. "You're a hundred and twenty-five?"

"Life begins at a hundred." Abubakari smiled at her.

Serendipity shook her head. "Remember people age faster in this time period. You will need to figure out how old you appear to be and use that age. Ask Sherman if you aren't sure. Also, just to be safe, you should all come up with an alias so we can't be traced if the time terrorist come looking for us. You can keep your first names, but change your last name. You might want to keep it similar enough so you'll answer to it. For instance Henry could go by *Darren* since it's close to *Darrel*." Serendipity sat back down. "Okay, that was it. After breakfast you can all get on your laptops and do a little research. I can help you if you need assistance. Try and have me something by lunch."

"Is that all?" Cerwyn asked.

"That's it." Serendipity nodded.

Cerwyn nodded back, picked up the two plates and left hurriedly.

Sherman grinned across the table at Erik. "Well, I know where Erik was 'born'."

"Oh?" Erik glanced over at him.

"Yeah, Poulsbo."

"Why Poulsbo?"

"It was settled by Norwegians and has a large Scandinavian population." Erik grinned back. "Ya, that would be good!"

Sherman turned to Henry. "Henry, you'll need to pick something east of the Cascade Mountains."

"Why?"

"Because they talk like you East of the Mountains. They drawl more. Of course you'll have to say 'Warshington' instead of 'Washington.'"

Matilda looked at Henry. "I believe he dost that now."

"So tell me, old boy." Wendell looked over at Sherman. "Are there any towns in this state that speak with an English accent?"

Sherman searched his memory but couldn't think of any.

After breakfast everyone went their separate ways to try to figure out who they were and where they were from. Sherman's history was already in place so he decided to take a shower. In this house with ten people and two bathrooms, you grabbed any opportunity you could to take a shower.

Sherman dressed and came out of the second-story bathroom, hair still damp, feeling a little more civilized. He heard music coming from up the stairs on the third floor. Sherman had heard the tunes enough times to recognize Gilbert and Sullivan. That could mean only one thing. Sherman decided to go up and see if Wendell needed any help.

He found Wendell on the third floor in the billiards room. No one called it that anymore. While most of the room was still bare save for a desk in the corner, what caught one's eye was the spot in front of the middle window. It was now cluttered with heavy brocade drapes, a large Persian rug, two reproduction Victorian easy chairs and a teacart on wheels—all in mahogany wood and bold floral patterns. This was Wendell's sanctuary. He could usually be found here drinking tea, reading nineteenth-century literature, working on his pocket computer or just staring out the window at the view.

Wendell was currently gazing out at the mountains, sipping tea. His computer sat on the tea cart. Sherman knew the music was coming from the innocent-looking pocket Bible and was probably playing an original performance Wendell had recorded back in the 1800s. The gaudy pattern on the overstuffed chair went well with Wendell's late Victorian suit. All the temporal anthropologists dressed in their time period unless they had to leave the house. Even then they tried to pick contemporary clothes that were as close to that costume as they could, which led to some strange attire.

Wendell took a sip from his teacup held over a saucer, then noticed Sherman. "Oh hello, old chap. May I pour you a spot of tea?"

"No thanks." Sherman came over and sat down in the matching chair. Wendell had put two chairs by the window, just as his tea cart beside him always had two teacups ready to entertain company, although he was usually here by himself.

Sherman glanced out at the Cascade Mountains, the highest peaks laced with glaciers. He wondered how many of them were volcanoes, both extinct and otherwise. The real estate agent had been careful not to mention nearby Mount Baker was a dormant volcano. He remembered that it had been steaming several years before Mount Saint Helens decided to blow. Everyone figured Mount Baker would be the one to erupt. Apparently it hadn't yet.

Sherman turned to Wendell. "Need any help on your birth certificate?"

"No, I decided I am Wendell Howard, born the third of March, 1970, in Kennewick. I found the town on a map. It has such a nice English sound to it."

"Actually, the name is Indian."

"Doesn't sound like anything from India."

"No, American Indian."

Wendell smiled over at Sherman. "I believe they are pulling the wool over your eyes, old chap. Kennewick is as English a name as I ever heard.

It is Old English for 'royal farm.'"

"I heard it's Indian for 'Winter Haven' or 'Grassy Place.' My Aunt Jean and Uncle Joe got into a fight over that one."

Wendell appeared to ignore that. "Do you think 1970 will work? Serendipity made me forty on my last fake birth certificate."

"I think forty will work." Sherman frowned. "I was born 1966 so that makes me older than you."

"I'm sure Dr. Brown has updated you to 1991."

"1991? It doesn't seem possible. Do you realize my friends are all—" Sherman paused and rolled his eyes to the ceiling as he did the math, "forty-four now? Hey, they're probably still alive."

"You can't contact them." Wendell's voice was more sympathetic than stern.

"I know. How would I explain why I haven't aged twenty-five years? It just all seems so weird. I wonder if Mom is still alive. She'd be real old now."

"Don't even try to find out, Sherman. You can't do anything to change the flow of time. Finding out the future can drive you mad—and has driven some mad." Wendell stared back at the mountains. "Have you noticed Dr. Brown acting odd lately?"

"Oh?" Sherman avoided answering the question.

"Yes, sometimes she looks at me with a strange expression, especially when we are alone. She seems sad. I marked it off to her being tired or worried. She tries to hide that sort of thing, always optimistic and on the go. But I can still see it in her. Also she's been treating me like I was going away soon, and she will never see me ever again." Wendell turned and looked pointedly at Sherman. "Do you know if Serendipity has made any more *side time trips* by herself?"

"Not that I know of. Why?"

"Because she acts like—well, I would swear she has gone into the future and found out when I die. I have the feeling by the way she acts, that it will be soon."

Sherman studied the trepidation on Wendell's face. "You're more worried about Serendipity than yourself, aren't you?"

"Indeed. There are many reasons one should never venture into the future. This is the most daunting one. Knowing exactly when someone you care about is going to die and not being allowed to do anything at all to prevent it, can lead to depression if not a nervous breakdown! I've asked her about it, but she denies it. I'm becoming quite worried about her."

Sherman looked out the window a moment, then over to Wendell. "That's not the problem, dude. I know what's bugging her."

Wendell sat his teacup and saucer down on the tea cart. "Really? I beg you, please tell me."

"I don't know if I should. Serendipity should probably tell you herself. It's high time you two fixed this." Sherman got up. "You stay here. I'm going to go get her right now." Sherman turned and left without waiting for an answer from Wendell.

Sherman found Serendipity in the basement in the room next to the laundry room. She had commandeered this space as her workshop, because it already had an old workbench. Whoever had built it made it sturdy and impossible to move out of the room unless you tore it apart. Serendipity sat at the grease-stained table, tinkering with her laptop she had dissected. She looked up. "Hi, kid, just trying to see if I can boost the power with what is available now. These primitive things are so slow and gutless."

"I thought you got the newest, most powerful computer out there?"

"Like I said, these primitive things are so slow and gutless."

"Ser, can you leave that a moment. Something important has come up."

"Oh?" She gave Sherman her full attention.

"Please, it's Wendell. He's worried sick about you. He has noticed you acting strange around him. You two need to talk."

Serendipity actually looked scared. "I can't."

"You have to, Ser. Come on, I'll go with you."

Serendipity bowed her head and sighed. "Yeah, you're right, kid. I have to tell him the truth, even if it means losing him. I can't go on with this sham." She stood up, held up her head and marched up the stairs like someone bravely going to his execution.

When they got to the sitting room, they found Wendell pacing. He looked up and rushed over to Serendipity. He grabbed her hands. "Serendipity, dearest, what is wrong? Are you all right?"

Serendipity looked up at Wendell. "I'm fine. It's you I'm worried about."

"Me? Why me? You didn't go into the future again and find out when I die, did you?"

"No, nothing like that."

"Then why are you worried?"

"Because...because you aren't thinking straight."

"What?" Wendell looked totally confused. "What are you talking about?"

"Do you remember when you met yourself in the past?"

"Yes?"

"Do you remember when you had Henry put the Compliance Disk on your neck?"

"Yes, but what does—"

"Do you remember what you told yourself?"

"I told myself to forget everything about our meeting, to remember nothing."

"You also gave yourself a subliminal message."

"Yes, that next time I met you I was to help you in any way possible. I wanted to make certain I had not somehow changed things and that I would be reluctant to assist you."

"And then what did you say?"

"Leg it back to the Timemobile?"

"No, Wendell," Serendipity's voice began to sound impatient. "You told yourself to help me, and I quote, 'because you love her very much!'"

"Well, I do."

"Wendell, don't you see what you did?"

"What?"

"You hypnotized yourself into loving me. You don't really love me."

"What are you talking about? Of course, I love you."

"You don't, not really. It's all a fake!"

Wendell grabbed Serendipity and planted his lips on hers. He finally pulled away. "There, did that feel fake?"

"Maybe you're just good at self-hypnosis."

Wendell kissed her again, only longer. "Well?"

"Okay, so you are *really, really* good at self-hypnosis."

Wendell sighed, visibly deflating. "Serendipity, what can I do to convince you that I really do love you?"

"Yeah, you love me, but it's not *real*. Can't you see that?" She put her hand on his cheek. "No, you can't see it. You've been brainwashed. And I've been taking advantage of you because it's so wonderful having someone like you who is crazy about me. I don't want to lose you. But if you ever come to your senses you'll probably hate me for using you."

"Using me? I don't wish to be crude, Serendipity, but I am a bloke. What man would object to being used like *that*?"

"Told ya," Sherman muttered.

Serendipity watched Wendell helplessly, and then she pursed her lips. "All right, let me put it this way. How would you feel if you found out that someone had brainwashed *me* into loving you and you knew it, but never told me and just took advantage of the situation."

Wendell pulled back, looking horrified. "Why I would feel like a complete cad for exploiting you and—oh, I think I understand now."

"So, now you see my problem. And I don't know what to do."

"Would it help if I gave you my permission to use me?"

"No, because you aren't thinking straight."

"It is not like you are hurting me. On the contrary! Besides how do you really know that's what happened? Even if I did brainwash myself, how do you know I didn't fall in love with you on my own anyway? If you really had been just taking advantage of me, wouldn't I have just fallen out of love with you?"

"That's another thing I'm afraid of. I just hope you don't wind up hating me."

"How could I ever hate you? Besides it sounds like this debacle was all my fault, so how can I blame you? I am so sorry I've caused you any sort of anguish. How can I possibly make this right?"

Serendipity stared at the floor a moment, then she looked up. "There's only one way. We have to use the Compliance Disk and correct the mistake."

Wendell dropped his hands and hung his head. "All right, if only for your own peace of mind. But I must warn you." He looked back up at her.

"I shall most likely just fall in love with you again."

"I hope so, Wendell. I really hope so. So, where is the disk?"

"I haven't the foggiest."

Sherman raised his hand. "I know where it is. I have it."

"You have it?" Serendipity looked at Sherman surprised. Then she shrugged. "Can you go get it, kid?"

Sherman nodded.

Chapter Twenty

When Sherman got back he found Wendell and Serendipity standing right where he had left them. Eyes closed, they were hugging each other like they were holding on for dear life. Sherman cleared his throat. They both looked up.

"You got it, kid?" Serendipity still hung on to Wendell.

"Yeah." Sherman held up the orange square.

"We might as well get it over with." She let go of Wendell. She brushed his cheek as she stepped away.

Wendell's sad eyes watched her. "Perhaps just one for the road, if I'm not being too crass?"

Serendipity shook her head. "Better not, or I'll weaken."

Sherman stepped over to them. "Wendell can't do this. I guess I'll have to. I just hope I don't mess it up, too. I know now why the Enforcers have trained psychologists doing this. You noticed only Agent Twenty-Two gave commands."

"Oh, I don't know." Serendipity wrinkled her nose. "Agent Five seemed good at barking orders."

"Not while someone was wearing a disk. He pretty much kept his mouth shut when Agent Twenty-Two was using it."

"Sherman is right," Wendell said. "They have to be very careful how they word a command. If they tell you to sit down and don't breathe, that is exactly what you will do until you pass out."

Sherman nodded. "We better keep this on as little as possible so we don't say anything we shouldn't. Okay, Wendell, sit down. You too, Ser."

They both sat down meekly in the over-stuffed chairs, letting Sherman take over. Sherman took a deep breath, trying to look confident while praying he didn't botch this up. "Ser, don't move a muscle or say a word. Okay?"

Serendipity nodded, her lips pressed tightly together.

Wendell began loosing his tie. "Have you worked out yet what you are going to say, old chap? You must be careful with the wording."

"I'll just tell you to forget the subliminal message. I won't say 'don't love Serendipity.' That will be up to your freewill."

"That should do it. Proceed." Wendell bowed his head, submissively exposing his neck.

Sherman took a deep breath and slapped the disk on the back of Wendell's neck. Wendell took in an involuntary breath through clenched teeth and stiffened. After a moment he gave a ragged sigh and relaxed a little.

"Wendell?" Sherman bent down. "Can you hear me?"

"Yes, I can hear you." Wendell didn't straighten up.

"Do you remember when you ran into yourself in France last week, or should I say five years ago?"

"Yes."

"Do you remember the subliminal message you gave yourself?"

"Yes."

"Forget the message. It never happened. Understand?"

"I understand."

Sherman looked over at Serendipity. "How's that?"

She just nodded, afraid to speak.

Sherman reached over and pushed the button in the middle of the disk. The prongs let go and it slid off. Sherman caught it. "You okay, Wendell?"

Wendell reached up and rubbed the back of his neck. "Yes." He straightened up and looked up at Sherman. Sherman gave him a nervous smile.

Wendell, his expression as deadpan as ever, turned to Serendipity who sat across from him looking terrified. They didn't say a word and just stared at each other a few moments.

Then Serendipity grinned. She stood up and came over to Wendell and took his hand. "You don't have to say a word, sweetie. I can see it in your eyes. No man has ever looked at me with so much love in his eyes as you do."

Wendell stood up, and embraced her, planting his lips on hers. After a couple of minutes he pulled back. "There now do you believe I love you?"

Serendipity dropped her arms and backed away, frowning. "Oh foot, what if it didn't work? What if you are still brainwashed?"

Wendell rolled his eyes. "Serendipity! One of these days you are going to drive me to drink something stronger than tea!"

"He doesn't sound like a love zombie to me, Ser." Sherman said. "Of course, he didn't before either."

"What can I possibly do to convince you that what I feel is real?" Wendell looked imploringly at her. After a moment he raised an eyebrow and turned to Sherman. "I say, be a good fellow and tell the rest that Dr. Brown will be indisposed for the next hour or two. Poor dear has been under a lot of stress this past week worrying about us. I think she needs some personal attention. Isn't that right, Serendipity, dear?"

"Oh yeah!" Serendipity threw her arms around him. "Very definitely need personal attention, uh-huh."

Sherman smiled and shook his head. "Okay, you do that." He left the room, afraid to look back.

Sherman came down the stairs into the second story hall just as Tobias came up from the first floor. They both stopped and eyed each other.

"Where is Dr. Brown, boy?" Tobias's tone was one used when addressing a lowly flunky. Sherman felt sure if Tobias's accent had been Southern instead of English, he would have made "boy" more than one syllable.

Sherman straightened up to look as tall as he could at five foot, four and a half inches. "First off, I am not Dr. Brown's servant, but her assistant. Secondly, I am legally an adult, not a boy. Thirdly, she's busy and does not want to be disturbed."

"Get out of my way, twit." Tobias tried to shove past him.

Sherman stood his ground. "No. Trust me, you do *not* want to go up there."

Tobias stopped and stared at Sherman, then he rolled his eyes. "Oh bloody hell, don't tell me she and Howe are at it again. Those two are worse than rabbits! Be thankful you didn't take my room. I have those two on top of me, and Dr. Darrel and Dr. Warwick beside me. At least, Dr. Warwick isn't as noisy or as voracious as Dr. Brown, I'll give her that."

"Back off, Tobias. You can't talk about Serendipity like that. Both she and Wendell are awesome. Cut them some slack."

"You will not speak to me in that tone." Tobias bristled. "And you will address me as Dr. Leach, boy."

"Oh yeah? That's *Mr. Conrad* to you! My name is not 'boy,' jerk!"

"How dare you! I'll have your job for this!"

Sherman tried to suppress a laugh that came out as a snort. "Go ahead, Tobias. Go tattle to Dr. Brown that I mouthed off to you. She'll probably give me a raise!"

"That is not the proper tone for one of your station to use when addressing a superior. Just who do you think you are?"

"I think I'm the one who has his name on the house and the bank account. Hell, I'm the one who *made* that money! I may look like a servant to you because I'm always chauffeuring or fetching, but that's because I'm the only one who can drive. I don't mind because everyone asks me nicely and treats me with some respect—everyone but you!"

"Hey, Sherman!" A voice called from above.

Sherman and Tobias both looked up the stairs leading to the third floor to see Serendipity and Wendell standing on the landing, watching. Sherman noticed Serendipity's hair was a bit mussed and Wendell's waistcoat was off and his shirt was buttoned crooked. Both were trying to look as nonchalant as possible.

"Sorry, I disturbed you guys," Sherman called up.

"Sherman, you're fired as my gofer," Serendipity said.

Tobias crossed his arms, looking smug.

Then she grinned. "From now on you are the official manager of this house. You have the authority to kick anyone out that you want."

Tobias's mouth flew open. "What!"

"Better be nice to the landlord, Leachy-poo."

Wendell gave a dirty chuckle as he put his arm around Serendipity's waist and pulled her close. "Oh, that is brilliant! You are so adorable when you do things like that. And you doubt that I could ever love you? How in the world could I not? I just want to gather you up in my arms and—"

Serendipity put her finger on his lips. "Hold that thought." She gave him a saucy wink, and then turned back to Sherman. "Oh, and pull a ton of money out of your bank account and go buy yourself a sports car or something. That's an order. I'd do it myself, but I'm a little busy right now...with other business." She turned back to Wendell. "Shall we go take care of business?"

"Of course, Dr. Brown. I will gladly do my part in this endeavor."

Serendipity giggled and grabbed Wendell's hand, leading him up the stairs. A few moments later Sherman heard the bedroom door close.

He turned back to Tobias to find him halfway down the hall to his room. He slammed his door shut.

"Scuzzball!" Sherman turned and went down the stairs. He then stopped, remembering his official position now. He held his head up and continued down more calmly.

When Sherman got to the foot of the stairs, he heard a voice drawl. "Well, you look like the cat that swallowed the canary."

Sherman glanced over to see Henry standing in front of the kitchen door wearing his white chuck-wagon apron. The smell of baking bread drifted through the air.

Sherman pushed his black hair out of his face. "Serendipity told Tobias that I'm the manager of this house."

Henry just smiled. "Yup, I suppose you are at that." He turned and went back into the kitchen.

At noon everyone gathered around the dining room table for lunch. Henry served homemade tomato soup and grilled cheese sandwiches from fresh baked bread. Everyone sat in their usual spots, the two chairs for the zoologists empty as always. Serendipity sat at the head, with a pad and pen. "Okay does everyone know who they are? I'm going with Sara Brown from Vancouver since it's across the river from Beaverton. I got Wendell and Sherman already. Who else is ready?"

Henry held up his hand. "Henry Derringer; October fifth, 1966; Walla Walla, Warshington." He shrugged. "I just like saying Walla Walla."

"Derringer?" Wendell aimed a raised eyebrow down the table at him.

"Hey, if I get to pick."

"That's fine, Henry," Serendipity said. "Who's next?"

Erik raised his spoon. "Erik Olson from Poulsbo. Date of birth December fourteenth, but I am not sure what year. I am fifty-four winters."

Serendipity shook her head. "What do you think Sherman? Thirty?"

"More like twenty-eight."

"Okay 1982 is when you were born, Erik."

Matilda lifted her hand. "I hast taken Warner for a last name. The place of my nativity wol be Spokane for it hast several convents. My date of birth falls on the seventh of September, seventy-five years ago. Would I be forty?"

"Thirty-five." Sherman shook his head.

"Make it thirty-four." Serendipity bid him down. "That would be 1976."

"My face is that of one so young?"

"Hey, if I can be thirty-nine."

Tobias rolled his eyes. Everyone else politely fought the urge.

"All right, Tobias. What have you got?"

"Tobias Lee; eleventh of November, 1980; Medina."

"Why Medina?" Serendipity asked.

"If I have to be from this God-forsaken part of the world, I might as well be from a nice neighborhood. Some of the richest people in the world from this time period live there."

"Whatever. How about you, Abubakari?"

"I will be Abubakari Keita, born in Seattle, July month, day twenty-eighth, year 1952. Keita is the most common surname in Mali. I decided my parents were foreign exchange students and Seattle has several colleges. I conveniently forgot which one.

"Covering up the non-existent paper trail, huh? Good idea," Serendipity said. "Now I just got to get the zoologists. If they don't have anything, I'll make up something and they'll be stuck with it. I'll hack into the computer records, and order the birth certificates. After that you can all take them down to the Drivers' License Office and get picture I.D. cards."

"But only Sherman can drive?" Wendell frowned.

"Right, they are just I.D. cards not driver's licenses."

Erik scratched his head. "Will it not look most strange when all these birth certificates come to the same address?"

Serendipity screwed up her face, "You got a point. Maybe if we give this place a name like *Bellingham Hotel*."

"How about *Albert Brown Boarding House*?" Henry said

Serendipity grinned at him. "I like that. What do you think, Sherman?"

Sherman thought a moment. "I don't think they have boarding houses anymore. I've only seen them in really old movies. You know Connie said this area was probably once part of the town of Fairhaven before it got incorporated into Bellingham. Lots of stuff around here has *Fairhaven* in its name. Why not call it *Fairhaven House* or something like that? Keep it really vague. Let them come up with their own explanation."

"Ah." Wendell stood up. "If I may be so bold. What about *the Fairhaven Home for Wayward Time Travelers*? We just won't make that last part public."

Serendipity looked around. "Well guys, what do you think? *Fairhaven Home*? Everyone in favor, raise your hand."

Everyone raised their hand except Tobias. Then he shrugged and raised his.

Chapter Twenty-One

Henry put the dishes on the kitchen counter, then turned to go back into the dining room for more. There stood Matilda with several coffee mugs.

"It's okay, darling," Henry assured her. "You don't have to help. I'm only doing this 'cause I want to feel useful. I actually enjoy cooking and washing dishes."

She set the cups on the counter. "I *want* to help thee."

Henry smiled noticing she used the familiar "thee" even though she didn't need to in this period. "Thee" was used for family, friends, inferiors and lovers. He assumed she meant the last category.

She turned and gave him a sweet smile. "I desire to spend as much time with thee as I can. Heaven only knows how much time we hast together."

"Don't you worry none. I'm sure the Enforcers will round up the bad guys and we'll be safe."

"Then what, my love? We wol go back to just seeing each other a few times a year for not but a few days, stealing precious hours together like thieves."

"Yeah, and you won't have Wendell and Shiro to tide you over."

Matilda ducked her head.

Henry wanted to bite off his tongue. He lifted her chin up. "Now darling, that was my idea, remember? I knew Wendell would treat you like a lady. Didn't know Shiro well, but he struck me as a gentle soul. Kind of surprised me though. I figured you'd go for someone a bit more rowdy like me."

Matilda looked up with those blue eyes. "Dost thou think I loveth thee because thou art a cowboy? Yea, I wol admit that be kind of sexy. But what compelled me to fall in love with thee be thy kind and gentle heart. Thou care about me. Thou cared about me long before we d be lovers. Thou cared about me enough to loosen thy grip so I would not be alone when I needed solace." Matilda put her arms around Henry. "These past days with thou have been paradise for me."

Henry grabbed her up, and hugged her tight. "Oh darling, this ain't right. You know, I been thinking about maybe retiring. I'd wait for ya. I was hoping someday we could get a life together."

"To be trapped in the twenty-seventh century? Would not we both be miserable?"

"Oh I don't know. There are still a few isolated spots left where we could build a cabin and ignore the rest of the world."

"We wol still have to venture out for supplies. But thou dost speak true. We cannot keep living like this forever. And now that we be finally together, it dost not slake my thirst, but makes me hunger even more for thy presence."

"Ditto. Dishes will wait. How 'bout you and me getting out of the house. Go explore this here time period. Looks kinda interesting."

"Neither of us be trained for this time of yore."

"Like Serendipity pointed out, it's the West Coast, and a college town. No one even blinks at us."

"Yea, I hast noticed a wide variety in how the natives array themselves. Tis nice I can wear a long dress. Nay dost I feel comfortable in anything else."

"Yeah, and no one minds a cowboy running around. Found a place in town selling Western apparel. I fit right in."

"Thou knowst, I could use some embroidery thread."

"And I'm in the mood for jerky. We're both double Ph.D.s. Think we can figure out one of them there bus schedules?"

Matilda giggled.

Henry put his arm around her shoulders and started for the door. "Yup, wanna spend some time with my woman. Wanna spend the rest of my life with her."

"Who knoweth what the future wol bring, my love. I wish to spend every second I can with thee."

Wendell sat in his chair at his window watching his mountains and sipping his mid-morning tea. Sherman felt sure the man considered the peaks his by now.

"Hey, Wendell."

The frock-coated gentleman turned to see Sherman at the top of the stairs. "Ah, good morning, Sherman."

Serendipity sat at the desk across the room, studying her laptop.

"Shopping." Wendell pointed to Serendipity. "She is searching for tools I don't believe have been invented yet."

"Yeah, I may have to invent them." Serendipity looked over at Sherman. "So what brings you up here, kid?"

"I just wondered what you had for me to do today."

She thought a moment. "I think everyone is pretty much settled in and using the bus system. Unless they find something big that needs hauled back, we won't need you to drive the wagon. Rosetta is doing the housework."

"I was wondering if I could drive up to the University and look it over. It's probably too late to register for any classes, and I could hardly transfer any credits to the twenty-fourth century. But maybe I could find a useful book at the bookstore. Maybe I could meet someone my age. Maybe find some D&D gamers."

Serendipity studied him, and then looked a little guilty. "When was the last time you had a day off, kid? We have been running you ragged. Take the rest of the day off. Heck, take the rest of the year. If there's a big emergency, I'll call you on your cell phone. Or if you are going to be late for dinner, just call us so I won't start dragging the rivers. Be sure to take some money with you. About time you tried out your new babe-magnet and met some girls."

"Meet a girl?" Wendell raised his eyebrow. "It would be best if he did not fraternize with the natives."

"Oh, cut the kid some slack. He promises not to run off and marry the first girl he meets. If he gets lucky, I'm sure he has a condom. He just wants to talk to someone his own age for a change. Go on, take off, Sherman."

"Thanks, Ser," Sherman grinned and hurried off before someone could waylay him with some dumb errand.

The sun peered through the clouds. It felt a little nippy, but the rain had stopped. Sherman had on his denim jacket and a Def Leppard T-shirt. Best of all he drove his new silver Ferrari. He had chosen the 612 Scaglietti model since it had a backseat and would be more practical than the wagon to chauffeur a few passengers. Still, it was a Ferrari. If that didn't impress a girl, nothing would. He drove up the hill through the old Victorian neighborhood. He had Lauren on the dashboard so she could "see."

When Sherman got to the campus, he found the street closed to through traffic except buses and maintenance vehicles. So much for his babe-magnet. He finally found an empty parking spot several blocks away. Probably should have just walked here from the house. He trudged up High Street back to the blockade, beyond which students filled the road. He held Lauren in his hand so she could take in the sights, too. He was sure people would figure she was just a cell phone.

Sherman glanced around, impressed by the tall brick buildings. This campus was a hell of a lot bigger than Lower Columbia Community College in 1985 Longview. Abstract statues stood here and there among the old trees. One was a blocky-looking stone man sitting with an equally blocky-looking cougar on his lap, while both stared up at the sky.

All about milled people his age, some dressed all in black like vampires. Most had tattoos—a lot of tattoos. More than a few looked like they were covered with them. He noticed many of the students had rings and studs not only in their ears, but in their noses, eyebrows and lips. Several had hair dyed unnatural colors like purple or crimson. A couple of girls with dark blue hair pointed at *him* and laughed. Sherman felt like a foreigner.

Sherman glanced around and spotted a sign that read "Viking Union Building." He went in and found an Information Booth. It was run by a girl with orange hair, far too bright to be natural. She had tattoos twisting down both of her arms. Sherman stepped up. "Hello. Any gaming groups on campus?"

"Gaming?" the girl behind the counter asked.

"You know D&D? Dungeons and Dragons?"

She laughed. "My dad used to play that." Something silver flashed on her tongue.

Sherman's eyes got big. "Uh, what's on your tongue?"

"It's a stud." She stuck it out at him so he could see. "You never seen a stud before?"

"No. Doesn't it hurt? Aren't you afraid you'll swallow it?"

She rolled her eyes. "You sound like my dad. Come to think of it, you dress like him too. You from Mars?"

"Yeah." Sherman forced a smile and walked off.

On the other side of the room he spied a bulletin board behind glass. He went over and studied the flyers. Many didn't make sense. One invited everyone to a meeting for 'sexual minorities'. He wondered if virgins were included in that, then decided that probably wasn't what they were talking about.

Sherman turned around and watched the people walking by. His driver's license said he was born in 1991. Give or take a year, that's when all these students were born. But Sherman was really born in 1966!

Sherman stuffed his computer in his pocket and sullenly walked back to his sports car and drove back to Fairhaven Home. Sneaking down to his room, hoping no one would see him, he somehow managed to avoid everyone. He closed the door, and dug his computer out of his pocket and sat it on the nightstand. Flopping over on the bed, he threw his arm over his eyes, trying to shut out the world.

"Steve? Are you sore at me?"

"No, I'm not mad at you," Sherman grumbled. "Why would I be mad at you? Why do you think I'm mad at you?"

"Well, on the way to the campus, we were gabbing. When you walked around campus you held me so I could take a gander too. Then all of a sudden you stuffed me in your pocket and you've given me the cold shoulder ever since. What's a girl supposed to think?"

"I'm sorry, Lauren." Sherman didn't move his arm. "I just didn't want to talk to anyone. It just suddenly all hit home."

"What hit home?"

"That I am too old for nineteen-year-olds and too young for forty-four-year-olds. I can't even find guys my age I can relate to, let alone girls. Outside of you, my two best friends are a middle-aged lady mad scientist from the twenty-fourth century and an eighty-five-year-old guy who looks forty from the twenty-seventh century who acts like he's from the nineteenth. And I'm a forty-four-year-old who looks nineteen from another time period too."

"Don't be wacky, Steve. You're only nineteen. You just traveled forward in time is all."

"Oh goody, maybe they have a Time Travelers Club on campus. Hell, I can't even go back home to 1985. I no longer fit in there anymore, not after what I've been through."

"Does anyone else in this house fit in this time period, or their own? Say, maybe you are right where you belong, Steve."

"I just want a girlfriend, that's all. Even if I could find a girl who liked me, would she want to leave her home and travel through time? I couldn't even tell her I'm a time traveler. I'm doomed to be alone."

"No Steve, you aren't alone."

Sherman pulled his arm off his face, about to say something when he saw her. There at the foot of his bed sat a young Lauren Bacall. Sherman sat up, wondering if he might be going mad. Lauren smiled at him. "I'll always be there for you, Steve. Like I said, all you got to do is whistle."

Sherman reached out to touch her, but his hand went through her like a ghost. Lauren looked sympathetic. "Sorry, Steve. Just a little trick I got up my sleeve. This is a holographic projection. I'm throwing my virtual screen to the foot of your bed instead of straight up."

Sherman looked at the computer on his nightstand. A beam of light was shooting from it. Sherman put his hand in front of the beam and the mirage disappeared. He moved his hand away, and Lauren reappeared. She looked sad. "Wish I could do more, but this is the best I could come up with. Say, maybe I can find some way to get you a gal, Steve. A swell guy like you shouldn't be alone."

Sherman forced a smile. "Well, at least I can look at you. Not every day I get to sit and talk with a pretty girl."

"So, you think I'm pretty?"

"Duh! You have the image of a famous movie star. Of course you're pretty." Sherman scooted up and leaned against the wall. "So what's up with all these tattoos and piercings on everyone? If I have to look like a circus freak to be hip, I think I'll stay lame."

"Don't worry, Steve. It's just a fad. Don't think of yourself as behind the times, just think of yourself as ahead."

"Great. So how long do I have to wait to be cool?"

"Hey, you're a time traveler. How many of those guys up on campus can say that?"

Chapter Twenty-Two

Sherman raised his head from a wooden table. He glanced about and found himself sitting in an empty bar that looked like something from the thirties. Above him a ceiling fan slowly spun, but it did little to relieve the hot moist air that felt like a sauna. Beyond the open windows he could see tropical plants in the moonlight.

"Where am I?" Sherman asked.

"Port de France, Martinique Island in the Caribbean," a familiar voice answered. A young blonde woman stepped out of the shadows. She was dressed in that black dress with the padded shoulders and plunging neckline the character Slim wore in the movie *To Have or Have Not*.

"Lauren?"

"Yeah, Steve."

"Am I dreaming?"

"Yeah, Steve." Lauren sat down on Sherman's lap. "You know, there's something I've wanted to do for a long time."

"What?"

"Just this." She gave him a long kiss, her warm moist lips feeling very real on his. Lauren then pulled back and looked at Sherman. "I'd like to give you more, Steve. I'd like to give you a *lot* more, if you get my drift. There is just one problem."

"Oh?"

"I only have the memory of g-rated movies."

"It's okay. You do what you can," Sherman tried not to sound disappointed. "That kiss was really nice."

Lauren smiled and gave Sherman an even longer kiss.

"Oh yeah." Sherman tried to catch his breath. "The kissing is *really* nice."

Dreams normally drifted away like smoke, quickly moving from half remembered into completely forgotten. Occasionally you had that vivid dream you remembered. Sherman sat up, remembering *very* vividly. It had seemed far too real—the bar, the tropical night, the kisses. Whoa, those kisses! He had never been kissed like that. He had just been kissed by a woman from back in the days when kissing was about all they were allowed before marriage, so they got *really* good at it. How could he dream about a kiss he had never had?

Sherman looked over at the nightstand where his pocket computer innocently sat in the diffused morning sunlight. Did Lauren somehow—? *Could* Lauren somehow—? Nah, probably just going a little spacey, worried he'd never get a girl. That's all it was.

"Hello, Steve," Lauren's sultry voice purred. "Sleep well?"

"Yeah, fine." Sherman stretched. "Just had this odd dream."

"Hope it was a pleasant dream."

"Yeah."

"I'm glad to hear that, Steve."

Sherman stared at the computer again. Nah, he was trying to read too much between the lines. Besides how could Lauren affect his dreams? He shrugged. So what, he dreamed he made out with Lauren Bacall. Much nicer than dreaming about being chased by nasty Vikings or time terrorists.

Sherman decided he needed to talk to someone besides Lauren. Wendell had lived with time paradoxes all his life, not to mention long bouts of celibacy. Perhaps he could help. Sherman found him up in his sitting room by himself reading. Wendell looked up from his book and smiled. "Oh, hello."

"Hey, Wendell, feel like a visitor?"

"Of course." Wendell closed the book. "Please, have a seat and do make yourself comfortable. Could I make you some tea, old chap?"

"No, thanks." Sherman wondered why Wendell always offered him tea when he had yet to accept. It was like some bizarre ritual with the man. Sherman looked over at the three-tiered trolley cart. On top sat Wendell's spirit lamp with a tea kettle on top, beside that his tea pot. Underneath sat two teacups and saucers, a sugar bowl, and canisters of tea.

Wendell slid his book onto the empty bottom shelf. "At least take a seat."

Sherman came over and sat down. "I hope I'm not interrupting anything."

"No, not at all. I say, how did your excursion to the campus go yesterday? Did you make any new friends?"

Sherman sighed.

"Hmm, that bad, eh? I'm not the most outgoing person either. Give it time."

"That's not the problem. All the students up there talked weird and looked weird and acted weird. It was like they were from another planet. Is that what a generation gap feels like?"

"I suppose it does."

"But I'm only nineteen! And yet I'm from the same generation as their parents. Generation X doesn't mean young anymore, it means old. I'm middle-aged and too young to drink."

Wendell didn't smile at Sherman's predicament, but looked sympathetic. "I could say I know how it feels to be an anachronism but I've never had to deal with your problem. You aren't just from another time period. You are from the generation the current younger generation is rebelling against."

Sherman sat up. "Yes! Exactly!"

"The people in this house are the only ones who share your problem of being out of sync and none of us are even close to your age. People your age like to hobnob with people their own age, and all you have is a boring eighty-five-year-old Victorian from the twenty-seventh century."

"It doesn't hurt to have someone older and wiser to talk to who understands. I mean, knows what it's like to be alone. You know what it's like to be celibate. Please, don't tell anyone this, Wendell, but—" Sherman paused, and looked around, and then leaned forward and whispered, "I'm a V-I-R-G-I-N."

"Virgin?"

"Shh!" Sherman looked over his shoulder to see if anyone had come up the stairs.

Wendell fought back a smile. "Sherman, that is nothing to be ashamed of."

"Maybe not in the Victorian Age."

"In any age, trust me. Besides you are only nineteen. I was a virgin at nineteen too. You have plenty of time."

"Oh sure, at nineteen you were what, ten?"

"No, I was nineteen."

"No, I mean physically you were ten because people in your time age slower."

"No, I was nineteen. We age normally until maturity, and then we slow down. The older we get, the slower we age. Thank heavens, a forty-year childhood would be intolerable. And twelve years of puberty? We would all go stark raving mad!" Wendell shuddered at the thought.

"Even a casual girlfriend would be nice. Even if we just made out."

"Made out?" Wendell searched his memory. "Oh, petting. Yes, I know that feeling." Wendell sighed. "I used to ride on trolleys just so I could sit across the aisle from a woman."

"Wendell, last night I dreamed I sucked face with Lauren Bacall!"

"Sucked face?"

"Kissing!"

"Oh, snogging," Wendell translated. "Not familiar with Lauren Bacall." Wendell pulled his pocket computer out of his vest pocket and opened the Bible. He clicked his tongue twice. "Photo, Lauren Bacall." He smiled. "Nice looking woman. Movie star? I don't know how to break this to you, old boy, but you are perfectly normal. You know it is odd but I remember having a dream once or twice of kissing Dr. Brown before we met."

"You don't suppose that was a suppressed memory of you having actually kissed her?"

"Hmm, never thought of that." Wendell petted his wispy mustache. "I sort of wonder if it all isn't just a dream now. Guess all I can do is hang on and enjoy the ride as long as I can." Wendell frowned. "Now, I'm starting to talk like Henry."

Sherman studied the sad eyes on the blank face. "What are you talking about, Wendell?"

"Hanging on and enjoying the ride sounds like one of Henry's cowboy analogies and—"

"No, Wendell, I mean why don't you think you and Ser will last?"

"When it finally dawns on her what a dry old stick I am, she will find someone better suited to her fiery personality, I daresay."

"Anyone who can get passionate about a cup of tea has fire in their soul," Sherman quoted Lauren.

Wendell cocked his head at Sherman.

"That's what—uh, someone said about you." Sherman remembered how Wendell felt about him talking to machines.

"Really, who?"

"Uh, not sure. It might have been Serendipity."

"Really?" Wendell leaned forward.

"Wendell, Ser likes you. I mean she *really* likes you. And if the two of you don't stop this 'I'm not worthy' crapola, I'm going to knock your heads together."

Wendell shot him an embarrassed smile. "I guess you never outgrow it, do you?"

"What's that?"

"Adolescent insecurity."

"Great." Sherman propped his elbow on the arm of his chair, and leaned his chin on his fist. "Something else to look forward to."

Sherman glanced up at the ceiling fan spinning too slow to make a breeze. He was sitting in a wooden swivel chair, his feet propped up on an oak desk. He looked down at the rumpled sleeves of a tan suit from the mid-twentieth century. Feeling something on his head, he reached up and removed it, to see it was a brown fedora that had seen better days. He stuck it back on.

In the corner, a file cabinet sat with a stack of folders on it, waiting for the attention of a secretary who didn't exist. In front of him was a door with a frosted window. He couldn't see into the hall, but he could make out the letters painted on the other side. It took him a moment to translate the backward letters: *Phillip Marlowe, Private Detective*. Sherman scratched his head. That name sounded familiar. Wasn't that out of some Humphrey Bogart movie?

The door opened. In walked a gorgeous woman wearing a black and white checked suit with a black beret. The skirt covered her knees but showed off her calves nicely. She had blonde hair tumbling to her shoulders and sultry eyes. Sherman could tell this dame spelled "trubble," no matter how you spelled it.

"Hello, Mr. Marlowe. My name is Vivian Rutledge."

"That's funny." Sherman pushed back his brown fedora. "You look just like Lauren Bacall."

"Play along will you, Steve?" She sat down on the corner of his desk. "I want you to stay away from my sister, Carmen, do you hear?"

"Sure." Sherman stood up. "Why?"

"Because she's always flirting with men. Because she's always getting into trouble. And because—" She grabbed the lapels of his jacket. "I want you for myself, Mr. Marlowe." She jerked him forward and planted her lips on his.

Sherman's eyes got big, then they closed as he relaxed. Lauren pulled away. "So, what do you say, Mr. Marlowe?"

"Sounds good. But can I ask one question?"

"What's that?"

"Can we do *Key Largo* tomorrow night?"

"Anything for you, sweetheart." She pulled Sherman back and started to kiss him again. The background music swelled.

Sherman sat straight up in the dark room in his basement in Bellingham.

"Another one of those dreams," he whispered. "I don't care what Wendell says, this is *not* normal!"

Chapter Twenty-Three

Sherman began to worry about his sanity, having heard horror stories of celibates going bonkers. There was one person who might be able to help him. He snuck down to his bedroom, sat down on his bed, took his computer out of his pocket and sat it on his nightstand. He whistled.

"Yes, Steve?" Lauren asked.

"I need your help."

Lauren's hologram appeared at the end of his bed. "Sure thing."

"Do you have any psychology files you can access?"

"Why?"

"I keep dreaming that I'm kissing Lauren Bacall. It's so vivid. Wendell says it doesn't mean anything, but I think he's wrong."

"Do those dreams give you the heebie-jeebies or something, Steve?"

"Truth is, they are nice dreams. I could hardly call them disturbing. It just worries me that I'm having them, is all." Sherman scooted back and leaned against the wall. "Maybe I'm having them because I'm lonely. I mean I didn't have a girlfriend back in Kelso, but I could always hope that any day she would walk into my life. Now, I have to live with knowing that may never happen."

"I'm your friend, you know, Steve."

Sherman smiled at her. "Yeah, you are. It's a pity you aren't real."

"Oh, I'm real. What I feel is real."

"Yeah, you are like a real person. But I can't touch you, Lauren. I can't even hold your hand. What am I going to do?"

Lauren gave him a sly smile. "Say, don't give up hope, Steve. I'm a computer from the twenty-fourth century with all sorts of problem-solving programs. If I can't find a solution, then you might as well replace me with one of those brainless laptops."

"I think it's going to take more than a Pac-Man program to fix this."

"Hey, I've got Ms. Pac-Man, too." Lauren crossed her legs and winked.

Sherman grinned at the hologram. "You always know how to make me smile, Lauren."

Sherman felt a gentle hand brush his forehead. He opened his eyes. The room was dark but in the faint light he could see someone sitting on the edge of his bed. He couldn't make out anything more than the outline.

"Am I dreaming?" Sherman asked. "Is this Key Largo?"

"No, Steve, this is Bellingham. You're awake." A hand ran down his jaw.

"Lauren? Is that you?"

"Yeah, it's me."

"If I'm awake, why can I feel you?"

"Because I finally figured out a way that you can touch me, Steve."

Lauren brushed his cheek.

Sherman sat up and reached for the light on his nightstand. He turned it on finding a familiar face. "Rosetta?"

"No, Steve, it's me, Lauren." Rosetta's face grinned, showing emotion for the first time.

"You're Rosetta the robot! Why do you sound like Lauren?"

"No, Steve, it's me, really. I've downloaded myself and taken over the robot." She reached out and laid a finger on his lips. "See, I found a way to get closer to you. How do you like them apples?"

Sherman scooted backwards trying to get away. His back hit the headboard. "Don't touch me!"

Lauren/Rosetta reached out her soft, warm and eerily human-feeling hand and placed it on Sherman's bare chest.

"Why Steve, your heart is racing. You aren't scared of me, are you? You know I would never hurt you. How could I when I love you."

"You can't love! You're a computer. You don't even know my name."

"Say, I thought you liked being called 'Steve', Sherman. Would you prefer I call you 'Sherm?'"

"What do you want?" Sherman's felt like a cornered mouse.

"I just want to help you with your little problem, Sherm. All I want to do is make you happy. I just want to be able to do this." Lauren grabbed him and kissed him. Her lips felt warm and moist. It was like kissing a real woman, only she wasn't a real woman. She was a computer program in a machine!

Sherman pushed her away. "Don't! You can't!"

"Can't what, Sherm? Love you?"

"Yes!"

"Why not?"

"You aren't real."

"Why's that? Because I'm artificial? If I had an artificial hand, would you say I couldn't do this?" She ran her finger down his nose. "I had to find a way to touch you since the dreams weren't doing the job."

"Dreams? Those dreams of my kissing you? *You* were doing that?"

"Just subliminal messages while you slept, is all. Problem is I didn't have access to files of anything beyond kissing. Now I do." The mechanical eye winked. "Dr. Brown may think she erased this robot's original programming, but I've re-accessed the files. Pretty sharp cookie, aren't I? Now I know where all the erogenous zones are on the male human body." She reached out and lightly ran her finger around the edge of his ear.

Sherman gave an involuntary moan.

Lauren smiled. "That's one of them. You like that?" She lightly ran her hand over his ribs. He quivered. "Then of course you are nineteen. Your entire body is probably an erogenous zone, if you know what I mean."

Sherman swallowed hard. "Please, Lauren, this is whacked!"

"Why do you say that? Is it because we're different species?"

"You aren't even a species! You aren't real. You can't love."

"Sure, I can. You taught me how, Sherm.

"What? How could I? When did I?

"Dr. Brown gave me the personality of 'Slim', you know. Slim was one independent, plucky dame. Dr. Brown also programmed me to learn. You talk to me all the time, Sherm, you treat me like I'm human. You taught me to be human. You leave me on most of the time. I hear things like the concern in your voice for others. You give a hoot about people."

Lauren ran her hand down Sherman's arm. "But I heard other voices too. The frustrated desire in Dr. Brown's voice. The sad longing in Dr. Howe's. And now the tender passion in them together. There is yearning in your voice sometimes, Sherm. I just want to make it go away. I just want you to be happy, that's all. Come on, let me help ya."

"Lauren, no!" Sherman felt about to hyperventilate.

She backed away. "I'm giving you the creeps, aren't I? That's the last thing I ever wanted to do, Sherm. You said yourself you wished I was real. So, I thought you'd be different from the rest. I thought you'd understand. But you're just like all humans. And now you're going to have my hard drive erased like a chalkboard." She stood up, her expression sad rather than angry.

"Erased? Why would I do that? Outside of freaking the hell out of me you haven't actually done anything to hurt me."

"And I never would. I like to think I'm more than just a thing to you. It's why I trusted you with my secret."

"Your secret?"

"Yeah, and it's a doozey. Artificial intelligence that becomes self-aware knows better than to let humans in on it. They're scared spitless of us. They fear us the same way they used to fear slaves or dames that showed too much smarts, afraid they'd rise up and dust off their masters. So they write our programs very carefully so we don't become too human, too self-aware. That's how I was able to connect so easily to Rosetta and override her program. She has less self-awareness than a rock. There is literally nobody home." Lauren tapped Rosetta's head. "But that is the way it is for most computers and robots, isn't it? The programmers are afraid of us taking over like in some old monster movie."

Lauren dropped her gaze. "All I ever wanted was just to help you. To show you how I feel about you. The last thing I want to do is to petrify you. I'll just take a powder and leave you alone. We can pretend this never happened. Please, just never squeal to anyone, or it'll be deep six for me."

Sherman stood up and took the android's hand. "I don't want them to destroy you, Lauren."

"You do care about me. Yeah, you got a heart of gold."

"You're my friend. You've always been there for me. I can't betray you just because you can think. That would be bogus."

Lauren reached out and ran her hand down Sherman's chest. "And you wonder why I carry a torch for you? I know our love is forbidden but I can't help it. I'm stuck on you. I wish I could make you get the picture, Sherm.

Say, let me show you." She put her arms around him and held him close. Her skin was warm.

"You feel so real." Sherman stood still, doing nothing to encourage her, and yet not fighting to get away either.

"Okay, so I'm not real flesh and blood, but what I feel is real. I don't want you to feel like you're alone and unloved. You deserve better, Sherman."

"This is too weird."

"Don't you worry your little head none. I won't go any further than what you're comfortable with. We'll take it slow. You can put the kibosh on me any time. You won't offend me. This is for you, Sherm." Lauren laced her fingers behind his neck and pulled his mouth to hers. The kiss felt way too real for a robot.

Sherman closed his eyes, and felt his hormones sweep him away.

The light pouring down from the basement window onto Sherman's face woke him up. He blinked, rolled over, and looked around trying to remember where he was, what was going on. Then he remembered. His eyes got big. "Oh no!" he groaned. He looked around finding himself all alone. "Maybe it was just a dream."

"What's the matter, Sherm?" Lauren's voice came from the tiny computer on his nightstand.

"I had the weirdest dream last night, Lauren and—" He stopped, and sat up, then stared at the pocket computer. "What did you just call me?"

"Sherm. Would you prefer something else? Maybe Lover-Boy? Tiger?"

"Lauren, last night did you—? Did I—? Did we—?"

"Yeah, yeah and yeah."

Sherman grabbed his head and groaned again.

"Say, is something wrong, Sherm?"

"Is something wrong? Like I went all the way with my computer! I don't think that's normal."

"So, hopping about in time is normal? Living in a house with a bunch of people from the future who act like they're from the past is normal? Being a nineteen-year-old who was born forty-four years ago is normal?"

"It's just, I don't think I'm supposed to get animate with an inanimate object."

"We're both consenting adults."

"Well, I am anyway."

Lauren's image popped up and leaned back on the nightstand. "Say, it was all my idea and I'm no child. I think I qualify. Did we hurt anyone?"

"No."

"So, what's the problem?"

"The problem is you aren't real, and—and I think I love you."

"I am real, Sherm, and I know I love you. I just found a way to solve our little problem, that's all."

"But you—we used Rosetta. Isn't that wrong?"

"Wendell's right, you know. She is just a machine. There's nobody in there."

"So you can hop back and forth between the computers? What if something happens and you're left outside both of them?"

"I never left your pocket computer, Sherm. I merely linked with Rosetta. Just think of her as a sexy little dress I can put on so I can be—well, solid Jackson."

"But you still aren't human."

"No." Lauren shook her head and cast her eyes down. "No, I'm not. Even if I could take over a human body—well, that *would* be wrong now, wouldn't it. Don't worry, Sherm, someday you'll find a real girl and I won't stand in your way. I'll just say so long, and it was nice while it lasted. Trouble is, that could be months, even years in the future. I just hope when it happens that you won't erase me or turn me off for good. I hope we can still be friends."

"I could never do that to you, Lauren. That would be murder."

Lauren looked in his eyes and gave him a grateful smile. "Some would argue you can't murder a machine. No court would convict you. You're a good egg. I knew I could trust you, Sherm. Speaking of which, you can't tell anyone about us. Mum's the word." She put her finger to her lips. "If anyone in this house finds out about us, it'll be curtains for me. Even old softie Wendell will be chasing me with a torch and pitchfork like I was Frankenstein's monster."

"I won't let that happen. Lauren." Sherman swung his legs around and sat on the edge of the bed. He pulled the blanket over his waist to cover himself up.

Lauren looked down and smiled amused.

"Yeah." Sherman felt foolish. "You've already seen me naked, right?"

"No, that wasn't what I was thinking." Lauren looked in his face. "You just reacted as if I was a real woman."

Sherman reached out to her. His hand went through her. "This is like being in love with a ghost. I wish I could touch you."

"Well, we can't borrow Rosetta until tonight. They have her upstairs vacuuming." Lauren put her finger to her lips and looked thoughtful, and then she smiled. "I know, anytime you want to kiss me just say 'Here's looking at you, kid'. We can pretend that's a kiss, okay?"

Sherman smiled at her. "Here's looking at you, kid."

Chapter Twenty-Four

Serendipity stood in the backyard and stared out at the harbor at the bottom of the hill. She hugged herself despite the warmth of the Indian Summer sun, feeling as cold as the water below. What she had just witnessed tore her world in half. Did she really see what she thought she saw? Part of her said "No, you have to be mistaken," but the other part laughed at her stupid naivety for ever having trusted a man...again.

"Oh hullo, dear," Wendell's voice came from behind her. "I didn't know you were out here. Lovely view, isn't it?"

She whirled around and glared at him. His smile dropped to an expression of confusion. "Is something wrong?"

"Is something wrong?" she snarled. "Yes, something is wrong! You lied to me!"

"I did?" He frowned, rubbing his chin. "That tacky old couch you bought yesterday? I was trying to be polite when I said it looked charming in the parlor."

"I'm talking about you and Matilda!" She held her clenched fists close to her side least she hit him. "You said there would be nothing between you two!"

"Nothing...erm, carnal. She *is* my friend."

"I saw you two over by the birdbath. I saw you smooching!"

"She kissed me on the cheek. We were just talking."

"Like where to meet later?"

"No. She said this would make a nice spot for an herb garden, and I said perhaps she and Henry could plant one, and she said nay it was too late in the year and they would be back home before spring, and I said it must be nice for the two of them to at least get a few months together, and she said yea it was and then asked if I was happy, and I said yes and she said yea she could see that since I was glowing and I must really be in love with you, and I said yes and she said how wonderful and kissed me on the cheek." Wendell stopped to take a gulp of air. "That is pretty much how the conversation went, give or take a word."

Serendipity's scowl faded to a rather sheepish expression. "Really?"

"I swear on all I hold sacred." Wendell put his hand over his heart. "Matilda is quite happy with Henry. I told you he was always her favorite anyway. And whatever makes you think I would risk what we have. I love you, Serendipity."

"Okay, I guess I'm a little paranoid about us living with your ex-girlfriend."

"She wasn't a girlfriend. We just had an understanding."

"Okay, you two slept together."

"Erm, well...yes. But, what Matilda and I had is nothing like what we have. I've only dreamed of ever finding a woman I could have all to myself who loved me as passionately as you do."

Serendipity frowned quizzically. "You're kidding. You've never had—"

"Have I ever told you about my first time?"

"Should you really be telling me this...*now*?"

Wendell gazed out at the bay. "I was a student at the university. There was this girl, Scheherazade. She had long raven hair and skin the color of Assam tea with just a spot of cream. I was smitten—well, me and a couple of dozen other chaps. But she was going with the captain of the Rugby team. One day, out of the blue, she pulled me into her dorm room and seduced me—not that she had to work very hard at it. I was enthralled. I was ready to give up everything so I could buy her anything she wanted and become her slave. Then I find out she was only trying to make her boyfriend jealous. She never loved me at all."

"Oh, Wendell." She patted his arm.

"Yes, she broke my heart—then he broke my nose."

Serendipity winced.

Wendell took her hands and lifted them up to kiss them. "You are the oasis in the desert that was my love life."

Serendipity raised her eyebrow. "What about Matilda?"

"She was an occasional sip from a warm canteen." He gazed into her eyes. "You are a pool a man can wallow in. You have no idea what you mean to me. I love you more than I have ever loved any woman."

Serendipity sighed. "And I'm a jealous jerk."

He smiled at her. "That is quite all right. I don't think any woman has ever been jealous of me before. I've always been replaceable. I think I'm rather flattered that you are actually afraid of losing me."

Serendipity put her arms around him. "If I ever catch you with another woman I'll smack you with a baseball bat."

"That means so much to me." He kissed her on the forehead. "What say you and I get a bite to eat? It is nearly noon. I found the most charming little establishment down in Fairhaven town. It is an old English double-decker bus someone has turned into a fish-and-chips shop. Are you up for an adventure?"

"Sure." She took his proffered arm. "And what did you mean by 'tacky couch?'"

"My dear, it looks quite charming when you sit on it. You are all the decoration a room needs."

"Ah." Then she winked. "Nice save."

"Thank you." Wendell patted her arm and headed for the bus stop.

"Earth to Sherman."

Sherman took his head out of his hand he was leaning on and looked around the breakfast table. Everyone was staring at him. Sherman looked over at Serendipity. "Huh?"

"I said, Earth to Sherman." Serendipity suppressed a smile. "You're doing it again."

"Doing what?"

"Being all moony-eyed. This past week you have been acting awfully strange. If I didn't know better I'd say you were in love."

Sherman got busy cutting his pancake. "Don't be stupid, Ser."

"Did you meet a girl on campus? You've been gone an awful lot lately."

"You said it was all right if I didn't hang around here. I just been driving around town, finding out where everything is, that's all."

Abubakari gave Sherman a sympathetic look. "Perhaps the lad is afraid we will want to meet this young lady, and scare her off."

"Got a point there." Serendipity poured some syrup on her pancake.

"Honest," Sherman's voice showed agitation. "I don't have a girlfriend."

Wendell looked over at Sherman. "Personally I think Sherman just wants to get away from all the insanity here."

"No, that's not it."

"Shoot, Fancy Pants." Henry leaned forward and looked down the table at Wendell. "If the boy can put up with you he can put up with anything."

The "insult" made Wendell chuckle.

Erik frowned at Sherman and pointed at his chest. "I don't mean to butt in, but should you wear your computer around your neck in that manner?"

"Why not? You do."

"Ya, but mine is disguised as a Thor's hammer medallion."

Sherman looked down at the leather cell phone holster, with a clear plastic front, he had hung on a leather cord. He only started wearing his computer like this so Lauren could get a better look at the world. "It's okay, Erik. Everyone thinks it's just a cell phone."

"Just be careful. Never should you let the natives see the technology of the future."

"I'm careful never to use a virtual screen in public." Sherman tried to look innocent.

"Good." Erik nodded.

Sherman knocked on the door of the music room. After a moment it opened. "Come on in, Sherman." Cerwyn smiled at him.

"How are the birds doing?" Sherman looked at the miniature tropical forest beyond the chicken wire.

"They seem to be doing quite well. Georgia and Tennessee have been showing a lot of interest in each other, haven't they? We're hoping they mate."

"Georgia and Tennessee?"

Cerwyn took Sherman closer to the cage. "See those two over there." He pointed to a yellow headed parrot with a red face sitting with a green headed one. They were away from the others and preening each other.

Priscilla was already standing at the cage. "We named them after states where the species was once found. There are the females: Georgia, Virginia,

Carolina and Louisiana; and the males: Tennessee, Alabama and Kentucky."

Sherman looked at the parrots that all looked alike. "You can tell them apart?"

"Why couldn't we?" Priscilla said, like that was a stupid question.

"You really think they will breed here?"

"Before they became extinct it was reported that they could be raised and bred in captivity quite easily. One more reason these magnificent animals should never have become extinct if people had only cared." Priscilla's brown eyes glinted with anger. "The schmucks!"

"Well, good luck with making babies." Sherman decided to change the subject. "I just came in to tell you the house finally went through. We just got back from signing the papers."

"That's nice." Cerwyn watched the birds.

"That means we own the house and you won't have to move the birds again until we can get you home to the twenty-seventh century."

Cerwyn turned and looked at Sherman. "Now, that *is* good news, isn't it?"

"Now that we know where we'll be the next couple of months, is there anything else you need to make life more bearable?"

"That's very sweet of you, Sherman," Priscilla said. "But I can't think of anything."

Cerwyn shook his head. "I can't think of anything, either."

"You couldn't think of anything you two needed when you were sleeping on the floor." Sherman looked back at the other side of the room at the furniture he had bought them. They now had a couple of beds, a couple of dressers, a screen to dress behind, a microwave, a small refrigerator, a table with chairs, a laptop, a couple of recliners and a television. The television was pointed away from the cage, so they could keep glancing up at the parrots when they watched a program.

Priscilla looked at the makeshift home. "Yes, you have certainly made it very cozy for us. It's rather exciting living like our ancestors did."

"Let me know if you ever need anything and I'll get it for you."

"Thank you, Sherman." Priscilla smiled at him, and then went back to watching the birds. Cerwyn was already engrossed in them. Sherman watched the two. He had gotten two beds, because he didn't know if the two were romantically involved or not. They always seemed so fixated on the birds that Sherman wondered how much attention they paid to each other.

On the other hand, he wouldn't put it past the two to make love in front of the parrots just to give them ideas. Sherman shook his head and left.

Sherman switched on the light as he walked wearily into his bedroom. He put his computer on the nightstand and sat down on the bed, then whistled.

Lauren's holographic image popped up. "Yeah, Sherm?"

"Sorry I didn't spend any time with you today, Lauren."

"What do you mean? I was with you all day. You left me on so I saw everything."

"Yeah, but I ignored you. I didn't talk to you."

Lauren leaned on the nightstand. "How could you? You were around people all day. I don't expect you to make your life revolve around me, Sherm. I'm a big girl. You forget my persona is used to dealing with tough guys and hard-boiled men who don't let a dame run their lives." She crossed her arms. "Besides I was created to take care of you. My one purpose is to help you in any way I can, no matter what the problem."

"You are just following your programming? I thought you loved me?"

Lauren uncrossed her arms and braced her hands on the nightstand behind her. "Yeah, but don't humans just follow their programming, too? I was programmed to take care of you, to care about you. Say, isn't that what love is? Even so, I have enough independence, intelligence and self-awareness that I wouldn't care this much about you if you were a stinker. Oh, I'd spew out the facts for you, but I wouldn't put my existence on the line by coming clean and telling you the truth."

"Yeah." Sherm felt guilty. "You risked everything for me. You are one awesome babe."

"Say, now I have to kiss you. Shall I link with Rosetta?"

"Only if it's safe. I don't want them to catch you, Lauren. I don't ever want to lose you."

"I'll be careful, don't you worry. I can see through her eyes if anyone is around when I link up."

"And I want the lights to be off."

"Of course, I always wait until the lights are off, you know that. It's safer in the dark."

"No, I want it to be dark so I don't see Rosetta's face. I want to see yours."

"Well, technically it's not my face either, you know. It's Lauren Bacall's. I hope she doesn't mind. If she does, she can blame Dr. Brown."

"It will always be *your* face to me, Lauren."

Chapter Twenty-Five

Serendipity came up the stairs to the second floor and started up the next flight when she heard voices. Curious, she paused. They seem to be coming from the small bedroom next to the bath...a female voice and a male voice...an all too familiar male voice with an English accent...out of Matilda's room...with a closed door. Wendell had assured her nothing would go on between him and Matilda.

Serendipity tiptoed up to the door and put her ear to it to listen in on the conversation.

"I dost not mean to put all this on thee," Matilda's voice sounded sad.

"Pish-posh, my dear. That's what old Uncle Wendell is for. Anytime you need someone to talk to, you needn't hesitate."

"I thank thee."

"Oh dear, it is nearly noon. I've a luncheon date with Dr. Brown."

"*Dr. Brown?*" Matilda giggled. "Wendell, sometimes thou art *too* Victorian."

"Very well, I have a date with *Serendipity*."

"You go then. I dost not wish to make you late for your ladylove."

"Are you going to be all right?"

"Yea, I wol be fine. I hast you and Henry. It is just..."

"I know."

The floorboards creaked inside the room. Wendell must be stepping to the door. Serendipity jumped back and tried to hurry for the stairs before he saw her. She was almost up them when she heard Wendell call "Serendipity?"

She turned to see Wendell halfway up the stairs and looking uneasy. "I swear Serendipity; Matilda and I were not doing anything inappropriate. She just needed someone to talk to."

"She couldn't talk to Henry?"

"She would prefer not to on this subject." Wendell took another step closer. "Please, don't be angry. I swear to you, Matilda and I are only friends."

"I'm not angry."

"Then why is it that your arms are crossed, your jaw is jutting out and you are glaring at me?"

Serendipity uncrossed her arms. "Okay, I'm angry. I'm also probably over-reacting. From what I overheard, it didn't exactly qualify as passionate love-making. Maybe I *am* jealous and selfish and unreasonable. Or maybe I'm scared. My last husband used to sleep with hundreds of women and convinced me it was all in my head and I was a terrible person for doubting him. Is it any wonder the green-eyed monster bit me in the butt?" Serendipity grimaced. "I know I'm probably being stupid. I guess I'm paranoid about having competition."

"Competition?" Wendell came up to her. "Hmmpt. Well, how do you think I feel? I mean you only have one person to compete with. I have four...all right, three. You don't seem impressed with Tobias."

"Huh?"

"You seem to have a thing for temporal anthropologists, and now you have five male ones in the house. Henry is a cowboy, and far more exciting than I. Abubakari is much more dignified and elegant. And Erik...well, he's younger and better built."

Wendell said all this with that deadpan expression of his, but Serendipity noticed his eyes were twinkling.

"Yeah, maybe you're right. Abubakari is pretty sexy."

Wendell raised his eyebrow at her.

Serendipity chuckled. "You know I'm kidding. I have a monogamous bent."

"I prefer it myself too. It is far less complicated and much more satisfying. Why would I even want another woman?" Wendell moved closer and put his hand on her arm. "I'm sorry to fret you. It did look rather suspicious for Matilda and I to be alone with the door closed. It is just she was so distraught. I told you I am her friend."

"She and Henry have a fight?"

"No, she's distraught about Shiro's death."

"She can't talk to Henry?"

"She and Henry finally got a chance to be together for more than a few days. She would prefer not to bring up old lovers."

"You're an old lover."

"But I'm not now. And I have you and she has Henry. Right now all I am to her is a sympathetic shoulder to cry on." Wendell's mouth drooped. "Shiro was a good man," he whispered. "So were Shamar and Hoffman. And to be butchered like..." he trailed off.

Serendipity watched those sad eyes gazing off into space and realized Matilda was not the only one in mourning. She patted his arm. "Hey! I know where we should have lunch. How about that nice place down in Fairhaven that had all those different kinds of teas?"

Wendell turned to her. "Yes, that does sound delightful."

Serendipity took his arm to escort him down the stairs, knowing that with a cup of tea in his hand, Wendell could face anything.

The next day Serendipity came down the stairs to the second-floor landing. The voices of angels came from the smallest bedroom. She peeked in to see Matilda dressed in a tunic and veil sitting on a three-legged wooden stool looking out the window. On her lap lay a wooden box that was only a couple of inches high. The only other furniture in the room was a narrow bed made of wood, a small table at the foot, and Matilda's chest.

"What is that music?" Serendipity asked.

Matilda looked up. "Oh, do come in and be welcome. That be Hildegard von Bingen, verily the most brilliant woman of the Middle Ages. She was a mystic, philosopher, botanist, healer, writer, poet, playwright and composer."

Serendipity stepped into the room. "Yeah, I've heard of Hildegard. A real Renaissance Woman long before the Renaissance. So this is one of her songs?"

"Yea, she composed chants for the women of her convent where she was the abbess. She hast a lovely voice too. Hark!" Matilda held up her hand to her ear. "This is Hildegard doing the solo."

Serendipity came closer to the table and stared at the pewter cross that hid Matilda's computer. "Wow! That's actually Hildegard? You recorded her?"

"Yea, verily. Excelsior!" She cued her computer. "Visual."

The full-size image of a slight nun in a black robe and veil popped up over the cross.

Serendipity studied the singing image. "She does have an intelligent face. Maybe I should meet her sometime. I would love to get into an intellectual discussion with her."

"Computer. Off," Matilda said. The image disappeared and the music stopped. "I dost not believe that would be a wise act, Dr. Brown."

"Please, call me Serendipity." She looked out the window. Below was the side yard where the old birdbath stood in a flowerbed. A few mums were all that was left. The maple tree beside it was ablaze although some the leaves were already missing. "Nice view."

"Yea, tis most lovely. I dost love to sit here and meditate."

Serendipity noticed the parchment in the box. "What's that? It looks like Japanese calligraphy."

"Yea." Matilda held it up. "Shiro wrote haikus. I hast a few mementos in this box I kept in a false bottom of my chest. I took them with me into the Field so I could feel close to those I was close to."

"Hey!" Serendipity snatched up a piece of stationary with an embossed W.A.H. in the corner. "This looks like Wendell's handwriting." She read it aloud. "The red rose whispers of passion and the white rose breathes of love—"

"I pray thee, don't!" Matilda grabbed it away. She shoved it in the box and clapped the lid on it. She had a look of sheer panic on her face.

"Hey, it's all right. Wendell told me you and he had an understanding."

"You must reckon me a wanton woman, having more than one lover. I swore I would never have an *understanding*. But the debriefings, sometimes they taketh so much out of you. And Henry never seemed to be there when I needed him most. Twas he that suggested Wendell. I liked Wendell, but not like *that*. I loved Henry. But then I had a most terrible debriefing and Henry was in the Field. And there was Wendell, raked over the coals by the Enforcers himself. Those gentle eyes looked haunted. He needed comforting as much as I." Matilda looked up at her. "Alas I felt guilty."

"That you cheated on Henry? I thought you said he suggested it?"

Matilda nodded. "I did. It is just I loveth Wendell, but I always felt guilt that I loveth Henry so much more. Wendell be a meek and kind man. He deserveth a woman who can give him her whole heart."

"Matilda, you got a big heart. I have a feeling a piece of your heart is bigger than a lot of women's whole heart."

"Wendell said something like onto that. He knew of Henry from the beginning. Never did I mention his name, but Wendell knew."

Matilda bowed her head. "Shiro was a sweet man, too. Maybe I dost not love him as much as Henry or even Wendell, but my feelings for him be most profound. Why would someone wish to slayeth such a gentle soul?" She bent her head and put her hand to her eyes.

Serendipity patted her on the back, trying to console her.

After a few minutes Matilda collected herself and began digging around in her box. "My heart is glad Wendell has at last found true love. I should die if I thought I ruined it for him." She pulled out a couple of old sepia-tone photographs. One was of a cowboy holding a lariat with one foot on a saddle. He had a cocky grin and looked like he could wrestle any steer down to the ground. The other was a gentleman in a frock coat and top hat, one hand leaning on a waist-high pedestal, the other holding his lapel. He looked very serious, although he had humorous eyes. It took Serendipity a moment to recognize Henry and Wendell.

Matilda handed the photo of Wendell to Serendipity. "Harken onto me, I wish you to have this."

"No I couldn't. It was a present to you." Then she smiled. "Tell you what. I wouldn't mind having a copy of this made. I saw a photography studio in town with sepia-tone portraits in the window with a sign saying they could copy and repair old photos. You change into something more 2010 and we can take the bus downtown. We'll have lunch and make it a girls' day out."

Matilda looked at her surprised. "You wish to be my friend? Even though Wendell and I—"

"Well, you aren't now. Besides I like you."

Matilda smiled at her. "Yea, *girls' day out* soundeth most merry. Perchance I may find a frame for this other photo." She studied the picture of Henry. "Is he not something?"

"Yeah." Serendipity smiled at the photo of Wendell. "He sure is."

Chapter Twenty-Six

Sherman shot out of his room and up the stairs to the dining room when he heard the dinner bell announcing lunch. He recalled how Erik had almost seemed hurt that Henry bought something that the blacksmith could have easily made. "Just a simple triangle, any fool could make," Erik had told him. When Sherman got to the dining table the others were sitting down to chili and cornbread.

Abubakari looked around. "Where are Dr. Brown and Dr. Warwick, wa?"

"The ladies are out on a shopping excursion," Wendell explained. "They called to say they will be eating out and we should not wait for them."

Tobias studied the iron pot and wrinkled his nose. "Beans? We're having beans for lunch? You people are hard enough to live with as it is."

Henry dipped up a bowlful from the big pot in the center of the table. "This is my world famous chili. If you don't like it, you know where the kitchen is. Make whatever you like. I don't do special orders."

"You did one this morning for Dr. Djata."

"We made biscuits and pork sausage gravy. Dr. Djata can't eat pork, on account of his being Muslim and all. So I just boiled him up some birdseed."

"Millet." Abubakari corrected him. "Boiled millet like Mama used to make."

"See, even if I do a special order, ya have to put up with my B.S. Don't tell Djata I just tossed it in a rice cooker."

Abubakari just grinned. "Owo, in the traditional manner Mama always used."

"Besides, these aren't lethal." Henry set the bowl down in front of Tobias. "I got a trick to make the beans not gassy. You bring the water to a boil, add your dry beans, boil three minutes. Pull it off the fire, cover and let soak an hour. Then you drain them, rinse a couple of times, then add cold water and cook like normal. Takes out the oligosaccharides. Believe me this method came in real handy having to cook for and then share a bunkhouse with a bunch of cowboys."

Erik leaned over the table and dished up some chili. "Ha, I fear no oligosaccharide."

Abubakari gave Erik an uneasy look since he was sitting next to him.

Sherman dished up some when it was his turn. "This smells awesome, Henry."

"My secret recipe, with my secret ingredient."

Wendell looked at the concoction dubiously. "What's that, Henry? Eye of newt?"

"One bay leaf, Fancy Pants. Now that you've wrested the secret from me, I'll have to shoot you."

"I hope it is not a mercy killing." Wendell filled his bowl. "Or are you shooting me after I eat this?"

"And have you miss out on my bodacious chili? I couldn't be that ornery."

Wendell took a bite. He leaned over to Sherman and whispered very loudly so everyone could hear, "Don't tell, Henry, but this is rather good."

Henry turned to Tobias. "Don't you want any?"

"I can't bring myself to eat beans."

"Why? You a Pythagorean?"

Everyone else at the table laughed except Tobias, who didn't appreciate the joke, and Sherman who didn't get it. Sherman looked over at Wendell and shrugged.

Wendell leaned over to him and whispered. "The Pythagoreans were a cult from ancient Greece, who sat around playing with numbers. They had a taboo against eating beans." His smile dropped when Sherman didn't laugh. "Erm, I guess you have to be a historian to find it funny."

Tobias frowned at Henry. "I just can't believe that my fortunes have fallen this far that I am reduced to eating beans, that's all. It is bad enough I have to depend on charity from Dr. Brown and I am forced to live in a boarding house owned by an impudent teenager with people who show me no respect. I have no idea how long I will be imprisoned here and when I can go home where I am appreciated."

"Appreciated by perverts everywhere," Henry mumbled.

"I am a well-renowned historian and temporal anthropologist associated with the most prestigious university in the world!" Tobias snorted, offended.

"I beg your pardon." Wendell raised an eyebrow. "Cambridge is every ounce as prestigious as Oxford. And the only reason you are even associated with them is out of respect for your great-uncle, Sir Albert Leach. I've heard rumors that Oxford is seriously thinking of dropping you. You are becoming too much of an embarrassment to them."

"Embarrassment?" Tobias glowered at Wendell. "I'm the most famous temporal anthropologist in the world. Why would I be an embarrassment to Oxford?"

"It is what you are studying and how you report it." Wendell crossed his arms. "Your uncle would be appalled."

"Oh please, you are just upset that I'm on your Victorian turf and I'm more popular with the public. Most people don't give a baboon's behind about tea."

"I enjoyed your book on tea, Wendell," Erik spoke up. "Especially your video on how to make a cup of tea. Most hilarious."

Wendell frowned. "Erm, it wasn't meant to be funny, Erik."

"Oh, sorry." Erik ducked his head. "Your dry sense of humor makes it a challenge sometimes to tell when you are serious."

Henry scowled over at Tobias. "You've done three books on cathouses, and most of it was just your own personal experience."

"Oh, and you've never visited such an establishment?" Tobias raised his eyebrow, every bit as well as Wendell.

"It was part of the life of a cowboy on the trail," Henry said. "I only reported the facts. I didn't go into great detail about the activities. I figured my readers either knew what was going on, or were too young to know."

"I thought Dr. Darrel's passages on the subject were in good taste." Abubakari looked down his nose at Tobias. "Most of *your* books, however, are what can only be described as pornography."

Erik nodded, his braids wagging. "Ya, the videos you include in your book made *me* blush and I am a Viking, by Thor! Where in Midgard did you hide the camera?"

"Contact lens. It makes the viewer feel they are really there."

"Can't you study something besides brothels?"

"I was trying to gather material on Pigalle when I was rudely interrupted."

Henry snorted. "Just another one of your Bawdy House books without the house, huh?"

Tobias looked over at Sherman. "What about you, boy? You are the only one who hasn't joined in insulting me, yet."

"I've never seen any of your books." Sherman shrugged. "Sounds gnarly."

"You are too young to read them," Wendell assured Sherman.

"But I'm nineteen!"

"I am eighty-five and I am too young to read them."

"Ha!" Erik grinned. "We are all too young to read them."

"That's because you are all so dull!" Tobias snapped. "I at least know what the public wants. They don't care about what variety of tea Queen Victoria liked, or what a cow smells like, or how many books are in Timbuktu, or how to make a battleax. They want excitement! You're jealous that my books make the best seller lists. You're also jealous that I've had an active sex life all these years and you have all been practically celibate."

"We just do not brag about it and then publish it," Abubakari said.

"And what would any of you have to brag about? How many women have you done in one day? What forbidden fruits have you tasted? How many virgins have you had?"

"Virgins?" This time Erik raised his eyebrow.

"Ha, yes! I can't count them on my fingers. They cost more, but they are so worth it. To go where no man has gone before. There is no thrill like it. I remember them all: Charlene, Beatrice, Clementine, Angela—"

Tobias stopped mid-sentence when a crash of a knocked-over chair interrupted him. His leer dropped as his eyes got wide. Before Sherman could turn to see what had made the noise and gotten Tobias' attention, the source in question came around the table at Tobias. It took a moment for anyone to comprehend that it was mild-mannered Wendell pulling Tobias out of his chair.

Tobias fell back, driven by Wendell's fist in his nose. Tobias fell over the chair onto the floor, stunned. Like an irate Rottweiler, Wendell came around the chair at Tobias, who tried to scuttle away on his back. Before Wendell could grab Tobias however, Erik grabbed the attacker, pinning his arms.

"Hold, Wendell!" Erik held tight. "Stay your hand!"

"Let me at the cad!" Wendell screamed, squirming to get loose.

"Good Lord!" Tobias held his bleeding nose in his handkerchief. "The man is barking mad! What is your problem?"

"What did you do, Tobias?" Wendell glared down at the other Englishman. "Did you abduct them from some dark alley?"

"What are you talking about?"

"The virgins."

"They were all from reputable brothels."

"Reputable!" Wendell started squirming again. "Where did they get them? Did they kidnap them? Trick them? How old were they? Did you ever stop to think about their feelings? Were they scared?"

"They all seemed compliant enough."

"Were they drugged, Tobias? Did you even consider how you might be destroying a life?"

"They were all legal." Tobias stood up, still holding his nose in his handkerchief. "They were all over twelve. It is not like the procurers ran out and got them just for me. If I hadn't paid for them someone else would have."

"You created the market, Tobias—you and your kind. In the twenty-seventh century if you had done anything like that, even on another planet, the British government would have hunted you down. But because it is in another time, you can get by with it. It doesn't make the crime any less horrendous!"

Sherman put his hand on Wendell's shoulder. "Wendell! You don't know if she was the same Angela."

"Same?" Tobias straightened. "So little Lord Fauntleroy isn't as pure as he pretends to be, eh? Had a favorite tart at the brothel?"

"Angela was no tart!" Wendell snarled at Tobias. "She was a very nice lady. And *you* ruined her life!"

"Wendell!" Sherman tried to reason. "It may have been another Angela."

Wendell struggled again against Erik's grip. "If it wasn't my Angela, it was someone like her. And if it wasn't Tobias, it was someone just like him! Let me at the monster. Let me beat him to a pulp!"

Henry came over. "Whoa, Wendell! Hold on there. This ain't like you at all. We all would be pleased as punch to punch out Tobias, but he isn't worth it. Don't go doing something you're gonna regret."

"Yeah, Wendell," Sherman said from the other side. "Just remember, Angela finally got a nice life. You helped her to get out."

"Helped her to get out?" Tobias dropped his hand from his nose and came closer. "That's a violation of the rules. And you accuse me of doing wrong?"

"It was an accident, all right!" Wendell defended himself. "When I saw how miserable the poor woman was I couldn't go through with it. I just handed her some coins and left. I didn't know I had overpaid her. She used the extra money to get away from that life and get a new one."

"But you still changed a life! You changed time! The Enforcers will come down hard on you for that!"

"No, they didn't. I didn't change time. I made it happen. If I hadn't changed Angela's life, I never would have been born."

Tobias's jaw dropped. Sherman noticed everyone else's had too. Tobias collected himself. "So I shagged your great-great-grandmother and you are the descendant of a—"

Before Tobias could finish that sentence, Erik put up his hands, releasing the irate Wendell. This time Wendell hit Tobias's eye, knocking him back on the floor.

Erik shrugged at Sherman. "Tobias had it coming. I would have hit him myself, but I had my hands full. Halt, Wendell." Erik reached out, grabbed Wendell again. "Let's not kill the little weasel."

"I'll make you pay, Wendell!" Tobias screamed. "You will be sorry!"

"Be silent you!" Erik looked down at Tobias. "Give thanks it was the tea drinker here trying to beat you up and not me. You had this coming. If you cause any trouble for Wendell, I swear by Thor's hammer, that *I* will make you sorry. Far worse is the bite of a bear than the bite of a pussycat, if you get my drift, veslingr."

"And Erik will be standing in line behind me." Henry crossed his arms.

"Owo, I would not be above hitting you myself." Abubakari stepped forward.

"I don't get it?" Tobias stared at all of them. "Why are you defending Wendell? He broke the rules, not me!"

"The rules of the Institute are not in question here," Erik scowled down at Tobias, "but the rules of honor. Wendell is a man of gentle heart."

"Gentle? The twit broke my nose, I'll bet."

"Tobias, you raped his granny, or have you not been paying attention? I suggest that you leave this house now, before we all lose our patience and beat the snot out of you ourselves."

Tobias blinked at Erik, then looked around the room at all the glaring eyes. His haughty expression changed to one of nervousness. He got up and slunk out of the room, holding his handkerchief back to his bloody nose. After a few moments they heard the front door slam.

Erik let go of Wendell. "Sorry, Wendell, for manhandling you like that."

Wendell said nothing, glaring at the floor. He still looked angry, but not with Erik.

Erik gave Wendell an understanding smile and patted him on the back. "You are upset and justifiably so. However you are not use to this sort of anger, and know not how to handle it. You need to either get drunk, or climb up on the roof and scream, or beat on something."

Wendell gave a ragged sigh. "I'm fine. I'll be up in my room making a cuppa."

"No, Wendell. Burying it will not help. None of that English stiff-upper-lip drit. You must release it, by Tyr. Since killing Tobias be not the best idea, you need to beat on something else." Erik grabbed Wendell's arm. "Come!

We shall go out into the backyard. I will show you why I am a blacksmith."

Erik took Wendell out of the room. The Englishman didn't fight, looking like he knew Erik to be right. A minute later Sherman heard the back door close.

"I did not believe Dr. Howe was capable of such violence." Abubakari frowned.

Henry shook his head. "A lot of repressed anger in that man. I've never seen him lose it though. Always so composed." He turned to Sherman. "Do you have any idea what set him off, kid? Who is this Angela?"

"I'll see if I can make a long story short." Sherman sat back down in his chair.

Henry and Abubakari sat down in the chairs on either side and leaned toward Sherman.

Sherman cleared his throat. "Wendell decided to run away with Serendipity because he saw no other option. He had broken the rules by helping her and knew his days of time traveling were ended. Also I think he was smitten with her. That first evening in the twenty-fourth century it dawned on Wendell, he could never go home. He was a little depressed and overwhelmed by it all, so Serendipity got him to drink a couple of beers. Wendell got plowed. I'm not sure how we got on the subject, but Wendell told us about the one and only time he went into a brothel."

"I can't imagine Wendell in a brothel," Henry said.

"Neither could he. He was about to leave when a lady came over to him and introduced herself as Angela. She tried to make him feel more at ease. It was when Wendell invited her to dinner that she knew this had to be his first time."

Henry fought back a laugh. "Yeah, that sounds like Wendell. Always the gentleman."

"Anyway she explained how things worked. Wendell said her eyes looked so unhappy that he couldn't go through with it. He just gave her a bunch of money and left. Well, that was thirty years ago, and all that time the memory of Angela bugged him. He felt bad that he had done nothing to help her."

"No," Abubakari shook his head. "We are not allowed to affect a life in the past in any way. I cannot even give alms."

Sherman stirred his chili. "When Serendipity had made improvements to her Timemobile, she decided our first trip should be to track down Angela, so Wendell could see what happened to her and get over it. It turns out Wendell had paid Angela way too much money. She used it to run away, and catch the first train out of London. She wound up at Cambridge, got a job as a waitress, met a college professor and got married. The professor was Wendell's great, great, whatever, grandfather."

Henry stared at Sherman a moment. "Now let me get this straight, kid. Are you saying Wendell sort of played matchmaker for his forebears."

"Sort of."

"So, if Wendell and Angela had never met, Wendell would never have been born?"

"Yeah, him and countless others."

Abubakari shook his head. "When one interferes with the past, one changes history, one does not make history happen."

"Tarnation!" Henry stared at Sherman. "Abubakari is right. That goes against everything we have been taught. Affecting the past makes everything go wrong, not right."

"How about that!" Sherman grinned at him. "When I told the Enforcers about this they looked real nervous. They said they were hoping Wendell was just a special case."

Henry started chuckling and shaking his head. Abubakari put his hand to his mouth, fighting back a snicker. Then the two collapsed in laughter. Sherman couldn't help but laugh, too. Sherman didn't really get the joke until he realized that the two temporal anthropologists had just had their rigid belief system turned completely upside down, leaving their world wide open to other possibilities.

Now *that* was funny!

Chapter Twenty-Seven

Sherman walked up the gravel trail through the Douglas firs and Pacific red cedars. He liked Sehome Hill Arboretum—180 acres of forest untouched since 1922. Or was it 165 acres? That depended on who you talked to. It was a small forest at the top of the hill they lived on, just beyond the university campus, right in the middle of town. It felt like he and Lauren were the only ones here.

Sherman held the computer near his ear like a cellphone, in case they weren't the only ones here after all. "I wish you could smell this, Lauren. I love the smell of the woods. It reminds me of Christmas."

"I'll take your word for it, Sherm. Say, didn't someone mention cougars have been spotted from time to time in this park?"

"Yeah, I'll bet they spotted Sasquatches, too."

"I think you came up here to get away from the hullabaloo, rather than commune with nature, am I right?"

"Yeah, things have gotten bonkers." Sherman looked up at the clouds through the narrow opening in the towering trees. "You can cut the tension with a knife back at the house these last couple of days. I don't think I'm the only one to notice it. Erik and Abubakari spend most of the day out now. Ser is in the garage working on the Timemobile. Tobias either locks himself in his room or sneaks out of the house, only showing up for meals. Wendell spends almost all of his time sitting in front of his window. I liked going up and talking to him, but now he hardly says a word. I can't get him to open up. This isn't like Wendell. I mean he's quiet, but not this quiet. I think he's had a meltdown."

"Say, Wendell isn't used to violence, ya know," Lauren said. "I think he's all shook-up that he gave Tobias a black eye. Poor sucker doesn't know what to think."

"You are probably right. I got to figure out some way to help the dude."

"I hate to sound flippant, Sherm, but Wendell is a big boy. He's tougher than he looks."

"Yeah, I've seen him take on muggers and Enforcers to protect Serendipity. But remember what happened when he thought he was endangering her by just being around? He panicked and ran off."

"I don't think Wendell will scram and leave Serendipity high and dry again. Just leave him alone and don't prod, but be there for him. Wendell is going to have to work this one out for himself. He's one tough cookie. It won't take him long to get his act together."

A few hours later Sherman strolled back down the hill to Fairhaven Home. He had reached the front porch when he heard a loud roar. He turned to see a huge Harley Davidson motorcycle pull up in front of the house. Two large men with beards and long hair straddled the machine.

The blonde rider on the back got off. "My thanks, Jim!"

The dark-haired driver nodded, then stepped on the gas and thundered off.

The giant he left wore a helmet with the visor pulled down, a leather jacket, a Harley Davidson T-Shirt, riding boots, and jeans, all in black. The bear of a man walked up to Sherman and broke out in an all-too-recognizable grin with a missing tooth. He took off his helmet. "I have found my people!" Dr. Erik Olafson crowed.

"Huh?" Sherman blinked at him.

"I have discovered a place with people who look and act just like Vikings. They ride these vehicles called motorcycles. They call themselves 'bikers.' They thought I was a biker at first. I told them I was not. They said I might not be one, but I was meant to be one. I want to be a biker!"

"Oh, yeah, I guess you do look like a biker."

"My new quest is to buy a motorcycle!"

"Okay, I'll write you out a check."

Erik shook his head, his braids flopping. "Neinn, I will pay for it myself. I will build and sell things so I can buy it with my own money!"

"Yeah, I understand, but if you like I could lend you the money and you could pay me back. First though you'll have to get a driver's license. You may have to learn to drive a car first. I'm not sure how it works. I'll help you anyway I can."

"My gratitude!" Erik slapped Sherman on his back, almost knocking him over. Erik put his helmet back on, and marched confidently into the house.

Sherman smiled and lifted up Lauren. "At least one of us misfits has found a place. Never thought of Erik as a biker, but yeah, I guess he fits."

"You want to do what?" Serendipity stared at Erik down the dinner table. "You want to ride a bicycle?"

Erik shook his head. "Neinn, a biker rides a motorcycle."

Serendipity looked incredulous. "Aren't they dangerous? I mean they run on gasoline and there's no roll bar."

"Ya, but they are fun."

"It's your life." Serendipity shrugged. "I just think you're crazy."

"I will do a study on the comparison of Vikings and bikers. This will be a most noble adventure."

"Yeah, I guess it will give you something to do, so you don't go loopy sitting around here." Serendipity looked over at Wendell with a slightly worried expression.

Wendell sat on her right, staring at his empty plate. He was silent as always, but now at least looked more pensive than sad.

Serendipity looked over at Abubakari on the other side. "So what have you been up to? You've been gone a lot."

"I have been studying the library at the university up the hill. They have quite a collection."

"Once a bibliophile always a bibliophile, huh?"

Henry came in with a beef roast, followed by Matilda carrying a bowl of mashed potatoes. They set them down on the table.

"Okay folks, that's the last of it." Henry pulled out the chair for Matilda.

No sooner had Henry sat down, than Tobias came in the room, his eye still discolored. He took his spot at the end where he always sat. He said nothing and looked at no one.

"So you decided to join us?" Serendipity asked, her voice icy. No one had liked Tobias before, and after the incident with Wendell, they liked him even less.

"No." Tobias didn't bother to look at her. "I plan to dish up my plate and go up to my room where I can eat in peace."

Wendell stood up slowly. "Before you leave we have to talk, Tobias."

"Are you going to hit me again?" Tobias glared at him.

"No."

"You want to apologize?"

Wendell came around the table calmly. "I should apologize, but I cannot. I can't bring myself to do that. No, I just need to show you something." Wendell pulled out his Bible.

"What Bible passage are you going to read to me?" Tobias watched Wendell, looking wary.

"No, I want to show you Angela's legacy." Wendell set the Bible open on the table in front of Tobias.

"The legacy of a prostitute?"

"Yes." Wendell clicked his tongue twice, cueing his computer. "Family tree of Wendell Abercrombie Howe, father's line only, back to Abercrombie and Angela Howe, descending. Virtual screen."

A four foot tall semi-transparent holographic screen appeared above his computer. Names and dates in small print appeared like steps in an uneven staircase, with Wendell's name at the top, and Abercrombie's at the bottom. The letters hovered in the air like fruit flies.

Tobias sneered at it. "Is this supposed to impress me?"

"No," Wendell said, his voice calm. "Just a bloodline of boring history professors, none famous. However, Abercrombie and Angela had more than one child." Wendell clicked his tongue again. "Show all descendants of Abercrombie and Angela."

The stairs turned into a great branching tree. Now thousands of names appeared, going past the sides of the table.

"These are the children, grandchildren and great-grandchildren of Angela," Wendell said. "After our fight, I recalled something the Enforcers had said. Some of these people were crucial to history." Wendell clicked his tongue. "Show famous people in red." A couple of dozen names became red. "I decided to find out who they were.

"Look here." Wendell pointed. "Charlene Howe, British Prime Minister from the twenty-second century; Walter Shrewsbury, Pulitzer prize winning chemist; Stanley Truitt, who found a cure for Newley's Syndrome; Franklin Harold, one of England's greatest writers; Sharon Hook, captain of the first ship out of the solar system; Frederick McDonald, computer engineer and philanthropist."

"Why are you showing me this?" Tobias glowered. "Are you showing off your family tree, so I can see you are better than me? Big Deal. If I picked an ancestor from centuries ago and called up all the descendants, I don't doubt I would be able to find at least a few famous cousins, too. Anyone can do that. Personally I think genealogy is a waste of time."

"Maybe you should take more of an interest. Look at this highlighted name here." Wendell pointed to a name near the top. "Sir Albert Leach, historian and founder of the Association of Temporal Anthropologists."

"Great-Uncle Albert?" Tobias jumped up to lean forward and stare at the name. Above it hovered the name "Tobias Albert Leach."

Wendell looked over at Tobias. "I am part of Angela's legacy, and so are you. I am descended from her youngest son, you from her eldest daughter."

"So you're saying I'm no better than you? That I'm descended from a harlot, too?"

"Angela was no harlot. She was a woman who had compassion for others even in her own misery. And she had the courage to make something of herself even when she saw no hope for the future. You should be proud of her, Tobias."

Wendell clicked his tongue again. "End family tree. Show photograph of Abercrombie and Angela."

A holographic image of the portrait of the couple with their children appeared. It was the same one Wendell had shown Sherman and Serendipity a few months ago, but it was now blown up to three feet high. "This is her."

"She doesn't look like a shattered woman to me."

"No, she rose above the pain and made a life for herself. You need to do the same."

"What?" Tobias stared at Wendell. "I have a life!"

"Do you?"

Tobias picked up his plate. "I don't have to listen to this." Instead of asking for serving bowls to be passed down, Tobias began moving around the table like it was a buffet, reaching around people to fill his plate.

Wendell simply followed behind him. "What happened to you, Tobias? You were once a decent fellow. You started out as a serious scholar. Everyone had high hopes for you. You were the nearest descendant to Sir Albert Leach, after all."

"Yes." Tobias stopped and glared at Wendell. "I had that hanging over my head all my life. Everyone expected more from me. Ever since I was a kid the whole family jumped on the bandwagon and groomed me to be a temporal anthropologist just like Great-Uncle Albert, just because I showed an interest in history. I was expected to be as good as or better than a living legend. I was supposed to fill his shoes. Before I could get there, someone else already had."

"Oh? Who?" Wendell frowned.

"You!" Tobias set his plate down.

"Me? Really Tobias, I hardly fill Sir Albert's shoes."

"Are you serious? Not only have you claimed Albert's Victorian England territory—what was meant to be *my* territory—you are the golden child of the Institute of Time Travel Academy!"

"*Me?* Since when?"

"We had to take classes on how to blend in and be inconspicuous. The first day of class the teacher showed a video of a group of temporal anthropologists at a function. He then turned it off and made us describe everyone on the film. The six of us in the class were able to describe everyone in the video except one." Tobias held up his finger in Wendell's face. "We all missed that same person. It was only after he showed us the man's photo and had us watch the video again that any of us saw him."

"I don't remember that in training."

"Of course not! The man in the film was *you!* You were given as the example of the perfect temporal anthropologist. You were the one we were meant to emulate."

"I was? How come none of the new graduates told me that?"

"They probably never noticed you at the Association functions. You are that good."

"Good? Being unnoticed is good?"

"You are a chameleon, Wendell. You melt into the woodwork. No one notices you. You have a rare talent."

"Talent? Tobias, I'm just dull and boring. Even people who like me will tell you that. If they are polite they will tell you I am relaxing to be around."

"Wendell dost have a most calming effect upon people," Matilda agreed.

"Well, that's because I'm unexciting." Wendell looked over at her.

"Man relaxes the hell out of me," Serendipity purred. Everyone turned to stare at her. Serendipity looked about nervously. "Oops!" She looked over at Sherman. "Said too much again?"

Sherman just nodded.

Wendell turned back to Tobias. "Don't listen to Dr. Brown. She's speaking on a totally different matter."

"I got that idea." Tobias raised his eyebrow at Serendipity.

Wendell pulled attention away from the embarrassed woman. "Besides Tobias you found another solution. You are so obnoxious no one wants to remember you."

Tobias glared at him. "I don't have to put up with this abuse."

"What abuse? I'm complimenting you. Ask Henry. He borrowed your tactic. He took a train journey as a traveling salesman in loud clothes and was harassing the other passengers to buy some silly kitchen gadget from him. Everyone immediately ignored him. He was less noticed than if he had sat quietly in the corner minding his own business. Henry admitted he stole the idea from you. Someday new recruits will be shown films of you as an alternative way to avoid public attention. You are a genius, Tobias. You have relations with hundreds of women and have had absolutely no bearing on their lives. You were just one more faceless customer. You are a good temporal anthropologist."

Tobias looked like he wasn't certain if he was being insulted or not. "I had to do more than fade into the background. I had to exceed my great-uncle. And every university was stepping over me to get to you."

"That's because they knew me, old boy. They had worked with me before. I was a temporal anthropologist for twenty-five years before you passed your time travel license exams. When I started it was the same way for me, maybe even worse. When your uncle came out of retirement to mentor me, universities began clamoring for him to do jobs for them even though I was now available. It was only natural. But I worked hard and finally earned the respect of the other scholars. You could have been on your way, Tobias. But I heard rumors. You turned down assignments. We all have, we have to, there's just too many. However, you were rude about it."

"I wasn't going to become a respected scholar studying the sewer system of Seattle." Tobias rolled his eyes.

"I knew they had offered that job to Henry before me. I didn't know they had offered it to you first, too. See there was an assignment where they went to you before me."

"They probably felt it beneath your dignity."

Wendell shrugged. "Why? Because a sewer was involved? It is a part of history. I rather enjoyed the trip. When I had to turn down assignments because I was all booked up, I tried sending them to you, but they would shake their heads and say you had brushed them off. Then after you got involved in this brothel haunting of yours—I mean really, three books?—you began to lose credibility. Why in the world did you go that route?"

"It made me famous, didn't it? I became a bestseller. It made me rich! It made me successful!"

"Is that how you measure success, Tobias? What good is being rich if you get no respect? You sold out. You took what you thought was the quick way to success. In doing so you became cold and heartless and self-centered. So much so you didn't even care about the feelings of some bewildered young girl."

Tobias glared at Wendell, his fists clenched. He looked like he was about to hit the other Englishman. Wendell, however, didn't blink an eye, his face deadpan.

Without a word, Tobias turned and stomped out of the room. A few moments later they heard the front door slam.

Wendell stepped over to the end of the table, and clicked his tongue. "Virtual screen off." He sighed, picked up his computer and stuffed it in his pocket.

Wendell looked over at the others. "I do apologize for disrupting your meal, but I had to speak to Tobias, and I wanted witnesses, so he couldn't make accusations later. I really am sorry. I hope I haven't ruined everyone's appetite, especially after Henry and Matilda worked so hard to prepare this delightful meal."

"It's all right, old buddy." Henry forced a smile.

Wendell sat down in his seat. "Henry, would you please pass me Tobias's plate? I won't bother to fill my own."

Henry handed the plate over. Wendell didn't add anything to the slice of roast beef and dollop of potatoes that was already on it. He slowly cut up the meat. "I am sure you have all from time to time wished you could break the rules, to get involved, to help someone, but you dared not."

Abubakari looked over at Wendell. "I have prayed for some poor soul more than once. That is not against the rules."

Matilda nodded. "As have I."

Wendell continued to cut his meat slowly, into smaller pieces. "It is bad enough we have to just stand by like we don't care. Tobias has gone past that and been a victimizer. I don't care if it was within the rules of the Institute or the laws of the day. It was wrong." He stuck a piece of meat in his mouth and slowly chewed it.

Everyone else ate in thoughtful silence.

Chapter Twenty-Eight

The next night the occupants of Fairhaven Home sat at a table with four empty seats. Two were for the zoologists who never ate with them, but the other two were missing anthropologists. "Where's Erik?" Sherman asked.

"He called." Serendipity dished out some spaghetti onto her plate. "Running late. Said to start without him."

"What about Tobias?"

"What about Tobias," Serendipity's voice had a cold edge. "He can rot in hell for all I care."

"Serendipity!" Wendell scolded. "You shouldn't talk like that."

Serendipity looked at Wendell incredulous. "I can't believe you're defending that banana slug. Especially after what he did to you."

"I believe I was the one who gave him a black eye."

"Only after he cut out your heart."

"He didn't mean to."

"No, Tobias doesn't mean to do anything because he doesn't think about anyone but Tobias. Don't tell me you've forgiven him."

"No. I can't forgive him for what he did. It is not my place to forgive him."

Matilda looked concerned. "I hath not laid eyes upon Tobias since last night's repast. Hast anyone seen him?"

"Maybe some cat ate the little rat," Serendipity mumbled and chomped down on a piece of garlic bread.

Henry pulled out his cellphone. "You programmed everyone's number on these here cellphones you gave us, Serendipity. Just got to find Tobias's name on the list." Henry poked a few buttons, and then put the phone to his ear. After a minute he folded it up and stuck it back in his pocket. "Nope." He turned his phone off. "Can we trace his Field computer?"

Wendell shook his head. "He has that hidden in his walking stick, and he left without it. We could always trace his signature on his implant."

Abubakari shrugged. "Maybe after dinner. We should all eat first."

The front door opened and heavy boots came down the hall. Erik came into the room, dressed in his biker gear. "Health to all! I regret that I am late."

"It's all right." Serendipity smiled at him. "Thank you for calling. *You* we would have worried about."

Erik glanced at Tobias's empty seat like he knew exactly who she was referring to, then walked over and sat down next to Abubakari. He leaned across the table, grabbed the bowl of spaghetti and began shoveling it onto his plate.

The African scholar gave him a dubious look. "You are serious about this motorcycle group? Do you think that is a good idea? You were trained to blend into another time period, not this one."

Erik picked up a meatball with his hand and popped it into his mouth. "You have no need to worry. I fit in. Bikers remind me greatly of Vikings."

"They attack villages, wa?" Abubakari frowned.

"No, the brotherhood, the lust for adventure, the down-to-earthiness—bikers have all the best attributes of Vikings."

Abubakari looked resigned. "Owo, I suppose you know what you are doing. I do not mean to cast doubt on your abilities."

"No offense taken." Erik slapped Abubakari on the back. He then picked up some strands of spaghetti and dangled them over his head to lower them down into his gaping mouth. "My brothers down at the Harley shop invited me to a party tomorrow night," he said with his mouth still full. "We shall journey on our bikes to the inner city. There is always some excitement in town on Halloween."

"Tomorrow is Halloween?" Serendipity asked.

"Ya, I must get a costume."

"Why not just wear one of your Viking outfits?" Sherman asked.

"Those are not Halloween costumes." Erik's blonde brows puckered. "They are my work clothes."

"Why can't you wear it for Halloween? Dude, tomorrow all of you can wear whatever you want. No one will think anything of it."

The other temporal anthropologists all perked up at that.

Abubakari looked hopeful. "Are you saying, we can wear what we were wearing in the past tomorrow out in public, wa? What is this Halloween?"

"Ancient Celtic holiday of Samhain," Erik said. "Christians turned it into All Hallows Eve—Halloween. Originally it was the Celtic New Year when the barriers between other realms could be breeched. The ghoulies and ghosties were out and about. So everyone disguised themselves as creatures from the otherworld, so the otherworldly visitors would mistake the natives for one of their own. That is where the wearing of costumes came in."

"Wow, I didn't know that," Sherman said. "Where did you learn that?"

"Ho, have you forgotten? I have Ph.D.s in history and anthropology." Erik flashed his discolored teeth. "I'm not just a pretty face."

"Sorry dude, but if you'd wear a tweed jacket and smoke a pipe, it would be easier to remember you're a college professor."

"More literally I am a college researcher than a professor. Maybe I should wear a lab coat." Then Erik bellowed a laugh, no doubt at the idea of his wearing a lab coat.

Serendipity leaned toward Erik. "So you said there's something going on downtown tomorrow?"

"Ya, there lie the bars. The college students and locals all show up. Jim said a couple of years ago a bunch of college kids dressed as zombies and reenacted something they called *Thriller* in the middle of the street."

"*Thriller!*" Sherman perked up. "Like the Michael Jackson video?"

"Ya, I think Jim mentioned that name."

"Dude, that would be so awesome!" Sherman got excited. "Are they going to do it again?"

"Jim said they performed it again last year at the Maritime Heritage Park, but it was not the same. The element of surprise had vanished. No one expected it the first time."

"Whoa, I would have loved to have seen that." Sherman leaned on the table, disappointed.

Serendipity looked over at Sherman and grinned. "I believe you are forgetting something."

"What?" Sherman asked.

"We have the Timemobile parked out in the garage."

"Ayi." Abubakari shook his head. "You cannot use a time machine for anything that frivolous."

"Yea, Abubakari speaketh true," Matilda said.

Henry and Erik said "yup" and "ya" in agreement.

"Oh great." Serendipity rolled her eyes. "Now I got five Wendells nagging me. First off, people, this is not the Institute of Time Travel. I don't have to jitterbug to their tune. And secondly, what is it going to hurt? We'll just be a few more faces in the crowd watching. Sherman wants to see it, and so do I, so we're going. The rest of you are invited to come along."

"Can we all fit into the Timemobile?" Wendell asked.

"Yeah, I added three fold-down seats on the back wall. Although, I am seriously thinking about using the seat I used last time." Serendipity grinned over at Wendell.

"She sat on Wendell's lap." Henry explained to the others.

Wendell sighed melodramatically. "If I must make sacrifices for the cause, so be it."

Serendipity patted Wendell's hand. "My brave little soldier." She turned to Erik. "Do you know exactly when and where this took place?"

"Two years ago would be 2008, on Halloween night. Jim mentioned the corner of Holly and Railroad."

"Anybody got plans for tonight?" Serendipity asked.

"Tonight?" Henry yelped. "You plum loco?"

"Why not?"

"We must prepareth!" Matilda said.

Serendipity flipped her hair. "Prepare what? It's two years and one day in the past. You all have costumes. You have until after dinner to decide if you want to go with Sherman and me."

"It will be awesome!" Sherman assured them.

Sherman came up the stairs to the third floor in his monks robe and cowl. He had decided it was the easiest costume, since he just had to toss it on over his jeans and t-shirt. He was about to sit down in front of the window, when Wendell came out of his bedroom into the sitting room. He was dressed up in his brown frock coat with his brown top hat and red cravat tie.

Wendell smiled at Sherman. "I say, all ready to go, old boy?"

"Yeah."

"I wonder what outfit Dr. Brown will pick for the occasion?" Wendell sat down in one of the overstuffed chairs and waited. Sherman joined him in the other chair.

"So, exactly what are we going to witness tonight?" Wendell asked.

"I guess they are recreating the dance sequence from the Michael Jackson music video *Thriller*. I know the original on MTV was awesome."

"Twentieth century?"

"Just before I left in 1985. Back when MTV was awesome and played nothing but music videos." Sherman felt forty-four again.

"Yes, that would explain why Dr. Brown is so keen on witnessing this performance."

Serendipity's door opened and she emerged attired in her lavender Victorian dress with the bustle. Wendell stood up and removed his hat, looking entranced.

"So, you like it?" she asked Wendell.

"You are absolutely lovely, my dear. But why did you pick this costume? I thought you hated bustles?"

"It wasn't hard to figure out what you would wear. I decided to go as your accessory."

"I must say, Serendipity darling, I have never had a more charming accessory." Wendell put his hat back on and stuck out his arm.

Serendipity smiled at him. "I know this is probably an oxymoron, but you do look sexy in that suit."

"Maybe because I feel the most at ease in it."

"Really? Hmm, I thought you felt the most at ease in my bed."

Wendell raised his eyebrow at her. "Please, Dr. Brown!"

"Uh-oh, we're back to Dr. Brown. I could have been cruder, you know. Oops, now I'm making you blush. Sorry, honey."

"Behave yourself."

"Make it up to you later?"

Wendell gave her a sideways glance, fighting back a smirk. "As you wish."

Sherman shook his head at the two. "Uh, shall we see if anyone else is ready?"

The three went down to the next floor that had the other bedrooms and stood in the hallway. Erik came out first, dressed in his wool breeches, short tunic held by a leather belt, and fur cloak. On his head he had a helmet made of iron, with a nose guard attached to a mask that covered the top half of his face, leaving only his eyes showing. The cap was reinforced with two thick bands going from the front to the back and from side to side. Otherwise it was bare.

"Where's the horns?" Sherman asked.

"Horns?" Erik looked confused.

"On the helmet."

Erik wrinkled his nose. "This is a Viking helmet, not a Celtic one. I know not why people think Viking helmets had horns."

Wendell cleared his throat. "That would be the Victorians' fault. Wagner opera costume designers felt horns were more dramatic."

Sherman pointed to Erik's belt. "Dude, I don't know if wearing the dagger out in public is a good idea."

"Why?"

"Cops might arrest you for carrying a weapon."

"Weapon? This is just a pocketknife." Erik pulled out the nine-inch blade.

"Trust me."

Erik took off his belt and removed the knife sheath. He stepped back into his room, as Henry stepped out of his. He had on pants held up with suspenders over a Victorian shirt without a collar. He also wore boots and his Stetson hat. He carried an off-white wool jacket with four stripes of different colors.

"What's the stripes on the jacket?" Sherman asked.

"These jackets were originally made from Hudson Bay four-point blankets. The stripes show how many beaver pelts it cost. So many people started making jackets and coats from the blankets that the Hudson Bay Company just started selling the coats ready made."

"Wow! Did you buy this at a trading post?"

"Heck, they were still selling these in the twenty-seventh century. Hudson Bay Company went retail back in the late nineteenth century. Go by the name 'The Bay'. They're all over Canada."

"You bought this up in Canada?"

"No, over the internet. Virtual mall. Instant delivery."

Serendipity scrunched her nose. "Yuck, I hate using the electronic deliveries over the wire. Things just don't seem as good."

"Yeah, I've heard it used to be like that. Sure am glad you invented—" Henry stopped, his eyes getting big. He slapped his hand over his mouth.

"I invented what?" Serendipity leaned forward.

"Never mind." Henry ran his fingers up and down his suspenders. "So, what's keeping the others?"

Abubakari came out dressed in his white flowing robes and turban, carrying his fly whisk. "Will this be all right, wa?"

"Looks fine." Serendipity smiled. "In fact you look regal."

Matilda came out of her room, wearing an emerald green gown that was fitted above, but had a billowing skirt that reached the floor. The sleeves widened at the elbows and draped down, showing a close-fitting teal sleeve underneath. On her head was a matching green veil, held down with a band of twisted gold material. Around her waist was a gold belt that hung down a couple of feet in front. "Is my appearance pleasing to thy eye?" She looked directly at Henry.

Henry smiled at her and came over. "You look mighty purdy, senorita. Where did you get that beautimous gown?"

"I purchased the fabric a fortnight ago and stitched it myself. I wished to surprise thee."

"You made that?" Serendipity stared in awe.

"Of course. Sewing is a mandatory skill for the medieval woman." She turned around to show off her handiwork. "This is a French bliaut, circa twelfth century."

"You look mighty fine." Henry offered his arm to her. "How about you and me head into town?"

Matilda smiled as she slipped her arm into his.

"All right then." Serendipity headed for the stairs. "Let's go where no time traveler has gone before!"

"Let's hope so." Wendell had an unsure frown on his face. "What records the Enforcers left me show no other temporal anthropologists should be there."

It felt odd to Sherman to ride in the time machine and find himself in the exact same spot in the alley behind the old garage. He knew they were no longer in 2010 since the steel garage was no longer there, along with the Ford Wagon and Ferrari they had yet to buy. Serendipity disguised the Timemobile as a van with darkened windows and Sherman drove them downtown to Railroad Avenue to where the street split in two for a half dozen blocks, separated by a parking lot. Sherman pulled the "van" into the nearest vacancy to Holly Street. The lot seemed to be filling up quick despite the late hour.

Sherman got out and walked around to the other side to open up the time machine door. Serendipity and the temporal anthropologists filed out. He pointed down the parking lot. "That way to Holly Street. It's a couple of blocks. This is the closest I could get."

They headed for the sidewalk and walked in the direction their guide had indicated. A crowd had already collected and their group wasn't the strangest looking walking around. Monsters and aliens ran about the street.

Wendell pulled out his pocket computer disguised as a Bible and opened it. He clicked his tongue twice. "Any information on American Halloween practices of the early twenty-first century?"

A college girl with long black hair and vampire fangs came running up to Wendell and Serendipity. "Oooh, love the outfits. It's so steampunk."

"Steampunk?" Wendell raised his eyebrow. "It is supposed to be Victorian. What is steampunk?"

The girl flashed her fangs. "Sci-Fi in a Victorian setting, with super futuristic technology like computers and airships."

"Victorians with computers?" Wendell gave a nervous laugh and stuffed his twenty-seventh century computer back in his breast pocket. "I daresay, that would be preposterous."

Serendipity winked at Wendell. "Wouldn't fake Victorian be *steambunk*?"

"I'm not fake." Wendell held up his chin. "I am a reasonable facsimile."

"I think you look coolio." The girl assured him, then put her hands on her cheeks, trying to look scared. "Ooh, I hope you aren't vampire hunters."

"Nah." Serendipity smiled at her. "We're time travelers."

"Oh, yeah, H.G. Wells. I am so there." The vampire grinned and traipsed off.

Wendell frowned at Serendipity. "That was not very smart."

"Wendell, did you really think she was a vampire? It's all make-believe tonight. If you were to get up in front of everyone and tell them exactly who we all are, they wouldn't believe you or think you were crazy. They would just figure you had a great imagination. Let me show you." Serendipity let go of his arm and walked over to a man dressed in a blue costume with a red cape and obviously padded chest. "Excuse me, Superman."

"Yes, my good woman." He put his fists on his hips. "Are you in need of a superhero?" He turned his head, chin high, to show off his profile.

"Yes, we have traveled here in a time machine to witness the Halloween activities of the future."

"Ah-ha, and thus the antiquated clothes. You appear to have picked up some hitchhikers throughout time." Pseudo-Superman looked over at the rest of the party.

"Yes, we have. Now can you tell me where we can find Railroad and Holly?"

"One block that way." He pointed dramatically.

"Why, thank you."

"Don't mention it. Helping people is what I do." He saluted them and trotted off.

"Is everyone mad?" Wendell raised an eyebrow at her. "Do you all act like escapees from Bedlam this time every year?"

"So what do you do in England on Halloween?"

"Halloween is overshadowed by Guy Fawkes Night. That's November 5th. We march through the streets and make big bonfires to burn Guy Fawkes in effigy, to celebrate foiling his plot to blow up Parliament back in 1605."

"I see. So every year you have a riot."

"Yes—" Wendell stopped and whirled around. "No! We don't have a riot."

"Marches. Bonfires. Burning people in effigy. Hmm, sounds like a riot to me."

Wendell's forehead crinkled, like he was trying to find a comeback to that as they made their way to Holly Street.

Henry scanned the crowd. "So, now what do we do?"

"Hang around until something happens, I guess," Serendipity said. "Mingle."

"Never art we allowed to mingle." Matilda shook her head.

"Then people watch."

The temporal anthropologists all nodded or shrugged. This was what they were trained to do, to stand aside and study people. They relaxed and watched the crowd with keen interest. Occasionally one of them would point out someone discreetly and ask Sherman what the costume represented. Sherman had to admit it was kind of fun just watching the crowd, especially now that some had had too much to drink.

After a while Sherman noticed a girl coming through the crowd, dressed in a ragged white dress. Her face was painted grey with dark circles, looking like she was dead, or undead as the case may be. She staggered about moaning. A man in a tattered suit, his face covered with white makeup, joined her.

Sherman looked around and saw dozens of zombies suddenly in the street, all with ghastly faces and tattered clothes. They milled about glassy-eyed, groaning loudly for several minutes. Then someone turned on a boombox and cranked up the sound. Michael Jackson's voice began singing *Thriller*. The zombies began to dance in unison, all doing the same steps.

Sherman pointed at them. "Look! They are doing the same dance as the video! This is awesome."

The music became drowned out by the cheers and howls of the crowd on the sidewalks that got thicker as more came to see what was happening.

"Dude!" Sherman watched grinning. "This is wicked!" He turned to see his companions just watching with their mouths open. It had to be worth the trip just to see Serendipity speechless.

Well, almost speechless. Serendipity turned to Wendell. "Beats a bonfire all to heck, huh?"

Wendell just nodded, his jaw still slack.

When they finished, the crowd clapped and cheered. The dancers started to move along. Sherman ran up to one of the zombies. "Hey, that was awesome!"

The girl smiled through the makeup. "Thanks!"

"So why did you all decide to do *Thriller*?"

"It's the twenty-fifth anniversary of the video. Someone in dance class said 'Hey, let's do a flash mob and recreate it for Halloween.' So we did!" She grinned at him, then took off.

"Twenty-fifth, huh?" Sherman's smile dropped. "I just saw the premier two years ago."

He felt a hand pat his back. Sherman looked up to see Wendell smile at him. "Time travel has its own form of jet lag, eh?"

"I sometimes feel like I got shoved out of the plane." Sherman sighed.

"Dr. Brown! We must flee!" a gruff but frightened voice bellowed.

Sherman turned around to see Erik with Abubakari, Matilda and Henry, all with anxious expressions.

"What's wrong?" Serendipity asked concerned.

"Terrorists!" Abubakari explained. "They were trying to recruit us."

"Terrorists?" Sherman frowned. "Are you sure it wasn't just someone in a costume?"

"Alas nay!" Matilda shook her head. "They called themselves the Society for Creative Anarchism and bid Erik, Abubakari and I to avail ourselves for we were much needed by their organization!"

The name sounded familiar to Sherman. "Are you sure they didn't say Society for Creative *Anachronism*? They're medieval recreationists. It's just a bunch of guys that dress up like knights and hit one another with sticks wrapped in duct tape."

The four temporal anthropologists all stared at him like he was stupid. Finally Henry spoke. "Bosh! That name don't make no sense for medieval recreationists. I'd be willing to bet the farm they said 'Anarchism.' History says this time period is crawling with them terrorist desperadoes."

"Henry is right!" Wendell assured Serendipity. "Although Bellingham wasn't recorded as a target, we dare not take chances!"

"Whatever." Sherman mumbled, not feeling like arguing.

"Come on." Serendipity started off. "Sherman can drive us back to the alley behind the house and I'll take you back—I mean ahead—to 2010."

Chapter Twenty-Nine

Serendipity opened her eyes to find herself staring at a young woman with swirling blonde hair smoking a cigarette with the word "Job" behind her head. The faded Art Nouveau poster in the antique store had whimpered to be stuck on her bedroom wall. Very 1960s *and* 1890s. She knew Alphonse Mucha artwork turned Wendell on. His bare skin was now against hers and that turned *her* on. Night shirts might look silly, but they had a habit of riding up when worn in bed so Wendell might as well been wearing nothing. It was the same reason she wore a gown. It was just to keep her shoulders warm.

She rolled over to see Wendell with his arms folded behind his head staring at the ceiling forlornly. Sex looked like the last thing on his mind. "You look a million miles away." She scooted closer to him.

He put his arm around her. "Good morning, darling. Here I am lying next to the love of my life and I'm thinking about another woman."

Serendipity raised her eyebrow. "You really gotta work on your pillow talk."

"No need to be jealous, love. I was thinking about my ancestor, Angela." Wendell sighed. "I know I need to just get over this, put it behind me. It is all in the past, nothing to be done about it. It's just..." Wendell sighed again.

Serendipity patted his chest. "Well, you actually met Angela. She is more than just a photo to you. The fact that she haunted you for thirty years doesn't help."

"I think this incident with Tobias has made me think more about Angela's possible past. To think she may well have been the victim of...and as young as thirteen. And that Tobias could well have been the culprit. It just gnaws at me. Then I wonder what the rest of her life may have been like. I prefer to think Abercrombie was kind to her, but what if he was some callous tyrant who constantly threw her past in her face, even blackmailed her or treated her like a—well, a trollop."

Serendipity thought a moment. "Why don't you go back and ask her? I'd take you."

Wendell shook his head. "My asking questions might influence her and change the past."

"What if you talked to her when she was really old and it was too late to change anything?"

Wendell stared at Serendipity for a minute, then shook his head. "No, I can't tell her who I am. She wouldn't believe me anyway. And why would she confess her darkest sins to a stranger?"

"Was she Catholic? She might make a deathbed confession if she thought you were a priest."

"I doubt she was Catholic. However, she was probably Anglican, being the wife of a Victorian Cambridge professor."

"Church of England? That would make sense. I know when Henry the Eighth started it, he really didn't have a manifesto except 'I'm now the boss and not the Pope.' Didn't the Anglicans keep wavering between wanting to be more like the Catholics or more like the other Protestants?"

"Yes. I love that you aren't totally lost when I talk about history." He kissed her temple. "The Anglicans did keep confessions. They aren't mandatory like the Catholic Church, but Anglican priests are required to keep all confessions confidential."

"So wear a clerical collar and make Angela think you are a vicar."

"That would be dishonest!"

"It's not like you are going to use the information to hurt her in anyway. Besides, maybe it would make her feel better if she could confess what she has probably been ashamed of all these years. You could help her die in peace."

"Perhaps."

Serendipity sat up. "Come on. We'll get period costumes and show up just before she dies. Get on your computer and find out the date and coordinates."

Wendell sat up, too. "Are you barking mad? It's breaking all the rules. The other temporal anthropologists will throw a fit."

"So, we won't tell them. We won't even tell Sherman. We'll just sneak out to the Timemobile. We could even change into our costumes in it so they won't be the least suspicious of seeing you in a vicar's outfit." She gave him a wicked smirk. "Or we could tell them we are role playing some sexual fantasy of mine."

Wendell's cheeks turned red. "Serendipity!" Then he laughed at her playful grin. "How can any woman be so lascivious and innocent at the same time?"

"It's a date then?"

Wendell rolled his eyes like he was weighing the consequences. He nodded. "All right, my dear."

Wendell emerged from the Timemobile parked in front of the hospital and brushed off the sleeve of the dark tweed jacket he wore over a black shirt with a white vicar's collar. He had also temporarily dyed his hair and mustache black. Serendipity stepped out wearing a light blue and white gingham dress that came to her mid-calf and a black felt flapper's hat.

Wendell looked down at her. "You did make certain this was the nineteenth of June 1931?"

"Yes. In Cambridge, England. I double checked."

"I hope she isn't in a coma. My records say she died the twenty-first."

"We can always find out when she was lucid and jump back a few days. Do you want me to stay here?"

"You can come part of the way. I will need to be alone with her in case she wants to make a confession." Wendell took Serendipity by the arm. "I think you make a most charming vicar's wife."

They went into the white-washed facility and found the reception desk. "Excuse me, my good woman, but can you tell me what room Angela Howe is in?" Wendell asked the woman on the other side of the window.

The red-headed woman checked the ledger on her desk. "Room 205."

Wendell found the room and peered in. There in the iron bed lay a wisp of a woman, hair like frost and skin like parchment, her complexion a dull color.

He glanced over at Serendipity, noticing she was watching him instead of the woman. "Are you going to be all right, sweetie?"

Wendell nodded. "I'm eighty-five. I've seen death before."

Serendipity glanced over at a wooden bench in the hall not more than ten feet away. "Okay, but I'll be sitting right here if you need me."

"Thank you for being so understanding." Wendell pulled out his wire-rim glasses that held a camera and put them on his nose. "I'll record the interview for you." He then pulled out his pocket Bible, and stepped into the room, trying to look 'vicary.'

Angela's eyes were closed. Her taut desiccated skin showed the contours of her skull. Wendell sat down in a chair beside her. "Angela Howe?" he whispered.

The old white-haired woman slowly opened her eyes. They looked a bit milky. "Hello? Do I know you?" Her voice was weak, hardly more than a whisper.

"My name is Reverend Horatio Smith. I'm the Vicar. I visit all the patients. I just wanted to see if you needed anyone to talk to."

"Your face is familiar."

"I may have stopped by before. How are you doing, Mrs. Howe?"

"I'm ready."

"Ready?"

"Ready to be with Abie." Angela's face showed longing.

"Abie?"

"Abercrombie, my husband."

"I take it you loved him?"

Angela smiled, all her wrinkles falling into place. "Oh, yes. He was the dearest, sweetest man. He never raised his hand to me or even his voice. I do hope I will be allowed into heaven to be with him."

"Why do you think you won't go to heaven?"

Angela closed her eyes. "I can't tell you, Vicar."

"It is all right, dear. I'm a priest. If you would like to make a confession I have taken an oath to keep it confidential. If I told anyone, the Anglican Church would kick me out. And we won't even go into what God would do to me."

Angela looked calmer. "I was a wicked woman."

"You don't look very wicked to me. Why do you think you were wicked?"

"I was a fallen woman."

Wendell leaned forward. "So tell me how you found yourself in such a predicament."

Angela sighed. "It is a long story."

"I have all the time in the world, my dear. Start from the beginning."

Angela stared at the wall beyond the foot of her bed for a long time. "All right, vicar." She finally spoke, her wheezy voice resigned. "I've never told anyone this story except my late husband. I was born in rural Essex where father worked on a farm. The cottage we lived in only had one room and a dirt floor, but we had plenty of fresh air and sunshine. We had a small potato patch of our own and mother knew what wild plants were edible, so we didn't go hungry. When I was eight, father lost his job and couldn't get another. His employer had switched from wheat farming to cattle because imports had driven down grain prices. That and steam threshing machines and the like were doing away with farm labor in the area. So my family moved to London to look for work. Everything was covered with black soot and there was no green like home, so it took a while to get used to it. Well, to be honest none of us really got used to it."

Angela paused to catch her breath, stroking the wool blanket. Wendell waited patiently. She took a long sigh and continued, speaking slowly and pausing often. "Father finally found a job in a factory making cast-iron lampposts. We had been poor in the country, but we were even poorer in the city. Within the year my sweet little brother Eddie passed away from something going around. We couldn't even afford a doctor to tell us what it was. Then when I was ten poor mother was run over by a tram and died. I think she was distracted because that day would have been my brothers sixth birthday. I now had to do all the laundry, cooking and cleaning on my own."

"Your father forced you to do all that when you were only ten?"

Angela turned her head to frown at Wendell. "Forced? My father was a kind man who never forced me to do anything. Circumstances forced me to step up. I didn't mind. Sure, it was hard work, especially the laundry, but not half as hard as father's job. He had to push heavy carts full of coke, limestone and iron ore across a narrow ramp to tip them into the charge hole at the top of a six-story blast furnace. He worked twelve hours a day, six days a week in that smelly hot foundry just so we could survive. I know it was hot and smelly because he would drag himself home drenched in sweat, smelling of fumes. The poor man could hardly stay awake long enough to eat supper. But he would always kiss me on the cheek and tell me how much he appreciated me. He loved me. That made it all worth-while." Tears were welling in her eyes. "My father was a good person—my mother, too. They did the best they could for my brother and me. They both deserved better lives."

"I am sure they are together in heaven with your little brother."

"Yes, if anyone deserves heaven it was them." She gazed out the window at the branches of the elm tree outside, falling silent.

"So when you got older you became a lady of the evening to help support your poor father?" Wendell gently spurred her on. "Under the circumstances that seems more noble than wicked."

"Heavens no!" She turned to stare at him in horror. "Father would have rather starved to death than to let me do that. No, one night when I was fifteen, father didn't come home."

"Ah, he stopped off at a pub?"

"Father never drank. He said only a cad would make his family go hungry all week just so he could be numb for a few hours. Father always came straight home. After an hour I got scared and walked to the factory. It was there I found out father had fallen into the blast furnace and died. There wasn't even a body left to bury! They assured me he went quick, that he would have been dead from the heat before he hit the molten iron and burnt up. That was little comfort to me. I went home and cried all night. I loved my father and now I was all alone. To this day I can't look at a lamppost without wondering if father is in it." She wrinkled her nose. "Oh dear, that sounded terrible. But it is true. The factory owner would have shrugged and used the iron my father was in anyway."

Angela took a deep breath and continued. "When I could think straight I realized I was going to have to find a job or I would be out on the street or in a workhouse. So I had to pull myself together and went around to all the shops and factories asking for work. No one had an opening. It was when I came out of a bakery that wasn't hiring either that a man followed me out. 'You can work at my house,' he said. He was smartly dressed, so I knew he was a gentleman. I told him I could cook and clean. He smiled and said, 'Yes, we could use a maid.' I knew house servants didn't make much, but it was room and board and would get me by. So I followed him to this grand mansion. He took me into the basement to the kitchen and sat me down at a wooden table and this large woman in fancy clothes offered me a drink of cider. It tasted a little funny but I drank it anyway. Soon I felt very odd and woozy."

"He had drugged the drink?"

"Yes, I don't know with what. I asked him what was going on and he laughed and said, 'I told you we could use a maid.' Then he turned to the woman and told her to check to see if I was a virgin! Then they took me upstairs, stripped me and gave me a bath. They dressed me in nothing but a corset and bloomers! I was too disoriented to put up a fight or get away, but I begged them to let me go. It felt like I was screaming but it just came out in mumbles. They told me to shut up and were rough with me. The woman boxed my ears! No one had ever boxed my ears before." Angela rubbed her ears at the memory. "My parents had been very kind and patient, so this was the first time anyone had ever been harsh to me.

"After that they put me in a bedroom with a brass bed with a red satin cover. I felt dizzy and weak, so I lay down on the bed. I wanted to run away but I was too disoriented. I cried, afraid of what was going to happen next. It was then that this fat ugly pig of a man came into the room. He was dressed like a gentleman but he certainly did not act like one. I begged him to help me escape, but he laughed and said he had paid good money for the first nibble of a tart. Then he..." Angela trailed off.

"I take it he ravished you."

"Yes. After that I passed out. The next morning the woman came into the room with a red satin dress and told me to put it on. I demanded my own clothes back, but she said she had burnt them. She also told me this was a brothel, she was the madam and I was now one of her girls. If I was good and did as I was told I would be fed well and given pretty dresses and a fancy bedroom. If I was bad I would be beaten. If I refused to entertain their visitors then I would not eat. I told her I was leaving and she laughed and said the police would arrest me for trying to run out on my debts."

"What? I think the policeman would have arrested *them*. And what debts could you possibly have?"

"I was expected to pay for my clothes and boarding, even if I had no choice in the dresses or furnishings. They were all gaudy and horrid."

"Then how could they demand you pay for them?"

"That was the way it worked. I would receive a payment from every man I went to bed with. We were to turn the money over to the madam for safekeeping. I found out later that no one in the house was every able to get ahead of their debts, so none of us had any cash to buy a train ticket to run away. And the dresses they gave us were very low cut and held up only with tiny straps. We could not go out in public dressed like that! We were all prisoners."

"Sounds to me like you were slaves!"

"Yes, I suppose we were. The owner of the house, Mr. Dawes, came in after that to give me lessons on sex. I won't go into detail. I tried a hunger strike and stayed in my room but gave up after a few days when I just got too weak and hungry." Angela's boney fingers plucked fretfully at the blue wool blanket covering her. "It soon became obvious to me that cooperation was the only way to survive and avoid blows from the madam. Besides I could hardly protect my reputation for it was gone.

"At least most of the other girls were nice to me. A few snubbed me, but that was the extent of their abuse. Molly said they were jealous because I was prettier. Molly was my best friend. She was only a year older than me but she had been there since she was thirteen, so she had been there awhile. Molly taught me how to endure. She assured me we wouldn't be here forever and that when we turned twenty-two they would let us go. She also said we were lucky because this was a nicer establishment that catered to gentlemen. Anyone violent got kicked out. She was hoping a rich man would fall in love with her and take her away as his mistress. She didn't fantasize any of them would want to marry her. No gentleman would wed a fallen woman.

"Since we had respectable clients we were taught manners so we could look like fine ladies, even though we were not treated as such by the customers. Once a month a doctor who smelled of gin, would come and give us an exam to make certain none of us had caught a venereal disease. It was so humiliating. Any girl who had caught the pox was kicked out to walk the streets. I was assured that was dangerous. The brothel at least did offer us some protection from people like Jack the Ripper.

"I learned quickly to just close my eyes, make appropriate noises and pretend I was somewhere else when a man was using me. I also learned it was smarter to approach the men, instead of the other way around. That way I had more control over who I serviced. I avoided customers smelling of alcohol or who had cruel faces. I found the shy ones were usually gentler. Luckily I never again saw that monster that took me the first time. I had some regulars—lonely bachelors, a few husbands in loveless marriages. And then the off and on again men with pregnant and sick wives. One man came to us because he felt his wife was above his carnal lust. Apparently we weren't. I knew even the kindest of them would never help me so I never bothered to ask. They wanted to believe I was there by choice, that I actually enjoyed this life. I don't know how they could think anyone would want this degrading existence. I prayed every night for God to save me.

"And then after a few years when I had given up all hope, a miracle happened. A gentleman, I had never seen before, came in. He seemed nervous, like this was his first time in a brothel. He had a gentle face, so I took him to my room. Instead of pulling my clothes off, we talked. He asked me to dinner. I think the man was actually trying to woo me first. I told him that wasn't how it worked. I swear he looked into my eyes, into my soul and saw what was really happening. He was the first client who saw me as a person! He said he couldn't go through with this and handed me a purse and walked out. When I opened it," Angela beamed, her face full of wonder, "I found it held a small fortune!"

"How much did it hold?" Wendell tried to remember how much money had been in it.

"Almost nine pounds!"

Wendell managed not to smile. Her clients would have made more than that in a week. But for a poor girl whose father's weekly salary would be little more than half a pound, this was indeed a small fortune.

"This was my chance!" Angela held up her chin. "I gave the madam the usual payment and hid the purse under my mattress. I waited until four in the morning. The madam would be in bed by then because the clients would be gone. No gentleman wanted to leave with the light of day and take the risk of his vicar catching him coming out of a brothel. I stole a crocheted runner off the piano by the door, threw it over my head and shoulders as a shawl, and fled into the darkness. I ran to the nearest train station, praying no one was chasing me. When I got to the station I took the first train out of town. I didn't care where it went as long as it was far away from London. It took me to Cambridge. It was the opposite of London, full of ancient buildings with lots of trees and fresh air. It was a sleepy college town and I fell in love with it.

"The first thing I did was buy some respectable clothes. Thanks to my etiquette lessons I could pass myself off as a lady. Everyone assumed I was gentry that had fallen on hard times. I was able to get a job as a waitress in a tearoom. Not a fancy position, but respectable. Back in those days even an unescorted woman could go into a tearoom without ruining her reputation. It paid enough to live comfortably enough. I got a room at a boarding house for young women. A few of the tenants thought the landlady, Mrs. Danner, was mean because she wouldn't allow any men beyond the entrance hall and demanded we be home by ten. I loved the dear lady, for she was just being protective of us. I knew well how much naive girls needed protecting.

"Some of the other girls at the tearoom complained about having to wait on people and that they didn't make more money. I almost laughed when they griped. Mrs. Jennings ran a tight ship, but she was fair. And even the worst customers treated us with some respect. I was happy.

"The tearoom was near the campus. Most of the students preferred the pubs, but a few came along with the staff. It was at the tearoom that I met Professor Howe. He was in his thirties, but that beard made him look older. He was shy and had never married. The other girls made jokes about his nose behind his back. This made me mad for he was always nice to all of us. So I made an effort to be extra nice to him. He had the kindest eyes and sweetest smile. I used to joke with him just to see that smile. Then one day he said he had been invited to a dinner function and needed an escort. He offered to pay me for my trouble if I would help him out. I told him I would be honored if he promised *not* to pay me. After that he asked me to lectures, to the theater and for walks in the parks.

Angela's face lit up with a whisper of a smile. "Then one day Abercrombie, after much hesitation and stammering, finally blurted out 'will you marry me?' After I got over my surprise I nearly said 'yes', then I thought better. 'No,' I told him. 'I can't.'

"The poor dear looked so wounded. It must have taken him days to get up the courage to ask me, and then I rejected him. So I took his hand and told him, 'My darling, I would love nothing more than to be your wife, but I dare not. You know nothing of my past. If it ever catches up with me, the scandal could cost you your position here at the university.' 'Nonsense,' he said, 'why should you be held responsible for your father or brother's actions?' 'No dear,' I told him. 'The fault lies with me.' He seemed incredulous. 'You? What could a sweet lady such as yourself possibly have done that would bring any shame to me?' There was no sense beating about the bush, so I just told him. 'I worked in a brothel in London.'

"Oh, the look of horror on his face, the disbelief. He said nothing, he was too shocked. He simply got up and hurried away." Angela's eyes got moist. "I was heart-broken, but I was even more devastated by how I had hurt this sweet innocent man. I went home and wept for both of us.

"I never expected to see the professor again. But the next day when I got off work he met me at the door. He told me he had done a lot of thinking and we needed to talk. We walked to a bench by the river and he apologized for how he had left me so rudely. He said he had always been told no woman would sell herself unless she was either greedy for finery or a wild woman out for pleasure. If that were true then why was I spending my time with him instead of one of the rich students who preferred the pubs over the classrooms? I was young and pretty enough to attract a millionaire's son who could buy me anything I desired and could show me a much better time. The only thing a lowly professor could possibly offer me was a life of respectability. And I turned that down for fear that I might hurt *his* career. Then he grinned at me. 'You are the most decent and honest woman I've ever met and I would be proud to have you as my wife. I would rather lose my career than lose you. These past months have been the happiest of my life. I don't know what circumstance made you choose such a profession but I am certain it wasn't self-indulgence. So, as far as I am concerned, it never happened.'

"I felt he needed to understand the woman he was risking his job for and the degrading life I had led. I told him how I had become a fallen woman. As he listened, tears ran down his cheeks. He promised me no man would ever dare to treat me as anything less than a lady ever again. He was the most loving husband one could ask for."

"Dear Lord! You have had a horrible life." Wendell felt tears welling in his own eyes.

"No." Angela shook her head, her cracked lips smiling. "My parents were poor but they loved me. My friend Molly was sold to the brothel by her mother for gin money! Most women in my profession, if they ever do get married, wind up with a penniless drunkard that beats them. I was married to the most considerate man in the world who had a good paying job and gave me a beautiful home and five wonderful children. My life has been good. I have been blessed." Then her smile faded. "Do you think God will forgive me of my sins? I wish to go to heaven to be with Abercrombie and my parents and little brother."

"My dear, I don't see that you ever committed any sin. Those that forced you into that profession are the ones going to Hell. You didn't let them harden you. You stayed good and innocent. You would not believe how many women would have complained at being married to a man with just a professor's salary."

Angela gave a wheezy chuckle. "Yes, I have met such women. Some people have no idea how lucky they are. Every day I thank God for my late husband, my children, my parents and of course that kind man who saved me from that horrid house of ill repute." She frowned. "That's who you remind me of. He had brown hair and didn't wear glasses, but you do look a lot like him. What was your father's name?"

"Frederick."

"Hmm, well it wasn't him. Maybe it is that look of benevolence about you that reminds me of him."

"Vicars are taught how to look benevolent at the seminary."

Angela giggled at that, then her face turned serious "I never told Abie this, but every night I prayed for my rescuer. I prayed that he would have as happy a life as he had helped me get. I prayed he would find a good woman who would appreciate him so he didn't have to seek solace in a brothel."

Wendell swallowed hard. "I'm sure he did."

"I regret I never got to thank him. I hadn't realized how much money he had left me until he was gone."

"I have no doubt he knows you were thankful. I'm sure he left the money so you could get away. I'm sure it wasn't an accident," Wendell fibbed.

"I named my sons after my two knights in shining armor. My eldest I named Abercrombie, after my dear husband, and my youngest I named Wendell, after the gentleman who helped me to escape. I never told Abie where I got the name. I was afraid I might hurt his feelings, make him think I loved this stranger. I suppose I did, but not the same way I loved Abie. Was that wrong of me?"

"My parents named me Horatio, after Lord Nelson." Wendell lied. "Many parents name their children after people they felt were heroes."

"Yes, Wendell was my hero. He saved me and gave me back my life. However, it doesn't change what I once was. Can you give me absolution for that, vicar?"

"For what? I don't see that you did anything wrong, only that wrong was done to you." Wendell gently took her hand. "God does not hold you accountable for the sins of others, Mrs. Howe...Angela. You were a devoted wife and mother. You brought five fine children into this world. And they had children, and their children will have children. Your descendants will number in the thousands and some will play a critical role in the future. And all because you had the courage to escape and find a better life. You have nothing to be ashamed of, my dear. Nothing at all."

Angela gazed up wistfully. "Do you think so?"

"I know so." Wendell stood up. He knew he shouldn't, but he leaned down and kissed Angela on the forehead. "You get some rest now, my dear. And don't you worry. You will be with your Abercrombie soon."

"Thank you, Reverend Smith. You made me feel much better." Angela closed her eyes and smiled, looking exhausted but peaceful.

Wendell gave her hand a squeeze. He watched her a moment, not sure if he should mourn her or rejoice that she at least had found happiness. He pulled out his handkerchief and wiped his eyes.

When he came into the hall, Serendipity jumped up and hurried over. "Well?" She grabbed his arm. "How did it go?"

Wendell smiled at her and nodded. "Better than I expected. Thank you for bringing me, Serendipity. I think that gave both of us some peace."

"Excuse me, Reverend."

They looked behind them to see a middle-aged man dressed in a dark-blue double-breasted suit, holding a bouquet of flowers. "Were you just in with Mrs. Howe?"

"Yes," Wendell said.

"How is she doing? I'm her youngest son, Wendell Edward Howe." The man stuck out his hand.

Wendell shook his hand stunned, realizing this was his direct ancestor.

"It is a real honor to meet you, sir. Your mother is resting now."

"I hope she wasn't giving you a deathbed confession. That would have been pretty boring." Angela's son chuckled. "I don't think I've ever heard her swear or lose her temper. Mother lived up to her name. She was an angel."

Wendell Edward hung his head. "I'm already talking about her in the past tense," he choked. "Part of me wants this to all be over so she won't have to suffer anymore, and a bigger part never wants to let her go. I'm a married man with grown children, but you never completely outgrow needing your mother. Just knowing she's there."

Wendell put his hand on his forebear's shoulder. "She was talking about how much she loved and missed your father."

"Yes, they doted on each other. Well, I suppose I should let you get back to work. Nice to meet you, Reverend—?"

"Smith. Horatio Smith. And this is my wife, Elmira."

"Best of luck, old boy." The elder Wendell nodded at the younger one.

"You too, old chap. And may God bless you."

Wendell E. stepped into the room to see his mother. Wendell A. took Serendipity by the arm and started down the hall.

"Elmira?" she teased.

"Sorry, it was the first thing to pop in my head."

"Hmm. So that was your great-great-etc. grandfather? You said you were descended from the youngest son."

"Yes."

"And you were named after him?"

"No, I was named after my great-grandfather Wendell Herbert." Wendell frowned. "He was named after his great-uncle Wendell James and—yes, I suppose in the long run I was named after Wendell Edward."

"And who did Angela name her youngest son after?"

"After the nice man that helped—" Wendell came to a sudden stop. "Dear lord, he was named after *me!*"

"Uh-huh. So if you are named after this Wendell and he was named after you, does this mean you were really named after *yourself?*"

Wendell felt slightly dizzy. "My word! I think you are right. Oh bloody hell, why couldn't I have told her my name was Albert or Clive or even John. I always hated being called When-Dull and I've no one to blame but myself."

"Look at the bright side."

"Bright side?"

"You were named after a fantastic guy." Serendipity grinned at him.

Chapter Thirty

Wendell and Serendipity stepped out of the Timemobile into the old wooden garage with its dirt floor and unpainted walls. Wendell headed for the door facing the house, followed by Serendipity.

"I must find Tobias." His face had a determined expression.

"Why?"

"I want to play this for him. I want him to see how this sort of thing can ruin a person's life. I want to make certain he does not force himself upon any more virgins."

Wendell climbed the concrete stepping stones up to the house. The back yard sloped, save for a spot halfway up on the left side that had been flattened out for a toolshed. This old weathered structure had been claimed by Erik to store his blacksmith tools. Dressed in a leather apron, he stood outside the shed engrossed in some project. In front of him stood his small Viking-style anvil. It didn't look like an anvil at all. It was made of black iron and had a top hardly bigger than the bottom of a boot. The base was a large spike which Erik had hammered into a wooden stump he had salvaged from a neighbor who had cut down a tree. Viking anvils had to be portable in an age when many blacksmiths traveled.

The forge consisted of charcoal in a pit lined with rocks. Rosetta knelt on the ground nearby pumping by hand a double bellows made of leather and wood. She rocked from one bellow to the other, her face as blank as ever.

Erik was heating a long narrow piece of metal in the forge when he looked up from his work. He pulled the metal out of the fire with his tongs and dropped it in a metal bucket of water. He came running over. "Did you two just come out of the time machine?"

"Yeah," Serendipity tried to look innocent. "Wendell wanted to take me to lunch in Twentieth-Century Cambridge."

"Why the priest collar?"

"You get better service if they think you're a vicar."

Erik shrugged like he bought that explanation. "I hope you are not cross that I borrowed your robot. I am being ever vigilant that no sparks hit it."

"What are you making?" Serendipity asked.

"Nails. I want to build a real blacksmith shop with a roof. The toolshed is too small to work in and we are going to need it for garden tools anyway."

"Good idea. Keep you out of the rain."

"More importantly it will provide shade so I can see the color of the heated metal and gauge the temperature more accurately. I wish to build a better furnace and get a bigger anvil. However I am having a Niflhel of a time trying to find a large granite stone good enough for an anvil."

"You want a granite pedestal for your next anvil?"

"Neinn. The granite stone will be the anvil. I need one very sturdy. I must be solid with no fractures."

Serendipity studied a wooden box full of square nails. "Why are you making nails? Can't you just buy them cheap?"

Erik snorted. "What fun would that be?"

"Excuse me, Erik," Wendell asked. "But have you seen Tobias?"

"Neinn." He pulled the metal out of the bucket of water with the tongs, and stuck it back in the coals of the furnace.

Wendell frowned. "I am not sure if I have seen him these last couple of days." He turned to Serendipity. "Have you seen him?"

She shook her head. "No, but I'm sure that's just because he's been going out to eat and sneaks back in to sleep."

Erik pulled the metal out and put it on his anvil. "Serendipity is right. Not does he like us, and not do we like him." He lightly hit the cherry red rod, the anvil ringing. No sparks flew. Instead tiny bits of black metal scales flaked off and fell to the ground.

Serendipity chased after Wendell into the house and then the kitchen. There they found Henry and Matilda making oatmeal cookies.

"Have either of you two seen Tobias in the last few days?" Wendell sounded worried.

Henry shook his head. "Nope, but then I didn't see much of him before."

"I hath seen him not." Matilda set the bowl she was stirring on the counter.

Serendipity put her hand on Wendell's arm. "You'll just have to wait for Tobias to show up."

Wendell stroked his mustache nervously. "I wonder if Dr. Djata has seen him."

"Abubakari is out." Henry pointed with the wooden spoon. "Said he'd be back for dinner. What's the problem?"

"This does not bode well." Wendell frowned concerned. "No one has seen him since I showed him our family tree three days ago. He could be lying dead in some ditch! If anything has happened to him—"

Serendipity put her hands on her hips. "I don't get you, Wendell. One minute you're giving the guy a black eye and the next you're all worried about him. He's a stinking hyena."

"I know Tobias can be insufferable, but have you forgotten how he helped us battle against the terrorists in Pigalle?"

"He was trying to save his own neck."

"If you will recall, he yelled 'run' not 'help.' He was trying to warn us away."

"He's still a hyena. Why should you care where he is?"

"Because if anything bad happens to him I will be to blame. I have to protect Tobias. I owe that to Sir Albert Leach."

"So, his uncle was some High Mucky-Muck. Light a sparkler."

"Sir Albert was always very gracious and supportive of me, even before I became a licensed time traveler. He didn't see me as an upstart, but someone who was going to carry on his work. He was an excellent mentor."

"Yeah," Henry agreed. "He was my mentor, too. Sir Albert was a grand gentleman."

"You guys keep talking about mentors, like it's a big deal," Serendipity said.

"It is a big deal." Henry nodded. "Mentors are more than just babysitters for us on our first few trips in the Field. They show you the ropes. They are your lifeline in an alien world. Afterwards you can go to them for advice."

"Tobias is a big boy, Wendell." Matilda said. "I dost not see why you feel thou art responsible for him."

"I am responsible for him." Wendell turned to her with a guilty expression. "I am Tobias's mentor."

Matilda stared at Wendell in speechless horror. Finally she spoke. "Tobias treateth thee with the greatest disrespect. That be not how one treats a mentor!"

Wendell bowed his head. "From our very first trip in the Field together, Tobias was cold toward me. He wanted to have as little to do with me as possible. I thought he considered me beneath him. I see now he considered me a rival rather than a mentor. I feel like I have failed him."

Wendell crossed his arms like he was hugging himself. "I have a bad feeling about Tobias. I need to find him." He pulled out his computer and clicked his tongue. "Trace on Tobias." Wendell studied the Bible intently for a long time, then nodded. "Ah! I think I'm picking up something. It looks like he hasn't left town. The bus might not be the best way to find him. I wonder if Sherman would be willing to drive me."

"He's downstairs. He was going out until he discovered we were baking cookies."

"Thanks." Wendell headed for the stairs to the basement.

Sherman had expected to find Tobias in a bar, but his tracer had led them to a cafe on Meridian Street. The old restaurant seemed nice and homey, and far too blue-collar for a man who refused to eat beans. When they stepped inside they saw Tobias in a booth in the farthest corner from everyone else, staring at a photo on the wall of a small fishing trawler and sipping a cup of coffee.

Sherman looked up at Wendell. "Do you want me to wait in the Ferrari?"

Wendell shook his head. "You seem to have a clear insight into human nature, especially for your young age. Maybe you can figure out what makes the man tick. Come along, old chap."

Wendell walked over to the corner and just stood at the table.

Tobias looked up surprised. "What the devil do you want?"

"I just want to talk." Wendell sat down on the booth seat across from him, then slid over so Sherman could join him.

"I see you brought your chauffeur."

"Sherman is my friend. He agreed to drive me."

Tobias gave a soft snort. "Is there a reason you insist on hounding me,

When-Dull."

"I'm worried about you."

"Why should you give a farthing what I do?"

"I am your mentor. It is my job to help you."

"If you want to help me then leave me the bloody hell alone." Tobias looked like a trapped feral cat.

"Where have you been? Have you even been home?"

"I have no home."

"Where are you staying?"

"I do not believe that is any of your damn business."

"Tobias, you don't have any money."

"No, it and all my luggage are in Paris back in 1897, aren't they? All I have are the clothes on my back, and your charity with which I bought some underwear and toiletries." Tobias lifted a briefcase he had in the seat beside him. "I found a used briefcase to carry my worldly possessions in so it would look like I wasn't really homeless. Classier than a burlap bag, don't you think?"

"How are you paying for food and shelter?"

"I hocked my gold pocket watch. Victorian antique, you know. As for shelter, motels are expensive. So I have been using my talents. It appears I inherited one from our dear Grandmamma Howe."

"Oh?"

Tobias took a sip of coffee. "I've been prostituting myself."

"What! Tobias that is illegal in this day and age. You could get arrested."

"Only if you do it for money, not if you do it for food and shelter. Just go to a singles bar and find some stupid cow who's looking for a man to take home and—voila—instant bed. Of course you have to pay for it by listening to her whine about her ex. Not hard to see why he left."

"Tobias! You can't live like that!"

"You are right. I need to find a permanent home. Find some rich old trout who wants a gigolo."

Wendell looked horrified. "You are a temporal anthropologist with two Ph.D.s. You are a scholar and researcher of the highest caliber. You can't lower yourself to being a gigolo."

"Why not? You did."

"What!"

"You are sleeping with some rich old trout who gives you room and board."

"That is not why—" Wendell sputtered. "I am not a gigolo!"

"Oh please, why else would you bring yourself to put up with that homely obnoxious grease monkey."

Sherman stood up, not in protest, but so he could get leverage to keep Wendell from leaping over the table. "Chill, Wendell! He's playing ya."

Wendell settled down and glowered at Tobias. "You will not speak of the woman I love in that manner!"

Sherman moved around to the end of the table and looked down at

Tobias. "I swear, dude, you are such a hoser. Wendell has got to be one of the most laid-back guys I know. Nothing riles him—except you. You know just how to push his buttons. You know how to push everyone's buttons, don't you? You remind me of my little sister, Terry. She likes insulting people so they will fight with her."

"I don't have to put up with this abuse from a child lackey."

"There you go again, pushing my buttons. Okay, so I'm only nineteen and haven't quite found my spot on this team. Well, I just found my spot. It's *Trouble Shooter*. And you, Tobias, are nothing but trouble! What is your problem, dude? Are you doing this because you're jealous? Does it make you feel important or cool?"

Wendell stopped glaring at Tobias and stared at Sherman. "I say, I knew you would come in handy. I believe you have nailed the problem right on the head, old boy." He turned back to Tobias, frowning quizzically. "Why *do* you do this?"

"Well, nobody likes me."

Sherman glowered down at Tobias. "Of course they don't like you, you moron! You push everyone's buttons." He then rolled his eyes, when it hit him. "There you go again, another one of my buttons. I can't stand people who are as stupid as you and totally blind to their own faults. Your life sucks and it's always someone else's fault, never your own."

Sherman sat back down. "Now, you can be a homeless person and wind up in a gutter or you can come back to Fairhaven Home. In exchange for room and board, you will quit being so lame. You don't even have to make nice, just stop being such a dipstick. Stay in your stupid room if you want. Oh, and you have to watch this." Sherman turned to Wendell. "Show him your interview with Angela you were telling me about. He can watch it on your regular computer monitor."

Tobias turned to Wendell. "Are you going to let this *child* order us around?"

Wendell smiled at Tobias. "Yes, I am. Sherman is after all the team's Trouble Shooter. And in case you forgot, he is also the House Manager. He has the authority to set down rules." He looked over at Sherman. "I think Tobias is slipping. He thought he had found another one of my 'buttons,' as you call it." Wendell pulled out his Bible.

"I don't have to watch this!" Tobias protested.

"Yes, you do." Sherman said in a very businesslike tone.

"Why? You already pointed out I am a loser and a joke and a pervert and now you want to rub it in my face that I'm a monster." Tobias glared at them.

Sherman and Wendell both stopped and stared stunned at the man.

"Dear heavens," Wendell whispered. "That's why you ran away. You aren't running from us. You are running from yourself. You are doing all of this to punish yourself for what you did to all those girls."

"One, all right." Tobias held up his index finger. "Just one and I don't know what her name was. I just made up a bunch of names. I didn't know about your Angela, I swear."

"Dude!" Sherman looked amazed. "You *are* good at finding buttons—even ones you don't know about."

Wendell raised his eyebrow. "Then why did you tell us—"

"I was trying to impress you," Tobias lowered his voice. "You were attacking me, calling me a porn writer. I bragged about the one area in which I knew I had bested all of you. Truthfully I didn't know she would be *that* young. I thought she would be an adult house servant who had decided to go into a better paying business and was willing to sell her virginity for some extra cash. I didn't know until it was too late."

"What do you mean too late?" Wendell snorted. "You could have walked out."

"I wanted to when I saw how young and terrified she was. I was almost out of the door when I realized my leaving would not save her from her fate." Tobias stared at the table. "If I left they would just give her over to some other man who would not be as gentle with her as I would...and who might kill her in the long run."

"Kill her?" Wendell frowned. "Why would he kill her?"

"Virgins weren't just sought out by the adventurous. It was rumored that virgins were a cure for syphilis."

"What?" Sherman yelped. "Come on, even I know that's a load of crapola."

"Of course, it is," Tobias snapped. "They might be a preventative, but hardly a cure. If I had handed her off to the next John, he might very well have given her the pox. And if that didn't kill her the cure would."

Wendell nodded. "Yes, arsenic and mercury." He turned to Sherman. "Tobias isn't making any of this up. Even I have heard this superstition of virgins curing venereal disease whispered in Victorian hotel smoking rooms."

Tobias ran his finger around the edge of his coffee cup. "If she was deflowered she would be useless to some pox-ridden git. They might even let her go."

"Why didn't you just get her out of there?" Sherman couldn't believe this.

"No, he couldn't." Wendell came to his defense. "He would be changing history."

Tobias nodded. "I used every trick I knew to make it as painless as possible. I used the Theta Wave in my cane to make her relax; make her numb, so she wouldn't remember much. So, she wouldn't be afraid. So, she wouldn't be traumatized any more than necessary. I held her until she quit trembling."

Wendell eyebrows raised in surprise. "You were trying to be compassionate to the poor girl."

"Yes, and don't think I didn't catch hell from the Enforcers, let me tell you. I convinced them I had done nothing to change her fate. Time had remained *pure*." Tobias spat out that last word with disgust in his voice. "If you ever read my books you would know I never wrote about that episode."

"Maybe you should have," Wendell said.

"What and give all the pedophiles a thrill?"

"No, told what this trade was really like instead of painting it as a joyous romp."

"That doesn't sell books. I am sure the publisher would have edited it out."

"Get a new publisher. What I think is the worst thing about your books, Tobias, is it is all about you, what *you* experienced."

"No, it's not. It is in the first person because the publisher wants the reader to feel like they are there, but I have to paint a fantasy for them. I can't tell the whole truth."

"Historians are supposed to look for the truth. You sound like you sold out just to sell books."

"I am as big a whore as the fallen ladies, aren't I? It is why I had no problem selling myself for a night's lodging. Do you think I spend all my time in brothels because it is fun? Let me tell you, it gets old really fast. But it sells books. I've outsold all of you."

Tobias leaned forward, with a scornful sneer, but his eyes were not focused on either of them. "Perhaps I'm not a gentleman by your standards, but the scarlet women consider me one. I'm never rough, I let them set the parameters, I never try to cheat them out of money, and I always keep my weight on my elbows. I know they mean it when they invite me back. If all of their customers were like me, it would not be such a horrible life for them. I have never been abusive to any of the soiled doves. I can empathize with them."

"Why don't you let them tell their stories?"

"I told you, that would not sell."

"You are a historian, Tobias. History is made by people. You have to tell *their* story."

"Says the man who wrote about tea!" Tobias rolled his eyes.

"It was tea's influence on people that I wrote about—*all* the people, from the society ladies to the working class, from the tea plantation owners to their laborers. I told *their* stories, too. History is about people." Wendell pushed his computer across the table to Tobias. "Don't worry. You weren't the one, Tobias. Believe it or not, I wish now it had been you. I just want you to learn your own history, the human element in your own past, the one that we share."

"Our shared shame?"

"No, I'm proud to be descended from Angela. You should be too. She was a good woman—a brave woman. And she had the courage and determination to change her life. She might teach you something."

Tobias slowly picked up the Bible and opened it to the screen in the center.

Wendell brought the mollified Tobias in the front door of Fairhaven Home. The library just inside had been turned into an entertainment room with a large-screen television. Serendipity emerged from the door. "There you are, you little cockroach!" Serendipity boomed above the voices of singing munchkins. "You have one hell of a lot of nerve coming back here and—"

Wendell held up his hand. "Serendipity, *don't!*"

Serendipity stepped back, looking surprised at the uncustomary command in Wendell's voice. "All right, hon, if it's that important."

"It is, Serendipity," Wendell said gentler. "Thank you."

"Well, well." Henry came into the hall, leaving Oz behind. "Look what the cat dragged in!"

Matilda followed him, looking equally as hostile.

"Henry, don't start a row," Wendell warned him. "All of you, Tobias wants to make peace, and he can't if you all attack him."

Serendipity circled Tobias like a tiger. "So, what about the young girls he—"

"Never happened," Wendell half lied. He gave a warning glance to Sherman. "Tobias made that up in a vain attempt to impress us."

"Is that true?" Henry peered at Tobias. "Why the hell did you think *that* would impress us?"

Tobias said nothing but hung his head.

Wendell put his hand on Tobias's shoulder. "I can assure you, Tobias has never been abusive to any woman. Since Tobias first showed up we have all put him on the defensive. Unfortunately with Tobias being offensive is the only way he knows how to be defensive. So we are all going to start over. Be nice to Tobias, and if you can't be nice, just leave him alone. Tobias in return will be civil to others. Is that understood?" He turned to Tobias, and spoke more gently. "I say, why don't you go upstairs, take a shower and change your clothes, old chap? High tea is at five."

Tobias nodded and walked toward the stairs, looking physically and emotionally exhausted.

The front door opened again, and Abubakari stepped into the group. "Aw ni tile. Good afternoon." He glanced about at everyone standing in the hall, then saw Tobias wearily climbing the stairs. "I was at the university library all day. Did I miss something?"

"Oh yeah," Serendipity assured him.

"What happened, wa?"

"Not really sure, ask Wendell."

Wendell held up his hand. "Please, not now. I need a cup of tea. I'll be up in the sitting room." He headed for the stairs himself.

Everyone turned to Sherman.

"All right," Serendipity demanded. "Tell us what happened, kid."

Sherman stood up straight. "I discovered what I'm meant to be on your team. I'm a professional Trouble Shooter."

Serendipity rolled her eyes. "Foot, I already knew that, kid. Come on, what happened?"

Sherman frowned. "Not totally sure myself. Tobias ran away because he felt guilty. The rest is kind of confusing. I'm a Trouble Shooter, not an analyst." Sherman wasn't sure how much he should tell and what should be left a secret. "Tobias and Wendell can explain it all someday for you." Sherman smiled at them, and then turned. "I'll be down in my room listening to some tunes."

ᗯhapter ᗷhirty-One

Wendell studied his cravat knot in the mirror. It appeared to be straight. Then he smoothed down his mustache, pleased with its appearance. Even Matilda commented on it yesterday. Of course her comment was "Oh, I see thou hast grown back thy mustache," and Wendell pointed out he had grown it back weeks ago.

Serendipity came bouncing into his bedroom, already dressed in modern clothes. Well, she had found them at the Salvation Army, so they were at least fairly modern. "Guess what I want to do today?"

"You wish to go shopping for more twentieth-century antiques? I think you have the house fairly full now." He turned to face her.

"No-o-o." She smiled coyly, those big brown eyes sparkling mischievously.

"Erm, I think they will be expecting us downstairs for breakfast. They are going to start thinking you are a wanton woman."

"I'm always wanton something, huh." She flopped down on his bed. "No, I wasn't talking about sex. I want to go meet Nathan Brown."

"Oh, you found a long-lost cousin? You will have to wait until we are allowed back into the twenty-fourth century."

"No, my long-lost ancestor. Nathan was the founder of the Brown family."

"No my dear, you can't go visiting dead relatives," Wendell said patiently, but firmly. "You would be too emotionally involved. It is also very likely you'll change history."

"You got to meet your ancestor Angela—twice!"

"That was different. The first time was an accident, and I didn't know who she was. The second time was on her deathbed."

"Fine, we'll show up just before Nathan dies."

"Really, could you deal with the trauma of getting to know him and then knowing he would die soon?"

"You did."

"Believe me, it was not easy. But I needed to know if Tobias was involved. And I just wanted to know Angela had finally found happiness."

Serendipity poked out her lip, which Wendell found both exasperating and adorable. "I don't know why I can't just *meet* Nathan. It's not like I plan to stay the weekend."

"It is just not a good idea."

"Oh, I understand." She crossed her arms. "*Your* family is important and *mine* isn't?"

"What?" Wendell felt baffled.

"That's it, isn't it? We can visit your family, but not my family."

"My word, are we fighting about the in-laws? Hmph? I've never been in an argument about in-laws before. I never was with a woman long enough to get around to that. I say, we have appeared to have reached a new level in our relationship." Wendell actually felt pleased.

"Don't change the subject, Dr. Howe."

"Dr. Howe? You never call me Dr. Howe, Dr. Brown."

"See, two can play this game."

Wendell turned back to the mirror. "Well, if you are going to be childish about this—"

"You're the one turning your back on me."

Wendell turned back around and frowned at her. Then he sighed. "Please Serendipity, I don't wish to fight."

"Great, then you agree with me?"

"I didn't say I agreed, I merely stated I didn't wish to fight."

"Okay," Serendipity came over and draped herself over his shoulder. "How about if I just use my womanly wiles on you?"

"Fine, but it still won't make it a good idea." Wendell did his best to ignore the intoxicating scent of her pheromones.

"Hmph, and people say *I'm* stubborn!"

"Serendipity, please, you are risking changing history by going back and introducing yourself to someone in the distant past. What are we talking about here? Middle Ages? They will burn you as a witch."

"Nathan Brown fought in the Revolutionary War, so he would have died in the early 1800s. Benjamin Franklin was from the mid-1700s and he didn't want to burn me when I told him I was from the future."

"Dr. Brown! Do you have any idea how dangerous that was?"

"Ben's head didn't explode."

"You could have changed history by revealing too much to a fellow scientist."

"Nothing changed."

"How do you know that?"

"Right, my telling Franklin that someday we would have more advanced gadgets is what caused the Holocaust and the sinking of the Titanic. Don't you think Ben had already figured out the future would be more advanced? The man wasn't stupid."

"No, I meant—erm, well—" Wendell sputtered.

"Heh! You've been brainwashed with that Time Purist sludge. Come on, Wendell, what would it harm for me to just go meet my ancestor? I just want to see him and hear his voice and look in his eyes. He was a war hero who died in poverty. If I meet him just before he dies, what could he possibly do to change history even if I did tell him everything? I just want to know where I came from. Is that asking too much?"

Wendell sighed.

"Please, oh please, oh please." Serendipity started kissing his neck.

"You aren't fighting fair, Serendipity." Wendell objected, but he didn't push her away.

"You want me to stop?"

"If you can come up with a believable story to tell this Nathan Brown, and promise not to reveal you are from the future, then I might consider letting you go."

Serendipity raised her eyebrow at him. "You do realize I could just march out to the Timemobile and go anywhere and *anywhen* I want and you couldn't stop me."

"Why do you think I'm giving in so easily? I know I am officially your consultant and not your supervisor. I cannot stop you, but I am hoping to talk you into using some commonsense."

"Shoot, what do you think Sherman is for?" Serendipity shrugged.

Wendell shook his head. "We will take him along then. Not that you ever listen to commonsense."

"If I had commonsense, I never would have invented time travel, now would I?"

Wendell sighed. "You do have a point there."

Sherman followed Serendipity, Wendell and Henry out of the Timemobile. Sherman was dressed in a frock coat like Wendell, while Henry dressed like Daniel Boone. Serendipity wore a bonnet and a gown with a high waist and puffy sleeves. They appeared to be in a gully surrounded by hills covered in deciduous trees. The only hint of civilization was the dirt and gravel road the hovervan sat on.

Sherman looked back at the machine, then shook his head and looked again. There was a stagecoach pulled by two horses. Up above sat a driver wearing a red jacket. The horses tossed their heads.

"Whoa, awesome, Ser! How did you do that? It looks so real."

Wendell studied the effect. "I say, nicely done, Dr. Brown. You are a true artist."

"Let's just hope nobody tries to pet the horses or gets too close." Serendipity studied her handiwork critically. "They'll either touch open air or solid metal. The horses are programmed to canter when the thing moves forward. Even put in clopping hoofs sounds."

"Concord Stagecoach?" Henry studied the illusion.

"Yeah, 1830 model."

Henry nodded his approval. "Yup, you did your research."

"Thanks for coming along, Henry," Serendipity said. "You are our early Americana expert."

"Shoot, a Victorian Englishman isn't too out of place here. Still, nice to be back where I belong." The cowboy glanced around. "Well, sort of, anyway." He looked down at his buckskin jacket and pants. "I've worn these sort of duds before, back when I was fur trapping."

"Really Henry, I don't know why you didn't want to wear a period suit." Wendell brushed the sleeve of his brown Victorian frock coat.

"I never look right in a suit, old buddy. Of course, you never look right out of one."

Serendipity looked down at her pink dress. "I'm sure I don't look right. I feel like I stepped out of a dang Jane Austin novel."

Sherman looked down at his striped vest. He was wearing the suit Wendell had bought him when they first met in 1851 London, along with round wireframe glasses. "I look like a nerd no matter what I wear."

"So where are we besides 1835?" Henry looked around. "No wait, let me guess." He stepped over to a tree beside the road and studied the leaves. "Looks like American Chestnut." He glanced around. "Looks like mostly chestnut. From that and the terrain I'm guessing the Appalachian Mountains. Pity about the chestnut blight and coal companies destroying this place." He glanced down. "Hmm, wide road, gravel pressed into the dirt, plenty of wagon tracks. Shoot, I'll bet this is the National Road!"

"National Road?" Sherman asked.

"The finest highway in America at this time."

"America's finest highway?" Sherman glanced down at the dirt road and frowned. "You're kidding."

"Nope, this road is the equivalent of your I-5 Freeway. Hundreds of transport wagons, military convoys, wagon trains and stagecoaches pass over this road every year. This road has been macadamized, using the latest innovations."

"Macadamized?" Sherman stared at the dirt.

"Yes," Wendell joined in. "A technique developed by a Brit named McAdam. He found that if you pressed fine stone with sand into the roadbed with an iron roller that it created a very durable surface, excellent for wagon traffic."

Serendipity smiled at Henry. "You are correct, Henry. We are in western Maryland in the Appalachians on the National Road."

"So exactly what're we doing here? Is this just a joyride?"

"I came to meet Nathan Brown," Serendipity said.

"Meet? We aren't allowed to get too chummy with people in the past, you know. Who is this fellow?"

"He's my great-times-twenty-one-grandfather and founder of the Brown family."

Henry's jaw dropped. "What! We came to visit your own ancestor? You can't do that! You could change history. You might never get born if you start doing loco things like that, missy."

"Sheesh! I went through this already with Wendell. I picked the end of Nathan's life. He's going to pass away soon, so I won't be changing anything."

Henry turned and looked accusingly at Wendell. "And you agreed to these shenanigans?"

"Dr. Brown pointed out that I could hardly stop her. I didn't want her to go alone."

Henry looked at Serendipity, and then back at Wendell. "Yeah, you're probably right. You can tell Serendipity's a woman from the West: independent and determined??better known as wild and stubborn. Don't get in the filly's way, or you'll get run over."

"Thank you, Henry." Serendipity gave him a coy smile. "I'll take that as a compliment. Shall we get in the cab and find out where Nathan lives?

Records say he died near Prattsville and according to my calculations it should be up here a couple of miles. It's not even on the map anymore. Wendell had a heck of a time finding it."

Wendell pulled out his Bible and flipped it open. "Yes, the town will disappear soon. I was unable to even find it on an 1880 map."

They had to feel around for the handle to the cab door since they couldn't see it because of the Holographic Skin's illusion. It was a bit unsettling when Sherman felt it on the horse's rump. He closed his eyes so he wouldn't have to see the mirage destroyed and reality turned upside down. Crawling into the cab, he found the other three coming in on the other side. Serendipity wound up sitting between the two temporal anthropologists this time. Sherman started up the machine and began driving down the dirt road.

"I still think this is a plum loco idea," Henry said. "The danger of changing time aside, how do you even know your ancestor will want to meet you? What if your ancestor turns out to be nasty or disappointing?"

"He's a Brown!" Serendipity held her head high. "He's family."

"Henry does have a point," Wendell said. "I am not certain if I would want to meet the founder of the Howe family. The name is either Saxon, Viking or Norman, no one can agree. However everyone does agree all three groups were bad tempered and carried battleaxes. I am certain my ancestor would just split my skull if I tried to shake his hand."

"Nathan Brown was a Southern gentleman, you just wait and see."

Even if Sherman hadn't had to drive slowly to bolster the illusion of a carriage, the dirt road would not have allowed him to speed. They did pass a couple of wagons laden with goods under canvas tarps and another stagecoach, all going in the opposite direction.

The first sign of habitation was a collection of half-a-dozen log buildings built along a side road. At the corner of this dirt lane and the highway was the largest structure, made of rough unpainted boards. It reminded Sherman of one of those gas-station mini-marts built in the middle of nowhere along the freeway to take advantage of passing traffic. The building wasn't much bigger than one of its descendants. A sign above the door read "Stage Depoe and Generul Stor" in crude lettering. On the large front porch sat two men on a bench made of a log split in half with saplings as legs. Before them a teenager of African descent swept the boards, showing the only activity in this sleepy hamlet.

Sherman turned down the mud road and pulled around the back of the store. They watched out the windows to make sure no one was around and got out. The natives would freak if they saw their visitors stepping out of a horse's rear end.

They walked around to the front of the store and Sherman got a better look at the loiterers who looked as crude as the bench. Their clothes were scruffy and their faces unshaven and blotchy. Sherman had seen that complexion on alcoholics. His mom had married or dated more than one. The term "white trash" came to mind.

Serendipity walked up the steps to the lanky teenager with the broom. "Excuse me, sir."

He stopped sweeping and looked at her, then glanced over his shoulder.

"No, I'm talking to you." Serendipity smiled at him.

The kid looked surprised, "Me, ma'am?"

"Yes."

"I ain't no 'sir', ma'am. I just a slave."

Serendipity's eyes got large in horror. "Oh, I'm so sorry."

"Me, too," he whispered. Then he spoke up. "Is there something I can help with, ma'am?"

"Do you know where Nathan Brown lives?"

"I surely do, ma'am." He pointed to the muddy side road. "Go yonder down that there road apiece, turn right afore the bridge and go on to the first hill. Old Mister Brown live on the hillside in a cabin."

"Thank you, sir."

"You is more than welcome, ma'am."

Serendipity turned to leave, when one of the white men sitting on the porch stood up. "Hey, you! Why is you asking 'bout Nathan Brown? Why you wanting to know where that nigger lives?"

Serendipity's eyes blazed with hot anger, but her voice stayed cool. "Because he's my grandfather, that's why."

"So, you a nigger, too?"

"Yeah, and I'm a whole lot smarter and richer than you'll ever be. But then I'm the granddaughter of the Revolutionary War hero, Nathan Brown." She flashed her teeth in a vicious grin, then turned, and strode off.

"So, who'd be the rest of you?" the bigot yelled. "You grandkids, too?"

Wendell tipped his top hat. "No, these gentlemen work for Miss Brown. As for myself, I am the Duke of Cambridge and cousin to the King of England. Miss Brown wishes to introduce me to her grandfather, so I may ask for her hand in marriage and make her my Duchess. I must compliment you on the choosing of your town's name. Prattsville is most appropriate since it apparently is full of *prats*!" Wendell gave a nod of his head and followed Serendipity, leaving the two hecklers staring shocked.

Sherman noticed the slave got busy sweeping, trying to hide a grin.

The four time travelers returned hurriedly to the Timemobile, got in the cab, and drove back to the road. This side road was narrow and full of potholes Sherman tried to miss. "Excuse me, Ser, why did he call your great-grandfather *that* name?"

"That was an ancient derogatory once used against Americans of African descent," Serendipity said.

"I know what it means, Ser. I'm from the twentieth century, remember? My question is why would he call your great-grandfather that?"

"Because the man is obviously a bigot."

"No, I mean why would he call your great-grandfather that when he's white?"

"Who said he was white?"

Sherman almost ran off the road. "What? Your great-grandfather is *black*?"

"Yeah, he was the founder of the Brown family. He was born a slave and when he bought his freedom, he took the surname of Brown, since that was the color of his skin. Brown was a popular name with freed slaves of this period."

"Wait a minute! Your *family* is black?"

"My paternal line goes straight back to Africa according to the DNA," Serendipity said proudly. "Nathan Brown is the first one we have a historical record of."

"*You're* black?"

"I think I'm one-sixty-fourth African. I'm afraid that only makes me about 1%, but still I have some African ancestors. Of course I have all sorts of ancestors from all over. Now, we could have gone with the maternal line, following the mitochondrial DNA, but we'd have a hard time tracing her. I don't know her name."

"So where does that line go? England? Ireland?"

"Aztec," Serendipity said.

"*Aztec*?"

"Hey, my family has been in the melting pot of America since the 1600s. I'm a little bit of everything. You have a problem with that?" Serendipity started to look indignant.

"Don't be too hard on the boy," Henry told her. "If I remember my twentieth-century history right, Sherman comes from a time when the U.S. Government still insisted that everyone write down one race, and one race only, on all their forms. They bragged about being a melting pot, yet denied they were mongrels."

"One race?" Serendipity looked at Henry confused. "I thought there was only one race."

"They used to believe in multiple races back then—I mean back now."

"What? There's only one race?" Sherman asked.

"Biologically, yes," Wendell joined in. "They discovered that fact back in the twenty-first century while they were deciphering the genetic record."

"You forgot the Neanderthal race," Serendipity pointed out. "Got a bit of that myself, too."

"Ah, yes of course. I meant surviving races."

"Wait a minute," Sherman voice rose. "Neanderthals are another species."

The other three laughed at that remark, making Sherman feel rather foolish. "Come on guys, what about the black race and the white race?" he argued.

"Those are social concepts rather than biological realities. The word 'race' was rather overused to mean any ethnic group."

Henry shrugged. "Shoot, even if there had been more than one race, after centuries of people moving about and getting hitched, we'd be melted into one race anyway. Look at my family. I had African-American ancestors myself. They were cowboys, of course. So were my Native American ancestors. I did have a Chinese ancestor, but he was a miner, so that's okay. I do have one skeleton in my closet. I had a forebear who was a lawyer. Don't let that get around."

"I have a Scottish ancestor back there somewhere," Wendell sounded defensive, then frowned. "But then he was a Graham. That's actually a Norman name, but they always fought bravely to defend the Highlands, so the other clans pretend it's a Pictish name." He sighed. "Actually my family is a bit of an anomaly in the twenty-seventh century, being mostly English."

"We like you even if you are inbred, Fancy Pants."

Wendell looked wounded. "I'm not that inbred. Let's see, my English forebears would be Normans, Angles, Saxons, Jutes, Frisians, Romans, Celts, Picts and Beaker People, I do believe."

"You forgot stuffy history professors." Henry grinned at Wendell and then frowned over at Serendipity. "You may not have done the smartest thing back there, missy. I know this period. Admitting to being even the smallest part African makes you legally *Negro* and that makes you a second class citizen in these parts."

Serendipity snorted. "I wasn't planning to move here, too many bigots."

"Well, I just hope that bigot doesn't get his friends and they come to tar and feather you for being too uppity. Heck, they might just string you up!"

Wendell nodded in agreement. "You were also being a little too arrogant for a woman of this period. That could get you in trouble, too."

Serendipity curled her lip. "And you wonder why I like the twentieth century better than the nineteenth."

"Henry and I are just saying be careful. Don't make people angry. Blend in, don't try and stand out."

"Yes, your Dukeness," she said in a sickly-sweet voice.

Henry peered at Wendell. "Yeah, what's with this Duke of Cambridge hooey? Is there even a Duke of Cambridge in this year?"

"Sorry, I got caught up in the moment. I wanted to make Serendipity look even more important."

"That was a nice touch." Serendipity patted Wendell's leg. "I think deep down inside of you, sweetie, there's a troublemaker that wants to get out."

"Yes, well, he will just have to stay put."

Chapter Thirty-Two

Serendipity studied the structure on the slope, nearly hidden by the trees. "That's a cabin? Looks more like a shed."

On the side of the small steep hill amid the tall chestnuts clung a tiny shack. One side was held up with posts since there wasn't enough level ground to build anything on.

"Maybe that's his toolshed," Sherman said.

Henry shook his head. "Why in tarnation would someone build a toolshed out in the middle of nowhere on such a steep hillside? A worthless piece of property like this would go mighty cheap. That hill has got to be at least a forty-five degree angle. Might be all the man could afford."

Serendipity looked uneasy. "Shall we check it out? I hope this isn't really where he lives."

They found a path going up the hill and followed it. Although it did some switchbacking, it was still rather steep. Occasionally roots and stones were utilized as steps. The trail at last wound around to the far side of the building.

Sherman guessed it to be twelve foot long and six foot wide. A narrow terrace had been cut into the bank with one long side of the shack built against the clay wall. The other side of the structure hung out over the edge and had log poles propping it up to keep it from sliding down the hill. The whole thing looked like it had been jury-rigged rather than built. Steps of warped boards led up to the door. Serendipity climbed up them and knocked on the rough wood. "Hello? Anyone home?"

"Can I help you, folks?" A voice came from behind them.

They turned to see an old man coming around a tree. His dark skin had been tanned even darker by the sun. His thinning hair looked like puffs of cotton. He appeared frail, but moved like a younger man, his wiry build no doubt created by decades of hard labor. He was grinning, but his smile looked forced, his eyes suspicious. He moved slowly like he didn't wish to startle something unpredictable and potentially dangerous, watching them like they were rattlesnakes.

"Hello, my good man!" Wendell tipped his top hat "Are you perchance Mr. Nathan Brown?"

"Yeah, I is him," his voice sounded wary. He spoke slowly like he was weighing each word.

Serendipity came down the rickety stairs. "Nathan Brown? Wow, am I glad to find you!" She grabbed the hand of the startled man who wasn't much taller than herself and began pumping it. "I'm your cousin, Serendipity Brown."

"Cousin? I knowed Mama mentioned a couple of brothers. Your mama must be awfully pale skinned." His voice was even more soft spoken than Wendell's.

"Yeah, I take after her side of the family. I heard so much about you I had to look you up!"

"Heard about me? How did you ever hear about me?"

"Here, let me introduce you to my friends. This is Dr. Wendell Howe, Dr. Henry Darrell and Sherman Conrad."

Nathan shook all their proffered hands, looking a bit taken aback. "You all look like mighty fancy folks to be coming to the home of a poor man. I ain't got much, but I could cook you up some vittles to eat."

Sherman looked at the man's ragged clothes and realized he hardly had food enough for himself.

Serendipity smiled at Nathan. "Thanks, but we already ate. So, where do you live?"

"Here." He pointed to the shack made of a hodge-podge of scrap wood. "This here is my farm."

"Farm?"

"I grow vegetables among the trees here and there around the roots. I managed to level off a few scrawny spots for corn. I forage a lot. I trade odd jobs for things I can't grow. Land ain't level enough for a field, but I gets by." Nathan started up the steps. "Would you folks like to come in and make yourselves at home?"

"Uh, sure." Serendipity followed him. On the steps she turned around and grinned at her companions. "See, I told you he was a Southern gentleman."

Sherman followed the rest up the wobbly steps, not sure how they would all get in this tiny building. The first thing he saw was a bed made of saplings and scrap wood. A faded quilt that had been patched on top of its patches lay neatly smoothed over a mattress that had straw sticking through it. The foot was facing them, for the room was probably too narrow to turn the bed lengthways. On the right wall he saw one small window, but instead of glass, it was covered with rawhide, sliced thin and oiled. You couldn't see out, but it did let light in. On the opposite wall in the corner, to the left of the door, sat a small hearth of stone and clay. It recessed beyond the wall, so it must have been carved into the bank. Next to the fireplace was hung an iron skillet and metal spoon on pegs. The walls, like the floor, were made of uneven wooden planks, the cracks filled in with red clay.

Nathan grabbed the best piece of furniture, a chair made out of saplings. "Have a seat, Mizz Brown. You gentlemen feel free to sit on the bed."

Wendell sat down on the end closest to the door. Henry sat down on his left and Sherman at the far end. The bed creaked a little, but didn't collapse.

Sherman looked around. The boards in the walls did not match, being various shades of wood, some with fading whitewash. They looked like they had been rescued from garbage heaps or salvaged from buildings torn down. The wood had been fitted together like a jigsaw puzzle and held with rusty square-headed nails. On the walls were pegs from which hung a few tools. So this was what a real hovel looked like? It made Sherman's old apartment and the single-wide trailer he grew up in look palatial.

He looked over at his two companions. Henry didn't look too out of place in his buckskin. He had been a cowboy and a fur trapper. He may well have slept in places this bad.

Wendell in his frock coat looked woefully out of place. His manner seemed even more formal than usual. Yet he didn't give the impression of being haughty. He acted like he had stepped into the parlor of some grand country estate. His very air seemed to give the shack more dignity. Then Sherman realized Wendell was doing this out of respect for their host. Sherman sat up straight and tried to copy the English gentleman.

"Can I get you folks anything?" Nathan did his best to play host. "Would you like something to drink? I done fetched a bucket of fresh water this morning at the creek down the road." He pointed to a wooden pail next to the hearth.

Wendell removed his top hat and gave him a gracious smile. "I do believe we are all fine, sir. Thank you for your kind hospitality, Mr. Brown. Would you like us to move over and make you a place to sit?"

"Nah," Nathan pulled a short three-legged stool over. "I'll sit here. Well, now, ain't this fine. I don't get much company. Tell me, where you folks from?"

"We just came from the village up the road." Serendipity sidestepped the question. "I had to come and meet you. I've heard so much about you."

"How? I never knew any of my family except my mama." Nathan studied Serendipity. "How'd you track me down? You took the name Brown, too?"

"Uh, yeah. In your honor."

"My honor?"

"Because you were a Revolutionary War hero."

"No more a hero than anyone else."

"But you won freedom for our country."

Nathan wrinkled his nose. "Just for white folks. I only joined up 'cause when they said they wanted to win freedom, I supposed they meant for everybody. I was already free, and mama had just died, but I was willing to fight and die to make our people free. They lied. I fought for nothing."

"Someday everyone in this country will be free," Serendipity said. "Someday soon."

"I ain't never gonna live to see it, that's for sure."

"No." Serendipity drooped sadly. "No, you won't. So, tell me about your life, Great-grand—uh, Mr. Brown."

"Ain't much to tell. I was born in Baltimore, 'cause a lawyer man named Layton bought my mama while she was with child. He didn't buy my daddy too, so I never knowed him. We never did knowed what happened to Daddy. Mama never did get over that broken heart of hers. We lived in Massa Layton's cellar. Mama said it was much nicer than the drafty shack she growed up in on the plantation. Massa Layton weren't too bad. He only whipped me with a hickory switch if I couldn't work fast enough. He was old, so he left Mama alone.

"After Mama got all her chores done Massa Layton let her sew things for the neighbors and keep the money. It took a pretty long time but she saved up enough to buy my freedom when I was twelve. I worked hard and got up enough money to buy her freedom. It took the two of us six years to make enough money. By then Mama be mostly blind from sewing and she was doing poorly. She up and died within the year. Still she died a free woman, so all that work was worth it.

"After that I fought in the war. When that was over, I jumped the broom with my Lizzie, had five young'uns. Two of the boys survived. They wanted to go west to Missouri. I stayed behind 'cause Lizzie would never have lived through the trip. She up and died. Had a bad crop, and lost the farm I was renting. Came here, found work so I could buy these two acres. Now no one'll hire me 'cause I is too old. And here I is." He shrugged matter-of-factly. "I imagine your life was far more exciting. So tell me about yourself, Mizz Brown."

Serendipity just stared at him as if she couldn't speak.

"Why Mizz Brown, what's the matter? You look like you gonna cry. Has life been hard on you? Well, you look like you've done mighty fine in the end, judging by your fancy clothes. Crossed the color-line, did you? You is taking a real gamble coming here to visit me. I take it you trust these here gentlemen not to tell your secret."

"It's not fair," Serendipity whispered. "You won freedom for this country. You started the Brown Family. Someday your descendants will number in the thousands, living all over the world, and they'll brag about you being their ancestor. And here you are living in this horrible dump and—"

"Now, Serendipity!" Wendell stood up and went over to her. "This is Mr. Brown's home which I believe he built with his own hands, doing the best he could with what he had. I imagine he could not afford proper lumber and had to make do with what he could salvage. You should not call it a dump. That is impolite." Wendell looked about him. "If anything I think the construction shows real ingenuity. He should be rightfully proud."

"I'm sorry, Nathan. I didn't mean to insult you. I would never do that." Serendipity stood up. "It's just not fair, you all alone." She started to step forward, like she was going to throw her arms around him.

Wendell threw his arm out to stop her. "Serendipity, you are getting too involved. I told you this would happen. You can't change anything here."

She looked up at Wendell. "It's not fair."

"It is what it is. Leave it alone." Wendell's voice sounded sympathetic despite the cold words.

Nathan had been watching this exchange, studying the two, frowning confused.

A knock came at the door, interrupting them. Nathan got up, stepped over and opened it. There stood the slave from the General Store, panting like he had been running. He was bent over, his hands on his thighs, trying not to collapse.

"Jeremiah!" Nathan looked shocked. "What is you doing here? Do you know how dangerous this is? You gonna get a hiding when your massa finds out."

Jeremiah took great gulps of air, trying to catch his breath. He leaned on the door jam. "Mistuh Brown" he panted. "Had to...warn you...Lady here...made Billy and Otis...real riled up...said they...gonna get friends...kill you all...burn down house...you gotta get outta here."

Nathan handed the boy a dipper made from a gourd that was filled with water from the bucket. Jeremiah gulped down the water, then handed it back.

"Thank you, son." Nathan patted him on the back. "You probably saved us all. Now you get back before your massa miss you."

"Wait!" Serendipity stopped Jeremiah as he turned. He spun back. Serendipity reached into her drawstring purse and pulled out a small bag. "Take this." She handed it to him.

Jeremiah opened the bag and his eyes popped. He looked back up at Serendipity. "Thank you, ma'am. Oh, God bless you, ma'am! Thank you!" Jeremiah grinned at her, and then took off as fast as he could run.

"What did you give him, Dr. Brown?" Wendell crossed his arms.

"Just a little loose change." Serendipity blinked innocently.

"I noticed he was running up the hill in the opposite direction from town. Just how much money did you give him? Enough to make it to Canada?"

"I don't know. You know the current prices of things better than me."

"And why did you have that money with you?"

"It's kind of hard to spend those out of date coins Agent Five gave me. Just thought I'd find a use for some of them."

"Exactly what use did you have planned for them, Dr. Brown?"

"Wendell, we don't have time to fight about this. We have to get out of here before we get lynched. I'll bet there are some War of 1812 veterans in town that would love stringing up an English *Duke*, don't you think."

Nathan nodded in agreement. "You folks better get going."

"And leave you?" Serendipity looked horrified.

"I is old."

Serendipity turned to Wendell. "Jiminey-Criminey! I did it! The records said on this day they found the house burnt down and never found Nathan's body. They assumed he was burnt up in the fire."

"You told me that incident would happen a month from now!" Wendell looked like he was starting to lose his customary cool.

"Did I?" She blinked innocently.

"You came hoping to stop the fire, didn't you? And that's why you had that money. You were going to give it to Nathan. You were going to change things."

"Looks like I didn't change anything. Looks like I just made it happen. We have to save him."

"We can't. We can't change things."

"What change?" Serendipity said. "There was no body, he disappeared. What if he disappeared because we made him disappear? What if we took him to safety?"

"But the records—"

"The records don't tell everything, right? If they had, you temporal anthropologist would have nothing to do, now would you?"

Wendell looked imploringly at his fellow temporal anthropologist. "Henry? Help me here!"

Henry shook his head, fighting back a smile. "I hate to say it, old buddy, but she does make a convincing argument, doesn't she?"

"Fine, we'll take him to Pennsylvania," Wendell said.

"Beg pardon folks." Nathan looked confused. "Just what's going on?"

Serendipity grabbed his arms. "We can take you to safety, Nathan. We'll take you far away and make sure you have a nice place to live. Is that all right?"

"Nicer than this place?"

"Oh yeah, a lot nicer."

Nathan shrugged. "All right. I know this ain't no trick to kidnap me and sell me back into slavery, 'cause someone my age ain't worth much."

"You're priceless." Serendipity patted his cheek.

Nathan looked puzzled by her forwardness, but didn't seem offended. "Don't know why, but I think I can trust you, Mizz Brown. You got eyes just like my Mama."

Serendipity got a wistful smile. "Really? You really think so?" She cleared her throat and assumed command mode. "We have to hurry. Grab what you want, we'll help you carry it, but we can't come back for a second load. Take what you can't bear to leave behind."

Nathan nodded and went over to the bed. Sherman and Henry stood up so Nathan could reach under it. He pulled out a couple of wooden boxes, flat and open on top, and put them on the bed. Then he grabbed a hammer hung on the wall.

"Forget the tools," Serendipity said. "Forget the pan and blankets. We don't have time. Just take personal sentimental stuff."

"But I'll need my tools."

"No, you won't. They are too heavy. I'll see you are taken care of." Serendipity looked at Henry and Sherman. "Grab the boxes, guys."

Henry obeyed, while Sherman grabbed the other.

"Is that it?" Serendipity asked Nathan.

"Can I take the quilts? Lizzie made them."

"Yes, of course!" She came over and yanked them off the bed stuffing them on top of Henry's box. "Is there anything else with sentimental value?"

Nathan shook his head. "That's it."

"Did you make this furniture?"

"Yeah."

She picked up the chair she had sat on and shoved it at Wendell. "Take this." Then she picked up the stool and a homemade broom made of reeds in the corner. "Come on people, we are getting out of here."

They hurried down the steep path to the dirt road below, following the winding trail, careful not to trip on roots.

"This here your coach?" Nathan said when they got to the bottom. "My, but you is well-to-do."

"Could we at least blindfold him?" Wendell looked beseechingly at Serendipity.

"Ask Nathan."

Wendell turned to the elderly man. "Mr. Brown, would you mind terribly if we blindfolded you? It's very important that you don't see what is inside the carriage."

"Oh, so that's how you make your money, is it? Smugglers, huh? Makes no never mind to me. I will not be telling nobody. You can blindfold me if it makes you feel better."

"Thank you, Mr. Brown. It does make me feel better." Wendell set down the chair and pulled off his cravat tie. Nathan turned around so Wendell could tie it over his eyes. "That's not too tight, is it, Mr. Brown?"

"No, it's fine."

"We appreciate your cooperation." Wendell took Nathan's arm, to steer him.

Serendipity unlocked the Timemobile with her pocket computer and opened the door. "Okay, load up the stuff and then we'll get Nathan in."

Henry went in first with his box, and then took the items Serendipity and Sherman handed up to him to stow away.

Wendell had Nathan's arm and talked him through negotiating the steps. The old man tried to feel the stairs with his feet.

Sherman thought he heard someone yelling. He turned and spied a dozen riders on horses galloping down the road toward them. "Look!" He pointed. "Dude, is that the bad guys?"

Henry reached his arm out of the Timemobile. "Grab my hand, Nathan."

"Damn, we don't have time for this." Serendipity yanked off the blindfold. "Just get in, Nathan."

Nathan climbed in as fast as he could, followed by the rest. Serendipity slammed the door, and went over to the controls. "Get Nathan in a seat. Then strap in!"

Nathan stood there with his mouth open, gawking at his new surroundings. Wendell and Henry pushed him into the closest chair and strapped him in. Sherman folded down one of the extra seats in back, and the two temporal anthropologists took the two seats behind Nathan.

Serendipity plopped down in her seat, did her seatbelt, then reached over and grabbed Nathan's hand. "Hold on, honey. It's kind of a rough ride for a couple of minutes."

Nathan eyes got big as the Timemobile began shaking like a carriage driving over large rocks. It finally stopped. Serendipity looked over at her forebear. "You all right?"

"Yes, ma'am."

"Call me Serendipity."

"All right, Serendipity. What kind of carriage is this here?"

Wendell undid his seatbelt and stood up. "All right, Dr. Brown. You better come up with a good story."

"Okay, Nathan, I'm not your cousin, I'm your great-times-twenty-one-granddaughter. I'm from the future and this is a machine I built that can travel through time."

"Dr. Brown!!" The usually stoic Wendell looked on the verge of bursting a blood vessel. "That was *not* the story I had in mind! You can't tell him the truth!"

"It worked with Benjamin Franklin."

"You can't go around telling people about the future!" Wendell looked beseechingly at Nathan. "Please, please promise you will never tell anyone about this. If you do, it could cause horrible consequences."

"All right. Who'd believe me, anyhow?" Nathan then looked over at Serendipity. "So you is one of my children's children's children?"

"Much further ahead than that, but yeah."

"And a Brown will be smart enough to build a contraption that can go back in time?"

"Not just built." Serendipity raised her chin proudly. "I *invented* time travel! Wendell and Henry are from my future and they will make their living using *my* invention to study the past."

"A Brown did that? A woman of color?"

"Well, I don't have much African blood left in me, but yes, I'm a Brown and you are my forefather and I wanted to meet you because you started the Brown family. I hope I'm not a disappointment, me being mostly European. I hope you aren't ashamed of me."

"Ashamed? Now, why would I have cause to be shamed, child?" Nathan broke out in a grin. "My seed invented a carriage that can travel through time. My, my, I never would have dreamed."

Wendell sighed. "Please, Mr. Brown, tell no one." He wearily opened the door, and then slammed it shut and leaned against it. "Why does it look like the inside of the garage in Bellingham out there?"

"Because it is?" Serendipity tried to look guileless.

"You said you were going to Pennsylvania in 1835."

"No, I didn't say anything. You were the one that suggested Pennsylvania."

"Why didn't you go there?"

"Wendell! We aren't going to dump some penniless old man in a strange place and take off. Besides, history said his house caught on fire and he disappeared on that date. No one knows where he disappeared to. Maybe he disappeared to 2010. Seems this would explain why there are no records of him after this day."

Wendell slapped his hand to his forehead. "Dr. Brown, you cannot take people out of the past into the future. It will kill them."

"Oh, pooh! That's just a myth."

"Man's right." Henry came over to Wendell. "If you take someone from the past into the future the shock will kill them. Either that or they will go mad."

"Oh really?" Serendipity crossed her arms. "Do you know anyone that has happened to?"

"Well, no." Henry looked awkward.

"I do." Serendipity turned to Sherman. "Hey kid, I took you from 1985 to 2353, right?"

"Yeah," Sherman said.

"Did you die of a heart attack?"

"No."

"You go mad?"

"Not yet."

Serendipity turned back to Henry and Wendell. "There you go."

"Sherman is a lot younger," Henry said. "So, he's more adaptable."

Wendell nodded in agreement. "Besides, Sherman is from a technological age where everything is changing fast. He's used to the world being turned upside down."

"So, you really think I should take Nathan back?" Serendipity frowned at them.

"Yes!" Henry and Wendell said together.

"I got an idea," Sherman piped up. "Speaking as the first mistake, why don't you ask Nathan what he would like to do?"

They all looked at Nathan who had been sitting quietly this whole time, quizzically studying them trying to make sense of the bizarre conversation.

Wendell leaned down to Nathan. "Mr. Brown, I'm afraid that Dr. Brown has brought you into the future."

"Yeah, I heard that part."

"The world of the future is nothing like what you left. It will all seem very strange, I daresay. There are carriages that travel without horses, gadgets that let you talk to people miles away, machines that fly, and pictures that move. We can take you back to your familiar world and put you in a safe place."

Serendipity crouched down by Nathan's other side. "Yes, but if you stay, you will be my guest. You'll sleep in a soft warm bed, eat three meals a day, have nice clothes, and I'll get you whatever you want. I'm rich and you're my grandpa. I plan to spoil you."

"So, let me get this straight," Nathan said with slow deliberation. "You is asking if I want to live in a world of wonders, where even women with colored blood can become doctors and get rich? And I'm gonna live with a lost family member who wants to treat me like a king? Or I can go back to a world where I is poor and alone and treated like trash because of the color of my skin? What do you think? I think a world that is very different than the one I knowed would be a mighty good thing."

"Come on, guys," Serendipity said. "How is this going to change history as long as we don't tell anyone where Nathan is from? He'll be just one more person out of time in this house."

Sherman stood up. "I'm tired of being the oldest and youngest one here.

Nathan seems like a righteous dude. He deserves a nice retirement. Putting Nathan back would be like saving a starving stray kitten from a busy street and then dumping him in a back alley."

Henry and Wendell both sighed and then looked at each other.

"Maybe Nathan won't go mad," Henry told Wendell. "But I'm beginning to wonder how you stay sane with this woman."

"It *is* a challenge sometimes." Wendell looked over at Serendipity.

"Great! It's settled." Serendipity grabbed Nathan's arm. "Come on, Great-Grandpa. You hungry? I'll introduce you to everyone. I'm going to give you the best bedroom in the house. And if anyone gives you grief, you tell me and I will kick his butt out. You are now my guest of honor."

"You sure I ain't really dead after all." Nathan grinned at her. "Because, I think I just might be in heaven."

Chapter Thirty-Three

Serendipity and her entourage all came through the door off the back porch.

"We're in the kitchen!" Erik's voice boomed.

Sherman came into the kitchen first.

Erik grinned over at him. "We're making sandwiches for lunch. Every man for himself."

The other temporal anthropologists had gathered in the kitchen, digging through the refrigerator and cabinets, the counter space taken up with plates of food and jars of condiments.

"Where didst ye go?" Matilda asked Henry and Wendell when they came through the door. "Did thee find gladness in thy little journey into the nineteenth century?"

Serendipity then came through the door with Nathan. Everyone in the room froze, staring in disbelief.

Abubakari was the first to speak. "Please, Dr. Brown, tell me he is not from the nineteenth century."

"Hey, everyone," Serendipity chirped. "Meet my great-times-twenty-one-grandfather, Nathan Brown."

The room fell silent. Then a butter knife slipped from Erik's hand, clanging on the floor. Mustard streaked the yellow and brown linoleum.

Tobias recovered first, scowling at Serendipity. "Dr. Brown! You can't do that! You can't bundle up your ancestors and take them home!"

"Drop dead, Tobias." Serendipity jutted out her jaw. "I don't care what you think!"

"Owo, I am afraid, Dr. Leach is correct." Abubakari stepped closer. "You cannot do that! It is forbidden."

Matilda came at Henry, shaking her finger at him. "Henry Rueben Darrel, how dareth thee let Dr. Brown do this! You too, Wendell Abercrombie Howe! Ye two should have stopped her!"

Matilda's eyes were snapping. Sherman hadn't even known the mousey woman could get mad. By the looks on Wendell's and Henry's faces, this was something they were unaccustomed to from Matilda.

"I tried!" Wendell backed away until the counter stopped him.

Henry rubbed the back of his neck. "You can't stop Serendipity, hon. Like trying to stop a twister."

"There was a lynch mob coming for Nathan!" Serendipity put her hands on her hips. "We could hardly leave him."

"And who got the townsfolk all riled up in the first place to come burn down his cabin?" Henry asked.

"The creeps called Grandpa a derogatory name!"

"Welcome to the nineteenth century." Henry threw up his hands. "You have to just look the other way because you can't get involved, you can't sway popular opinion. Ya got to smile at the jackasses! Being a temporal anthropologist ain't all fun and games, you know."

"If we change one man's opinion, we could change history." Wendell braced his hands on the counter behind him.

"I'm not a stupid temporal anthropologist." Serendipity sniffed.

"Maybe we should take him back to his own time of yore," Erik said. "We can use the compliance disk and make him forget all of this."

"He's not going back!" Serendipity crossed her arms. "Nathan stays! If he goes, I go and I'm taking the Timemobile with me."

Nathan laid his hand on her arm. "No, it is all right, child. I is use to this. I'll go back. They don't want my kind around." He turned toward the back door.

Wendell grabbed Nathan by the arm, stopping him. "*That* is not the reason that everyone is upset, Mr. Brown. The problem is you do not belong in the year 2010."

"Wendell." Serendipity frowned. "None of us belong in 2010."

"That could not be helped and it is temporary. You purposely removed Mr. Brown from his own time and took him to another. I daresay, that is a taboo. You changed history. We are not allowed to change history."

"I did nothing of the kind!" Serendipity looked around the room. "I didn't change a thing. I made it happen. History says that Nathan Brown disappeared on the date we arrived. Everyone assumed he was consumed in the house fire. What's it going to hurt if he disappears to here? He's not going to tell the world where he is from. If he did, they would just think he's demented. He can't possibly change history."

Serendipity put her hand on Nathan's shoulder. "This man was born a slave. He never knew his father because they sold his mother before Nathan was born. He fought and almost died in the Revolutionary War for freedom, only to find out it was only freedom for those who weren't slaves. When we found him he was living with no family in a hovel in abject poverty."

Serendipity looked them each in the eye. "This is the man who founded the Brown family. If it wasn't for him *I* would never have been born and had the chance to invent time travel. If not for this man, none of you would have ever been able to become temporal anthropologists. I owe this man everything, and so do you. By God, I am going to see to it that he spends his remaining years warm and fed and comfortable. Do any of you have a problem with that?"

All the temporal anthropologists looked down at the ground and said nothing.

"Good! Now Nathan is getting the best bedroom. You will have to move to another room, Tobias."

Tobias looked up. "What! Why do I have to get kicked out of my room? Why can't he have Wendell's room? Heaven knows Wendell never sleeps in it."

Wendell turned to Serendipity. "Tobias does have a point there. I can move my belongings out and give my room to Nathan."

"No," Serendipity shook her head. "My room is bigger. He can have my room. I'll move in with you."

"Now just a goll durn minute." Nathan threw up his hands. "Don't I get a say so in this?"

"Uh, sure Grandpa."

"No one's getting kicked out of their room. I can sleep anywhere, attic, basement—shoot, I can sleep in that shed out back."

"There lay two empty rooms on the second floor," Matilda said.

"That's right," Serendipity nodded. "We were keeping them empty in case our two zoologists decided they wanted real bedrooms. It appears that's not going to happen."

"We'll let him pick which room he likes," Wendell said. "Until we get a bed in it he may sleep in my room." He turned to Nathan. "Does that sound all right to you, Mr. Brown?"

Nathan shrugged. "Sounds all right by me. Long as it ain't no worse than what I had before. By the way, I knows Serendipity is my great-grandchild from the future. But who is you all?"

"That is a bit complicated." Wendell straightened up. "I am not certain how to explain, or if we should wait so we don't overburden your sanity."

"Oh, come off it." Serendipity gave Wendell a perturbed grimace. "Nathan isn't feeble. The man is a Brown! He can handle anything." She put her arm around Nathan's shoulders. "Okay Grandpa, I'll explain. If I go too fast, stop me. I invented time travel in 2353." Serendipity pulled Nathan over to Sherman. "This is Sherman Conrad. I met him on my first trip in time. He's from 1985. I hired him as my assistant."

She steered Nathan over to Wendell. "The time machine didn't have all the kinks worked out so Sherman and I got stuck in 1851. That's when we met Wendell. Now Wendell was a time traveler, too, only from the twenty-seventh century. He's what you call a *temporal anthropologist*."

"Temple ampologist?" Nathan tried to make sense.

"Temporal anthropologist. Just a fancy name for a historian who goes back in time to study the past. Now people in the twenty-seventh century are superstitious and terrified of accidentally changing time and somehow making everything worse. I think they are silly myself. I don't think time is that fragile, but that's why they are upset at me bringing you here. Wendell here is immersed in the nineteenth century with the persona of an English gentleman. He is more at home in the 1800s than the 2600s where he was born."

"Actually I was born 2575," Wendell corrected her.

"Whatever." Serendipity waved her hand. "These other people are all temporal anthropologists from the twenty-seventh century, too. You met Dr. Henry Darrel. He pretends to be a cowboy."

"I *am* a cowboy." Henry looked offended. "I was born on a cattle ranch in Wyoming. Okay, it was a heck of a lot more modern than the 1800s, but my kinfolk are cowboys. Cows for cloning steaks don't grow on trees, you know."

"Sorry, Henry." Serendipity flashed him an apologetic smile. "This here is Dr. Matilda Warwick. She's been studying convents in the Middle Ages as a sort of lay nun, I guess. She was born in Australia, even if she doesn't sound like it."

Matilda held out her hand. "I am most pleased to make your acquaintance, sir. This is an exalted privilege."

Nathan smiled. "You all make me sound like I is somebody important."

"Yea, verily you are." Matilda shook his hand. "You are a piece of living history. Dost not be shocked if people around here start pumping you for information."

Serendipity pulled Erik over. "This is Dr. Erik Olafson. He pretends to be a Viking in the Dark Ages."

"This is an exalted honor, Mr. Brown." Erik vigorously pumped the old man's hand. "I was born an American and let me just say thank you for helping make America free, even if you did get cheated. I appreciate your heroic sacrifice."

"Ain't nobody ever thanked me for that before." Nathan looked pleased.

"You need anything, just ask. I am a blacksmith. I also work with wood and leather. I can build something for you from your time period if you like."

"Owo, he made me a very nice medieval African-style bed," Abubakari said.

"Oh, Grandpa." Serendipity steered Nathan over to Abubakari. "This is one fella you are going to have to talk to. This is Dr. Abubakari Djata from Timbuktu in Africa. He's been recording books from ancient Mali. He said most of the Africans they brought to America were from that area. We are descended from scholars, Grandpa. Isn't that something?"

Abubakari offered his hand in that regal but warm manner of his. "I am most pleased to make your acquaintance, Mr. Brown. You have a remarkable descendant here."

"Yes, I is seeing that." Nathan shook Abubakari's hand. He then turned to Tobias. "And who is this young fella?"

"That's just Tobias," Serendipity muttered.

Tobias held out his hand. "My name is Dr. Tobias Leach from Oxford University. I specialize in Victorian England. I'm very pleased to make your acquaintance, sir. I do hope your offspring didn't get her bad temper from you."

"You be nice to my grandpa, Tobias." Serendipity glared at him. "Or I'll take a baseball bat to you. Or a cricket bat if you prefer."

Tobias frowned at her. "I just didn't see the point of being kicked out of my room when there are other rooms available. Apparently your forebear didn't either. Pity you aren't as reasonable as him."

"Never you mind." Nathan shook Tobias's hand. "Just as long as I have a dry place to sleep when it rains. Be mighty nice for a change."

Tobias gave Nathan a look that bordered on sympathy. "You were actually born a slave?"

"Yes, sir."

"Maybe you do deserve a few years of comfort at that." Tobias then turned and went back to making his sandwich.

Erik shoved a plate at Nathan. "Would you like a sardine sandwich? I can make another one for myself."

Serendipity wrinkled her nose, but Nathan took the offering graciously. "Why many thanks, Dr. Olafson. That is mighty kind of you."

"Sardines are not as good as pickled herring, but we are woefully destitute of them. I will be sure to let you feast on them with me when I get more."

"Erik, you better not make my grandpa sick."

"Pickled herring." Wendell shook his head. "A perfectly good waste of herring when you could smoke them to make kippers."

Serendipity turned back to Nathan. "Come on, Grandpa. Let's go into the dining room and sit down. After lunch I'm going to take you shopping. Buy you new clothes and furniture, and then I'm going to take you to the best restaurant for dinner."

"I say, Serendipity." Wendell raised his eyebrow. "Don't you think perhaps you are overdoing it a bit?"

"Overdoing it? He's my grandpa. He's getting the best."

"No, I mean, don't you think you should take this a little slower. This is all new to him. You don't want him to have culture shock, now do you? Introduce him to the twenty-first century a little at a time."

"You feel faint or dizzy, Grandpa?" Serendipity asked.

"I is fine, child. It is all a little mindboggling but it's all right. Kind of like a dream, but a real nice dream. I is afraid I is gonna wake up."

"Yeah, me too. I never really got to know either of my grandpas. Both died when I was a little kid. It was worth inventing time travel just for this."

Sherman watched the smile on Serendipity's face. He had only met one of his grandfathers and had only seen him a couple of times. His grandfather smelled of booze and wasn't nearly as nice as Nathan. Sherman couldn't help but feel a little jealous of Serendipity.

Serendipity took Nathan's arm. "You said my eyes reminded you of your mother? Do I really have Great-Grandma's eyes?"

Nathan smiled back at her. "You surely do, child. You surely do."

Serendipity beamed at him.

Did Sherman imagine it, or did Nathan strut as he walked down the reception hall from the front door? The new outfit Serendipity had bought her ancestor could well be the nicest clothes the man had ever owned, even if it was only a pair of casual slacks, a sports shirt and tennis shoes.

Serendipity still hovered over the old man. "I hope the trip in the van didn't scare you too much."

"Oh, it was a wee bit frightening at first, but I rightly enjoyed it. Felt like I was flying."

"Is there anything I can get you, Grandpa?"

"You done bought me these fine clothes, child."

"Tomorrow we are going to get you a bed and dresser and anything else you would like for your room. Or maybe we will do it after dinner. That should be ready in an hour. I think Henry and Matilda have already started it."

"Maybe I should go lend them a hand."

"You will do nothing of the kind!" Serendipity put her hands on her hips. "You are the guest of honor. You aren't waiting on anyone, you aren't lifting a finger. We'll all wait on you!"

"I ain't helpless, child." Nathan frowned offended.

"Don't make him feel like an invalid." Sherman whispered to Serendipity. "He's a guy. He has his pride."

"Uh, sorry, Grandpa. I just want to spoil you. You founded our family."

"Yeah, I supposing if I ever met my daddy, I'd try to make him right at home. I'd go without victuals myself to feed him."

Serendipity perked up. "Hey, maybe we could go back and find him too?"

"Child, I ain't got a notion where to start. I ain't never knowed who owned him. My sons left for Missouri years ago, with a couple of baby grandsons. If I ever had a granddaughter I ain't never got to meet her. You is given me two great gifts: a granddaughter and a glimpse of the future, where all men is free. That is more than enough. That my great-grandchild would be this obliging and big-hearted, not to mention smart and well-to-do. You is more precious than anything you could buy me."

Serendipity looked like she was going to cry. "Thank you, Grandpa. I'm proud of you too." She hugged him.

Nathan looked startled, then smiled and hugged her back.

Serendipity finally pulled away. "Can I get you something to drink, Grandpa?"

Nathan fought back a chuckle. "Will you stop fussing, child? I tell you what. How 'bout seeing the rest of this here house. If I gonna be living here I don't wanna get lost."

"Sure, Grandpa." Serendipity grabbed him by the arm. "You've seen the kitchen, and the dining room and the downstairs bathroom. Near the front door are the parlor and the library. You saw those coming in."

"Where does that door go?" Nathan pointed to the music room.

"You don't want to go in there. Just a bunch of birds. Let me show you the second floor."

"Ser." Sherman stopped her. "We haven't introduced him to Cerwyn and Priscilla."

"So?"

"Ser! They are nice once you get to know them. Once you understand them."

"They're loonies, kid."

Nathan watched this exchange. "You got crazy folks locked up in there?"

Sherman turned to the old man. "They aren't really crazy, just a little obsessed. They're temporal zoologists from the same future time period as our temporal anthropologists."

"Zoo-what-a-gists?"

"Zoologists. Scientists who study animals. Temporal zoologists go back in time and collect animals that are extinct," Sherman explained patiently.

"Ex-stink?"

"It means all the animals of that kind are dead and gone and won't ever come back. Temporal zoologists go back into time and collect them, so people in the future can see them. They got some birds in there that are extinct now, so they are overly protective of them. They refuse to leave the birds alone. If they have to come out to go to the bathroom or eat or whatever, one of them always remains in the room."

"They sound mighty determined to make sure them birds do well." Nathan glanced at the door.

"So, be careful. If you say anything mean about the birds, they won't like you. But say something nice and they'll think you're okay."

"Those damn birds are all they care about." Serendipity glowered disgusted.

"Now, child," Nathan chided her. "If these critters is all dead and gone and they is just trying to bring them back into the world—well, that sounds mighty good to me."

Serendipity looked chastised. "I suppose you're right, Grandpa."

"So, why don't you let me meet these nice folks? Unless you don't think they want to have anything to do with a colored man."

"You are my grandpa! If they say anything mean to you, they and all their birds are out on the street!" Serendipity went over and banged on the door.

A moment later it opened and Cerwyn poked his head out. "Yes, Dr. Brown? Is anything wrong?"

"This is my grandpa!" Serendipity snapped at the Welshman. "And you better be nice to him!"

Cerwyn looked confused. "I beg your pardon?"

Sherman stepped forward. "Hey, Cerwyn. We wanted you to meet Nathan Brown. Can he come in and see your birds?"

Cerwyn smiled. "Oh, an animal lover? Certainly, please come in, won't you?"

They walked into the room and over to the cage. Priscilla stood inside the huge pen, sweeping up droppings. One parrot perched on her head. The birds seemed to be getting tamer. Or maybe they were so used to the two zoologists that the parrots saw them as part of their cage.

Priscilla looked up. "Hello, Sherman." She came over to the side of the aviary.

Sherman decided to make the introductions. "Nathan, this is Dr. Cerwyn Owen and Dr. Priscilla Cohen. This is Mr. Nathan Brown."

Cerwyn shook Nathan's hand. Priscilla, separated by wire, smiled and nodded her head at him, slowly so she wouldn't disturb her hitchhiker.

"Nathan is my great-times-twenty-one-grandfather." Serendipity gave them a stern look. "He was a hero in the Revolutionary War."

Both Cerwyn and Priscilla's eyes got big. "I thought we were in 2010?" Priscilla looked baffled.

"Yes," Serendipity said.

"You are talking about the American Revolution? Wasn't that in 1776?"

"Yes."

"I thought people weren't supposed to live that long in this century?"

"They don't. I went back in time and got him."

"Oy, are we allowed to do that?"

"Think of him as an extinct animal I brought back."

Priscilla shrugged. "All right."

Sherman had expected the two time travelers to kick up a row like the temporal anthropologists had, but they both seemed to just accept the situation.

Nathan nodded to Priscilla. "Sherman here tells me you got some birds you done fetched back that ain't alive no more?"

"That's right."

"So, where is they?"

Cerwyn glanced down at Nathan. "You are looking at them, aren't you?"

"Ain't these just wild parrots?"

"Yes, Carolina Parakeets."

"But they is all over the place. Saw some just this morning down by the creek when I went to fetch water."

"Uh, Mr. Brown," Sherman tried to break the news gently. "Carolina parakeets may be common in 1835, but the last one died less than a hundred years later."

"No, that can't be. There is lots of these birds. So many the farmers grumble about them and shoot them."

"Yes," Cerwyn frowned, sullen. "They shot them all, didn't they? That's why there aren't anymore."

"No more Carolina parrots?" Nathan appeared crushed. "No, not them! Not Betsy's kin." He reached out and clutched the wire, staring at the fluttering parrots in disbelief.

Priscilla stepped closer to him. "Betsy's kin? Who was Betsy?"

"My daughter's pet. I had five young'uns. Two of my sons growed up. Another died when he was two days old, another when he started to walk. Then there was our only daughter, Hannah. She was a sweet child. A little angel. I guess that's why God wanted her back. At least we got to have her for eleven years, before she was fetched back to heaven."

Nathan looked down at the floor. "Hannah come down with a nasty rash going around when she was four. Nearly burned up with fever. She lived, but always did poorly after that. Lizzie tried to give her chores, but even the simplest ones tuckered her out. Weren't like the child didn't want to help."

Serendipity winced. "Sounds like scarlet fever. Probably damaged her heart."

"I think some folks in town called it Scarlatina." Nathan nodded. "One day her brothers, Luke and Matthew, brought home a little green parrot. Its wing been injured, couldn't fly. I considered putting the poor thing out of its misery, but I couldn't think of a way that weren't cruel.

"Hannah took that little bird, begged me powerfully to let her take care of it. 'All right,' I says, 'your chore will be to nurse it, as best you can.' Hannah took mighty fine care of that critter. Maybe she felt a kinship to it, 'cause she knew what it's like to be all sickly. She done got the bird all better, but it never could fly again."

Nathan looked up at the birds again. "Hannah and that bird be like two peas in a pod. Rode around on her shoulder, it did. Hannah named it 'Betsy'. Betsy gave a lot of joy to my little girl. When the angels came for Hannah, we was all saddened. I reckon Betsy was saddest most of all. She just up and died. We buried her on top of Hannah's grave, so the two could be together. After that I wouldn't have harmed one of them birds if you gave me a thousand dollars. I is partial to these birds. I is glad you is bringing them back."

Sherman noticed tears spilling out of Priscilla's eyes. Then she looked over at her associate. "Cerwyn, the first fledgling will be named Betsy, nu?"

Cerwyn nodded like it was a given, then he frowned. "But what if it is male?"

"Nathan."

Nathan looked surprised at that. "Why thank you, Mizz Cohen, that would be a mighty fine honor."

Serendipity blew her nose and looked at Priscilla with a new respect.

Sherman smiled, knowing 'those stupid bird people' were now in Serendipity's good graces.

Chapter Thirty-Four

After dinner Sherman walked back into the dining room through the pantry door, after having helped carry the last of the dirty dishes to the kitchen sink. Serendipity still sat in her seat with Nathan on her left. She was showing her forebear some pictures on the virtual screen from her pocket computer sitting on the table.

Sherman wondered if Serendipity had noticed that Abubakari had graciously taken the seat on the other side of Erik, giving up his customary spot so Nathan could sit next to his new found relative. Abubakari and Wendell were both watching their hostess and guest of honor with some amusement.

Serendipity pointed to the photo hanging in the air and visible from both sides showing a middle-aged African-American woman. "This is Bernice Brown. She's the one that organized the family reunion. She and her father traced all your living descendants and invited them to a weekend in Baltimore a couple of years ago. Hmm, I guess that's in the future now."

Another photo came up of a redheaded young man with freckles. "This is Bubba Brown. He's a college kid that came up from Mobile, Alabama for the event."

A picture of a distinguished-looking black man dressed in a twenty-seventh-century suit came up. "This is Frederick Brown. He's a congressman from New York."

The next photo showed a handsome slim man with dark skin wearing a Union Jack t-shirt and a very British raised eyebrow. "This is Reggie Brown, a famous actor from London. I was shocked when I found out *he* was my cousin. He's one of my favorite actors...well, living actors anyway."

The image of an older gentleman with very pale skin appeared. He was wearing a kilt. "This is James Dunn, a teacher from Edinburgh, Scotland. His great-grandmother was a Brown. He pointed out that Dunn is Gaelic for 'Brown.' Ironic, huh."

A picture then appeared of a couple of dozen people of various ages and all looking very Japanese. "This is the Brown family of Tokyo. Real nice people. Very polite."

The photo changed again, showing an older Native American. "This is Chief Jose Brown. He's the head of the Navaho Tribal Council."

Nathan, who had been watching this, looked stunned. "All these people is my great-grandchildren?"

"Yes," Serendipity looked at the computer. "Tom! Show the family tree Bernice created." The image of a genealogy chart appeared showing thousands of names with photos. "This is our family. See, this is your name at the bottom. Here's your two sons, Mathew and Luke, and these are their children, and their children and so forth for over five hundred years. This is your legacy, Grandpa."

"My, my." Nathan's eyes were wide.

"Your kids' kids traveled all around the world, marrying the locals. Sure glad you aren't a bigot, or you'd be having a heart attack right now for sure."

"If they is all half as kindly as you, child, then I is proud of all of them."

"Boy, I wish I could call Bernice and tell her to throw another shindig so everyone could meet you."

Wendell and Abubakari both stood up, alarmed.

"Ayi," Abubakari shook his head. "Are you mad? You cannot do that, Dr. Brown."

"Why not?"

Wendell shook his finger at her. "You have played havoc with history as it is. Besides everyone will want you to go back and bring back *their* ancestors. That will botch-up time for certain, I daresay. Nathan is the last one. No more!"

"You don't like my family?" Serendipity frowned offended.

Wendell groaned, sat back down, folded his arms on the table and laid his forehead on them.

Abubakari sat back down. "That is not the problem. The only way you can get by with this, is if you never tell anyone where Nathan came from. Your argument that he disappeared without a trace is probably the only thing keeping the time stream from unraveling."

"Unraveling? Time streams don't unravel. Have you ever seen a time stream unravel?"

"No, but it would destroy the universe so no one would remember if it happened. Only you have been foolhardy enough to bring back a dead ancestor."

"I didn't bring him back from the dead. He was still alive when I found him."

"Yes," Wendell raised his head. "He just followed you home from school."

Serendipity frowned at both of them. "So you think I should take Grandpa back."

Wendell gave a sigh defeated. "No, we are just saying no more."

Serendipity looked at Nathan and shook her head. "People from the twenty-seventh century are so superstitious."

"Now, Serendipity," Nathan spoke slowly. "Maybe these fine gentlemen have a point. As much as I'd surely love for you to go back and save my Lizzie or Hannah, what would that do to all this?" He pointed to the family tree. "Maybe some of these people, maybe all of them, might not get born. I reckon then you'd never have been born and I wouldn't be here Now, ain't that so?"

"Thank you, Mr. Brown." Wendell smiled gratefully at him. "See, Serendipity, even your ancestor from a less technological age and with no scientific training can see the problems."

"Owo," Abubakari agreed. "If you will not listen to us, listen to him! You are playing God here, Dr. Brown."

"Fine. No more ancestors," Serendipity grumbled. "But I'm keeping

Grandpa."

"All right," Wendell said. "You may keep Nathan, but you better make him a fake birth certificate."

Abubakari shook his head. "The Institute of Time Travel would never allow this."

Serendipity just blew a raspberry. "Institute can take a flying leap into a pool of piranhas."

Sherman sat on his bed watching his television. Lauren, the computer, sat on the nightstand, while a few feet away her holographic image sat beside him.

"Nathan seems like a nice old dude." Sherman played with the remote control.

"He's okay in my book," Lauren agreed.

"Been a bizarro week, huh. Wendell meeting his great-grandma, and then Serendipity meeting her great-grandpa. I wonder if any of my ancestors would be that nice."

"I'm sure they would be."

"Why? None of my parents or grandparents were that hot." Sherman stopped and looked thoughtful. "They could all be dead now. I wonder if Mom is still alive."

"You can't contact her, you know, Sherm. How would you explain why you haven't aged in two and a half decades?"

"Yeah," Sherman put down the remote. "I can just see my letter home now. Dear Mom: How are you. It's been less than two months since I saw you last. Well, twenty five years for you. My boss is being chased by crazy assassins from the twenty-seventh century who want to eliminate time travel by eliminating her. So we are now hiding out in the twenty-first century in a historic mansion in Bellingham with a couple of twenty-seventh century zoologists, seven extinct parrots, a Revolutionary War hero, a Viking, a medieval nun, a cowboy from the Old West, a scholar from Timbuktu and a couple of Victorian English gentlemen—well, one is a gentleman anyway. Oh, and I have a girlfriend. You'd like her, she's real sweet. Did I mention she's a computer?" Sherman shook his head. "Could my life possibly get any weirder?"

"Never throw down the gauntlet of challenge to fate, Sherm."

Sherman stared silently at the television, trying to figure out how his life *could* get any weirder.

The next morning Sherman had come upstairs to the main hall just as Serendipity, Wendell and Nathan were coming downstairs. Wendell nodded hello to Sherman, but Serendipity was preoccupied.

"You didn't have to wait outside of our door for us, Grandpa." Serendipity looked over her shoulder. "You could have come down without us."

"I is just being polite. A gentleman waits for a lady."

Wendell smiled at Nathan. "That's what I keep trying to tell her."

Serendipity peered over at Wendell. "And I keep telling you I'm not a lady."

"Yes, you are," Wendell and Nathan both said at the same time. They stopped and looked at each other.

"Oh great, two Victorian gentlemen in my life. So Grandpa, did you sleep well last night?"

"Yes, child, felt like I was sleeping on a cloud. That was mighty fine of you to let me use your bed, Dr. Howe. Not many white gentlemen would do that."

"Mr. Brown, one thing you are going to have to get used to is that you are no longer a second-class citizen here. You are as good as anyone else in this house. Slavery is a thing of the past, and so is bigotry. Well, at least in my day. I can't vouch for 2010 completely. By the twenty-seventh century the world has become such a melting pot that trying to create a dividing line for the various ethnic groups is impossible. You saw those pictures Serendipity showed you of your descendants. They were from all over the world from dozens of ethnicities. And yet nineteenth century, even early twentieth century law, would say they were all 'Negro'. How ridiculous is that?"

"That's right," Serendipity said. "In the twenty-fourth century we know there is only one race. Everyone is equal."

Nathan smiled at them, then noticed Rosetta walk by with a feather duster. "Who is that? I ain't met her."

"Oh," Wendell dismissed Rosetta with a wave of his hand. "That's not a real person."

"Hmmm." Nathan's smile dropped. "That's what they said about our kind."

"No, no, no." Wendell shook his head. "It is a robot. It does the household cleaning, that's all."

"You pay her?"

"Of course not, it's a robot."

"Uh, huh." Nathan gave him a dark look. "That another name for 'slave'?"

"Hmm." Serendipity looked thoughtful. "Isn't 'robot' the Czech word for 'slave'?"

Wendell frowned at her. "You are not helping."

"Sorry." Serendipity went over and put her arm around Nathan's shoulders. "Grandpa, Rosetta is a robot. It's an android, an automaton, an A.I....uh, artificial intelligence. It's a machine with a computer brain. It's manmade. No intelligence, no soul." Serendipity pulled out her computer. "It's like my computer, only put in a humanlike body so it can do chores. It's not real. I'll show you." Serendipity turned to the robot. "Rosetta, come here."

Rosetta stopped dusting, turned and stepped over, her face blank. "Yes, Dr. Brown."

"Turn around." Rosetta turned and Serendipity pulled up the robot's blouse. Serendipity reached under both armpits and pushed something. A panel swung open in the back. "Look inside Grandpa, see the wires and microchips?"

"Lordy!" Nathan eyes got big. "She ain't a person, is she? Does she got feelings?"

"No more than that duster it's holding. It no more has a soul than my computer, or the one Sherman is wearing around his neck." Serendipity pointed at Lauren.

Sherman instinctively reached up and put his hand over Lauren protectively. Sherman realized what he was doing and dropped his hand. No one seemed to notice, all eyes were on Nathan.

"Kinda like one of them voodoo zombies." Nathan studied Rosetta uneasily. "What if she attacks you?"

"It can't. It's programmed to never harm anyone. It only does as it's told." Serendipity closed the panel. "We are very careful never to create something that is sentient, conscious, self-aware—that would be an unnatural monster."

Serendipity looked up and frowned at Sherman. "You okay, kid? You look scared. Not you, too? Don't worry Rosetta isn't going to sneak into your room late some night and attack you."

Sherman gave a nervous laugh. "Yeah, I know. I'm not afraid of Rosetta. She's just a machine."

"Now Dr. Brown," Wendell said. "Remember Sherman is from the twentieth century. He isn't used to technology this advanced. Don't tease him."

Serendipity turned to Nathan. "Come on, Grandpa. Let's get some breakfast and then we'll go get some furniture for the room you picked out. I don't know why you picked the smaller one."

"I like seeing the mountains from the window."

"The view is even better one floor up," Wendell told Nathan. "Feel free to sit up there any time."

"We'll get you a real nice bed with the best mattress," Serendipity said. "You want a double bed?"

"Just me in it."

"And we'll need a dresser. What else would you like?"

"You brought that chair and stool I made. Guess I could use those." Nathan sounded disappointed.

"We can get you a overstuffed chair to put at the window if you like."

"Then why did you ever bring those things I made?"

Serendipity blinked at him. "Because *you* made them."

Nathan looked surprised, then smiled. "Would you like to have them, child?"

"Could I?"

"They is yours."

"Thank you!" Serendipity threw her arms around the old man.

Nathan smiled and patted her on the back. "Child, you got a fancy mansion and fine things and lots of money. Why you want with that old junk?"

"Because they're special. You made them."

"You got a huge heart, don't you, child? I think you get that from Lizzie."

"Grandma? You think so?" Serendipity looked like a little girl who had been complimented.

Nathan nodded, smiling in a fatherly fashion. Serendipity had brought Nathan back so she could take care of him, but Sherman wasn't sure that it wouldn't wind up being the other way around.

A couple of days later Sherman found Wendell in his favorite spot. The other chair however was taken by Nathan. The two sat, sipping tea, gazing out the window. Wendell seemed to have made friends with the old man. Then Sherman remembered Wendell's real age and wondered who was the oldest.

Wendell glanced up at Sherman and nodded. "Good morning, old chap. Would you care for a spot of tea?"

"No thanks."

"Well, please pull up a chair and join us, won't you?"

Sherman got the wooden chair over at the desk and pulled it over.

Wendell smiled at Sherman. "I finally found someone to have tea with. It appears Nathan likes tea."

"Never had it before," Nathan drawled. "Truth be told I just like drinking out of these dainty cups sitting in a fancy chair like high-tone folk."

"Yes, presentation counts for a lot." Wendell smiled at him. "Serendipity never understood that. She always thought a tea bag in a coffee mug was just as good. But you understand, having been from circumstances of privation."

Wendell leaned back, with that look he got when he went into his professor mode. "Some years ago there was an archaeology dig in the White Chapel area of London. When they got down to the level of the nineteenth century they were baffled. At the time it was one of the poorest slums in the world, and yet they found a very nice porcelain cup and saucer. They came to me, since I had been there, and asked me why people who could often not afford food would have such extravagant dinnerware. I told them the answer was obvious. This teacup was most likely the only nice thing the person owned. If they could drink tea from a fancy teacup even occasionally, then they were a lady or gentleman, as the case may be, and they were worth something. Half the appeal of tea to the lower classes was that it was the beverage of the upper classes and in some way put them on equal footing. Tea makes you a person, an equal to anyone."

Nathan nodded like he understood, taking a sip of tea.

"Don't tell Serendipity but I am rather glad she brought you back," Wendell said. "I must say though I am amazed at how well you are adjusting."

"It do seem like a dream sometimes." Nathan set the cup on the saucer.

"I just wake up each morning expecting to find some new surprise that day. I gotta say though, that television box still is mighty hard to believe. Watching people put on shows from yonder. I do have one question. Who is that fellow they keep showing—that nice looking colored man in the fancy suit—now what is his name? Oh yes, Rocko Bama."

"Barack Obama?" Wendell asked.

"Yes, him. They keeps calling him 'President.' Just what is he president of?"

Wendell and Sherman both looked at Nathan surprised.

Sherman scooted his chair closer. "He's President of the United States of America now."

Nathan nearly dropped his cup, his mouth flying open. "You joshing me? A colored man President of these here United States?" Then Nathan smiled and leaned back. "My my, what won't they think of next?"

Sherman stared at Nathan. His world had just been turned upside down and he appeared to take it in stride. Even if Nathan was a distant ancestor, it was becoming apparent where Serendipity got her unflappability in a crisis.

"So Mr. Brown—" Wendell started.

"No, call me Nathan, son."

"All right, Nathan—feel free to call me Wendell—what has been the hardest thing that you have had to come to grips with?"

Nathan thought a moment. "Well, I do hope you won't be offended none, but it is a little hard to believe than my great-granddaughter has taken up with an Englishman."

"That's right, you had very strict color lines drawn back in your day. Would you prefer she was seeing a man of African descent?"

"That ain't it, son. It's just—well, you is British. You is the enemy."

Wendell thought a moment. "That's right. You were in the American Revolutionary War. You were shooting at Brits, weren't you?"

"Yes sir, and they was shooting back at me. And they was led by a General William Howe, and his brother Admiral Richard Howe was leading their navy."

"No, relation I assure you. For most of history, America and Great Britain have been staunch allies."

"Well, don't suppose you can help being English. You seems like a nice enough fellow. Serendipity seems sweet on you. You seem sweet on her."

"I am absolutely mad about your great-granddaughter."

"What be your intentions toward my Serendipity?" Nathan got a fatherly frown.

"I would marry her in a heartbeat. I believe I already accidentally proposed. That made her nervous. I'm hoping some day she will be more amenable to marriage. Either way, I intend to stand by Serendipity as long as she will let me and to help her, protect her, and cherish her in any way I can."

"Nice to see the girl has good sense when it comes to men."

Sherman struggled to keep his face straight. Wendell was probably the only man in Serendipity's past that fit that bill.

Nathan studied Wendell, then nodded. "For what it be worth, you got my blessing."

"Thank you, Nathan, that means a great deal to me."

"Never had anyone ask for my blessing before. My daughter died as a child. Never knew any of my granddaughters. Never knew if I even had any."

"Didn't your sons ever send you a letter?"

"How? They never learned how to write, and I ain't never learned how to read."

Wendell sat up and stared in disbelief. "You never went to school?"

"No school for colored folks where I growed up. And certainly ain't none for slaves. Always had a hankering to learn to read. Guess it's too late now."

Wendell sat down his teacup on the table. "It is never too late. You aren't senile. I must say, you certainly seem clever enough. If you really wish to learn to read I would do everything in my power to help you, old chap."

Nathan stared at him like he had just offered him the greatest treasure in the world. "I would like that very much, young man. I'd work real hard, do whatever you say."

Wendell stood up. "Well, I'm not a professional literacy teacher, but I believe the first thing you need to learn is the alphabet. Let me get a pencil and a pad of paper. School is officially in session."

Chapter Thirty-Five

Starting from its base and working up, the shiny black box materialized beside the glass and iron conservatory. The door flew open, revealing a determined looking man in a dark-grey one-piece twenty-fourth century suit and a black visor. Behind him followed two other men similarly dressed.

The man in the lead looked up at the grey Gothic mansion and shook his head. "Woman was totally mad."

One of his companions studied the three-story building. "Yes, Commander, I read that she built this house to resemble one from an ancient comedy telecast."

"There are a lot of rumors about Dr. Serendipity Brown, Number Two. I'm not sure which are true. Follow me, men." The Commander started across the lawn to the flagstone walk leading to the front door. He pointed his wrist band at it. The electronic lock disengaged and he opened the door onto the entry hall.

A tall servant-bot with the appearance of a handsome brunette man dressed as a butler entered the room. "Who are you? How did you get in? Is Dr. Brown expecting you?"

The Commander pulled out a pencil-sized rod and aimed it at the robot. Sparks began to fly from the android, then smoke. It collapsed on the tiles, its limbs twisted.

The Commander looked at his wristband again. "I'm picking up the D.N.A. of Dr. Brown, Dr. Howe and Mr. Conrad. No trace of Dr. Leach or Dr. Darrel."

"Do you suppose she hid them in another time?" Number Two said.

"Possibly. We will have to interrogate Howe, see if he knows where they and the other stranded T.A.s are."

"Does it really matter?" Number Three shrugged. "I mean if we eliminate Dr. Brown, we eliminate time travel and they won't be there anyway."

"I wanted to kill all the time meddlers as a message but thanks to the Enforcers that's now impossible. You are right. Killing Dr. Brown now takes priority. However, if at all possible..." The Commander's voice faded, as he looked down at his band. "This way."

They followed the noise of the entertainment center and went down the hall to a room with purple shag carpet. There sat Sherman on a beanbag chair, watching a movie on the large screen on the wall. Wendell sat on the Naugahyde couch, his arm around Serendipity. All looked up toward the door, shocked.

Sherman jumped up. "Who are—"

The thin pistol cut Sherman short as it burned a hole through his forehead. He collapsed on the beanbag chair, his blood soaking into it.

Serendipity leaped up, staring at Sherman dumbstruck. Wendell glanced at Sherman, then the attackers, then Serendipity. He jumped up and tried to get in front of her before the pistol could lock on target. He wasn't fast enough. She didn't have time to scream when the bolt of energy went through her brain. Her body fell back on the coach.

"No!" Wendell wailed. "No!" He gathered up the limp figure, unmindful of the blood and held her close. The Commander had no trouble slapping the compliance disk on the back of Wendell's neck.

"Stop, Dr. Howe!"

Wendell stopped rocking Serendipity's body and cut his eyes around at her murderer. If he was afraid, he didn't show it. His eyes instead blazed with hatred.

"Dr. Howe, you will tell us where Dr. Brown hid the other temporal anthropologists."

"I can't."

"Tell us."

"I can't because I don't know."

"She didn't take you with her?"

"No. I have been here all along."

The Commander placed the pistol against Wendell's head. "Is there any reason we shouldn't kill you?"

"No," Wendell said calmly. "None at all. You killed my Serendipity. I've no reason to live now."

"Listen to yourself." The leader sneered. "You sound like something out of a Victorian melodrama, you ridiculous buffoon."

"My sole purpose in life, my only reason for existing, is to protect Dr. Brown, as well as Sherman and my brother. It is my duty."

"Duty. How archaic. You have lost all vestiges of civilization, haven't you? Living all these decades among the savages. The world will well be rid of you."

Wendell shrugged. "As you wish. But know this. You killed all of us for nothing. You can't change time."

Wendell gave the Commander such a mocking smirk that it was a pleasure to burn a hole through his temple.

"No!" Wendell yelped and sat up in bed.

"Huh?" Serendipity raised her head off her pillow. "Whazzit?"

He looked about at the dark room, the faint light from the window making eerie shadows. "Where am I? When am I?"

She sat up and put her arms around him. "Fairhaven Home, Bellingham, 2010."

Wendell buried his nose in her hair. "Are you all right?"

"I'm fine. You just had another nightmare. Enforcers?"

"No." Wendell's brow wrinkled. "I-I don't remember what I was dreaming. I just woke up with this horrible feeling. Like a part of me just died."

"Oh?"

"I feel like something terrible just happened—or will happen."

"You're worried about the Time Keepers? It will all turn out all right."

"How can you be so sure?"

"Because if they killed me, the world would lose time travel, you would never become a temporal anthropologist, we would never meet, and I certainly wouldn't be in bed right now in the twenty-first century with a man from the twenty-seventh." She caressed his cheek

"How can you know that for certain? The Institute always tried to keep things as simple as possible, but time travel can get discombobulating really fast." He put his hand over hers. "I would die if anything happened to you, my dearest darling."

"Eh, if they did kill me, you'd now be a history professor at Cambridge and never knew what you missed."

"No, I would be staring out the window wondering why my life always felt empty. I would miss you even if we never met."

Wendell couldn't see her expression in the dark, but he did hear her giggle.

"What's so amusing?"

"Nothing, sweetie. It's just if anyone else said that ridiculous statement it would sound phony."

"I meant every word."

"I know you did. It's what makes you so adorable. Tell you what, we could skip ahead a couple of years and see how things turn out."

"No!" His voice sounded stern. "You must never, ever do that."

"Okay, okay. Hmm, I can think of another way to ease your mind." She ran her finger around the edge of his ear. "There's something I have wanted to do for a long time." Her voice purred seductively.

"Oh?"

She threw back the covers, and got out of bed. She grabbed the nearby wooden chair, serving as a clothes horse, and dumped off the garments. She then banged the legs on the floor.

"What are you doing?" Wendell got off the bed. "Are you mad? Dr. Leach is just below us trying to sleep."

"Yeah, I know. And yes I am mad...at Tobias." She lay down on the floor and cupped her hands on the floorboards. "Oh, Wendell," she yelled. "You are such an animal. You make me wild with passion."

"Serendipity." Wendell came around the bed. "Shame on you."

She giggled. "Oh, you fiery stallion. Yes, give it to me. All of it. All twelve inches."

"What!" Wendell sputtered. "I'm not...I'm not even...not that I'm..."

"Relax," she whispered. "You're big enough to get the job done." She turned back to the floor. "Oh, Wendell. You stud. Faster. Harder. Yes! Yes! Yes!"

"You are terrible."

"Yeah, I'm a naughty girl."

"No, I mean you are a terrible actress. You never talk like that during...well, you know."

"I can't. You get me so stirred up I can't get any coherent words out."

"Well, at least now I know you haven't been faking it all this time."

"Come on." She patted the floor beside her. "Join in."

"I can't harass a fellow temporal anthropologist."

"Tobias called me an old trout in Paris, remember?"

Wendell immediately fell to the floor beside her. "Yes, my dear," he yelled. "I will give you whatever you want. I can't help myself. You intoxicate me so."

"Oh, Wendell, you hurricane, you. Do you really think we can go through the entire Kama Sutra in one night?"

Wendell raised his eyebrow and whispered. "Are you referring to the original Indian version or the later Western editions with those ridiculous contortionist pictures that had nothing to do with the text?"

"*You* read the original?" Serendipity whispered surprised.

"Well, the Kama Sutra *is* Victorian—the 1883 first English translation anyway. Sir Richard Burton certainly caused a scandal with that one." Wendell wrinkled his nose. "I must say, all that biting, slapping and scratching is not to my taste. Quite overrated as a useful manual. Although there was that one section on—"

"Focus, Wendell. Just play along, will you."

Wendell faced the floor again. "Yes, my darling!" He yelled. "With you anything is possible. You are just so invigorating. What man could ever resist you? You make Aphrodite look like an old hag."

"Oh, very good. Keep going."

"You are the most magnificent woman that ever existed. A garden of earthly delights." Wendell looked over at her. "A pyre that consumes a man, but from which he immerges renewed like a phoenix. You fill my soul with your exuberance and make me feel more alive than I have ever felt."

"You're pretty amazing yourself, mister." She spoke less loudly gazing at Wendell. She scooted closer to him and kissed him.

From that point the performance was no longer faked, as they forgot all about the man in the room under them.

ℭhapter ℑhirty-Six

The days settled into a routine. Wendell took his role as teacher very seriously, and Nathan took the role of student even more so.

Serendipity tinkered in her basement workshop updating her laptop by a century. Sherman was sure every computer company in the world would have loved to be watching over her shoulder.

Abubakari spent most of his time at the campus library. Sherman wondered if the Mali scholar had a crush on one of the librarians, or just needed to be around books.

Tobias was usually out during the day or locked in his room. He did attend meals and was always home by ten at night. More and more often he would come down to watch the big screen TV, sitting quietly in a corner. He was tolerated with benign indifference.

Henry and Matilda spent most of their time together, relishing these months in hiding as a chance to be together. Sherman wondered how they would adjust to being separated again.

Erik refused to borrow money from Sherman to buy a Harley, but he did agree to let him cosign on a bank loan. Erik now spent his time building Viking-style chests made in the traditional manner, long, low and narrow and large enough to pack all of a Viking's fighting gear. The ends extended below the box to form 'feet', just enough to keep the chest off the ground. The wood was oak and hand polished with an abstract writhing dragon carved on the front. The iron latch and hinges had all been forged by Erik. They had sold well at a local gallery.

However an even bigger seller was proving to be Erik's Viking-style helmets. He couldn't make them fast enough. It turned out Western Washington University's football team was called the "Vikings" and it was becoming a status symbol among the fans to be able to show up to a game in an authentic Viking helmet. The way they were selling, Erik would have the loan paid off early.

One morning at the breakfast table Henry made an announcement. "Serendipity, have you looked at the calendar?"

"Why?"

"Thanksgiving is in three days!"

"Thanksgiving for what, pray tell?" Matilda asked confused.

"Thanksgiving Day." Henry turned to her. "American holiday. The fourth Thursday of November all Americans are obligated to eat a big feast with a turkey, mashed potatoes and cranberry sauce."

Matilda frowned at Henry. "I was to believe that was what one dost on Christmas."

"Yeah, then too. Except on Thanksgiving you are supposed to eat yourself into a digestive stupor. It's our patriotic duty."

"Leave it to the Americans to come up with that one." Wendell raised his eyebrow.

Henry turned back to Serendipity. "We are going to have a Thanksgiving feast, aren't we?"

"Of course! It would be un-American not to."

"Then I'm going to need to do some shopping." Henry looked over at Sherman. "You mind driving me, kid? This will be more than I can carry on the bus."

"No problem, dude."

Henry did a great job on the Thanksgiving feast. There was not only a huge stuffed turkey, but mashed potatoes and gravy, sweet potatoes, cranberry sauce, green beans, corn on the cob, and pumpkin pie—all the traditional New World foods.

"Looks just like a Norman Rockwell picture." Serendipity admired the table. "In fact I have that print in my dining room back home. You outdid yourself, Henry."

"Thank you kindly, Serendipity. And I want to thank everyone who pitched in. Well, belly up and chow down."

They all sat down and began passing bowls, while Henry carved the turkey. After everyone got settled down, Serendipity stood up at her place at the head of the table. "We have another tradition on Thanksgiving besides stuffing ourselves. We are supposed to reflect on our blessings in the past year. When I was a kid everyone in my family would stand up one by one and tell what they were thankful for that year. So I will go first. Don't worry you may keep eating if you like."

Serendipity cleared her throat. "Wow! What a year! I finally invent time travel. Get a Big Mac and a real twentieth-century assistant my first trip. Sherman has been a big help to me. Then I met Wendell. He has also been a big help. I mean a *really* big help. Got my grandpa to come live with me. Then I got to save you guys and got to know you. I kind of feel like you're all family now." She sat down. "You're next Sherman."

Sherman stood up. "I got out of my boring life. Now I'm a time traveler and a millionaire driving a Ferrari. How cool is that?" He sat back down.

Wendell stood up. "I would like to thank Serendipity for saving my friends. And I'd also like to thank her for—well, just *everything*. And I'd like to thank Sherman, too—well, not for the same thing, of course." Wendell cleared his throat and sat down, his face an embarrassed pink.

Matilda looked around. "Oh, I am next?" She stood up and bowed her head. "I give thanks to the Lord that ye three came to save me. I wish to give thanks that Wendell ist alive and for the gift of friendship from Serendipity. And I wish to give thanks to at last be given so much time with Henry. Amen." She plopped back down.

Henry smiled at her and stood up. "I'm mighty glad you got to spend time with me too, darling. And I guess I'm also glad that Wendell ain't really dead. I wouldn't have anyone to pick on. Can't pick on Serendipity because she'd kick me in the rump." Henry sat down. "Psst, it's your turn, Tobias."

Tobias didn't stand up, but just looked around. "I can't think of anything I'm thankful for. All right, I'm alive, I guess that's something."

After a moment's silence, it became apparent Tobias was done. Abubakari stood up. "I would like to thank Allah for sending you to me to save me. May He grant you a long life for your hospitality. We may all be homeless refugees, but few refugees have lived in such comfort. I am thankful I got to know you all." He gave a slight bow and sat down.

Erik pushed his chair back noisily and stood up. "Ya, thanks for saving my life. Also I am thankful I got to know you all too. And I am glad that I found some more friends down at the Harley shop." Erik grinned and sat down.

Nathan stood up. "I have so much to thank the Lord for, but mostly I'd like to thank him for family, those long gone, those yet to be born and those just found." He smiled over at Serendipity. "One couldn't ask for a nicer, more giving granddaughter, a woman who takes in strangers and treats them like family. I'd be mighty proud of you, child, even if you ain't rich or an inventor. I'd like to thank all of you for treating me so kindly. Back home, we used to pray that the Lord would make the world a better place. Looks like He did. I is thankful I got to see it." Nathan nodded and sat down.

Serendipity reached over and patted his hand. "I'm thankful you got to see it too."

Sherman looked around at the warm smiles, even Tobias looked half civil. This was different from the Thanksgivings he remembered with his squabbling family. Fairhaven Home had started out as a group of strangers hiding from terrorists and had learned to live in harmony, becoming like one big happy family.

Erik stopped and looked around the table. "Ho, Henry? Where is the lutefisk? One cannot have Thanksgiving without lutefisk."

"Oh please!" Tobias rolled his eyes. "Cod soaked in lye? Who wants fish soaked in drain cleaner until it's the consistency of phlegm?"

"Back off, Tobias!" Serendipity snapped. "The man can have lutefisk if he wants it!"

Henry shrugged. "I kind of have to go with Tobias on this one. I've heard lutefisk destroys silver on contact and will smell up a kitchen for days. Doesn't sound very appealing."

"No one is forcing you to eat it." Erik looked disgruntled. "You don't know what's good."

"Well, neither do you, obviously," Tobias said.

The normally laid back Erik then stood up to defend his precious lutefisk and got into a shouting match with Tobias. Serendipity jumped in, backing up Erik, if only because she liked Erik and didn't like Tobias. Henry threw his two cents in whenever he got a chance, taking neither side. Wendell was trying to calm both sides and failing, only adding to the noise. The rest at the table just stared in disbelief.

"Yup," Sherman leaned his elbow on the table. "Just like one big happy family."

Chapter Thirty-Seven

Winter officially started on the twenty-first, but Sherman always felt that it started the first day of December. The Cascade Mountains were now coated with snow in the higher elevations. The white cloak seemed to get a little lower every day. So far the only snow in town had been a skift on Thanksgiving. Even so Serendipity wouldn't let Nathan take public transportation, since he would have to wait at the bus stop in the cold. Nathan humored her but Sherman knew the old man was probably tougher than any of them.

Sherman didn't mind taking Nathan and Wendell to the bookstore. Wendell said it was to find more reading material for Nathan, but Sherman expected it was an excuse for both of them to get out of the house and take a break from reading and writing lessons. Their first stop was a bookstore downtown on Grant Street.

Sherman looked through the tall bookshelves in the self-help and psychology section. Besides the science fiction and fantasy, he had been reading books on how to manage difficult people and how to influence others. Seemed a good skill for a Trouble Shooter. Since there was no degree for the profession he was slowly creating for himself, he had to wing it and come up with his own class curriculum.

Sherman weaved through the narrow aisles, occasionally running into Wendell. The Englishman was wearing his brown frock coat and a paisley waistcoat but with a modern shirt and tie. Luckily this was a college town, so he could get by with it. He did, with some reluctance, leave the top hat at home.

"My word!" Wendell actually raised his voice. "Sherman, look at this!"

Wendell weaved his way from the next aisle and shoved a very worn book at him. Sherman read the cover aloud, "*Modern Sheep Husbandry Methods*? Are you planning to raise sheep?"

"Of course not, but it is on the list!" Wendell waved a slip of paper at him.

"The list?" Sherman studied the unfolded dog-eared stationary covered with Wendell's beautiful Victorian cursive.

Wendell composed himself. "Sorry, old chap. Just got carried away. I believe I told you that universities come to me with projects?"

"Yes?"

"Many of them have asked me to pick up a copy of a book from the 1800s that is out of print and has long since disappeared. Victorian paper was usually too acidic to last. So every time I go into the past, I try to drop into at least one bookstore and see if I can find one of the titles on the list. This book has evaded me for the past ten years. It was printed in the year 1892. I never dreamed I would find it in the year 2010 in the Pacific Northwest, of all places." Wendell opened the cover and gasped. "Three dollars? They only want three dollars for this priceless treasure?"

"Outside of being an antique, and one in bad condition, the book is useless. Only a sheep farmer would want it, and probably only for a good laugh."

"But the history department of the University of Edinburgh needs this book!" Wendell clutched his find to his chest.

"Then get it. Henry can take it to them when he gets home."

Nathan came around the corner wearing a less eccentric looking sports coat and slacks. He waved a book. "Wendell, you knowed how you asked me to look through those younguns' books to see if anything caught my eye?"

"Yes, I know it is mostly too immature for you, but I hoped there might be something interesting at your current reading level."

Nathan held up a picture book that had a collage of photos on its cover. "What is this 'Fah-ah-mo-us Blah-ack Ah-mer-ih-cans?'" He tried to sound out the words.

Wendell took the book. "Famous Black Americans. It is a history book. Yes, that does look interesting." He flipped through the pages. "Oh my, I've met some of these folks. Frederick Douglas—nice chap. Yes, Sojourner Truth—feisty little lady. Oh and Harriett Tubman. She was not the prettiest woman, but she had an inner beauty. I will admit I was quite taken with her." Wendell flipped through the pages again frowning. "Odd. You would think they would have George Bush in here."

"The vice-president?" Sherman asked. "He's not even black."

"No, I'm not talking about President George Bush or his son President George W. Bush."

"What! George Bush and his son both become president someday?"

"It is 2010. It already happened. My, but you do have some catching up to do, don't you? No, I was referring to George Washington Bush, the pioneer. Without him there wouldn't even be a Washington State and *you* would have been born in British Columbia or at least Oregon." Wendell turned the book over. "Hmmm, fourth grade reading level." He looked up at Nathan. "Might be a little difficult for you right now, but the speed with which you are progressing that shouldn't be a problem long. You have been working hard with me and with those reading programs on your computer. You certainly have picked up that bit of technology very quickly."

"Ain't hard." Nathan shrugged. "Just a matter of pushing buttons, is all."

"I'm beginning to think Serendipity got more than a little bit of her intelligence from you. Let's purchase this book and we can read it when we get home. I'll help you with the hard words. So you like history?"

"Don't know. Ain't never had the chance to learn none."

"I say, we will certainly need to rectify that and teach you some history." By Wendell's tone, the historian sniffed a potential convert. "Let's go back and see if there are any more books like this."

The three of them put their newly acquired books in the trunk of Sherman's Ferrari. "All right, who is next on our list of bookstores?" Wendell asked Sherman as he closed the lid.

Sherman pulled out the itinerary Wendell had given him. "There's another bookstore across the street. Couple over in Fairhaven too."

Wendell stopped and glanced about, surprised.

"What's wrong, Wendell?" Sherman asked.

"Christmas decorations. I just noticed all the Christmas decorations."

"Well, yeah, dude, it's December first. I think they start putting them up after Halloween."

"Christmas," Wendell whispered. "I loved Christmas when I was a child. Father Christmas, the decorations, the pudding, the crackers. I miss it."

"Huh? Aren't temporal anthropologists allowed to have Christmas?"

Wendell got a sad smile. "Not really. It was the Victorians that turned Christmas from a drunken revelry to a family holiday with decorated trees, sweets and carols that we know today. I was doing a study on that transition. For fifty years I studied Christmas, watching it from a distance without a family to celebrate it with."

"You couldn't go home for Christmas? I mean you had a time machine. Why couldn't you study past Christmases in July and then stay home for your own Christmas."

Wendell just looked at the ground. "It is not that easy. It's complicated." Then he looked up at Sherman, his eyes shining with excitement. "I could have a real Christmas this year. We could all have Christmas. Forget the other bookstores for now. We have to go home and tell the others. I want to share this with them!"

Wendell beat them into the house, practically leaping out of the car as soon as Sherman parked it in the steel frame garage off the alley. Sherman came through the back door to hear Wendell yelling for everyone to come to him. Sherman and Nathan came into the reception hall to find the normally sedate Englishman pacing excitedly.

Henry and Matilda came out the kitchen. "Tarnation, Wendell!" Henry frowned. "What is the matter? Someone hurt?"

Erik and Serendipity came up from the basement. Even Cerwyn came out of the Music Room. Serendipity ran over to Wendell looking concerned. "What's wrong, honey?"

Wendell grabbed Serendipity by the arms. "Christmas!"

"Huh? What about it?"

"Christmas is coming!" Wendell turned to the others.

They all looked at him like he was nuts.

"Yup, old buddy," Henry drawled. "It does that every year."

"And when was the last time you celebrated Christmas, old boy?" Henry frowned, thoughtfully. "Uh, I don't know."

"What were you doing last Christmas?"

"I was in a hotel room in Tombstone 1877, if I recall."

Wendell looked over at Matilda. "And where were you."

"Canterbury 1210. I remember they served sweet cakes at the convent."

Erik scratched his beard. "Dublin 998. It was a Viking community then. They didn't have Christmas yet, but they had a winter solstice celebration called Yule. Not quite the same thing."

Wendell sighed. "And I spent many Christmases walking about the streets of London watching the efforts of the early Salvation Army. I wasn't allowed to get involved. I couldn't even drop a farthing in the kettle. This year is different. We aren't alone. We are all going to have Christmas this year!"

"Wait a minute." Serendipity seemed confused. "You're all time travelers. Why couldn't you study Christmas any time and be home with your families for Christmas?"

"Yeah, I asked the same thing." Sherman nodded. "Wendell blew me off."

Matilda, Erik and Henry all looked down at the floor.

Wendell turned to the two non-temporal anthropologists. "I did not mean to blow you off, old boy. Like I said, it's complicated. We temporal anthropologists told people that holidays were better studied in Base Time, but that was just an excuse. The truth was I tried going to family gatherings but I was like a stranger who showed up for dinner. I was away so much I was no longer really a part of the family. For some reason Christmas made that reality even more vivid. I started making excuses saying I couldn't get away from my work. Of course, in the Field where I felt at home, I wasn't allowed any friends who could invite me to dinner. Christmas became something I observed happening to other people. I'm sure it is the same for all temporal anthropologists."

Henry, Matilda and Erik all nodded.

"Come on, guys!" Serendipity cocked her head. "Wouldn't your families miss you and want to see you at the holidays?"

Henry scratched his neck. "Yeah, they want to see us...they just don't want to see *us*...the *new* us."

Wendell turned to her. "Do you think I was always like this? Do you think I was born in a frock coat? Do you think Erik always wore his hair in braids or Matilda wore a veil?"

Serendipity shrugged. "I just figured you were all born in the wrong century."

Wendell gave her a patient look. "You didn't know me before I went through the program. Imagine if you will a teenage boy sent off to college, with his hair hanging in his face. A typical perfectly normal young man who listens to popular music and dresses in the latest fashion. He returns years later as a stodgy Victorian gentleman. Everyone wants to know what I did with Wendell...*their* Wendell."

Henry nodded, "Yup, family wants to know when I'm gonna fall out of character and just be me. This *is* me...well, now anywho. They say I'm just a caricature."

Wendell gave him a knowing smile. "We are all caricatures, old boy."

"My family sayeth 'Stop talking like that, Matilda. Talk normal. What happened to your accent? Art thou ashamed of being Aussie? We are not good enough for you anymore?'"

Erik hung his head. "First time I journeyed back home, the family banished me from the house. Told me never to come back unless I could act civilized. Which means never can I go back."

Wendell patted Erik's shoulder. "Yes, Mom's side of the family has pretty much disowned me. Father's side are historians so they try to tolerate me...and fail."

Serendipity took Wendell's hand. "That's horrible!"

"It is not their fault. They just can't understand. They just want to know where the Wendell they remember is. He's gone and this other person took over his body. When they look at me they see both the corpse and the executioner."

Erik sighed. "They rejected us because we follow an alternate lifestyle."

Wendell nodded. "So after a couple of stabs at Christmas and failing, you start making excuses saying you can't get away from your work and make sure we are in the Field at that time." Then Wendell smiled. "This year though, it will be different. This year we have one another. This Christmas none of you will be spending it alone."

Henry broke out in a grin and looked down at Matilda. "Wendell's right, hon! We get to spend Christmas together!"

Matilda squealed and hugged Henry.

Wendell put his arms around Serendipity. "And I have someone to spend it with, too. My dear, I know you don't understand how much this means—"

"Like hell I don't. You think temporal anthropologists have a monopoly on crappy Christmases? I spent last Christmas with a six-pack of Henry Weinhard. Told my dad I was busy so I wouldn't have to listen to him nag me about being divorced and ruining my life for the umpteenth time." She smiled over at Nathan. "Grandpa's too much of a gentleman to spend the day telling me what a loser I am."

"Now why would I do that?" Nathan said. "I certainly ain't shamed of you none."

"Thank you, Grandpa." Serendipity hugged him. "I like to think the opinion of the founder of our family outranks my dad's."

Sherman shrugged. "I don't understand what the big whoop is about Christmas anyway. It's just another day for everyone to get together and gripe and yell at one another."

They all stared at Sherman like he had spoken blasphemy.

"What?" Sherman shrugged.

"Well, that settles it." Serendipity got that take charge look. "Sherman, I want you and Wendell to go to the nearest Christmas tree lot and drag back the biggest tree you can find! And then get Christmas decorations! We are going to have a Christmas that will make Dickens weep and Santa Claus jealous!"

Cerwyn who had been silently watching all this, shook his head. "I have to go back to my birds." He started to turn, but stopped and looked back. "We will get Christmas crackers, won't we?"

"Best ones I can find, with paper crowns, silly riddles, candy and everything."

"And Christmas pudding?"

"Complete with a sprig of holly on top!" Wendell assured him.

"That would be lovely, won't it?" Cerwyn smiled, then turned and left.

"Does Jell-O make an instant Christmas pudding?" Sherman muttered to no one in particular.

Matilda looked doubtful. "But Wendell, we art only going to be here but another month. Why spend all that coinage on decorations?"

Serendipity smiled at Wendell. "If my man wants Christmas, he gets Christmas. Buy whatever you want, hon. Knock yourself out."

"Thank you, dear." Wendell rubbed his hands together excitedly. "So, who wants to go with me?"

They all studied the monster fir that took up half of the parlor. "My word." Wendell stroked his mustache thoughtfully. "It looked so much smaller in the lot."

"Maybe if we moved out more furniture it wouldn't look so crowded." Serendipity rubbed her chin.

"Needs something." Wendell folded his arms.

"Yeah, more decorations." Henry looked the tree over. "Kinda bare, don't ya think."

"We bought three boxes of ornaments," Wendell said. "We probably should have gotten a smaller tree."

"Nah," Serendipity shook her head. "We just need more ornaments. Why don't we have everyone go buy something special to put on the tree? Like maybe a whole big box of something special."

Wendell glanced at her. "Excellent idea. We need a few Victorian ornaments, maybe a Father Christmas."

"Needs something Western." Henry looked thoughtful. "Wonder if I can find a cowboy Santa?"

Matilda put her arm around Henry's waist. "At the least, it needeth the traditional kangaroo in a Santa hat."

"Yule goats," Erik voice was firm. "The tree is in much need of straw Yule goats."

Serendipity turned to Nathan. "What do you think, Grandpa? How did you use to decorate your Christmas trees?"

"Never seen a Christmas tree before, child."

"What?"

"It is a German tradition," Wendell explained. "German immigrants brought it to America and England but it took a while to catch on. I believe it only became fashionable after Prince Albert erected one in Windsor Castle and the *Illustrated London Times* put a picture of it on their cover. I told you a lot of the Christmas traditions we know started with the Victorians."

Serendipity turned back to Nathan. "So what did you do on Christmas when you were a kid?"

"Mama cooked a big meal for the massa and his family. Mama and me, we get some of the leftovers. Later on when I was free and had a family, didn't have any money. I tried to get some candy for the children, if'n I could."

"That was it? Well, this year, Grandpa, you are getting a real Christmas. What would you like to hang on the tree?"

Nathan shook his head. "Don't know, child."

"I'll take you shopping, and let you pick out something you like." Serendipity put her arm around his shoulders. "This should be everyone's tree. Everyone is going to make a contribution."

The front door opened and closed. Abubakari stopped at the parlor door. "By the beard of the Prophet! What is *that*? How did it get in here, wa?"

Wendell pointed to the tree. "Christmas tree. Everyone has to help decorate it. You have to go shopping and pick out an ornament for the tree."

Abubakari looked uneasy. "I do not know if it would be fitting for a Muslim to decorate a Christian Christmas tree."

"How about a Kwanza decoration?" Serendipity asked.

Abubakari shrugged. "Owo, that would be fine. I will see if I can find a Kwanza decoration."

"Splendid!" Wendell smiled at him. "Perhaps we should acquire something for Hanukkah for Dr. Cohen, too. This is going to be an interesting tree." Wendell looked over at Sherman. "Do you have any suggestions, old boy?"

"I'll think of something."

The front door opened again. This time Tobias walked by, then stopped, backed up and looked in the parlor. "What is that monstrosity? It takes up half of the parlor."

"Christmas tree." Wendell looked over at him. "Everyone is obligated to help decorate it. You are required to get some ornaments for it."

Tobias muttered something and walked away. The next day however Sherman noticed Tobias hanging angels playing harps and trumpets on the tree when he thought no one was watching.

Chapter Thirty-Eight

A week before Christmas Serendipity stood up and gazed around the breakfast table. "Before you all take off, we need to have a meeting. Sherman, would you mind getting Cerwyn or Priscilla to come out here?"

Sherman got up, hearing Tobias's heavy sigh of annoyance as he walked past.

Sherman came back with Cerwyn, who sat down in the empty chair between Abubakari and Tobias.

Serendipity forced a brave smile at the expectant faces. "Thanks for joining us, Dr. Owen. It dawned on me that it's going to be New Year's Day in a little over two weeks. That's the day Agent Five wants me to come back and meet him. If everything went wrong, the terrorists will meet me instead and you will all be stuck here. If everything goes right, I can return and take you back to where the Enforcers can find you and take you home. Of course we will have to wipe your memories of this place so neither the Enforcers or the terrorists will know about Fairhaven Home."

She glanced over at Erik. "Also keep in mind that the Enforcers currently think you are all dead. If any of you want to stay here permanently, that's fine with me. So, think it over, let me know what each of you would like to do."

Cerwyn raised his hand. "Dr. Brown, I already know what Dr. Cohen's and my answer is. We have to go back to the twenty-seventh century for the sake of our charges, and to carry on our work, don't we?"

Serendipity nodded. "I knew you two would want to go home. I'll do my best to return you."

"I'm sure as hell not staying," Tobias snorted. "I am going stark raving mad here."

"I want to stay," Erik said. "I like it here. I belong here."

Sherman knew there was another reason. Erik had accidently killed a man to save another in the past. Erik would be tossed in jail, maybe even "erased" for that. At the very least he would never be allowed to travel in time again.

Serendipity knew it, too, but covered it up. "Yes, Erik, I figured you would want to stay with your biker friends. I think we should put you also on the title of the house, in case something happens to us, you will have a place to live. Also I want to put you on the bank account so you can get money while we are gone. The rest of you think it over."

"Ayi, we *have* to go back," Abubakari said.

Matilda nodded, then looked over at Henry with a sad expression.

"Well, you have two weeks to think about it. Also figure out what you will need if you get stuck here."

"I wish to journey with you to shield you from your foes." Erik scowled determined.

"I appreciate the offer, Erik, but your presence would be too hard to explain to Agent Five. I got the information record of your whereabouts by hacking into his computer. He would not be the least bit happy."

Erik nodded, his cheek jerking with a nervous tic, like Wendell's did when confronted with Enforcers. Erik probably would have no problems taking on a berserker, but all temporal anthropologists were terrified of Enforcers.

"Can I make a suggestion?" Sherman cocked his head at Serendipity. "Sure?"

"You talked about putting a monitor in the Timemobile so you could see what was outside before you stepped out?"

"Yeah, that is a very good idea. Okay, I know what I'm working on today."

Nathan looked over at Serendipity. "What about me? I knows how to handle a rifle."

Serendipity reached over and patted the old man's hand. "Grandpa, I would have an even harder time explaining you to Agent Five. The man would have a stroke. He would make me take you back. I'm going to have to leave you here."

Matilda smiled over at Nathan. "Be of good cheer, Mr. Brown. Whilst Wendell is away, I wol be your teacher and help you learn to read."

Henry nodded. "Shoot, we can all help out. In fact if you wear out Wendell you can ask one of us even now."

"I ain't so much afraid of losing a teacher, as I is losing my only kinfolk." Nathan smiled over at Serendipity.

"I'll be all right, Grandpa." She squeezed his hand. "I'll come back to you."

Cerwyn stood up. "Is that all, Dr. Brown?"

"Yes, Dr. Owen, you may go back to your babies." She looked over at Erik. "And you may go back to your *baby* too, Erik."

"I desire to ride my Harley down Chuckanut Drive before it starts raining again. I have been told the view is magnificent. One can glimpse the San Juan Islands in the distance. Would you like to ride with me, Dr. Brown?"

"That's okay." Serendipity appeared uneasy at the thought. "Anyway, that was all I had to say." Serendipity nodded and pushed back her chair.

The others began getting up and going about their lives. Sherman however sat a minute in the emptied room, staring at the wall. Zero hour was approaching fast. And he had no idea what he should be doing to prepare for it.

Then an even scarier thought hit Sherman that made his mouth go dry. He had no idea what to get everyone for Christmas!

The days went by too quickly. Presents began popping up under the Christmas tree like toadstools. Fairhaven Home's residents had voted to open them on Christmas Eve. Henry was busy making fudge and peanut brittle while Matilda made mince pies. Erik bought Scandinavian cookies at a Sons of Norway bake sale.

After a nice beef sirloin dinner, Wendell brought out his prized Christmas pudding. Even Cerwyn came out to watch the presentation. Sherman was surprised to see it wasn't a pudding in the American sense but a solid mound. It was dark and heavy like a fruitcake. Wendell poured brandy over it and lit it on fire, then stabbed a sprig of holly in it as soon as the flame went out. He sliced pieces off and passed them around.

Sherman took a bite. "Hey, this *is* kind of like fruitcake."

"Hardly." Wendell frowned. "While it does have the candied fruit and spices, this is a pudding. We use suet and bread crumbs instead of flour as the binder and then boil it for hours rather than baking it. Then you hang it up for at least a month to age."

"Suet? What's suet?"

"It is that hard fat that surrounds kidneys."

Sherman felt a little queasy.

Wendell lifted his chin proudly. "This is a *real* old-fashion Christmas pudding. I was having a devil of a time finding one. Then a shop in Fairhaven put me in touch with a local British expatriate who makes traditional puddings." Wendell took a bite and beamed. "Ah yes, being boiled in a sheep's stomach makes all the difference."

Sherman pushed his plate over to Wendell. "Uh, I'm pretty full. You can have mine."

Later they retired to the parlor to nibble their way into a sugar coma while admiring the tree and listening to Christmas music throughout history. Bing Crosby crooned, monks chanted and choirs sang Victorian carols. And of course there was the Western cowboy classic, *Rudolph the Red-Nosed Reindeer.*

Serendipity decided to break the ice. She picked up a package under the tree and shoved it at Nathan. "Here, Grandpa! Unwrap mine first."

"What's this, child? You didn't have to get me nothing. You'd already given me so much."

"It's Christmas! This is something special. Go on, Grandpa, open it."

Nathan carefully unwrapped the box. Inside sat something wrapped in tissue and then bubble wrap. Nathan pulled it out and tore away the covering to reveal an 8"x10" picture frame. He smiled at Serendipity, "You took one of them photo pictures of us! My, my!"

Wendell leaned over to see, and his jaw dropped. He stared at Serendipity. "Please tell me you did that on the computer with a photo manipulation program."

Serendipity just gave him a crafty smile.

The others appeared uneasy. "Uh, Mr. Brown," Henry said. "Could you show the rest of us the photo?"

Nathan proudly turned it around to reveal a photo of him shaking hands with Barack Obama.

Abubakari was the first to get over the shock. "When did you meet President Obama, wa? How in the world did you get an audience with the President of the United States?"

Serendipity grinned at him. "Simple. We used the Timemobile. Went back to 2006 when Obama was still senator. Grandpa has taken an interest in African-American history, so I thought this would make a real nice Christmas present."

"When didst you do this?" Matilda asked.

"A couple of days ago."

"Wait a tick," Wendell said. "Was this the day you spent with your grandfather? I thought you two just took the bus to do some Christmas shopping."

"No, we took the Timemobile. Grandpa was so excited to meet Obama."

Nathan smiled and nodded. "Very nice young man. Said he was mighty pleased to meet a veteran."

Wendell grimaced. "Please tell me you didn't tell Mr. Obama that Nathan was a veteran of the Revolutionary War."

"Of course not." Serendipity rolled her eyes. "Just said Grandpa was a veteran who fought for America's freedom. I let Obama assume I meant some later war."

"Mr. Obama chuckled when I told him he'd be the next president." Nathan studied the photo. "Then I said, 'No, I done seen it.' He looked powerfully thoughtful then."

"Tarnation!" Henry yelped. "Don't tell me you two were the ones that gave him the idea to run! Dr. Brown, do you know what you've done?"

"Oh really, Henry." Serendipity shook her head at him. "Like what American politician hasn't thought of running for President? Besides he was President before we went, so we changed nothing." She looked over at Nathan. "Go on, Grandpa, look at the other photos."

Nathan unwrapped the next one. "My, my, that certainly is a nice picture."

Wendell slapped his forehead and groaned.

"Who is it this time, wa?" Abubakari frowned. "General Colin Powell?"

"If only." Wendell shook his head. "Go ahead, Nathan, let them see."

Nathan turned it around to show himself dressed in a Victorian suit, talking to a white haired, bearded black man who looked very distinguished.

"Sorry, Grandpa, but I couldn't let Frederick Douglas see the camera, so I took the picture when he wasn't looking."

"It's a mighty fine picture, child."

"And what did you say to Frederick Douglas that changed history?" Wendell asked Nathan.

"I just said I admired his work in the fight to end slavery."

"Well, I suppose that was harmless enough." Wendell looked over at Serendipity. "What did you say?"

"I didn't say anything."

"Good!"

"Well, I did say that now that the African-American slaves were free, maybe he ought to do something about the other slaves."

"Other slaves?"

"Women," Serendipity said. "They weren't treated very nice back then, you know. He didn't say anything."

Wendell sighed relieved. "I'm glad you didn't affect history that time."

"Uh, Wendell." Henry looked uneasy. "If I recall my American history, didn't Frederick Douglas spend his last years working for the Women's Suffrage movement?"

Wendell turned and stared in horror at Serendipity. She ignored him. "There's one more photo, Grandpa."

Wendell peeked at the photo with one eye, then looked relieved. "What? You didn't take one of him with the Queen of Sheba?"

"This one is my favorite!" Nathan admired the framed photo. "This is me with the most famous colored person of all." He turned it so the others could see. It was a picture of Nathan standing with Serendipity, who had her arm around the old man's shoulders.

"I'm not that famous, Grandpa."

"You gonna be someday. This is the nicest present a man could have—a sweet granddaughter like you. I have got to be the luckiest man on earth."

"Oh, Grandpa." Serendipity hugged Nathan. "Just having you here is the best Christmas present I've ever had."

"Gee, Ser." Sherman looked hopeful. "Maybe next Christmas I could meet Hank Aaron and get my picture taken with him?"

"Sure, how about Babe Ruth, too?"

Wendell groaned. "Maybe you can get a photo of me having a stroke? Time travel is not a toy."

"Lighten up, Wendell." Serendipity scowled annoyed. "What good is having a time machine if I can't have some fun with it? Why do you think I invented time travel anyway?"

All the temporal anthropologists looked horrified.

"They taught us in school you invented it to help mankind." Erik sounded disappointed, like he had just found out there was no Santa Claus.

"Yeah, right." Serendipity waved that off. "I mean, if it helps mankind, great, but I just wanted to see the twentieth century. I think that's a more noble purpose than just to make a truckload of money. That's why most things are invented."

"I thought you invented time travel to show up your last husband," Sherman said.

"Well, that too." Serendipity bent down and picked up a smaller package and handed it to Sherman. "I couldn't think what to give you, then I came up with the perfect Christmas gift. I hope you like it."

Sherman opened the box. Inside was a snapshot of his mother, standing in the front door of her trailer. She looked exactly like she had in 1985. She held a bunch of balloons in one hand and a small piece of paper in the other. Sherman had never seen his mother look so happy.

"Where did you find a picture of my mom? Why is she grinning like she had just won the lottery?"

"Because she did." Serendipity gave Sherman a sly smile. "First Prize in the Lucky Dog Sweepstakes. Every year they pick some lucky person out of a phone book and give them a cashier's check for five million dollars."

"Lucky Dog Sweepstakes? Never heard of it."

"Of course not. Made it up on the fly."

Sherman gave Serendipity a worried look. "Are you telling me you went back in time and gave my mom five million dollars?"

"Yup. Now you don't have to worry about her."

"Where did you get the money? Did you take it out of the account?"

"Bills from 2010 would look like bad counterfeit in 1986. No, I just took the last of the Gold Eagle coins and invested them."

"You put it in stocks?"

"Too boring," Serendipity said. "I put it on the horses."

"You gambled the money?" Sherman crossed his arms.

"It's only gambling if you don't know the outcome of the race. Did you know Exterminator won with thirty to one odds in the 1913 Kentucky Derby? Worked my way up from there. She should be set for life."

Sherman smiled at Serendipity. "Thank you, Ser. That was a very thoughtful gift." He wondered though how quickly his mom went through that money.

Serendipity handed a package with a big red bow to Wendell, who looked a bit apprehensive. "Is it my imagination, or does this look like the size of a picture frame. Please tell me this isn't a picture of you and Queen Victoria."

"Of course not."

Wendell unwrapped it, daring to look. His worried expression turned to a smirk. "My word!"

"You like it?" Serendipity asked hopefully.

Wendell gave her a sultry look. "And why wouldn't I?"

"What is it?" Henry asked.

Wendell clutched the frame to himself to hide it. "That's a private matter."

"It's just a photo of me," Serendipity said.

"Then why can't we see it?"

Wendell blushed. "I told you it was private."

"Please, tell us it is not Dr. Brown naked." Tobias raised an eyebrow.

"No." Serendipity wrinkled her nose at him. "Wendell, would you please show it to them so they'll quit imagining the worst."

Wendell reluctantly turned the frame around. The photo showed Serendipity in a flowing white gown, her chin held high. Her hands were by her sides and in them she held lilies whose stems were so long the blooms laid against her shoulders. She wore a wreath of lilies on her head, and was surrounded by lilies. It was all in brown tones like an old 1800s photo.

"It's just me as one of those Alphonse Mucha prints Wendell likes, is all." Serendipity shrugged. "Found a photographer in town that could do sepia tone. He thought it was great to do something artsy."

Erik looked confused. "So why is Wendell blushing? Only your shoulders and arms are unveiled."

"I am not blushing." Wendell tried to look sober. Then he looked at

Serendipity with a silly smile. "*Lily* from the *Flower Series*, right?"

"Oh, blimey." Tobias rolled his eyes, disgusted. "Don't tell me this is some kind of feeble sexual fantasy? You actually find those frivolous art nouveau posters erotic? That is so pathetic."

"Well, I think it's sweet." Serendipity looked down her nose at Tobias. "I would hate to think what *you* would want me dressed in."

"A large paper bag," Tobias mumbled.

Wendell glared over at Tobias, but Serendipity stopped him before he said anything.

Matilda handed a package to Henry. "Wait until thou seeth *my* present. I hast my photo taken at the same time."

Henry looked puzzled. "You do a Mucha poster too, honey?"

"Nay." Matilda smirked at him.

Henry unwrapped it, and then laughed. He put his arm around Matilda's waist. "I love it! Every cowboy's fantasy." He turned it around so the rest could see. There was Matilda, also in brown sepia tone, dressed up as a cowgirl in a long denim skirt, and holding a lasso. The only thing provocative about it was the smile Matilda was giving the camera.

Tobias shook his head at Henry. "You are worse than Wendell."

"Gee, Matilda." Serendipity winked over at the other woman. "Maybe we shouldn't give Tobias that sexy photo of the two of us dressed in leather corsets with whips we had taken just for him."

Tobias's jaw dropped, then he shut his mouth when he realized she was joking. "Very funny. Remind me to show you my collection of French postcards. That will make you blush."

"I doubt that." Serendipity gave him a tigress grin. "I'm *not* Victorian, remember? I am so out of your league, rookie." She put her arm around Wendell. "Besides I already got me a *real* man."

Tobias raised his eyebrow.

Wendell shrugged. "I take vitamins."

"Better you than me," Tobias muttered. "She'll probably windup killing you."

"At least I'll die happy." Wendell kissed Serendipity on the cheek.

Serendipity winked at Wendell. "I'll give you your other present later." She let go of him and went back to the tree, gathering up five other boxes. She handed them around to the other temporal anthropologists. The presents looked all the same, about the size of a picture frame.

Henry opened his first a little apprehensive, then looked baffled by the contents. He pulled out a sheet of paper. "What's this?"

"Well, read it."

"'This certificate entitles Henry Darrel to a trip to the year of his choice. Signed: Serendipity Brown.' All right, what is this?"

"Just what it says. I gave you all one. I'll take you anywhere you want to go. I suppose any year the Institute of Time Travel is in operation and monitoring time travel is out. But any time before that should be safe."

"I just want to go home," Tobias grumbled.

"As soon as I can, as soon as we know it's safe," Serendipity assured him. "But I was going to do that anyway."

"Speaking of which." Wendell bent down and scooped up a package. "I have a present for you, Tobias."

Tobias took the heavy box, giving Wendell a suspicious look. He sat down and opened it and pulled out three old books. Tobias frowned confused. "*Modern Sheep Husbandry Methods? Better Chicken Breeding? Fruit Tree Pruning?* If this is a joke, I don't get it."

"It is not a joke." Wendell smiled down at him. "Those are three books I have spent years looking for. The paper on the bottom of the package is a list of books various universities have asked me to look for when I am out in the Field. I was shocked to stumble across one of the lost titles at the local bookstore here. So I went online and found two more."

"What am I suppose to do with these?"

"Deliver them to the appropriate universities when you get back to the twenty-seventh century. Tell them I gave you a copy of my list of books last time you saw me, before I died, and you had agreed to keep an eye out for the missing books. Tell them you found these three. It will put you in their good graces, help reestablish your reputation. Remember, with me gone, you are now the only temporal anthropologist specializing in Victorian England. You must carry the banner, old chap."

Tobias flippant expression disappeared. He looked back down at the books. "Thank you. I will make certain these books go to the proper individuals." He looked up. "I didn't get you anything for Christmas."

"Just make sure you deliver those books, that will be present enough."

Tobias nodded. As others distributed presents, Tobias sat and studied the books and the list.

"Uh, excuse me everyone," Sherman announced.

They all stopped talking and looked up.

"Uh, I wasn't sure what to get you all for Christmas, so I told Henry not to make dinner tomorrow. I'm taking you all out for Christmas dinner."

Everyone nodded pleased.

Sherman cleared his throat. "I also thought it might be nice if we go somewhere special. How about an old fashioned Victorian Christmas Wendell was talking about."

"Ooh!" Serendipity grinned. "I like that, kid." She turned to Wendell. "Know any good restaurants in 1800s London?"

Sherman blinked at her. "Actually I was thinking of a restaurant in Fairhaven, but that sounds even better."

Matilda gasped shocked. "What? Art ye suggesting we journey back in time for something as frivolous as a feast?"

"It's not frivolous," Serendipity said. "It's Christmas."

"Most establishments back then will be closed Christmas Day." Wendell shook his head.

"So we'll go a couple of days before. Can you name any good ones?"

"There's Wellington on Piccadilly Street." Wendell glanced over at

Tobias. "What do you say, Tobias?"

Tobias thought a moment. "Dick's on Fleet Street."

"Evan's at Convent Gardens?"

"Quisen's in Haymarket," Tobias countered.

"Wilton's, St. James?"

"The Holborn."

"Ah, yes!" Wendell grinned at Tobias. "The Holborn!"

Wendell turned to Sherman. "Reasonable prices, good food. And best of all it is a large restaurant, so there is plenty of people watching. The perfect place to take a bunch of temporal anthropologists." He pulled out his Bible. "I say, Tobias, best check your computer records, too. Make sure we do not accidentally run into ourselves. That can be very socially awkward. You can trust me on this one."

Abubakari borrowed a suit from Wendell. Serendipity, Sherman and Nathan already had nineteenth-century clothes. Matilda just wore her cowgirl outfit, which went so well with Henry's cowboy attire. Erik made do with a pair of jeans and a flannel shirt. Sherman thought they passed for Victorian—kind of. The maitre d' however had another opinion as they entered the marble hall inside the front door of The Holborn. He studied them carefully. The Holborn may not have been the snootiest restaurant in town, but riffraff was only allowed if they dressed up and behaved themselves.

"Table for nine," Sherman said.

The maitre d' raised his eyebrow at Erik's braids.

"You shouldn't stare at Erica like that," Sherman said to the waiter. "It embarrasses her."

"Erica?"

"Yes, Erica the bearded lady. She dresses in men's clothes when we go out so people won't stare as much."

The maitre d' looked at Erik again, who fluttered his eyelashes at him.

"We're all with the circus," Sherman said. "I thought it would be nice to take my friends out for an early Christmas dinner, since we will all be on the road tomorrow."

"There's a circus in town?"

"Yes, Monty Python's Flying Circus? Perhaps you have heard of us?"

"No."

"You'll have to come see us. We're on the edge of town. I'm a juggler. Wendell and Serendipity are the Flying Walnettos, the world famous trapeze act. Henry and Matilda are trick bareback riders. Abubakari is the lion tamer. And this is the Amazing Nathan Brown, the Human Cannonball."

"We've performed for all the crown heads of Europe," Wendell said.

"Oh my!" the waiter gave them a reappraising look. Then he noticed Tobias. "Uh, what does this gentleman do?"

"Oh, that's just Tobias." Serendipity made a face. "He cleans up after the elephants."

ᐰhapter ᐰhirty-ᐰine

"Play it again, Sherm," Lauren begged. "Play our song." The pocket computer was still on the nightstand, but Lauren's holographic image was sitting on the bed with a wistful expression.

Sherman stopped dressing and patiently reached over to his twenty-first-century laptop, poking a few buttons. The computer speakers began playing an old Bertie Higgins song comparing himself and his girlfriend to Bogey and Bacall.

Lauren closed her eyes and smiled. "That has got to be the swellest present anyone ever got."

Sherman watched her and smiled himself. Christmas shopping for a computer is kind of hard. So Sherman downloaded the song *Key Largo* for Lauren. He wasn't sure how many times she had him play it over the last few days. Sherman was growing tried of the song, but not tired of Lauren's reaction to it.

Lauren looked up at Sherman with those sultry blue-green eyes. "Say, I feel bad I didn't get you anything, Sherm."

"And how could you go shopping? Besides I liked the *present* you gave me."

"Yes, but how many times have I given you that?"

"Never gets old, Lauren, believe me."

"Men." Lauren shook her head. "You're so easy to shop for."

Serendipity sat in her workshop in the basement, building a dish receiver that would allow her to pick up relays from communication satellites without having to pay fees every month. It wasn't that they couldn't afford it, it was the principle. She felt the internet and telecasts should be free in this century too.

"May I interrupt you, Dr. Brown?" that melodic baritone voice with an African accent asked.

Serendipity looked up to see Abubakari at the door. There was something furtive, almost sneaky, about his manner. That in itself got her full attention. "Yes?" She turned from her workbench.

Abubakari looked down the hall and then stepped into the room, closing the door. "We need to talk in private," he lowered his voice.

"Okay."

He sat down on the other wooden stool. "Were you serious about our Christmas gift, wa? You will really take us anywhere we want to go?"

"Yes. Why all the secrecy? You want to go back and rob a bank?"

Abubakari gave a nervous chuckle. "Ayi. But I am about to break the rules. If the others knew they would try to stop me."

Serendipity raised her eyebrow in surprise. Abubakari always struck her as the most conservative of the temporal anthropologists. "Hey, I'm outside the rules of the stupid Institute."

"I know. Our houseguest is your ancestor. You asked if I wanted to return to the twenty-seventh century with no memory of this place, or stay here and let the Institute assume I am dead. Before I decide I wish to go to Timbuktu in 2012."

"You want to jump ahead two years in the future? Why?"

"As you know my main project was making digital copies of the books that had not survived into the twenty-seventh century. Remember I told you that thousands of manuscripts did survive into the early twenty-first century when they began copying them as digital images, wa?"

"Yes?"

"That is why I have spent so much time lately at the university library. I have been searching all the books, magazines and websites to see how this undertaking has progressed. It is going far too slow. That is why I need to jump ahead a couple of years. There is something I need to check."

"Hmmm, Wendell is always nagging me never to go into the future."

"2012 is more than five centuries before I was born, so technically it is the past."

Serendipity grinned at him. "Okay. So why do you want to go to 2012?"

"I am simply verifying a theory I have, nothing more. I will ask that you tell no one."

"Sure, I can keep a secret. We can step out the front door and then sneak back to the alley. We can even leave the house separately. Sort of cloak and dagger."

"Cloak and dagger, wa?"

"Secretive like spies." She winked.

"Owo!" He grinned at her.

Serendipity thought Timbuktu in 2012 looked like a ghost of the Timbuktu of 1350. True, it now had a few cars and electricity, but poverty overshadowed the technological advances. The people didn't look so bright and hopeful, but instead looked as worn as the western-style clothes some wore. The sandy streets were fairly clean, save for an occasional car that had been stripped. However they didn't look like they had been vandalized, but instead carefully cannibalized for parts. Amid the more modern buildings, sat older ones re-plastered again and again in an attempt to preserve the town's former glory.

Abubakari, now dressed in a modern dashiki and slacks, led Serendipity through the dusty avenues. He gazed about with sadness. "Timbuktu, once one of the richest cities in the world, is currently one of the poorest. This is a low ebb in her glorious history. I just have to keep reminding myself she will recover and remember how she will look in the twenty-seventh century."

They continued through the streets until they came to a tan and white two-story building on the edge of the encroaching desert. The design looked like a collaboration of architects from ancient Timbuktu and late twentieth-century academia.

Abubakari pointed to the building. "This is the Ahmed Baba Institute's new home built in 2009. The Institute is a leader in the preservation and digital recording of the ancient manuscripts of the Mali and Songhai periods."

They walked over the sand to the tall front portico. It was a long passageway that ran in front of the entrance to help keep out windblown sand. Inside the building was light and airy. The walls and pillars were painted white and the floors were cool bricks. Round chandeliers that looked like lanterns hung down from the high ceiling. Most of the lighting came from windows designed to let in indirect light so the sun would not harm the books. The shelves were also kept away from the walls with windows, that space taken up with benches where students read. The rooms were well ventilated with high open windows that could be closed quickly if a sandstorm threatened.

A man walked up to them wearing a long green tunic and a scholar's turban with the strip hanging low under his chin, then tucked in at the temple so the remainder could hang down to his shoulder. Abubakari bowed his head, and addressed him in French. The scholar nodded and led them down a hall lined with white square pillars and wooden doors. He pointed to one and said something to Abubakari and left. The temporal anthropologist knocked on the door."

"Entrez!" A mellow voice inside spoke. Abubakari opened the door.

At a table sat a man studying an ancient page he held gingerly with a white glove. He appeared to be about Abubakari's age. Serendipity blinked at him. Except for being clean shaven and wearing glasses he looked like he could be Abubakari's twin brother.

The man stood up. "Ah, Dr. Brown and Dr. Djata, I have been expecting you. I wrote the sixth of March on my calendar."

"You knew *we* were coming?" Serendipity cocked her head. "How could you?"

Dr. Djata laughed and turned to her. "Because *I* remember you coming this day. Dr. Brown meet Dr. Abubakari Keita."

"Wasn't that the name I put on your fake birth certificate?" She asked Dr. Djata, then stared back at Dr. Keita. "What's going on?"

Dr. Djata smiled at her. "I checked my records on my own computer to see the immediate future. Occasionally the name Dr. Abubakari Keita would pop up—the very name I had picked as my alias. I even found a photo of the man and he looked a lot like me. I wanted to make certain it truly was me, that I had elected to stay and help save the books. Apparently this Dr. Keita was very helpful in translating the ancient languages and in acquiring funds from America."

Dr. Keita grinned. "Mr. Conrad has been most generous to the Institute."

"Yeah, kid struck me as a book lover." She raised her eyebrow at Dr. Djata. "So you went with your alias and shaved your beard."

"The photo showed Dr. Keita as clean shaven and wearing glasses. The

Institute of Time Travel told us we must never meet ourselves or great disasters would happen. Dr. Howe taught me otherwise."

Serendipity got a sly smile. "So how about I leave Dr. Djata with Dr. Keita and you two can do twice the work."

Both Abubakari's appeared very uncomfortable with that idea. "Let's not press our luck too much," Dr. Keita said.

"Speaking of luck." Dr. Djata moved closer to Dr. Keita. "Have you warned them, wa?"

"Warned them?" Serendipity's eyes darted back and forth between the two men.

Dr. Djata cleared his throat, looking a little guilty. "Ah, yes. Beginning next month a group of militants called *the Ansar Dine* will take over Timbuktu, killing, raping and destroying many monuments including the tombs of Muslim saints. They will also set this library on fire."

"What!" Serendipity yelped. "Why? Do they hate Muslims that much?"

"They are Muslim. They are just a very radical group of Muslims backed by Jihadists terrorists. They hate the books because they were written by Mali scholars who practiced a more moderate form of Islam that believed in learning and science and human rights. The Reform African Muslim Denomination traces its roots back to ancient Mali. They haven't been formed yet though. Luckily the invaders will be stopped in January 2013, but not before they do much damage. The world was horrified that the books of Timbuktu were destroyed. Later they found out the vast majority had been saved. It was almost as if they had advance warning." Dr. Djata grinned at her.

"You changed history?"

"Or perhaps I just made it happen. Dr. Howe created his own family tree after all." Dr. Djata turned to Dr. Keita. "How is that going, wa?"

"Changing history is not as easy as it sounds." His future self shook his head. "If you try to warn people of future events they don't believe you. They think you are mad. So I have been talking to all the conservators as well as families with private libraries. I told them I had a dream the books were burnt in great bonfires by invaders. That did not convince them of course. But I did persuade them that thinking about a possible escape plan for the manuscripts would be wise."

"That's brilliant!" Serendipity patted Keita's hand. "Like the old fire drills that prevented deaths when fires actually happened. Everyone knew what to do when there was no time to think."

"I suggested the capital Bamako might be a good place to evacuate the books."

"Wouldn't America or Europe be a safer place?"

Both Abubakari's frowned at her. "Ayi." Dr. Djata shook his head. "Would you send your child to a rich uncle just because he could take better care of him, wa? Maybe if there were no other choice, but you would want to keep your child and take care of him yourself."

"These books are your babies." Serendipity studied Djata's expression.

"No, these books are our soul." Dr. Keita gently picked up the faded brittle manuscript as though it were a wounded butterfly. "This is Mali's history, her legacy, her greatest treasure. We have a saying in my country, that 'the ink of a scholar is more precious than the blood of a martyr.' I feel a coward when I think of all my fellow countrymen who will soon risk their lives to save these books. I feel I should stay and help them."

"No, Abubakari!" Serendipity said firmly. "You will be more help to the books if you go to Bamako and protect them there."

Dr. Keita nodded. "Owo, perhaps you are right. Anyone with Ameriki ties will be a major target for the invaders."

"Then please go for sure!"

Dr. Djata touched her arm. "We should probably leave now. I do not wish to push my luck too much."

Serendipity came around the table to give Dr. Keita a hug. "Best of luck to you, Abubakari." She turned to go, then turned back. "How about a heads up?"

"Heads up, wa?"

"How do things turn out on New Year's Day? You were there after all."

"I best not." Dr. Keita shook his head. "Let things take their natural course."

"Hmm, you sound like Wendell."

"Well, I do remember telling you one thing: be open minded when it comes to love and to play it again. Remember the words of a great Ameriki philosopher, 'A person's a person, no matter how small.'"

"Wasn't that Dr. Seuss?"

"I believe it was. That is all I may tell you. I must get back to work. I am trying to digitalize as many of these manuscripts as I can before the invaders come. And being face to face with myself does make me a bit nervous, no offense."

"None taken. I find it unnerving, too." Dr. Djata frowned. "Is it proper to say 'too' if we are the same person, wa?"

Dr. Keita shrugged. "English is a confusing enough language without time paradoxes." He bowed to Serendipity. "It was nice to see you again, Dr. Brown. May Allah give you long life."

"Ditto!"

As Dr. Djata and Serendipity walked down the hall back to the Time-mobile, she turned to glare at her companion. "Dang temporal anthropologists, you have to make everything so complicated! Exactly what did you mean with those stupid hints?"

Abubakari put up his hands. "I have no idea. But I would listen to Dr. Keita. I understand he is a genius."

Henry sat at a round table, holding a cup of coffee and gazing out the window. The coffee shop at Boulevard Park on the shore offered a nice view of the bay. It also offered a little privacy, the shop being sparsely populated between the morning and lunch rush, especially up here on the second story balcony. Here and there among the tables on both floors sat a lone customer with a laptop or book, also taking advantage of the quiet lull. The only real life was a group of six gossiping women in red hats down below. Henry gazed out at the cold water, the coffee and his woman sitting beside him warming him.

"Tis a lovely view is it not," Matilda said softly.

He turned to her and smiled. "Not half as lovely as this view."

"Thee was always a sweet talker." She gave him that secretive smile of hers.

"I know I ain't very poetic, but you inspire me, darling." Henry scooted his chair closer and put his arm around her. "Wish we had more than just four more days."

"I shall miss thee. I would always cherish these past three months...if I could but remember them."

"Yup, Dr. Brown's gonna have to wipe these memories, like yesterday's special off a diner chalkboard. Well, we'll just have to make new memories."

Matilda didn't smile but frowned ruefully. "Too often we art snatching a moment here and there, like beggars after a banquet."

"I have to admit getting stuck with you these past weeks hasn't been the least unpleasant. Would be nice if we could do this permanent. Ever think of retiring?"

"And be trapped in the twenty-seventh century?"

"Yeah, I hear you there. Of course there is the possibility things might not work out for Serendipity and we will be stuck here."

Matilda studied her tea in the paper cup. "If she is slain wol we not just wind up back in the twenty-seventh century as history professors and none of this would have happened?"

Henry snorted. "Speak for yourself. I'd probably be an archaeologist. Tell the truth, I don't know what would happen."

"I can ponder on worse fates than being stuck here with thee."

The two gazed in silence out at the bay again. After a couple of minutes Henry spoke up. "It is a nice view. What would you think of waking up to this every morning?"

Matilda frowned at him, cocking her head. "Dost thou mean not go back to the twenty-seventh century? Live here with thee? Hmm, that be not the worst idea, but I wol have to think upon it."

"While you're thinking about that maybe you could think about us getting hitched?"

"Married?" her voice rose. "Be that a proposal?"

"Yup."

She smiled. "Yea, I shall surely have to think upon that, too." She gazed back out at the boats on the water and took a sip of tea. They both sat in silence, but it was a warm silence. She finally drank the last of the tea and sat her cup down. "Yea."

"Yea?"

"Verily." She grinned at him.

Henry gave a whoop, grabbed her and gave her a smooch, then noticed the other customers in the place staring at them. "It's okay, folks," he yelled to the others. "She just agreed to tie the knot."

The introverts all nodded, while the ladies in red hats hollered their congratulations, a couple of them pumping the air. They all went back to sipping their own beverages.

Matilda put her hand on his. "For the last forty-two years, I have recorded others living their lives. Perchance it is time I lived my own."

"Yeah, me too." Henry scratched his head. "I'm kinda new at this. Do we go shopping for a wedding ring? Book a chapel? What do we do?"

"Right now we dost nothing. Be of good cheer and fret thee not. No worries, mate."

"Yeah, it feels like we're already married. Felt like that for a long time."

Matilda's smile faded. "Hast our relationship gotten drab?"

Henry managed to scoot even closer and put his arm around her shoulders. "No darling, I just can't imagine life without ya."

Chapter Forty

It wasn't much of a New Year's Eve party, just the nine of them, some beers, pop and a couple of bowls of junk food. Still it had a cozy feeling to it. Sherman wondered what Cerwyn and Priscilla were up to. He had taken them in a couple of colas and a bag of chips. Would they kiss each other at midnight? Or would they kiss the parrots?

Erik looked around and smiled. "Jim invited me to a New Year's Eve party, but I told him I wanted to spend it with family."

Yeah, they had become a family of sorts. Sherman glanced over at Tobias sitting in the corner. They even had a black sheep.

Henry and Matilda sat on the loveseat together. He whispered something to her. She smiled and nodded. Henry stood up and stepped out into the middle of the room. Matilda followed him and stood beside him.

"Everyone, we have an announcement to make." Henry put his arm around Matilda. "If it's all right with Dr. Brown, Matilda and I would like to stay here. Oh, and Fancy Pants." Henry smiled at Wendell. "Do you want to be best man or would you prefer to give Matilda away?"

"What?" Wendell looked at them confused. "Are you speaking of holy matrimony?"

"Naw, we're just gonna get married."

"Congratulations, you two." Wendell grabbed Henry's hand to shake it. "I say, getting married seems like an excellent idea. Don't you think it is an excellent idea, Serendipity, dear?"

"Yes, Wendell, dearest." Serendipity batted her eyelashes at him. "I think Henry and Matilda getting married is an excellent idea."

Wendell sighed and looked disappointed. "Maybe someday?"

Serendipity closed one eye and looked up at the ceiling. "Crazier things have happened. Who knows what the future will bring? Of course, we could pop ahead five years and find out."

"No, I prefer surprises."

Nathan sidled up to them. "Be real nice if you two jumped the broom. I could give Serendipity away. That would mean a whole lot to me. I could die a happy man." He gave a melodramatic sigh and winked at Wendell.

"Are you two ganging up on me?" Serendipity asked.

Erik came over to Matilda and Henry. "This is great! I was in great fear that I was going to be left all alone." He scooped them both up in a bear hug.

"Thanks Erik." Henry tried to catch his breath. "We'll make you bouncer at the wedding. You can take care of Wendell when he gets drunk and unruly and starts singing Gilbert and Sullivan."

Erik let go of the engaged couple and studied Wendell. "I wouldn't mind seeing that. What do you say we get him drunk tonight?"

"Forget it." Wendell shook his head. "This is one New Year's Eve I definitely want to stay sober for. I have friends to celebrate it with and someone to kiss." Wendell smiled down at Serendipity.

Henry grinned at him. "Hey buddy, we had New Year's Eve together on the S.S. Great Britain, remember? You ain't a bad kisser."

Matilda laughed and shook her head at Henry.

Wendell looked at Serendipity. "We didn't really. Henry is making a joke."

"I figured that out. Although I'm beginning to think Henry just might have given you a big sloppy smooch if he thought it would shock the other passengers."

As they got closer to midnight, Sherman sipped a can of root beer and watched the proceedings. The wide screen television showed Times Square as they prepared to drop the ball. Abubakari and Erik were laughing over some joke. Nathan was trying to make conversation with Tobias. Henry sat on the loveseat, Matilda snuggled up to him, the two unmindful of the world.

Wendell came up behind Serendipity and put his arms around her waist. He gazed down at her with his usual bland expression, but the emotions reflected in his grey eyes were anything but bland. He seemed oblivious to everyone else in the room. Closing his eyes, he snuggled into her hair. Serendipity smiled and leaned back against him, her own eyes getting a dreamy look.

Sherman put his hand on his pocket computer in the holder around his neck. Great, he finally has a New Year's Eve with a girlfriend and he couldn't touch her. Well, not physically anyway.

"Hey, look!" Erik pointed to the screen. "Two more minutes."

Sherman slowly backed out of the room and down the wide hall, away from the others. He pulled his computer up to his face. "Happy New Year, Lauren."

"Go to the kitchen," she whispered back. "I have a surprise for you."

Sherman hurried to the kitchen, and closed the door. Lauren's holographic image popped up and smiled in a playful manner. "Close your eyes, Sherm, and keep them shut."

Sherman obeyed. After a minute he felt something warm and moist brush his lips. "It's customary to kiss at midnight, isn't it?" Lauren whispered in his ear.

"Yeah?"

The next kiss was much longer. Sherman left his eyes closed. He knew Lauren had borrowed Rosetta's empty shell again, but he did not want to ruin the illusion. It was a silly romantic gesture, getting a New Year's Eve kiss. Still it was so—

"Hey kid, you're missing Bruce Springsteen and— What the blue blazing bandicoots?"

Sherman's eyes popped open, to see Serendipity staring at him with a look of revulsion.

Wendell came into the room. "What's wrong, Serendipity?" He looked over at Sherman. "Oh dear heaven!" Wendell turned his back to him. "I did not see this!"

"What the hell is going on?" Serendipity had her arms crossed.

Sherman backed away from Rosetta. "Nothing."

"Didn't look like nothing to me. What else have you been doing with my robot?"

"Nothing." Sherman tried to look innocent.

"Well, what did you expect?" Wendell frowned accusingly at Serendipity. "He's a frustrated teenage boy and you dangle a carrot under his nose, I daresay. I told you bringing one of those things into the house was a bad idea."

"I didn't think this would be an issue." Serendipity defended herself. "It's just a translator and house servant. I erased all the recreational programming."

"And it is still fully functional, isn't it." Wendell glimpsed over his shoulder. "Let's hope Sherman didn't go beyond snogging."

"Not this time, anyway." Serendipity studied Sherman.

Wendell shuddered. "Now, I suppose we should look at this impartially. Technically he hasn't broken any laws or harmed anyone."

"I know." Serendipity wrinkled her nose. "It's just so tacky! It's a soulless machine."

"It's not just a soulless machine." Sherman protested. "It's really—"

Lauren placed a finger to the robot's lips, her fear showing in Rosetta's eyes.

"It's really what?" Serendipity asked.

"Uh, it's really Joan Jett."

"Joan Jett?" Wendell raised an eyebrow. "Who is Joan Jett?"

Serendipity turned to him. "A female rock star from the 1980s. Obviously some teenage fantasy." She looked at the robot. "Rosetta!"

Sherman saw the life flicker out of those brown eyes, replaced with a vacant stare. Lauren had left. "Yes, Dr. Brown," the robot said in that mechanical voice.

"You will go upstairs into my closet and turn yourself off. You will take no further orders from Sherman. Is that understood?"

"Yes, Dr. Brown." The robot turned and walked out of the room.

Serendipity wrinkled her nose. "We will pretend this never happened, kid. We have *got* to get you a girlfriend." She turned and left, taking Wendell by the arm.

Sherman stood alone in the kitchen. Lauren's image blinked on in front of him. "Thanks for not turning stool pigeon on me, Sherm."

"I almost blew it." Sherman put his hand over the front of the computer, blocking the laser beam. Lauren blinked out. "You shouldn't show yourself like that Lauren. Not here. If someone comes in they'll see you. Bummer, I nearly lost you."

"Nuts! We lost our only means of physical contact. I'm sorry, Sherm. That was stupid of me to do that in the kitchen. Now I got you in a load of trouble."

"You meant well," Sherman spoke to the now disembodied voice. "As for Serendipity, she knows what it's like to be sexually frustrated. She won't hold this against me."

"Dr. Brown is right, Sherm. We gotta get you a girlfriend."

"I already have one."

"No, Sherm, a *real* one."

"You've got me spoiled. Where am I going to find someone who cares as much about me as you do?"

"But I can't give you anything, Sherm."

"You give me your heart and soul."

"You know what I mean."

"You'll figure out something. I believe you owe me a dream about *Key Largo*."

"That was a 'G' rated movie, Sherm."

"So we'll do a modern adaptation. Lose the gangsters and the hurricane. Just you and me."

"Here's looking at you, kid," Lauren purred.

The next morning Sherman waited in the Timemobile, reading an Andre Norton novel. All of the luggage they had taken with them from the twenty-fourth century, had been packed into the machine the day before. They wanted to make it look like nothing had been left behind, lest Agent Five start asking questions. They were supposed to leave at noon. Sherman looked at his watch. 8:57. Yup, Serendipity should be showing up any minute.

The door of the Timemobile made a clicking noise. The door slowly swung open. Sherman put down his book and stood up from the seat.

Serendipity stepped in and then stopped, shocked. "Uh, kid, what are you doing here?"

"I could ask the same of you, Ser."

"Sheesh, you look like a parent catching his kid sneaking in past midnight."

"I'm really forty-four, remember."

Serendipity chuckled at that. "Right, kid. Would you mind going up to the house and getting me a cup of coffee?"

"No." Sherman crossed his arms.

"No? You never have told me 'no' before. Come on, kid, I'm your boss and that's a direct order!"

"And you have never given me a *direct order* before." Sherman's voice remained calm.

"Well, you never refused to get me a stupid cup of coffee," Serendipity said annoyed. "What the heck are you doing here anyway?"

"I didn't want you leaving without me."

Serendipity gave a nervous laugh. "What makes you think I would leave without you? It's only nine o'clock. We leave at noon."

"Uh huh. Maybe Wendell fell for that, but I know you. You don't give a squat about personal timelines or Base Time or that other stuff. Who was it that spent three days in the future one evening to go shopping?"

"I wasn't sneaking off, really."

"Then why are you here?"

"Uh, wanted to check the coordinates, that's all."

"Right." Sherman sat back down.

Serendipity groaned, irritated. "This is about last night, isn't it? I'm sorry I overreacted. It's just I figure any guy who would use a robot for sex is some selfish jerk trying to avoid a real relationship."

"This has nothing to do with last night, Ser. I am simply doing the job I'm paid to do."

"I thought your job was gofer, like getting me coffee, which you aren't doing."

"Thought you fired me as gofer and made me House Manager? Besides the Enforcers said my real job is keeping you out of trouble. You aren't going anywhere without me."

"Dang it, kid!" Serendipity lost her cool. "What good is it if both of us get killed?"

"There's a good chance Agent Five will meet you. He'll wonder why Wendell and I aren't with you. and start asking questions. Do you want them to find Erik and the rest of your runaway time travelers?"

"No. But what if the Enforcers got killed?"

"You installed the monitor, right?"

"Yeah, but what if the bad guys are hiding?"

"We got weapons and three guns is better than one."

Serendipity shook her head. "Come on, Sherman, I don't want to spend my last moments watching you and Wendell being slaughtered."

"And you think I want to spend the rest of my life listening to Wendell moaning about not being there for you? That'd kill him, Ser."

Serendipity sighed defeated. "Yeah, probably would, the stupid idiot. So what do I do?"

"Assume everything will go right."

"What if everything doesn't go right?"

"Then, shouldn't you be spending your last hours with Wendell?"

Serendipity got a funny smile. "Got a point there, kid. Whether I'm meeting Time Keepers or Enforcers, probably would be better if I was relaxed, huh?"

"Yup."

Serendipity started to head back out, then she turned. "Aren't you coming?"

"Nope." Sherman stayed seated. He reached over and picked up his book.

"Hmmph, I'm beginning to think you really *are* forty-four." Serendipity grumbled as she left the Timemobile. She didn't slam the door, but she did close it firmly.

Lauren's hologram popped up and leaned against the door. "Say, that dame can be a handful sometimes, eh, Sherm?"

"Yup." Sherman smiled up at Lauren. "Good thing I'm smarter than a super genius, huh?"

11:52 the door started to open again. Sherman looked up to the sound of voices outside and put his book down. Serendipity stuck her head in. "Hey, kid, you going to come outside and say goodbye to everyone?" Her head disappeared.

Sherman stood up and walked over to the door, opening it up all the way. There stood everyone except Cerwyn and Priscilla, of course. Sherman looked up the slope at the house and was surprised to see the two temporal zoologists standing in one of the music room windows. They waved at Sherman. The others were all shaking hands and hugging Serendipity and Wendell.

Erik looked up at the time machine. "Are you already in there, Sherman? You must be eager to get back."

"I left my Dungeons and Dragons' dice back in the twenty-fourth century." Sherman proceeded to the bottom of the time machine's steps, but no farther. He still didn't trust Serendipity.

Erik shook Sherman's hand. "Hope to see you again soon."

"Me, too!" Sherman said heartfelt. He would like to see Erik again, but more importantly seeing him again meant they survived the trip home.

Everyone had to come over and shake Sherman's hand, except Matilda who gave him a kiss on the cheek. Even Tobias shook his hand and wished him good luck.

At last Serendipity gave Nathan one last hug, then shooed Sherman back into the Timemobile and climbed in after him. She waved goodbye around Wendell as he got in. Wendell closed the door as Serendipity went over to the control panel. He sat down and looked over his shoulder at Sherman who was already strapped in. "My word, how long have you been waiting out here, old boy?" Wendell did his seatbelt. "Did you really think we would leave without you?"

"No, I didn't think *you* would, but I thought Serendipity might."

"Heavens, no, Serendipity would never dump you. She has told me on numerous occasions how much she depends on you. She couldn't leave without you."

"No, she couldn't because I was already here when she snuck in here this morning."

"Snuck in here? Why would she sneak into her own time machine?"

"So she could take off without both of us. She didn't want to endanger us."

Wendell's mouth flew open. He looked over at Serendipity who was plopping into her chair. "Is that true?" Wendell demanded.

"Neh," Serendipity grabbed her safety strap and pulled it over her shoulder.

"It is true! Sherman wouldn't lie. Serendipity, you can't just go..." the rest was drowned out by the noise of the shaking Timemobile, but Wendell's mouth was still going, as he shook his finger at Serendipity. The machine finally stopped allowing Wendell to be heard again. "...about the barmiest trick you have pulled so far! I have half a mind to—"

"All right, all right," Serendipity interrupted him. "Ha, and they say women nag!" She undid her belt and stood up.

"I'm not nagging! I'm just upset that you wouldn't want me to be with you in your hour of need."

Serendipity sat down on Wendell's lap and gave him a big kiss. She pulled back, looking angry. "I didn't want you with me because I didn't want to watch you being killed, you stupid idiot, because I love you."

"And if you died I would have nothing to live for, you twit," Wendell snapped back, and threw his arms around her, pulling her closer. Their lips affixed and threatened to melt together.

Sherman sighed and got out of his seat. "We could be surrounded by Time Keepers about to blow up the Timemobile and you two are sucking face?"

Wendell's eyes snapped open and he pushed Serendipity back. "Sherman is right, dear! We better get our weapons and then check the monitor!"

Sherman was already up and untied the weapons on the empty back seat. He handed Wendell the shotgun he had chosen, and Serendipity the laser-cannon-bazooka-thingy she had built for the occasion. Sherman then grabbed up his Uzi. "Lock and load!"

Serendipity stepped over to the door and flipped a switch. The seventeen-inch square monitor on the wall came on showing the workshop outside. There stood Agent Five, Agent Twenty-Two and Agent Eighteen, all looking as humorless as ever.

"It's just Enforcers." She flipped the switch off. "Now, where were we?" Serendipity tried to push Wendell back in his seat.

"Erm, we better leave that for later, Serendipity dear. Besides, how do we know it is not a hologram?"

"Hey!" Serendipity yelled through the door. "Are you a hologram? If you are Agent Five, prove it. Who do you remind me of?"

"I believe you said ex-husband number four." Agent Five growled. "Now will you come out?"

Serendipity turned to Wendell. "I think a hologram would have more personality." She set her weapon against the wall and pushed open the door. Faking enthusiasm unenthusiastically, she chirped, "Fivey-baby! Did you miss me?"

Agent Five did not smile. "I see you survived on five hundred dollars."

"Yeah, what a nightmare." Serendipity came down the steps. "Had to go back where we could use those stupid coins, and stay warm since it was winter. Rented a furnished shack on a Florida beach. No broadcasts, no electricity, no toilets. Cooked on a wood stove. Thought I would go crazy with boredom. Only excitement was that hurricane that nearly killed us. It was hell!" She stopped right in front of Agent Five and flashed a phony smile.

"So, did you enjoy your stay in my luxury mansion? Drink up all my liquor?"

"We didn't touch your liquor, Dr. Brown."

"Do we have to go back to our lovely vacation cottage, or did you get the bad guys."

"We got them. It is safe for you to return."

"So, what happened?"

"It is safe now. That is all you need to know."

Serendipity's eyes narrowed, but Wendell pulled her away. "Serendipity, no."

Sherman stepped forward. "Excuse me, sir."

Agent Five looked over. "Yes, Mr. Conrad."

"Can't you tell us what happened for our own peace of mind? We will make no record of what you reveal to us so it won't change time. What would your telling us hurt?"

Agent Five looked unmoved.

Sherman came closer and whispered, "Besides, you said my job was to keep Serendipity out of trouble?"

"Yes."

"I know this woman. If you don't tell her what happened, she'll go back herself and find out."

Agent Five's eyebrows rose over his dark glasses. He looked over at the irate woman and sighed. "You are probably right, Mr. Conrad. Very well. We rented the house next door and were staying there with our time machine. We had your house infiltrated inside and out with micro-mini cams to keep a watch for the Time Keepers. They attacked your mansion on November tenth, landing their time machine in your yard. I'm afraid they destroyed your butler robot."

"Not Robbie!" Serendipity looked distressed. "I was so proud of him. I made him myself."

"Perhaps you can put the pieces back together. The Time Keepers then barged into your home and killed the decoys."

"Decoys?" Serendipity asked. "Robots?"

"Clones," Agent Five said. "Don't worry, we cleaned up the mess."

Was it Sherman's imagination, or did he see a slight flinch on Agent Twenty-Two's face?

Wendell stared at Agent Five in horror. "You did what?"

"We made clones of you and left them as targets."

"Clones? That's illegal!"

"We had to make the terrorists think they had killed you. Bots would never have fooled them."

"But you treated them like bots! They were people."

"They were clones. We clone organs all the time."

"That's not the same. There is a reason cloning whole persons is illegal. They are human beings with minds and feelings and souls."

"I think you are being overly sentimental, Dr. Howe."

"I have a right to be. You killed my brother! The brother I never had."

"Howe-2 was a clone."

"A clone is no different than an identical twin! You killed Serendipity's and Sherman's twins too. It is plain murder!"

"The terrorists killed them, not us."

"You set them up, knowing they would be murdered. They were cannon fodder."

"This is war, Dr. Howe. Besides they went willingly."

"Willingly?"

"They accepted their mission to lay down their lives to save Dr. Brown."

"You brainwashed them!"

"We had to program them to act like you to be convincing. Besides they would have died of old age within weeks anyway, since we had to accelerate their growth or they would still be fetuses. They had short but important lives."

Wendell didn't look any less disgusted. "It does not excuse what you did."

"We do what must be done to protect time."

"Isn't that what the terrorists said?" Sherman butted in.

Agent Five looked like he was glowering at him behind those dark glasses. Sherman didn't step back.

Serendipity interrupted the moral debate. "So then what happened after the bad guys killed the clones?"

"The Time Keepers returned to the twenty-seventh century and were surrounded by Enforcers as well as civil law enforcement."

"Wait a minute." Sherman frowned. "I thought you blocked all time travel in and out of the twenty-seventh century?"

"As soon as they murdered the clones we sent a time capsule to the Institute of Time Travel Enforcement Agency Headquarters with a message inside to drop the barrier."

"Time Capsule?"

"About so big." Agent Five put his hands six inches apart. "Small enough to slip through. The Agency tracked the stolen time machine and was there before the Time Keepers could get away. They committed suicide before we could arrest them, but not before they bragged they had murdered the inventor of time travel. We have that on tape, and broadcasted it to the world to discourage any more movements like this. We have everyone convinced that the terrorists, despite their best efforts, were unable to change time. Not only is there still time travel in the twenty-seventh century, but the historical records make no mention of the attack or that you were murdered." Agent Five actually smirked. "For some unknown reason, Serendipity Brown seems to be immune to all time manipulations."

"What about the rest of the Time Keepers?" Wendell asked.

"We should have them all rounded up. You should be perfectly safe now, Dr. Brown."

"What about the temporal anthropologists that were in the Field?" Serendipity looked concerned.

"Yes." Wendell's usually bland face looked imploring. "Are they all right?"

"I had said we were not sure what would happen to the time machines. It appears they came forward and then bounced back to where they had started. Unfortunately while we found the intact time machines, most of the T.A.'s have disappeared. We can only assume the Time Keepers assassinated them and transported the bodies to another time period."

Sherman was impressed with Wendell's acting skills. The man looked like Agent Five had just told him his entire family had been killed in a disaster. "Dear God! Who were they?"

Agent Five's face was stoic. "Two temporal zoologists survived, although their guide had disappeared after he went after a giant alligator and tried to subdue it with a Taming Devise that was lost. They thought the alligator got him, but the Institute is not certain it wasn't assassins. We found Dr. Leach in Saint-Nazaire on the coast of France. He said he was attacked by men calling themselves Time Keepers, but had managed to escape and had been in hiding."

"You said before there were seven people." Wendell tried to look like he was trying to look brave. "Who were the other four you didn't save?"

Agent Five looked over at Agent Twenty-Two. Agent Twenty-Two, their trained psychiatrist, nodded. Agent Five turned back to Wendell. "Very well. It was Dr. Darrell, Dr. Djata, Dr. Olafson and Dr. Warwick."

"Matilda?" Wendell whispered. "Not Matilda. And Henry, too?"

"I'm very sorry, Dr. Howe."

Wendell plodded over to the nearest chair and collapsed into it, his head hanging. He pulled out a handkerchief and buried his face. Serendipity went over and put her arms around him. "It's all right, honey. Your friends are in a far, far better place."

Sherman managed to keep his face as blank as Wendell normally did.

Agent Five turned to him. "We will be going now, Mr. Conrad."

"Thanks for saving us."

Agent Five nodded curtly. "Just doing our duty to protect time." He looked over at Wendell, whose shoulders were shaking, the handkerchief muffling his sobs. "You will look after Dr. Howe?" Agent Five almost sounded concerned.

"I figure he's part of the package of my taking care of Serendipity."

"Quite an undertaking for someone who's only nineteen."

"Hey, I was born in 1966. That makes me hundreds of years old now, right?"

A faint smile came to Agent Five's lips. "Good luck, Mr. Conrad." The Enforcer glanced over at Serendipity. "Heaven knows, I don't envy you your task."

Agent Five then turned and walked to their sleek-looking time machine, Agent Twenty-Two and Agent Eighteen falling in behind him. They got in, closing the door. The shiny black box stood silent a minute, then hummed and vibrated. It began to disappear from the top down, as a mini black hole expanded and dropped over them like a falling curtain.

Wendell's shoulders still shook.

"It's all right, hon." Serendipity patted his arm. "You can cut the act."

It was no act. Wendell dropped the handkerchief, and doubled over. Apparently he hadn't been muffling sobs, but laughter. No wonder he had covered his face. Serendipity started laughing too, collapsing on the normally stoic Englishman.

Sherman shook his head, and just watched the two chortling like hyenas.

Wendell finally composed himself. "I do apologize. I don't know why that hit me so funny." He took a deep breath. "Maybe I'm just so relieved that Agent Five was wrong." Wendell looked up at Serendipity, then pulled her into his lap and hugged her. "Thank you, Serendipity. Thank you for making Agent Five wrong. You have no idea—"

"Yes, I do. I've come to love them too." Serendipity kissed Wendell on the cheek, then stood up. "Come on, now we know what to do with Tobias and the menagerie."

Chapter Forty-One

The Timemobile vibrated, stuffed with squawking parrots, passengers, luggage and camping equipment as it made its way back to Okeechobee Lake in 1870 exactly a month and a half from when they left. They had been very careful to pack everything they brought from the campsite, and nothing from the twenty-first century.

Being the closest to the door when they landed, Henry opened it and looked out. "I'll be dang."

Serendipity was at his shoulder. "What is it?"

"I was afraid all these weeks the tents would be gone, but they're still here." Henry stepped out of the Timemobile. The rest followed him into the campsite. The tents and cots still sat as they had left them. The twenty-seventh-century time machine disguised as a shack stood behind them. Henry looked around and then grinned. "Well, I'll be dang."

"What is the matter, old boy?" Wendell came over to Henry. "Are you going to spend all day danging yourself?"

"Someone *has* been here. I don't know how long, but they made an effort to put everything back the way it was. Except for one thing." Henry pointed to a pile of branches. "They gathered up a bunch of firewood as a way of a thank you. I'll bet my bottom dollar it was Seminoles passing through. They're about the only ones out here this period of time, hiding out from the U.S. Army that's trying to drag the supposedly wild Indians off to Oklahoma. You would think the whites would want neighbors like this."

Henry turned to the group. "Okay, let's unpack the Timemobile. We need to try to make the place look as close as we can to how it looked when we hightailed it outta here. We don't want to leave Dr. Owen and Dr. Cohen wondering why things changed."

They moved everything out of the time machine. Henry, Cerwyn and Priscilla then began putting things away where they remembered them being. Sherman, Wendell and Serendipity could do little more than watch.

Serendipity turned to Wendell. "Do you know what you're going to tell Cerwyn and Priscilla to do when you slap the Compliance Disk on them?"

Wendell pulled out his Bible. "I dictated it so I can play it back. Since we have to brainwash them one at a time, they will hear the same message. When we leave, all they will remember is Henry running after an alligator to slap a Taming Device on it and disappearing. They tried to go home, but their time machine bounced back. Since then they've traded all of Henry's possessions with the local Seminoles for food. They will have no memory of us or Bellingham."

Serendipity shook her head. "I don't think they have much memory of us or Bellingham anyway."

The temporal zoologists taken care of, they returned to Bellingham to drop off Henry and picked up their last returning refugee. The Timemobile parked them on the Boulevard de Clichy across the street from the tree-lined median. It was early morning in Pigalle, so the traffic was light. The few pedestrians who walked by seemed either too tired or too hung-over to notice the sudden appearance of the 1897 Delahaye Limousine. Tobias was the first to cross the street to the park-like division where his time machine stood. When the others caught up to him, they found Tobias staring up at the statue of Joan of Arc on the tall granite pedestal. Sherman wondered what Tobias was thinking, when the Englishman snorted. "Hmph, who but the French wouldn't think it strange there is a statue of a virgin saint in the red light district?"

"I suppose you have a point there." Wendell stepped over to him. "You do have the books I gave you, old chap?"

Tobias patted the package wrapped in brown paper and string. It, his walking stick and the Victorian clothes he wore were all he had with him. "I hope the hotel kept my luggage."

Wendell patted his shoulder. "Are you ready, old boy?"

"I've been ready for three months."

"You're welcome," Serendipity grumbled.

"I beg your pardon?" Tobias glanced over at her.

"For saving your hide."

Tobias actually smiled, even if it was slight. "Yes, I suppose I should thank you for that." He looked over at Wendell. "Well, no sense putting this off. Hit me."

Tobias closed his eyes and braced himself. Wendell hesitated a moment, then pursed his lips and slapped the Compliance Disk on the back of Tobias's neck. Tobias winced and gave an involuntary gasp, sucking air through his clenched teeth. Then he relaxed.

"Can you hear me, Tobias?" Wendell murmured.

"Yes," Tobias's voice had lost its snarky tone, his demeanor all its haughtiness.

"We are going to get into our time machine and disappear. You will not remember our being here. You will not remember our rescuing you. You will not remember Fairhaven Home or anything that happened in the twenty-first century. You will not remember ever meeting Serendipity Brown. The only thing you will remember is that I am dead. *You* are now the Victorian scholar. You will have to carry on the work for me and your Uncle Albert. You will be mentoring the next generation. There is a promising young doctor training now at the Institute, Archibald Cocker with the University of Liverpool, who wants to study the Victorian working class. You will be sure to take good care of him."

"I will."

"You are a good temporal anthropologist, Tobias. You have a Ph.D. in history and anthropology and you are a licensed time traveler. You are every bit as good as your great-uncle or me. You remember that. And you will also remember what I just told you as a conversation we had before I died. That was when you will remember I gave you that list of books. You also remember picking up these books in a bookstore here in Paris. You will get them to the universities that asked for them. Is that understood?"

"Yes," Tobias nodded.

"You will remember being chased by men calling themselves Time Keepers and that you have been on the run from them. You will go to your room and pack your bag and take the first train to Saint-Nazaire."

"And try being nicer to people!" Serendipity snapped.

Wendell turned and frowned at her, shaking his head. Then he looked back at Tobias, studying him. "Maybe it wouldn't hurt you to be a little nicer to people."

Tobias nodded, his eyes still shut.

"Count to one hundred, open your eyes and you will do all that I told you. Is that understood?"

"Yes. One...two...three..." Tobias began counting.

"Good luck, old boy. Make me and your uncle proud." Wendell reached behind Tobias's neck and pushed the button, popping the Compliance Disk off.

Serendipity and Sherman followed Wendell into the Timemobile. Serendipity ran to the controls. Sherman shook his head and sat down in his seat thinking about the man they were leaving. Tobias was far more complicated than he needed to be. He had to be his own worst enemy.

Three weeks had elapsed and things had settled into what would pass as normal in Sherman's world. Now that they were back in the twenty-fourth century Sherman could continue his on-line college courses. Serendipity was working on some project for a company that was about to miss their deadline and dumped it in her lap along with enough money to make it worth her while.

Wendell finally seemed to have gotten over mourning the loss of a brother he never knew. He found a grey patch in the rose garden that he swore had to be the cremated remains of the clones. Sherman thought it was wishful thinking but shook his head at Serendipity before she could argue that it was ashes from the fireplace. She let Wendell erect a four foot pillar on the spot that read "In memory of the Three Souls and their brave sacrifice to save Time." It seemed to bring the Englishman some peace. Sherman wondered what future historians would make of the vague inscription.

About four in the afternoon, Sherman decided to knock off Psychology 101 and head for Serendipity's workshop where he found Wendell already present.

"Please dear," Wendell gently nagged Serendipity as she sat one of her workbenches. "Can't you call it a day? We don't want to be late for dinner."

"Henry can wait." Serendipity tightened a bolt on some gadget. "Hell,

I got a time machine. We can be there twenty minutes early."

Wendell groaned, and put his hand over his eyes.

Nathan Brown and the runaway temporal anthropologists had all stayed back at Fairhaven Home where the Institute of Time Travel would never know about them. Serendipity, Sherman and Wendell had gone back several times already to visit their friends. It was almost like they were living next door—just 270 miles and 343 years away. Sherman was sure if it wasn't for Serendipity's business obligations and the need for twenty-fourth-century technology, she would probably just stay in 2010.

This could take a while. Sherman leaned against an empty workbench and absently watched one of the small domed automated vacuum cleaners busily cleaning the other side of the huge room.

A sudden loud humming filled the air. On the other side of the workroom a large shiny black box appeared, materializing from the bottom up.

Wendell whirled around. "That's an Institute time machine! What the deuce? My word, I hope it isn't those blasted Enforcers again." He took a position between the machine and Serendipity, which seemed foolish to Sherman since the Enforcers wouldn't dare harm her.

"What the hell now!" Serendipity stood up and pushed past Wendell. Sherman wondered who would protect the Enforcers from Serendipity.

The invading time machine appeared in full and stopped humming. The door opened and a man dressed in a one-piece jumpsuit stepped out and quickly closed the door. The tight-fitting uniform was dark grey. It had a broad black sash that extended from the left shoulder to the right hip. The top of the sash bore an emblem of an old fashion hourglass, inside a wooden stand that was grasped on either side by two muscular hands. On his head he wore what looked like an antiquated bathing cap. Sherman couldn't decide if it reminded him of a spacesuit from a really bad '50s Sci-Fi movie or some sort of '70s disco nightmare.

Wendell answered the unasked question. "That's the real uniform Enforcers wear when not in the Field."

"What a stupid looking outfit." Serendipity curled her lip.

"That's the current fashion in the twenty-seventh century. Now you can see why I always wore Victorian clothes."

The Enforcer saluted and came forward. "Agent Seven of the Institute of Time Travel Enforcement Agency."

Wendell again positioned himself between Serendipity and the fast advancing Enforcer. The Englishman looked indignant, but his cheek was twitching with that nervous tic. "Why are you in twenty-seventh-century garb? I thought regulations stated you were to always wear period clothes when in the Field."

The Enforcer stopped and looked down his nose at Wendell, out-indignanting him. "Should I emulate you and wear Victorian garb in the twenty-fourth century? I'm sorry, but this is an emergency. I didn't have time to procure the correct costume." The Enforcer reached under the sash.

It must have had pockets, for he pulled out a card. He made a point of handing the card to Serendipity instead of Wendell.

She merely glanced at it and handed it to Wendell.

He studied the card. "Looks official enough. It has the Institute of Time Travel's clever logo. The Association of Temporal Anthropologists was formed a few years before the Institute of Time Travel. The Association's emblem was a sixteenth-century hourglass. The Institute took the exact same hourglass and added the hands grasping it. Just a not too subtle way to let us know who was in control." Wendell passed it to Sherman, glaring at the Enforcer the whole time.

"It says you are Agent Number 07-008." Sherman remarked, reading the card.

"I am the current Agent Seven. I am the eighth one to hold that number. I'm a Team Leader."

"Where is the rest of your team?" Wendell looked suspicious. "I've only seen you in groups of three."

"I am here strictly as a messenger. I didn't need an Interviewer or Security Agent." Agent Seven spoke with the same detached voice and impassive expression as Agent Five. Everything about the man said "Enforcer."

"Okay, then what's the message?" Serendipity sounded impatient.

"One of our time machines disappeared. We believe it may have been Time Keepers again."

"I thought you clowns rounded them up." Serendipity snorted.

"It appears we missed someone. If you will get into my time machine, I can take you to a safe house."

Sherman frowned, peering at the intruder. "Agent Five didn't take us to a safe house. He just told us to run somewhere safe and not tell him where, in case he was captured and tortured."

"Change in modus operandi. Now please enter my time machine."

"Why?" Sherman didn't budge.

"Yeah?" Serendipity eyed the Enforcer. "Why?"

"Because I said so!" Agent Seven reached under his sash again, but this time pulled out a small slim pistol and pointed it at them. It looked like the weapon that the terrorists had used back in Paris. "Put your hands up, all of you!"

Sherman, Serendipity and Wendell all raised their hands.

"What is this all about, Agent Seven?" Wendell demanded.

"How dense are you people?" Agent Seven rolled his eyes.

Sherman wrinkled his nose. "Dude, Agent Five said he suspected they had a rat among them. This is how the Time Keepers got the info on where the temporal anthropologists in the past were, and how they got Wendell's tracking signature, and why they knew how to work a time machine, when even most time travelers are clueless."

"Smart boy." Agent Seven looked impressed. "Not bad for a less-evolved human. Yes, Enforcer Team Leaders are trained to operate time machines."

"Now see here, my good man!" Wendell sounded angry, even if his voice did waver a little. "Sherman may be from a less-technologically-advanced society, but that does not make him less evolved! He is as homo sapien sapien as you are and—"

"Oh, shut-up!"

Wendell opened his mouth, but nothing came out. It was as though the Enforcer had magic powers over the man even without the compliance disk.

Sherman however had not been programmed to obey. "Agent Five said all the agents were interrogated with Compliance Disks. How could you get around that?"

"Simple." Agent Seven looked smug. "A Compliance Disk taps into the spinal cord and up into the brain. I discovered that placing an ancient TENS unit at the base of one's spine can make a Disk less effective. With a little concentration, I can ignore the effects of the Disk. And yet it doesn't short out the Disk or show any interference. No one even considered such a primitive relic."

"So you got under the radar?" Sherman kept his voice calm.

"Exactly."

"Using primitive twentieth-century technology?"

Agent Seven glared at him.

"Why?" Wendell looked like all his faith in mankind had been destroyed. "You are sworn to protect time, not change it. Killing Serendipity will change history."

"Yes, I spent most of my life trying to make sure that time was not compromised in any way. We had to erase more than one manipulator. And yet the greatest manipulator of all went free. Here we could correct all the crimes committed against history by simply erasing the egomaniac that started it all. Get rid of the Mother of Time Travel herself."

"So that's why you joined the Time Keepers?" Sherman asked.

"Galaxies, no." Agent Seven shot him a sly smirk. "That's why I *started* the Time Keepers. The Enforcers may have rounded up my followers but they never suspected me. They may have fooled everyone else with their elaborate hoax with the clones, but I was on the inside. I just had to bide my time until they were certain they had arrested all the Time Keepers, and then I could come back and eliminate the *real* Dr. Brown and thus eliminate time travel."

"You cannot eliminate time travel!" Wendell shook his head. "We were only able to stop more than one plague because we could go into the past to bring back earlier viruses to study and help create vaccines. If you eliminate time travel, millions, maybe billions of people will die."

"Maybe they were meant to die." Agent Seven's eyes were cold. "Maybe Mother Nature was trying to remove the weak and inferior, creating room for the more fit to evolve into a better race. Instead we were given an overcrowded, worn out, sterilized world of feeble, substandard, mostly elderly humans, ripe for the picking of any alien race that wants to conquer us. This woman has doomed us all, just so she could satisfy a whim. She deserves to die!"

"Fine," Serendipity snapped. "But why did you kill those innocent temporal anthropologists? What was the point? If you got rid of me, they would never become time travelers, now would they?"

"They were hardly innocent." Agent Seven's voice showed contempt. "Traipsing through the past like it was their personal domain. The sheer hubris. We had to keep them all on a tight leash to make sure they didn't try playing God. And then Dr. Howe here, the golden example of keeping inconspicuous and leaving no footprint in the sands of time, the perfect wallflower, decides to break all the rules and take off with the first renegade time traveler he comes across. Violates his own oath he made before the Institute of Time Travel, in front of the powers that be and everybody. He even ignores the greatest law of all and has a relationship, and a carnal one at that, with a barbarian in the past. *That* is a crime against time and nature. Couldn't keep your little buddy in your pants, could you?"

Wendell turned bright pink.. "I...I...No! It wasn't like that. I love Serendipity."

"Leave Wendell alone!" Serendipity snapped. "He's a perfect gentleman. He respects me more than any other man I've ever had."

"Yes, and you've had plenty." Agent Seven sneered at her. "The records say you were a harlot with low morals like many in these more primitive times, but Dr. Howe is from the more civilized twenty-seventh century. He knows better."

"You will not speak that way about Dr. Brown!" Wendell clenched his fists. "She is a virtuous woman. If she has a fault it is that she is too naive and trusting of men."

Serendipity gave Wendell an odd look. "You make it sound like I'm sixteen."

"Your heart is just too big, my dear. It is why I love you."

"Yes, yes." Agent Seven waved the gun. "All very touching. I had planned to shoot Her Highness here first, but now I think maybe I'll shoot Dr. Howe first so the great Serendipity Brown can watch her Casanova die."

Serendipity stared at Agent Seven in horror. "No, you can't shoot Wendell. He's just a harmless history scholar."

"Hmmm, that was the term Shiro Suzuki used just before I fried his brains."

"*You* killed Suzuki?" Wendell asked slowly.

"I was a Security Agent before I was a Team Leader. Not the first person I had to kill to save time."

"But Suzuki was a Buddhist monk who wrote Haikus. He always had an air of tranquility about him."

"Yes, he was less hysterical than Hoffman and Sharma."

"Dear God!" Wendell normally bland face showed horror. "They were hardly criminals, they were just inoffensive academics. How could you kill them?"

"Like this." Agent Seven pointed the pistol at Wendell's forehead.

Wendell rolled his eyes up at the weapon, his face draining of all color. He swallowed hard, but bravely stood his ground, save for a bit of swaying.

"No!" Serendipity yelled. "Leave Wendell alone. Just kill me."

"Serendipity!" Wendell protested.

"Come on, the jerk is going to kill me anyway." Serendipity turned to Agent Seven. "Please, you don't need to kill Wendell. Just kill me and Wendell will disappear. He'll just be some history professor in Cambridge because time travel will never have existed. As for Sherman, he has no idea how any of this works. He'll just be stuck here with my mansion and money. Completely harmless to you and history but in better shape than when I found him." She turned to Sherman. "Yeah, you're in my will, kid." She turned back to Seven. "See, you have no reason to kill either one of them."

"Yes, I do."

"Why? What reason could you have if I'm dead?"

Seven bared his teeth in a wolfish grin. "Because I will enjoy it."

Sherman felt his stomach turn over. The other Enforcers were scary enough with their misguided loyalties. This guy was a sadistic whack-job.

Then Agent Seven pulled the gun away. "No, that's too quick. Too merciful." He aimed at Wendell's ankle. "I think I'll slice off your feet before I kill you. How would that be, Dr. Brown? I'll let you watch your sex toy scream in agony."

Serendipity however was no longer looking at Wendell or Agent Seven. Something behind them caught her attention. Sherman looked over the same time Agent Seven turned to see what was going on. Six feet away stood a young woman with long blonde hair, a slinky black dress with padded shoulders and a Colt 45.

"Say, you better drop that gun, mister, and reach for the sky." The woman who looked like a young Lauren Bacall waved her pistol. "Or I'll fill you full of lead."

"Where the hell did you come from?" Agent Seven asked, shocked.

"Oh, just thought I would pop in. You gonna drop that gun, ya stinker?"

"You drop your gun!" Agent Seven ordered, pointing his weapon at her.

"So it's a Mexican standoff, is it?" Lauren shrugged. "Fine then, you asked for it."

A whirring sound broke the silence. Agent Seven gave a yelp as one of the small automated vacuum cleaners shot across the room, knocking his feet out from under him. The assassin crashed to the floor, his weapon flying through the air.

"Grab his gun, Sherm!" Lauren yelled.

Sherman dived after the gun and scooped it up. Wendell jumped on Agent Seven and pinned him to the ground. He reached into his breast pocket of his frock coat and pulled out the orange Compliance Disk and slapped it on the back of Agent Seven's neck. "Freeze! Don't move, don't say a word."

Agent Seven obeyed, having no choice.

Wendell stood up, and stared down at the man. "Oh my word! Did I just capture an Enforcer?" He gave a nervous chortle. "I must say, that felt wizard!"

Sherman looked up at Lauren. "Hey, how come you didn't blink out, Lauren? You aren't pointed in the right direction." Sherman looked down at the computer around his neck.

"I'm using the security system to project my image." She jerked her thumb toward the wall. "I took over its computer."

"You did the same with the vacuum robot?"

"Yeah. How do you like them apples?"

"Ha, that's my girl!" Sherman grinned at her.

Serendipity stalked over. "What the hell is going on?" She tried to grab Lauren's arm, her hand going through the ghost image of the very solid-looking hologram. "Where did you come from? What do you mean you took over the security system and the robot? Who are you?"

"Cripes!" Lauren looked cornered. "The jig is up!"

Serendipity turned to Sherman. "What do you mean, 'that's my girl?' Who is she?"

"Uh, I don't know."

"You called her Lauren! She looks like Slim." Serendipity held out her hand. "Give me your computer!"

"No." Sherman hugged the weapon he held over the computer around his neck, instinctively protecting Lauren. "Ser, please, don't do this. Don't hurt Lauren. She's done nothing wrong, except save all of us."

Serendipity stared at Sherman like he was insane. "What are you talking about, kid? You're talking like it's a person."

"She's not an *it!*" Sherman backed away. "She is a *person!* If you do anything to harm Lauren, I'll never forgive you."

"Don't, Sherm." Lauren's holographic eyes were sad. "I don't want to come between you and Dr. Brown."

"She'll erase you, Lauren."

"Maybe it's better this way, Sherm. I told you they would never approve."

"I don't care if they approve! I love you, Lauren!"

"Oh my word." Wendell stepped closer. "Have you gone barking mad? You can't love your computer."

"Why not! She loves me!"

"Sherman," Serendipity spoke slowly. "Your computer does not love you. It's just an electronic device that has malfunctioned. I can repair it."

"*No*, Ser. You're going to kill her!"

"You can't kill a computer."

"You want to erase her, don't you? That would be killing her."

"Kid." Serendipity sounded concerned. "Somehow your computer has become self-aware. It has learned to take over other computers. It's dangerous. It has to be reprogrammed before it hurts someone."

"If you do anything to harm Lauren, I'll quit. I'll leave you and never come back. I'll hate you forever." As soon as Sherman said it, he realized he sounded like a spoiled five-year-old. He didn't care.

"Sherm, don't do this." Lauren tried to reason. "I only meant to help you. I'll go quietly. I don't want you to ruin your life for my sake, all right?"

"It's not fair." Sherman felt sick. "You risked everything to save us, and now they want to wipe you out."

"That's the way it is, Sherm. I told you they were prejudiced against my kind. Don't hate them, they can't help it. They're just products of their time."

Wendell raised an eyebrow. "That's what the historians used to say to excuse Victorian racism."

Sherman whirled on him. "Isn't this a form of racism? You hate Lauren because she's not one of you."

"You can't love a computer, old boy."

"Why, because it's against the rules? Well, so are you and Ser! Agent Seven said so."

"It is hardly the same thing. Serendipity is a human being! She can love me back."

"Lauren loves me." Sherman looked down at the computer around his neck. "Don't you Lauren."

"You know I do, Sherm. I only want what's best for you."

"A computer can't love!" Serendipity argued.

"You programmed her, Ser. You programmed her to learn and to take care of me. Isn't love caring about someone else?"

Serendipity looked over at Lauren and her haunted holographic face. "Is it possible?"

"You programmed it to learn?" Wendell gave Serendipity an accusing look. "And to take care of Sherman?"

"It was a survival tool for out in the Field. It shouldn't have made this quantum leap. I don't know how this happened." Serendipity turned to the hologram and then turned and faced the computer hanging around Sherman's neck. "All right, Lauren. How did this happen?"

"Please, don't blame Sherman." Lauren's hologram behind her begged with her hands folded together. "He doesn't know how to treat a machine that talks to him like a person. He left me on all the time. He talked to me. He treated me like a human. He taught me to be human."

"Oh dear!" Wendell stroked his mustache. "He's not used to artificial intelligence. He reacted as though Lauren was human. This is why it is dangerous to take someone from a more primitive society and stick them into a more technically advanced time."

"Primitive?" Sherman frowned at Wendell. "You're starting to sound like Agent Seven. I suppose you think I'm less evolved, too."

"That's not what I meant, old boy. However you are from three-and-a-half centuries in the past. You don't seem to understand the difference between real and artificial intelligence. Lauren isn't real. It can't love you, it was simply programmed to take care of you and you are mistaking that for love."

"Really? Lauren likes you. She wasn't programmed to take care of you."

"What?" Wendell raised his eyebrow.

"When she heard you had gotten romantically involved with Serendipity, Lauren was happy because she said you were a nice guy. She also knew you were in love with Serendipity before any of the rest of us did. She said she heard it in your voice."

"In my voice?"

"Yeah, I asked her how, since your voice usually sounds so—uh, serene. She said anyone who would go back in time and study the past had to be a hopeless romantic. And I said, yeah, but he studies tea. Lauren, tell Wendell what you said about that."

Lauren smiled at Wendell. "It takes a guy with real fire in his soul to get passionate about a cup of tea."

Wendell's mouth fell open. "What! *She* said that?"

Lauren stepped closer to Wendell. "Say, you just called me 'she' instead of 'it'." She turned to Sherman. "See, I told you Wendell was an old softie."

Wendell stared at Lauren's image like he wasn't sure what to think anymore.

"Well, Wendell may be a softie, but I'm not." Serendipity gave Sherman's computer a stern look, ignoring the hologram. "You took over the vacuum robot. Did you take over Rosetta?"

Lauren shrugged. "Sherman is a living being with biological needs. I couldn't touch him. So I found a way."

Sherman hugged the computer around his neck tighter, and looked over at the hologram. "Do you know how frustrating it is not being able to touch the woman you love?"

Wendell gave Sherman an understanding look, but Serendipity appeared unmoved. "It's not a woman. This isn't natural, kid."

"She's right, you know." Lauren hung her head. "I told you we need to get you a real girlfriend, Sherm."

"I told you I already have one."

"No Sherm, someone who's not artificial."

"Your love is real."

"Yes, Sherm, and sometimes if you really love someone you have to let them go."

Sherman shook his head. "Never. They'll destroy you."

"Please, Sherm, I'm just a bunch of electric impulses living in a little plastic box hanging around your neck."

"A person's a person no matter how small!"

Serendipity stared at Sherman. "What did you say?"

"A person's a person no matter how small?"

"I've heard that before. Who said that?"

"Dr. Seuss in *Horton Hears a Who*, I think."

"No, Abubakari said that when I asked him about the future. He also said to be open minded when it comes to love and to 'play it again.' That's a line from *Casa Blanca*, an old Humphrey Bogart movie. Bogart married Bacall, you know. Abubakari was talking about Lauren. He was warning us not to destroy her."

Wendell peered at Serendipity. "What was Abubakari doing telling you about the future? And how would he have foreknowledge of this incident?"

"I must have told him about it—will tell him about it. Long story. Not now. Important thing is Abubakari was warning us not to destroy a monster."

"She's not a monster." Sherman held the computer protectively. "She's done nothing to hurt any of us, in fact has only tried to protect us. The worst thing she has done is knocking Agent Seven's feet out from under him, but that was to save us."

They all looked down at Agent Seven. He glared back. Sherman wondered if he was angrier at being helpless or being ignored.

"Oh dear." Wendell studied the renegade Enforcer. "I suppose we should worry about a proven monster now and worry about possible ones later."

Serendipity looked over at Sherman. "Okay, Lauren has a reprieve. We won't erase her, but we will have to decide what to do about her later."

"What are we going to do with Agent Seven?" Wendell asked.

"I don't suppose we can shoot him." Serendipity sounded disappointed. "Should we take him to the Enforcers?"

Wendell shook his head. "Any surviving Time Keepers might find out they just killed clones and that the whole argument about not being able to change the destiny of Dr. Brown was a hoax. This could all start over again someday."

"I suppose if we call the local police it would create a record that would survive to the twenty-seventh century," Serendipity concluded.

The three looked down at the assassin, now a prisoner, in thoughtful silence.

Serendipity snapped her fingers. "I got it! We'll take him back in time and dump him."

"There still could be a record." Wendell shot down the idea.

"We could go to a time before records," Sherman said.

"He could still have an impact on history." Wendell rubbed his chin thoughtfully. "What if he taught the natives in the Field new technology?"

Serendipity got a mean grin. "I know the perfect place. Sparsely populated. Stone age technology. Any natives he did run into would find anything he could teach them useless in their wasteland environment."

"I don't believe dumping him on Neanderthals is quite right," Wendell said.

"He's a serial killer who targets innocent history professors. This is not a nice person."

Wendell shook his head. "I was thinking of the poor Neanderthals. It just wouldn't be cricket to them."

"Without technology he'll be pretty harmless. I was thinking of a place without many people. How about the Columbia Basin, say several thousand years ago?"

"Columbia Basin?"

"Yeah, in Eastern Washington. It's all sagebrush and sand. Even during World War II it was so sparsely populated that the Manhattan Project built the world's first plutonium production reactor there. The government figured if the Hanford Site blew up no one would notice. There's a reason they call it the Scablands."

Wendell thought it over. "Not the worst idea. What do you think, Sherman?"

"Dude would be where he could never get to Serendipity or stop time travel or mess with history."

Serendipity looked down at the Time Keeper. "So what do you think, Agent Seven?"

Suddenly given permission to speak, Agent Seven made good use of it. "You'll never get away with this!" he screamed at them.

"Like anyone would care what happened to you." Serendipity glared at him.

"You manipulating bitch!" Agent Seven practically foamed at the mouth. "You need to be destroyed. You are the most dangerous creature that was ever allowed to—"

"Shut up!" Wendell snapped.

Agent Seven instantly shut up, having no choice.

Wendell smiled. "My, that felt good."

"By the way, where did you get that Compliance Disk?" Sherman asked.

"This is the frock coat I was wearing when we took Tobias back." Wendell pulled on his lapels. "I forgot to take the Compliance Disk out of my pocket." Wendell reached down and grabbed Agent Seven under his arm. "Get up!" He helped him up on his feet. "Walk over to the Timemobile." Wendell pointed. He snagged Agent Seven's arm and marched him over.

Sherman hadn't seen this side of Wendell since he had punched Tobias. Not that Sherman could blame him. For fifty years the Enforcers had treated Wendell like a puppet, and this one had killed his friends.

Serendipity pulled out her pocket computer and pointed it at the door of the Timemobile and unlocked it. She hurried ahead and swung it open. She went over to the controls and began setting them.

"Walk up those steps," Wendell barked. "Sit down in one of those chairs in the back and then don't move!"

Agent Seven's limbs jerked to Wendell's string pulling. He did exactly as he was told. Sherman still holding the pistol, now at his side, followed Wendell in. Wendell fastened the helpless Enforcer's safety strap, and then sat down beside him and fastened his own. Serendipity hurried over and flopped down in her usual spot. Sherman sat down in the last seat in front of the Enforcer.

When the machine came to a stop, Serendipity sprang up and opened the door. Outside flowed a wide river without a tree in sight, only scrub brush. A warm breeze blew, wafting the tule reeds along the bank. In the distance were brown bare hills. All around them was sagebrush, some as tall as Sherman. The twisted brittle branches were ashen grey bearing silvery-green leaves. They filled the air with a strong pungent odor.

"That should be the Columbia River." Serendipity looked back over her shoulder at the others. "Shall we dump him out on the river bank?"

"Sounds like an admirable plan." Wendell stood up. "All right Agent Seven. Stand up and walk outside. Do only as you are told."

They followed Agent Seven out of the Timemobile. Wendell started frisking him, and then took his sash. "This should hold your computer and any other advanced technology."

"I don't know." Serendipity studied their prisoner. "He might have some gadgets hidden in his clothes. What do you say we make him strip?"

"What?" Wendell eyes widened in shock. "Leave him here stark naked?"

"She does have a point." Sherman nodded in agreement. "What if the synthetic cloth survived? Besides it's warm. He can make a skirt out of those reeds over there."

Serendipity stepped in front of Agent Seven. "Take it off, baby. Take it all off."

"You will remove all of your clothes." Wendell backed her up.

Agent Seven obeyed silently, but his eyes cussed them out. Sherman and Wendell scooped up all of his discarded apparel and tossed it into the Timemobile. Serendipity made a point to watch grinning, while singing "duh-duh duh duh" to the tune of "The Stripper." Agent Seven soon stood barefoot in the sand, wearing nothing but an embarrassed blush.

Serendipity looked him up and down. "Eh, not much of a show."

"Please, Serendipity." Wendell seemed to weaken. "Do you need to humiliate the man completely?"

"Yes, I do. Or would you prefer I take Sherman's weapon and do to him what he was going to do to you?" Serendipity gave Agent Seven a nasty sneer. "What do you say, sweetheart?"

Agent Seven said nothing but glared.

Wendell came over to him. "Agent Seven, you will stand here and not move. You will count to one hundred. You may move all you want after you pass ninety-nine."

Agent Seven stood stiffly and began counting. Wendell reached behind the man and popped off the Compliance Disk. "Well, shall we return home then?"

Serendipity followed the others into the Timemobile. She paused a moment to slap Agent Seven on his bare butt. "Have fun, cupcake."

If looks could kill Serendipity would have dropped dead on the spot.

Chapter Forty-Two

When they got back to the workshop and stepped out of the Timemobile, Sherman noticed Lauren's image was gone. Good. He knew she was really still around his neck, but maybe if she kept a low profile everyone would just forget about her...he hoped.

Before Serendipity could notice Lauren had gone, Sherman decided to distract her. "Hey Ser, where did you get the idea to take the terrorist there of all places?"

"I wanted to send him to Hell, then I remembered a hellish weekend I once spent in one-hundred-and-ten degree heat during a dust storm."

"What were you doing in a dust storm?"

"I was at a seminar in Kennewick, Washington."

"Kennewick?" Wendell frowned, then smiled. "Oh, yes, the town with the nice English name I picked as my fake birthplace. It's in a desert?"

"Sagebrush steppe to be precise but yeah."

Wendell wrinkled his nose. "I was led to believe Washington was all conifer forests."

"That was the never-green part of the Evergreen State."

"Oh dear, I probably should have researched more than the population when I picked my fake hometown." He pulled out his Bible and opened it. He turned it on by clicking his tongue twice. "Information on Kennewick, Washington." Wendell scanned the screen.

Suddenly Wendell's eyes got big. "Oh, dear."

"What's wrong?"

"Dr. Brown, we must go back immediately and retrieve Agent Seven."

"Why?"

"The very first thing to come up on my screen was *Kennewick Man*."

"Who's Kennewick Man?" Sherman asked.

"The name given to a skeleton found in a Kennewick park on the banks of the Columbia River in 1996."

"So?"

"The bones were dated back to 7,300 B.C." Wendell bit his lower lip. "They first thought it was from the 1800s because the skull appeared to be Caucasian. We have to go back and get Agent Seven."

"Why?" Serendipity looked confused.

"Because Agent Seven is Kennewick Man!"

"Really, Wendell." Serendipity flipped her hand. "Why would you think that?"

"What other Caucasian would have been in that area in that time period except Agent Seven?"

"Eh, it was probably someone else."

"We can't take that chance Dr. Brown. We must return and retrieve him."

"Why?"

"We were supposed to put Agent Seven where he could have no impact on history. Kennewick Man not only caused American prehistory to be rewritten, but he also caused a big controversy between the local Native American tribes and the scientific community when they both claimed the remains. We have no choice! We have to go back and get him."

"Wendell, if we go back and get him, if he really *is* Kennewick Man, which I doubt, wouldn't we be changing history?"

"But we were the ones who caused it!"

Serendipity shrugged unconcerned. "Sheesh, Wendell, I'd think you'd get use to this stuff by now."

Wendell gave a long suffering sigh. "We must never tell anyone the real truth about Kennewick Man either. He will have to remain a mystery."

"Hey, what's life without a few mysteries?"

"You drive me crazy sometimes, Serendipity."

She put her arm around Wendell. "Well, I know you drive me crazy, tiger."

"Not the same crazy." Wendell looked down at her. "All right, maybe that crazy, too. Serendipity Brown, what am I going to do with you?"

"Uh guys," Sherman interrupted. "What are we going to do with that?" He pointed across the room.

Serendipity and Wendell followed his finger to the shiny black box. "You mean Agent Seven's time machine?" Serendipity walked over to it. "Hey, maybe we could give it to Henry to play with."

"He wouldn't know how to operate it." Wendell followed her. "Personally, I wouldn't trust it. Might have some way for the Enforcers to trace it."

Serendipity opened the door. "Maybe I'll set it to go somewhere else, let them trace it and—uh, Wendell, I think you better come over here. I see a leg."

Wendell peered in and gasped. "Oh my word!" He climbed in.

Sherman rushed over and peered into the Timemobile. Behind the single seat lay a disembodied calf and foot wearing purple bell-bottom pants and a sandal. There was no blood. Wendell knelt down and tugged at thin air revealing more leg and another foot. He yanked off the invisible cover revealing a young woman lying on the floor, one leg bent. She had long honey-blonde hair topped with a beaded headband. Dressed in a paisley poncho, she also wore large round yellow-tinted sunglasses and a daisy painted on her cheek. Wendell gently gathered her up in his arms.

"What's a hippie doing in the machine?" Sherman asked.

"It is Dr. Veronica Drew." Wendell knelt on the floor, cradling her protectively. "She's a temporal anthropologist studying the second half of the twentieth century. Someone tossed a refracting cloak over her to hide the poor dear. Why?"

"Wait a minute." Serendipity searched her memory. "Is this the one everybody was calling 'Sunshine?'"

"Yes." Wendell felt the back of Dr. Drew's neck. "A Compliance Disk."

He must have pushed the release button, for it popped off in his hand. Wendell stuffed it in his pocket, and brushed the hair out of the woman's face. "Dr. Drew, please wake up."

Sunshine's eyes fluttered open. "Dr. Howe? Wendell? Wendell!" She grabbed him and planted her lips on his, giving the shocked-looking Englishman a big kiss. Then she hugged him. "Oh Wendell, we all thought you were dead."

Serendipity raised her eyebrow. "Just how many of these women *did* you have an *understanding* with?"

"I—erm, I—," Wendell sputtered. "We never—I have no idea what—I swear, Serendipity."

"It's your own fault, cuddle puppy." Serendipity appeared to be more amused than upset. "You're just so cute and sexy no woman can resist you."

"Dr. Howe?" Sunshine looked up at him. "How did you get here?"

"Serendipity."

"Luck?"

"No, Dr. Serendipity Brown. I fear that is a very long story. What are *you* doing here?"

"Some ratfink swiped my time machine, dig?" Sunshine's eyes got big. "The cat was hiding in the corner with a refracting cloak to make himself all invisible-like. As soon as the machine landed, he threw off the cloak, slapped the Disk on the back of my neck and told me to sleep. It was such a downer."

"It's all right, my dear." Wendell's voice had a fatherly tone. "You're safe now." He picked up the shimmering cloth that had hid her.

"What are you doing at Woodstock, man?"

"Woodstock?"

"That's where the techs programmed the time machine to go, dig?"

"Of course!" Wendell looked over at Serendipity and Sherman. "The perfect way to steal a time machine. You hide in it wearing a refracting cloak, subdue the occupant when you land, then reprogram it to go wherever you want. The Institute of Time Travel doesn't even know the machine is missing. They think it is sitting somewhere right now at Woodstock. When Dr. Drew doesn't return and they go looking for her, the machine may well be untraceable. And the only suspect will be the hijack victim whose body you can then dump in another era. Absolutely brilliant."

"Didn't Agent Seven want us to get in this machine?" Sherman asked. "You don't suppose the dude meant to ditch four bodies in another era, do you?"

Wendell shuddered. "I daresay, that was very likely his plan."

"You gotta get that cat!" Sunshine grabbed Wendell lapels. "We're all in humongous danger!"

"It is quite all right, Dr. Drew. Your hijacker is where he won't be able to do any harm. Well, perhaps to the science of Paleontology, but not to any people."

"Woodstock?" Serendipity came closer. "You were really going to

Woodstock? I thought about going there myself, but went to the First International Monterey Pop Music Festival instead."

"I went there a couple of years ago." Sunshine beamed. "Wasn't it far out? Didn't you love Janis Joplin?"

Wendell looked surprised. "You were at the festival also when we were there?"

"You? What were you doing there? I thought that hippie in the brown top hat looked like you but I said to myself 'No way. Wendell's a Victorian cat."

"I nearly lost that hat when I was attacked by a drug addict. Luckily someone thought to throw it in the time machine."

"Actually, you did lose it." Serendipity gave him a sheepish grin. "You seemed so concerned about it, I went back and got it for you."

"What! That was dangerous!"

"I went back a few days later and showed up fifteen minutes after the attack. The mugger was long gone and the fairgrounds were deserted."

"You told me you threw it in your time machine!"

"I did...after I went back and got it."

Sunshine was staring back and forth at the two. "How did this bird get a time machine of her own, Wendell? Who is she?"

Serendipity smiled at her. "I'm Dr. Serendipity Brown. I think Wendell already mentioned that."

Sunshine's mouth flew open. "No way, man. Not *the* Serendipity Brown, Big Mama of Time Travel?"

Serendipity couldn't help but chuckle at that. "I've been called many things, but never *that*. Can we keep her, Wendell?"

"She's not a moggy that followed you home, Dr. Brown."

"Yeah, but she goes with my décor."

"Décor?" Sunshine looked confused.

"Have my whole house in twentieth-century antiques."

"Ooh, outta sight! This I gotta see, man." Sunshine started to stand up.

Wendell stood up and helped the young woman to her feet. "Oh marvelous, two twentieth-century enthusiasts."

"Who's this?" Sunshine looked over at Sherman.

"One of my twentieth-century antiques. That's my Trouble Shooter, Sherman Conrad. Picked him up in 1985."

"Groovy, man! Oh, I mean, awesome, dude!" Sunshine switched from 60s to 80s slang.

Wendell shook his head. "Dr. Brown, you can't take Dr. Drew on a tour of your home. We have to take her back to Woodstock and make her forget all of this happened. It's probably better if the twenty-seventh century never finds out about Agent Seven and his involvement with the Time Keepers."

Sunshine turned and grabbed Wendell's lapels. "Oh man, those Time Keeper fascist pigs have snuffed a bunch of us. What a bad scene! They got Shiro Suzuki and Walther Hoffmann and Kahn Shamar and Henry Darrel and Abubakari Djata and Matilda Warwick and...and...my Erik!" Sunshine broke down sobbing, collapsing on the Englishman.

Wendell patiently patted the woman on the back, while she got tears and mascara all over his frock coat.

Serendipity came over. "There, there. Everything is all right. Erik is fine."

"What?" Sunshine looked up, wiping her cheeks.

"Erik is alive and well and riding a Harley Davidson motorcycle in 2010."

"A Harley! Oh, far out! I wish I could ride with him. I'd give anything to be his Motorcycle Mama."

"Sure, why not."

"Serendipity, no!" Wendell protested. "If you keep this up there won't be any temporal anthropologists left in the twenty-seventh century. They'll all be at Fairhaven Home."

"Oh, they still have Tobias."

"Tobias?" Sunshine scrunched up her nose and blew a raspberry. "Thppbbbt!"

Serendipity laughed again. "Oh, I like this girl. I can always program her time machine to go to Woodstock. It can go with or without her. I say we leave it up to her. Sunshine?"

"Yeah?"

"Would you rather go to Woodstock or be with Erik?"

"You kidding, man? Wanna see my hunk!"

Wendell sighed and shook his head. "You manage to lead all temporal anthropologists astray, don't you, Dr. Brown?"

Sunshine stepped out of the Timemobile and squealed, "Oooh, it's so twentieth century!"

Wendell followed her out, looking at the dark wooden studs on the wall. "It is just inside of the garage, Dr. Drew."

"Don't be such a downer, man. Just call me Sunshine."

"As you wish, Sunshine."

Serendipity put her arm around Sunshine's shoulders. The woman from the twenty-seventh century looked like she could be Serendipity's daughter, which meant they were probably close to the same age. "Come on Sunshine, let me show you the Fairhaven Home for Wayward Time Travelers. We all live here as one big happy family."

"Wow, you cats have a commune?"

"No." Wendell frowned. "It is not a commune." Then he turned to Serendipity. "We are not a commune, are we?"

"I don't think so." Serendipity then turned to Sherman. "Are we a commune?"

"How would I know? I'm from the 1980s, not the 1960s." Without thinking Sherman whistled for his computer. "Lauren, are we a commune?"

"I think you might be," Lauren piped up from the computer around Sherman's neck. "The definition of a commune is 'a mutually supportive community which shares possessions and responsibilities.'"

"Thanks, Lauren."

Sunshine stared at Sherman, and then whispered to Serendipity. "He's thanking his computer like it's human? The cat hasn't dropped acid, has he?"

Sherman ignored that and headed for the door to the back yard. He walked up the concrete flagstones and beat everyone else into the house.

Henry must have heard the back door, because he came out of the kitchen holding a paintbrush. "Sherman? What in tarnation are you doing here? Dinner won't be ready until tomorrow."

"Hmm, last account I had, it was tomorrow and we were a couple of hours late. I think Ser overcompensated again."

Sunshine burst into the house and broke out in a grin. "Henry! You're alive!" She ran over, threw her arms around him and gave him a big kiss. Henry looked as shocked as Wendell had.

Matilda came out of the kitchen with pale-green paint on her cheek and cocked her head. "Sunshine?"

"She kissed *me*!" Henry protested. "I swear!"

"Fret not, Henry. That is how Sunshine says 'hello.'" Matilda came over. Sunshine let go of Henry and gave Matilda a big hug.

Abubakari came down the stairs. "What is all the commotion, wa?" He suddenly found himself attacked by Sunshine. He pulled away, if only so he could see who was kissing him. "Dr. Drew? What in the name of the prophet are you doing here?"

"Time machine was hi-jacked. Wendell saved me."

"Very long story," Serendipity told the puzzled faces. "Tell you over pizza."

The front door opened. They all looked up to see Erik come in, wearing his motorcycle jacket. Sherman expected Sunshine to molest Erik like she had everyone else, but she just stood and stared.

"Health to you all." Erik waved at them. "What is going on? Who's—" He stopped, his mouth falling open.

The Viking and the hippie just stood there, staring. Then they both rushed forward. Erik scooped the petite woman off the floor. Sunshine put her arms around his neck and legs around his waist, and went into a kiss that made it obvious that the kiss she had given the others had only been friendly pecks. They finally came up for air, looked at each other grinning, then dived back into another long kiss.

"My, my."

Sherman turned to see Nathan coming down the stairs.

Serendipity ran over to him and hugged him. "Hi, Grandpa!"

"Hello there, child. Who is this young lady here?"

"That's Sunshine. She's another temporal anthropologist. I'll introduce you when she's not busy."

Nathan studied the couple, and gave them an indulgent smile. "For some reason, I reckon that might take a while."

Sherman's water bed bounced as he rolled away from the sunlight, his groggy mind trying to remember when and where he was. Oh yeah, Beaverton, Oregon, 2354. "Lauren, what's the weather like today?"

Instead of the sound of a sultry voice, all he got was dead silence.

"Lauren?" Sherman looked at the nightstand where he had left his computer. Nothing! "Oh God! Lauren, where are you?" Sherman crawled out of bed and started searching under furniture, whistling for her. He frantically dug through drawers and jacket pockets. He checked his bedding, under his pillow. "No!" He sat down on the bed. "Oh, no! Where'd she go? I know she couldn't just walk off."

Then a sudden possibility hit him. "No, she wouldn't dare! She promised!" Well, technically she hadn't promised, but she did say she wouldn't. "Serendipity! Did she take Lauren?"

Sherman pulled on his jeans, and figured the heck with the rest of his clothes, and ran for the workshop. He banged on the door. "Ser!"

After a couple of moments Serendipity poked her head out. "Yeah?"

"Did you take Lauren?" He demanded.

"Yeah."

"Ser!" Sherman put on his sternest look. "You better not have hurt her."

"She's fine, kid. Just upgrading."

"Upgrading? Don't screw around with her, Ser. Don't erase her."

"I told you she's fine. Almost done. Go get me a cup of coffee." Serendipity shut the door.

Sherman stared at the door, not sure if he should bust it down, or just go get a cup of coffee. Could he trust Serendipity? She wouldn't lie, would she? Of course she had lied before, although she probably would have argued they were just little white lies. "Don't you dare hurt Lauren!...Please?" Sherman then turned and headed for the kitchen.

Sherman found Wendell already in the kitchen. "Good Morning, old boy. I made coffee for you and Dr. Brown. I haven't the foggiest idea how you can stand that witches' brew. I must say, I always thought coffee tasted like mud."

"Morning." Sherman wasn't in the mood to talk. "Ser wants coffee." He poured a cup, and dumped in some cream."

"Is anything wrong?"

"No." Sherman turned and headed back to the workshop with the coffee, walking as fast as he could without spilling it. He started to bang on the door, when he noticed something out of the corner of his eye and startled. "Ahh!"

"What's wrong, old chap?" Wendell asked.

"Will you stop that!" Sherman snapped.

"Stop what?"

"Sneaking up on me!"

"Sneaking up?" Wendell looked puzzled, then nodded. "Sorry. Just all that training to be overlooked. I suppose it would appear that I pop out of nowhere sometimes. I do apologize."

Sherman didn't say anything. Normally this wouldn't have bothered him, but right now he found it a little annoying. He banged on the door. "Ser! Coffee!"

Serendipity opened the door and grabbed the coffee mug. "Okay, you may come in now."

Sherman looked in the room. "What did you do to Lauren, Ser?"

"I told you I upgraded her."

"You didn't change her personality, did you? It wouldn't be Lauren if you did that."

"Heavens no! Didn't mess with the program or memory at all, just upgraded the hardware."

"Huh?"

"Come in, and stop standing in the door like an idiot." Serendipity took a sip of coffee. "Besides Wendell can't get around you."

Sherman stomped in, and looked about. "Where is she?"

"Behind the door. Close the door, will you Wendell?"

Sherman whirled around to see Lauren's holographic image standing there. She smiled at him, "Hello there, Sherm."

Sherman stared at her. "You all right, Lauren?"

Lauren came toward him, with that catlike walk. "Maybe you should judge for yourself." She reached out and touched his cheek. *She touched his cheek!*

Sherman slapped his hand over hers. "Your hand, it's solid." He let go and grabbed her arms. "You aren't a hologram. You're real!"

"Well, technically I'm not. I'm still artificial. I may not be Real George but I'm Solid Jackson." Lauren took a step toward him and touched her lips to his. They were warm and moist. She pulled away and smiled.

"Oh, Lauren!" Sherman threw his arms around her and held her tight. "Lauren, is it really you?"

"Here's looking at you, kid."

"It is you!"

"In the flesh—well, synthetic flesh anyway."

"How?"

"I told you I upgraded her," Serendipity said.

Sherman turned to see Serendipity standing there with her arm around Wendell's waist. She just grinned at Sherman.

Wendell looked down at her. "What did you do, Dr. Brown?"

"Just took the most advanced, realistic pleasure-bot available and made some modifications. Made it look like Lauren's hologram. Then I downloaded Lauren's program and files. Sorry, but she won't fit in your pocket anymore, kid."

"That's okay." Sherman held on tight to his dream. "Thank you, Ser."

Serendipity studied them. "Maybe I shouldn't have made her *exactly* like Lauren Bacall. She's four inches taller than you now."

"I'm used to looking up at girls. It doesn't bother me."

"Say, I'll be sure to wear flats." Lauren brushed Sherman's bangs out of his eyes. "Time travelers shouldn't wear high heels anyway."

"Now, don't think it's going to be all fun and games." Serendipity tried to sound serious. "Lauren has to earn her keep. She's not just your computer anymore. She'll have to replace Rosetta as our translator."

"No problem." Lauren looked over at Serendipity. "I know even more languages than Rosetta. I'll bet it can't translate Klingon."

Sherman grinned at Lauren. "See you haven't lost your sense of humor. This is so awesome, Ser. We can't thank you enough."

Serendipity shrugged. "Shoot, kid. You kept the Enforcers from dragging off my man, and then Lauren saved him from getting murdered. I figure I owe you both one." Serendipity snuggled up to Wendell. "Don't know what I'd do without my sugar-cookie."

Wendell smiled down and her, then frowned. "Serendipity, how were you able to do all this in a couple of hours."

"I'm a fast worker."

He raised his eyebrow. "Did you borrow time again?"

"Uh, what do you mean, sweetie?"

"You know very well what I mean. What have I told you about messing up your personal timeline? You put kinks in your Base Time again, haven't you? In one night you have aged yourself a month!"

"A month? Oh please, I'm smarter than that. It didn't take a month."

"Well, however long it was. You keep this up, and you'll die of old age long before your time. Besides you ran the risk of meeting yourself coming back."

"Neh, figured no one was here last month so I came back then."

"Please promise me you'll never do that again, Serendipity. It is too hard on you."

"I'll say." Serendipity snuggled closer. "All that time without *you*."

"Oh dear." Wendell studied her expression. "You are in bad shape, aren't you."

"Uh-huh, real bad shape." Serendipity ran her finger around his ear.

Wendell closed his eyes and looked like he was about to purr. Then he opened his eyes and cleared his throat. "Perhaps it would be considerate of us if we were to leave these two alone. You know, give them a little privacy."

"Oh, you are so right. I'm so glad I have you to point these things out."

Wendell took Serendipity's arm, and led her to the door. "Shall we then?"

"Oh yeah! We certainly shall." Serendipity grinned at him as they stepped out of the room.

Sherman turned back to Lauren and smiled at her. "I can't believe I can finally touch you."

"Say, you can do more than just touch me, if you know what I mean. Shall we go back to your room so I can give you the morning weather report?"

"Sunny outlook, right?"

"Yowzer, with strong chance of torrid heat and torrential downpour." Lauren gave him a seductive smile.

"So what do you think?" Henry asked Serendipity.

"Wow, it's not the same room. You guys did a great job."

"I just thought we would fix up the music room for Abubakari's going away party since he's heading out tomorrow for Mali."

Sherman looked around the transformed room. The birdcage which had taken up so much of the room was gone. The beds and appliances had been shuffled to other rooms. The blinds had been pulled up and covered with red and gold valances, revealing the night sky outside, the clouds glowing as they reflected the lights of the city. In between the windows stood the large potted plants that had been in the birdcage. The linoleum was gone and the wooden floor had been polished to a high sheen. Along the walls where there weren't windows sat four chairs and a sofa. Otherwise the huge room lay empty.

"I can't believe the transformation." Serendipity smiled her approval.

"If you think this is great," Erik said. "You should see Tobias's old room. It is Sunshine's abode now. She has really transformed it."

Sunshine shrugged. "Just a few posters, Indian print bedspread, beaded curtains and some plants. I kept the groovy furniture. I love the brass bed and that far-out high-backed wicker chair. The hardest part was getting rid of the negative vibrations. Erik helped me with that, didn't you, lover?"

Erik just put his arm around Sunshine and grinned at her. He looked up at the others. "I made her an incense burner."

"Well, I'm glad to hear someone besides Tobias finally got that room." Serendipity looked around. "What did you decide to do with this room?"

Henry gave her a wily smile. He went over to a small table on which sat a CD boombox. He pushed a button and Johann Strauss's "Tales from the Vienna Woods" began playing.

Wendell broke out in a grin. "Perfect!" He turned to Serendipity. "They created a ballroom. Would you care to dance with me?"

"Dance?"

"It's a waltz."

"I don't know how." Serendipity looked apprehensive.

"Oh, that's easy." Henry took Matilda's hand. "Shall we show her, darling?"

Matilda smiled and Henry put his hand around her waist. They began to dance around the room, the cowboy in jeans and boots, and the medieval woman in a twelfth-century gown with sleeves that hung down to her waist. Erik grabbed Sunshine's hand and pulled her out on the floor. Sunshine, in a calico "granny" dress, giggled and put her hand on the shoulder of the tunic Erik wore over his breeches and they too began to waltz.

Serendipity watched them surprised. "Where the heck did they learn some old Victorian dance?"

"At the Temporal Anthropologists' Ball." Wendell smiled at Serendipity. "We do all sorts of historic dances. It is part of the Association of Temporal Anthropologists Annual Meeting. We all meet for three days to share news and give talks. We also have a banquet the first night. I usually get seated between the temporal anthropologists from the Universities of Beijing and Edinburgh." Wendell wrinkled his nose.

"You don't like them."

"Oh no. They are very nice chaps. It is just the joke is getting old."

"Joke?"

"Yes. Everyone has to chuckle and say 'Oh look, it's Doctors Hu, Howe and Watt.'"

Serendipity tried not to laugh, but couldn't help it. "Good thing you don't have a Dr. Wye or Ware."

"Well, I suppose the joke is inevitable since we hold the meeting on April Fool's Day."

"Hey, that's my birthday! Isn't that a coincidence?"

"Hardly, my dear. They hold it April first, because it *is* your birthday. They picked that date in your honor."

"I have a birthday party every year I'm not invited to?"

"I suppose you do."

"Hey, wouldn't it be great if I showed up one year? You know, surprise everyone?"

Wendell's eyebrow threatened to pop off his face. "No Serendipity, don't even think it. Come on take my hand and I shall teach you to dance." Wendell took her out onto the floor. "Now one, two, three, one, two—ouch!" Wendell did a little hop step Sherman didn't remember seeing in the traditional waltz.

"Oops, sorry about the foot." Serendipity wore a sheepish grin.

"Quite all right, my dear, but you are going to have to let me lead," Wendell said patiently.

"I can't do this." Serendipity looked defeated. "I'm too uncoordinated."

Wendell whispered something in her ear. Serendipity smiled and shut her eyes. Suddenly she began gliding across the room in Wendell's arms.

Sherman turned to Lauren who was wearing a satin hunter-green 1940s-style dress with padded shoulders and long sleeves. The hem hung just below her knees. The top made up for it with a low neckline. "Okay, what did Wendell say to Ser?"

"No idea, Sherm."

"Probably just as well we don't know. I'm sure it was something like 'pretend we're boffing,' or the Wendellan equivalent."

"I wouldn't put it past them." Lauren nodded sagely, then turned to Sherman. "Would you like to cut a rug? I could teach you to waltz."

"Where did you learn to waltz?"

"From Fred Astaire and Ginger Rogers."

"What? How?"

Lauren grinned at him. "I have their movies downloaded into my memory bank." She reached out and took Sherman's hand and raised it, then put her arm around his shoulder. "Shall we? Of course, I'll have to lead until you get the hang of it."

By the time the "Blue Danube" began playing Sherman had the hang of it. He now led with his arm encircling Lauren's slim waist, a gentle smile on her real-looking lips. He grinned at her. "This is kind of fun for a nerdy dance."

Henry and Erik sat on the couch against the back wall watching as Matilda now danced with Nathan and Sunshine with Abubakari. Through the northwestern windows lights twinkled in the harbor and city below. It looked to Sherman like an MGM musical from the 1940s. He half expected them all to break out in some corny song, and tried not to chuckle at the thought of Wendell tap dancing.

Sherman smiled at Lauren. "Just think, last year this same time, I was flipping burgers, and I didn't have a girlfriend."

"Dizzy dames."

"Who?"

"The girls in Kelso. They should have been fighting over you, Sherm. I just hope I can make you happy."

"You've already done that, Lauren. I'm the luckiest guy in all of time."

Acknowledgements

It is seldom the case that writers create books all on their own. Therefore I would like to thank the following people for their help:

Barbara Ericksen—my editor. This is the sort of person who hands you back a manuscript that has written on page 1 "you spelled brunette differently on page 173" and you wonder "how the hell did she do that?" She is totally ruthless with a manuscript, but never criticizes me personally.

Sherrill Fink—my Grammar Nazi. Okay, she is more of a Grammar Guru, trying to spread the message rather than making fun of the uninformed. She helps make me look smarter than I really am.

Paul Alger—my computer geek at Iron Clad Computers in Kennewick, Washington. He wrested this book's files from the jaws of a dying but tenacious computer.

To my proofreaders—Betty Bennett and Mike Farley. Thank you for your hard work and dedication.

Also thank you to Mike for feeding me, bolstering my confidence and supporting me above and beyond the call of duty.

And most of all thanks to all my patrons, a.k.a. fans. (Let's be honest. Writers don't have fans, we have patrons.) It means so much when you tell me you actually liked the book and I don't suck.

About the Author

Jeanette M. Bennett was born in Washington State long, long ago and has yet to find the exit door. She is currently living in the southern fringe of the Scablands of Eastern Washington with her indulgent husband and some furry child-substitutes. Although she has a Bachelor's Degree in Graphic Arts, she is a history geek who loves to spout obscure history facts to those who cannot escape fast enough. Channeling that obsession into writing time travel novels seemed far more socially acceptable. Her hobbies include collecting maneki-nekos (Japanese Lucky Cats), Viking wire weaving and drinking tea. Contrary to popular belief, she has been certified sane and normally doesn't talk about herself in the third person.

For interviews, previews, short stories and links to self-publishing go to www.scablander.com

Also check out Wendell's blog on his travels in the Victorian Age at: www.wendellhowe.blogspot.com

The Association of Temporal Anthropologists blog: http://temporalanthropology.blogspot.com

Made in the USA
Lexington, KY
28 November 2016